D1524317

Amazing Grace

Amazing Grace

by
Judith Davis

NAL BOOKS

NEW AMERICAN LIBRARY

TIMES MIRROR
NEW YORK AND SCARBOROUGH, ONTARIO

Published simultaneously in Canada by
The New American Library of Canada Limited

The author wishes to acknowledge the following sources for permission
to quote material in this book.

HONEY by Bobby Russell. Copyright © 1968 Bibo Music Publishers,
c/o The Welk Music Group, Santa Monica, Ca. 90401. International
copyright secured. All rights reserved. Used by permission.

Material from "To a Friend Whose Work Has Come to Nothing" and
from "The Choice," both in COLLECTED POEMS by William Butler Yeats.
Copyright 1924 by Macmillan Publishing Co., Inc. Renewed 1952 by
Bertha Georgie Yeats.

Material from ON THE ROAD by Jack Kerouac. Copyright © 1955,
1957 by Jack Kerouac. Reprinted by permission of Viking Penguin, Inc.

Material from IN THE SHADOW OF TOMORROW by J. Huizinga.
Reprinted by permission of the Huizinga estate.

Lines from CARMINA BURANA. Copyright by B. Shotts Sohne, Meinz,
1937. Copyright © renewed 1965. Sole U.S. agent European American
Music Distributors Corporation. Used by permission.

Lines from "Ghosts" in SIX PLAYS BY HENRIK IBSEN.
Translated by Eva Le Gallienne. Copyright © 1950 Random House, Inc.

Material from THE COMPLETE POEMS AND STORIES OF
EDGAR ALLAN POE, WITH SELECTIONS FROM HIS WRITINGS,
Volumes I & II, by Edgar Allan Poe. Edited by Arthur Hobsen Quinn,
1946, Alfred A. Knopf, Inc.

Material from THE RED AND THE BLACK by Stendhal. Translated by
C. K. Scott-Moncrieff. Copyright © 1954 Liveright Publishing Corporation.

Material from MOURNING BECOMES ELECTRA by Eugene O'Neill.
Copyright 1931. Renewed 1959 by Carlotta Monterey O'Neill.
Reprinted by permission of Random House, Inc.

 NAL BOOKS TRADEMARK REG. U.S. PAT. OFF. AND FOREIGN COUNTRIES
REGISTERED TRADEMARK—MARCA REGISTRADA
HECHO EN CRAWFORDSVILLE, INDIANA, U.S.A.

SIGNET, SIGNET CLASSICS, MENTOR, PLUME, MERIDIAN and
NAL BOOKS are published in the United States by
The New American Library, Inc.,
1633 Broadway, New York, New York 10019,
in Canada by The New American Library of Canada Limited,
81 Mack Avenue, Scarborough, Ontario M1L 1M8

Library of Congress Cataloging in Publication Data

Davis, Judith.
  Amazing grace.
  I. Title.

PS3554.A934915A8   813'.54   80-26220
ISBN 0-453-00399-0

Designed by Leonard Telesca

First Printing, April, 1981
1 2 3 4 5 6 7 8 9
PRINTED IN THE UNITED STATES OF AMERICA

To Matthew and my mother
with gratitude and love

I wish to express my thanks for the dedicated editorial help given to me by Joan Sanger and Jill Freeman.
For their librarian skills, I am obliged to Sara Whildin and Susan Ware.

Publisher's Note

The intellect of man is forced to choose
Perfection of the life, or of the work,
And if it take the second must refuse
A heavenly mansion, raging in the dark.
—W. B. Yeats

Bred to a harder thing
Than Triumph, turn away
And like a laughing string
Whereon mad fingers play
Amid a place of stone,
Be secret and exult,
Because of all things known
That is most difficult.
—W. B. Yeats

Prologue

After the brilliant light of a chill December day, swift
dusk had brought with it wet snow. In the crowded living room of Nick's townhouse, Jane lingered before the
long windows to watch the snow's slow descent, illumined by the street lamps. Behind her, logs crackled in
the fireplace and Floyd, black face somber, passed
drinks among the guests. In the clatter of dishes, cutlery,
glasses, there was only the confused noise of party
voices, no mention—Jane listened, almost idly—of
Nick's name.

That was, she supposed, a common pattern following
burial. After the solemn church service, the melancholy
processional to the graveyard, emerged this regression
to the mean, a return to ordinary deportment and concerns. Only she, perhaps, would watch the wet snow
shining in the dusk, imagine its hesitant impress on that
newly dug grave.

It would be strange, Jane told herself—she lit a cigarette and decided that, when it was finished, she could
reasonably leave—strange not to discuss the day's
events with Nick, not peruse in detail his final starring
role. He'd have approved—he'd left all the handling of
it to her—the closed casket, its message that he be remembered not in the sad ruin of his last years but as the
shining presence that had dazzled spectators in the past.

There'd been, of course, many eulogies at the
church, masses of flowers. James Hooper had spoken:
"Always he sought to find the richest depths in every
character he played. When Nick Spenser had portrayed
a role, one knew one had seen—whether on the stage
where he began, or on the screen where he was working
when he died—the definitive depiction of that charac-

ter. I considered myself fortunate indeed that Nick, still not much more than a boy, interpreted the role of Erin O'Neill in my play...."

Those words—"where he was working when he died"—had caused Jane to contemplate. No one present, aside from herself, from Floyd, had made that possible. The one who had: *she'd* called, weeping, the day before, from Paris. She couldn't face his funeral. Not that, after everything else. Nick would have understood Gloria's inability to accept the fact of his death.

Jane turned for a moment from the window to meet Walter Raney's patient, worried regard. He'd not wish to leave her by herself tonight; she wondered how, without hurting him, she could just slip away. He'd been, as usual, staunch at her side through the day, had grasped her elbow firmly as they'd moved among the crowd— few had recognized her anymore—and up the church steps.

That had been quite a scene. Warren Lantz, the producer, maneuvering his fat belly against gravity and swept close by the crowd, had paused long enough for a triumphant smile. The jostling had reminded Jane of an Academy Award night—the award they'd denied to Nick four times—but the winter sky, one of those incredibly pure, translucently blue skies so seldom seen in New York, had resembled those of Wellfleet, so many summers ago.

The memory of Wellfleet had unsteadied Jane. Walter had helped her up the remaining steps. He'd pointed out how many there were inside, not only stars, directors, producers but also technicians—cameramen, grips, gaffers, film cutters. That they'd left their work to pay a last tribute to Nick indicated, Walter had murmured in consolation, the esteem in which Nick had still been held.

She'd nodded. So had the many notes accompanying those masses of flowers. "We won't see another star like Nick for many years to come...." "All our lives have been enriched by the life of this one man...." "Great actor, great friend, great victor...."

Why had none said it? He was only a man, like any other. Suffering had brought him pain.

The benediction had, perhaps, expressed it. "Accept into Thy fold this, Thy servant, Nicholas Spenser, whose life ended, as men measure years, still in its prime. He was noble in his calling and noble in the tragedy that befell him—perhaps the worst that can befall an actor, and certainly one whose singular beauty the world so admired. . . ."

As the music began—"Amazing Grace"—one bagpiper, accompanying the organ, had stood in a dappled circle of colored light thrown by the stained-glass window. Only the skirl of the bagpipes sounded the last four lines. The benediction, and that moment, had rocked Jane as nothing before.

Her life had orbited Nick's so long. Objects hurtling through outer space, when they reentered earth's atmosphere, disintegrated, burned to ashes.

The music had accompanied them from the church, but the sound converted now to the renewed shrieks of the crowd. In the press of those outside and the noise and the sight of the casket bobbing above the heads as it made its way to the hearse, Jane had stood motionless a moment, her breath forming a vapor in the cold. She'd gazed at that translucent sky shining above Fifth Avenue, above the buses that lurched sideways into the stream of traffic, the gas fumes rising, the curious bypassers on the opposite side of the street, the salespeople standing in the doorways of their stores, the trail of a jet overhead, and had felt adrift, weightless.

As Walter Raney held her, someone else had taken her other arm. She hadn't expected *him*.

"You're not alone, Jane," he'd said, as though reading her thoughts. "Remember: you're not alone."

The press of the crowd had separated them, he hadn't gone on to the cemetery, hadn't appeared here where, in all this company—Jane smiled reassuringly toward Walter's obvious concern—she felt perhaps more solitary than she ever had. The sense of loss was suddenly overpowering and, as Steve and Kathy Hearn engaged Walter in conversation, Jane moved swiftly, gathered up her wraps, and slipped outside into the wet snow.

In the blue dusk turning to night, she stood hesitant a moment. Her own townhouse was only two doors down. The black veil she slipped over her dark hair was thin, her feet in the slim alligator pumps felt the cold. But an abrupt determination made her pull on the long angora gloves, tuck the collar of the sable coat firmly about her neck.

She began to walk, not toward home, but up to Third Avenue and heading west.

Part One

Chapter 1

1

They were still living, when she was ten, in the six-room, fifth floor apartment on Eighty-first Street and West End Avenue in 1935. Even though Papa had "lost" all his money. The loss was connected to "the Depression"—which was different from what Mama had. Had had, in fact, even before the money was "lost."

The Depression had something to do with those men who drew horses in colored chalk on the pavements the next block up on Broadway. It was why Papa, who'd owned "stocks" but no longer did, and who'd owned a men's clothing store and employed six clerks, now sold insurance, when he could. And that only through the kindness of Uncle Ben.

In fact, it was through the kindness of Uncle Ben that they retained the lease on this apartment, although the maid's room was now unoccupied, and Mama couldn't bestir herself to stop the dust from gathering on the crystal chandeliers, or the lint from curling in gobs on the Oriental rugs. The velvet and brocade furniture, no matter how hard Jane and her twin, Peter, tried to keep five-year-old Joanie off it, showed traces of grime, saliva, food.

Jane and Peter didn't much care that Papa had suffered a misfortune. They didn't much care for him, never had. A tall stern man, whose cane alone rendered him suspect. Also, they were also a little ashamed: his bony hand fondling the naked lady on its knob: they wondered that Mama allowed it. And who else wore such glasses, trailing a black ribbon and pinching the top of his nose so cruelly? If he could inflict pain on himself, what might he not be capable of toward others?

Not that he'd ever struck them. When angry, Papa

elongated in a frightening way and hissed, "Go to your room!" In the years since they'd done without Emmy, the maid, it appeared to them they'd spent much of their time closed in there, with Joanie. As Joanie grew out of her crib and into childhood, she was always butting in.

Like now.

Papa had come home early, in the same hour they'd trailed one another in from school. Nobody wanted to buy insurance. He'd returned expressly, it would seem, to fight with Mama. Jane and Peter didn't understand the waves of sadness that inundated Mama, but they believed in them. It looked as though she kept the escape hatch of suicide in her mental pocket, patted it each day to make certain it was there.

That was one of the reasons they hastened to coddle her, to keep Joanie out of her way. As recompense, Mama always had the money on Saturdays for them to go to the double feature at the RKO Eighty-first Street or Loew's Eighty-third—bringing Joanie, of course. Years ago, when Emmy had taken them, they'd sat in a box. Fred Astaire and Ginger Rogers had sung "Flying Down to Rio" and they'd stood and sung it with them, been asked to leave.

Now: they didn't know, as usual, how it had begun. But they could hear the voices, strident, strangled, rising and falling across the hall in their parents' bedroom. Jane and Peter were squeezed into the too-small chairs at the too-small round table, part of the maple furniture that crowded their bedroom. Everything was maple, including their twin beds, except for Joanie's narrow couch against the wall. Joanie was tucked onto Jane's lap and sucked her thumb while she played with her blonde curls—like Mama's; Jane and Peter were dark, worse luck, like Papa. She kept butting into the refereeing comments the twins exchanged. Through the window drifted the sounds of the apartment house children who played in front of the building. Jump rope, roller skates, the triumphant shrieks of the marble players.

They weren't allowed, by Papa, to play with those children, who were all Jewish. Another reason to be grateful for one another.

But it was exactly the bed arrangement that caused

Papa's uproar now. Why should all three children be crowded into the one bedroom when the maid's room went empty? It was time, he shouted, that Peter and Jane slept apart. His voice cracked: they were old enough.

"Only someone who wears a pince-nez would worry about stuff like that." Peter's tan elfin face wore an adult amused expression.

"What's a pants-nez?" Joanie wanted to know.

Jane removed the thumb from Joanie's mouth. "Why doesn't she go to Uncle Ben for money to leave him? Instead of taking money to stay here?"

"Listen. If she could let him fuck her—even five years ago . . ." Peter indicated the result of that action as its subject reinserted the thumb and demanded:

"What's fucker?"

"Uncle Ben just gives what he wants to give for *what* he wants," Jane conceded. "He's never even had us all up to the resort for one stinking week in any hot summer, has he? He just wants to keep up appearances, here."

"Maybe I should call him. 'Hey, Uncle Ben! Papa wants to stick me in the maid's room!' " His dark eyes —her identical eyes—held a sardonic glow.

"Oh, Peter!"

It was bad enough they no longer attended the same school. P.S. 9 on the next block had separate entrances, as it was, for boys and girls from first through fourth. "They don't want us to knock you girls up," Peter had explained. Once one entered the halls that smelled suspiciously of pee—the years frightened children had wet their pants?—the sexes were also segregated in the classroom. By fifth grade, the girls went into blue serge skirts and middy blouses, the boys into another school, *only* for boys, ten blocks north.

Now Papa wanted to keep them apart at night, too? Jane didn't know why Peter had always been braver. Because he was older, he told her. But she still counted on being able to crawl into his bed when the fire engines shrieked up Broadway or the shrill voices of newsboys echoed fearfully through the dark, calling: "Wux-tree! Wux-tree!" Then, in the morning, it was nothing: no war, no epidemic. She didn't understand how Joanie man-

5

aged to sleep through those night noises, but she never had. And never will, she told herself now, staring at Peter as though she'd already lost him.

"Never mind," he said. "Mama doesn't give in easily, you know."

That she did! Mama had very definite opinions. When she wasn't drowning in the swamps of her depression, she could become quite noisy, even violent. Then she'd hurl herself through the house with the vacuum cleaner, curse as the plug came loose. She'd enter their room, throw everything off the beds and tables onto the floor, demand that each thing be put in its place—or else. Marlene Dietrich was one film star she didn't permit them to see. The woman wore pants, was obviously evil. Had even kissed a woman on screen right on the lips. . . . Um. Would they ever get to see her?

But it was, now, exactly on her refractory side they must rely. If Papa wished to separate them, Mama would find a way to stymie him. In fact, they could hear her already.

"If anyone should be moved out, it's the baby. After all, the twins have homework. She has to go to sleep with the light on. She hears them talking about God knows what till all hours. . . ."

"That's just what I mean. If they were separated, they wouldn't *be* talking about God knows what till all hours."

"Wonder what—and when—we're going to eat." Bored, Peter turned the pages of a book.

"Um." Jane's knees were killing her from holding Joanie. She set her down and reached for a book herself.

But Joanie wanted to play school. She was at the blackboard that hung inside the closet door and she demanded Jane give her different letters of the alphabet to print.

"Oh, for Christ's sake." Jane glanced at her Mickey Mouse watch. It had been a Christmas gift from Uncle Ben years ago and, by now, far too childish for her. Still only four o'clock. Though the wind whistled up the side streets from the river, a weak sun shone. "Let's take Joanie to the park and get out of this madhouse," she suggested.

Peter considered this. Lately, he and one of the Jewish kids from the house, a boy a year or two older, had been running into one another in the park at Riverside Drive and batting a ball back and forth. The bat and ball belonged to the Jewish kid. Meanwhile Jane played catch or hopscotch with Joanie, or pushed her on the swing. It wasn't that Peter cared for baseball, or any sport, for that matter. It was the chance to socialize with another boy, and one of whom Papa would disapprove. One had, occasionally, to study how to disobey.

So Peter nodded and they simultaneously told Joanie they'd take her to the park, so go pee. "Just don't be in such a hurry you forget to wipe," Jane added, sternly. Joanie, easily ecstatic, nodded.

In the elevator, Fritz was on duty. He was the one operator who still treated them halfway decently, and that just because they were the only non-Jewish kids in the building, and he was German. He made his usual big fuss over Joanie—"Germans like blondes, you know," Peter had explained to Jane—while Jane and Peter made horrible faces at one another behind his back.

They paid scant attention to the children playing around them as they walked away from the building. Joanie was inclined to linger to watch a girl Jane's age jump between double ropes while those turning recited a verse faster and faster. Another shouted to the girl she was huddled with, "But that's a *name* card I'm trading you!" Jane pulled Joanie along, pointed to the top of a freighter that could be glimpsed on the river as they crested the hill and walked down to the park against the wind.

"Keep your mouth closed," Jane ordered, "and you won't be so cold." It was still only late March.

Once onto the cement paths between the scrubby grass, the prospect before them was wintry dismal. From this level one could no longer glimpse the river; dust blew into their smarting eyes. A man on a bench battled a newspaper. A nursemaid, head lowered, pushed a baby carriage rapidly up the path. A couple of shabby side-street children—all the wealthy ones lived on the avenues, on West End and Riverside Drive—scuffled in the dirt of the small enclosed playground. Otherwise, the park was deserted.

Or, so it seemed, till they heard the shout, "Hey! Peter!"

There was Danny Edelman coming toward them. Peter gave a slow casual wave down near his waist. Immediately, the ball came sailing to him and Peter leaped. To Jane's relief, he managed to catch it, and she trailed Joanie toward the swings but walking backward to watch how Danny—a damned good-looking kid, she told herself—swung the bat. She didn't see why she couldn't be included once in a while. Maybe after Peter was more secure with Danny, he'd suggest it.

She certainly wouldn't, she resolved, as she made Joanie pull herself up into the swing—this child has to learn some self-reliance, she argued silently—and began to push. She could hear Peter and Danny, no longer visible from here, call to each other good-natured insults. Things were loosening up between them. Punching at one another, the two children from the side street had left.

Suddenly, the ball sailed into the playground and Jane darted off, crying, "I'll get it!" At the same time Peter called:

"Hey, Janie! Find the ball!"

It had crashed into the scrubby bushes beyond the iron grating that surrounded the playground. Jane stooped and felt with her hand, but it was too far beneath. She looked around, found a stick, and after a good deal of probing—and yelling back: "I'm *getting* it, wait! It's stuck!"—she finally saw the ball roll out within reach. For a moment she considered trying to throw it. With her skill, it would only land back inside the playground. So she trotted out to where she could see them. Peter was occupied hurling stones to Danny, who batted them into the ground while they talked, man to man.

"Here you go," Jane called, and let the ball sail. Though it felt as though she'd given a fabulous hurl, it fell almost immediately, rolling the rest of the way toward the boys, who laughed. She turned and went back to Joanie.

Who was gone.

8

The swing still moved from the pushes—or was it the wind?—but Joanie was gone.

"Damn!" Jane muttered, and called out. No answer. Probably hiding. Jane left the playground, began to circle around it. The brat could be in any of these bushes and she called out warningly, "I'm in no mood for games, Joanie"—Mama's phrase—"so you better come out right now or I'm going to leave you here"—a long-ago threat from Emmy.

No answering giggle. The wind, turned increasingly raw, picked up swirls of dirt and smacked it into her eyes as Jane gazed up the paths. The boys remained oblivious. The man with the newspaper was gone. They were the only ones left in the park and the sun had slipped behind the Palisades.

Joanie wouldn't have left the park by herself, would she? Cross Riverside Drive and West End Avenue all alone? Assuming she'd even know how to make her way home? And why? Jane's heart began a slow hard thumping that made it difficult to breathe.

Kidnapped! Some band of gangsters, figuring they were rich kids, had followed them from the apartment house, awaited their chance to grab her!

"Peter!" Her cry was feeble.

At bat, awkwardly intent on a good showing, he didn't answer.

"Peter!"

He swung and connected. Began to run but Danny, in midair, caught the ball. "Damn!" Peter commented goodnaturedly. Then, not so, "What do you want?" to her.

"Joanie's gone." Her voice trembled. So did her knees.

"What do you mean—gone?" But Peter's quick glance about, the immediacy of his response were at once soothing and frightening. He came toward her, trailed by Danny, whose interested gaze at her loose knee socks and frayed coat made Jane blush, even while the slow, measured thud of her heart continued to sicken her.

Peter reassured himself that the playground was empty. Danny mentioned the bushes. Jane let them repeat her poking around, but she knew Joanie couldn't keep herself hidden that long. There was a long eerie blast from a tug on the river. As though in answer, the wind assumed a voice and threw more dust in their faces.

"She must have lit out for home by herself, the little brat." Jane saw Peter struggle to keep his lips steady, for her sake or Danny's she didn't know. "We better hightail it after her before she's killed by a bus."

"How come you always have to watch out for your little sister?" Danny asked. He didn't appear perturbed. Perhaps his reaction was the more rational one, she and Peter just highly emotional, being the children of their parents. Still, there was a taste of vomit in her mouth as they hurried back up the side street, the wind at their backs now. Danny assured them traffic would stop for a five-year-old.

"Besides," he argued, his steps brisk, "you didn't hear any ambulances, did you? You don't see any crowd gathered around, do you?" That, Jane thought with admiration, would be the "shrewdness" that Papa singled out as one of the many hateful traits of Jews.

The children were off the street now in front of the building. The doorman was nowhere in sight and Fritz no longer on duty. It was John, the long melancholy fellow that Mama said was alcoholic. No, he responded languidly as he took them up, he hadn't seen Joanie come in. Danny appeared to pity them as he leaned against the elevator wall. Something in Jane's throat made it difficult to swallow. She could tell from the way Peter breathed that he had it, too. Just let Joanie be in the apartment and it wouldn't matter what they got from Mama and Papa for being careless.

Peter let them in with his key. They tiptoed to the bedroom but, in silence, were already agreed she wasn't there. The argument appeared to be over because the only noise was that of pots being banged around in the kitchen. That sound stopped, too, and Mama appeared in the hallway as they returned to it.

"Where's Joanie?" she asked. Her eyes were red and she held a cut finger to her mouth to suck it.

Peter looked at Jane. She shook her head.

"What's the matter? Where's Joanie?" The voice, always ready to rise, did so. Papa emerged from the living room with his newspaper.

"We don't know," Jane whispered.

"We were in the park with her," Peter said, very low. "We were all playing and she—she disappeared."

"What do you mean?" Papa advanced. The pince-nez dropped from his nose and swung on the black ribbon. "How could you all be playing and Joanie disappear?"

"Well, I had her on the swings," Jane put in hoarsely. "Peter was throwing a ball back and forth against the wall . . ."

"Wall? What wall?"

"What does it matter what wall?" Mama wailed. "How could a five-year-old child who's sitting on a swing disappear?" She began to wring her hands in the damp apron.

They both spoke at once. The ball had rolled under some bushes. Jane had gone after it. Joanie had disappeared. They had looked. Everywhere. There was no one else in the park. They'd come back. John was on duty. He hadn't seen her. They . . .

"Oh, God!" Mama wailed. "Where's my baby?" She was digging frantically in the hall closet for her coat.

"What are you doing? Don't be stupid! We have to call the police," Papa admonished coldly, and glared at them both a moment. "Responsibility!" he hissed, and elongated in that way of his. "Get to your room!"

They fled. More wailing from Mama, punctuated by two gasping sobs. The front door slammed. From the other bedroom they heard Papa's haughty voice at the telephone. A flurry of wind-borne dust flew into their faces as they leaned out the window and saw Mama hurtle toward the side street, toward the river, her blonde hair flying, her coat open and flapping about her. They sank back and looked at one another, their pallor mirrored in the other's face.

When the two policemen, unsmiling cardboard figures, showed up, Jane and Peter repeated the story. Then, for some reason, Peter was taken into Papa and Mama's room by one of them, Jane retained in their own by the other, to be questioned separately. Had Papa told the police he suspected that Peter played with some Jewish kid, that the Jewish kid had had a hand in the kidnapping?

Mama was back. Up and down the hall she flung herself, crying out: "Where is she? *Where is she?* WHERE IS SHE? I want my child!" Jane shivered uncontrollably and cringed as she stared up into the policeman's impersonal eyes.

It wasn't until later that she and Peter understood the police suspected *them*—tired of playing nursemaid—of foul play. This they realized when Danny—they'd both "squealed," just like in the movies—and his parents showed up in the apartment later. Mr. Edelman, round, shaken, his bald head perspiring. Mrs. Edelman, stuffed into a corset, her high bosom heaving with sympathy and fear. Danny appeared so puzzled, so different, unfamiliar, the way he kept shaking his head to the policemen's questions.

By now there were two other men also, with hats on their heads and, in the hat ribands, small cards that said "Press"—again, just like in the movies. Danny couldn't honestly say, he told the assembly reluctantly, that he'd even noticed Joanie at all. Sure, he knew what she looked like from other days. Papa's eyes rolled. But Danny couldn't remember seeing her, one way or the other, today. A new policeman had appeared, very white-skinned, with pale red hair, colorless lashes. He gazed upon Jane and Peter.

"You're sure," he put to them, gravely—one last chance?—"you had your sister with you when you entered the park?" A pause. "Or by the time you ran into your young friend here? ... I mean, you hadn't—let's say—stashed her away by then?"

Sweat and tears ran into Jane's untasted glass of milk. "I was pushing her," she repeated monotonously. "I was pushing her in the swing."

Meanwhile, the wind howled up from the Drive and the sounds of traffic rumbled below, and somehow a lost hurt voice called her name in terror. But that last only in her mind. What was really shrilling was the telephone and one of the policemen answering, then scribbling on his pad as he listened. Lights blazed in every room as though either Joanie would be revealed or the worst terrors held at bay. What was the policeman scribbling? Had her body been found?

No, it was Uncle Ben, who'd heard on the evening news. Was it that late already? Why was Fritz here, ashen, lips stiffened so he could barely speak? And John? Why did the two quibble about what time they'd changed shifts? "You were fond of the little girl, weren't you?" the policeman with the colorless lashes asked.

"No!" Fritz protested.

"Yes, you were," Peter said, low.

"You be quiet," from Papa.

Uncle Ben appeared, bearing his cologne scent and the diamond ring on his pinkie. Big and blond like Mama, but officious, in command. He'd get to the bottom of this, he assured the police, demanded to know why the newsmen were there.

"Mister, we're on your side," one explained in a tired voice. Jane noticed how his cigarette ash dropped rhythmically to the rug.

Not that it mattered. If only they were all quiet: was it possible that was Joanie's voice crying in the night, crying her name? For Uncle Ben, they went over the story again. The swing. The ball coming over the grating. The bushes. How she'd gone out only for a moment to throw back the ball. The empty swing. The search . . .

. . . They were in bed. The room was dark. They must have fallen asleep immediately because Jane didn't remember even crawling under the covers. There was light still visible beneath the crack of the door, the sound of voices, of the telephone. Jane sat up to stare toward Joanie's bed. She sensed that Joanie was there, had somehow crept in unseen.

"Joanie?" she whispered.

Silence.

Jane, arms extended as though blind, moved from her bed toward the narrow couch. Her hands met the rough texture of the spread. A groan, and she sank down by the bed, her teeth tearing into the spread. She saw Joanie's body sprawled, frozen, bloody, under some bench where nobody had thought to look. How could Peter sleep? Why was he braver than she? Because he was a boy? Was it possible—what he used to tell her when they were small—that every month they'd changed places inside Mama: one month he was the girl and she the boy, the next vice versa? It had just happened to be his turn to be the boy when they'd popped out?

She didn't believe it. How could she let Joanie know they were searching for her, that she'd be found, she'd be all right? Jane whimpered and Peter's arms were around her. He was pulling her to her feet and steering her, sobbing, while he, too, cried, to his bed.

They held each other tightly. They began to count off the places nobody had thought to search. Suppose she'd headed off downtown—supposing she knew the direction—to get to the Roxy Theatre? They'd been there once, Joanie enthralled by the stage show. Suppose she'd come out on Riverside Drive and a man had stopped his car and told her he'd take her to the Roxy and she'd climbed in, forgotten the times she'd been told never to talk to strangers. Suppose. . . . Their tears mingled as they clung to one another.

The door crashed open. Mama, a swaying giant who bellowed, was there between their beds.

"What did you do with her? What did you do with Joanie?"

Uncle Ben and Papa were pulling at her and Uncle Ben demanding of Papa, "Do they always sleep in one bed like that?" Papa, his spittle shining in the light from the hall, his voice breaking—fatigue? anger?—"What the hell are you doing in Peter's bed?" yanked Jane out by the arm, flung her across her own bed. For the first time he swung his hand backward hard against her face and back again, then the same to Peter.

"Jew-lovers!" he hissed. The door slammed.

Sometime the next day, Saturday, they saw a copy of the *Daily News*. Again, Jane had that sense that all of them were in a movie. The paper swirled on the screen, came to rest in focus. The whole front page was the picture taken of Joanie on her birthday. In tall black letters the headline blared, GIRL, 5, MISSING. Beneath the picture: "Have you seen this child?" On page three they found the story, with the new constant sense of unreality, read it.

"She could be Shirley Temple's younger sister. The same blonde curls, the same shining eyes, even though hers are blue, the same snub nose and engaging smile. But her bed was empty last night at the apartment of Arthur and Beatrice Belmont. And nobody knows why. Not even her sister and brother, ten-year-old twins Jane and Peter, who apparently took her to Riverside Drive late yesterday afternoon and then, busy playing ball with pal, Danny Edelman, from the same apartment house, lost sight of the little girl. Or so the twins have said. . . .

"Questioned in the disappearance were. . . ."

There were all the names. Danny. His parents. Fritz. John. Benjamin Crandle, owner of the extravagant summer resort, High Hills. Dr. Osman, called on to give the grieving mother a sedative. Papa, an insurance salesman down on his luck. . . .

The phone kept ringing. Each time one of the new policemen picked it up, they listened in ominous silence. It turned out to be Joanie's kindergarten teacher expressing concern, a crank call from somebody who wanted to know why Mama hadn't looked after the child herself, a former friend of Mama's, one of Papa's old sales clerks. . . .

"Did any of your former employees have reason to hold a grudge against you?" the policeman asked Papa. The poor guy, who'd probably done it just to be in on the excitement, had got himself in trouble, making that call. The sun was brilliant today. Sirens shrilled by on the street below and Jane, dizzy with fatigue, closed her eyes, imagined the sirens closing in on a small figure somewhere far uptown in Harlem. Joanie, Joanie. . . . She felt the wool cap she'd pulled over the blonde curls before they'd set out.

Again, it was night. They were afraid, in the darkness, to go to one another, but lay whispering reassurances. To each other, to Joanie. Some lonely woman had seen her with her blonde curls, her cheeks rosy from the cold. Despite warnings, Joanie had accepted the proffered candy. Perhaps the lady had told Joanie she had a kitten at her house—Joanie had always begged for a kitten—and taken Joanie off with her.

Joanie was there now, not too scared anymore, not too lonesome anymore, because the lady was really kind to her. It was just that somehow she knew how to keep Joanie hidden so no neighbors and no police and no store people glimpsed her. She had a fire escape that she would let Joanie out on to get fresh air and she did exercises with her so Joanie wouldn't get stiff. She was poor, but somehow had enough money to buy Joanie all the paper dolls she'd ever want. She'd buy the paper dolls at Levine's on Broadway—perhaps they'd pass right by her and never know—where the Jewish girls at school bought Nancy Drew books for one another's birthday parties. And she really did have a kitten—an orange one—maybe she'd run out and got it for Joanie after enticing her to the cramped rooms she lived in— and Joanie was really quite happy by now. . . .

"Oh, do you think so? Do you really think so?" Jane begged. Then, fearful of Papa, but more so of that empty bed behind her, Jane was again pressed up against Peter and now they could hear Papa and Mama shouting at each other, all the recriminations of all the years. They shivered against each other, neither believing what they'd told the other, but Jane whispering against Peter's chest, trying not to hear the bellicose voices: "We'll never get married, will we? Promise me. . . ."

In the dark, with the traffic noises an ominous bellow from below, a swelling like threatening ocean waves, Peter promised. From the small play table that had been Joanie's—had been?—he seized her favorite doll, a Raggedy Ann, and placed it between them as though to keep it warm between their frigid bodies.

Everything that had seemed unreal about these last two days now settled on them, like a shroud. Jane wondered if Peter sensed it, too. Like a heavy band of iron about her head, a brand of doom.

2

Strange they could grow accustomed to it. Sunday, the visit to the Eighty-second Street police station. Reporters. Crank calls. Sympathy calls. No ransom note. Awed stares in the elevator. They didn't go to school all week and nobody suggested they should. The days passed. They began to live with the idea that Joanie wouldn't be found. In the night they heard Mama's groans. Jane was aware of her pacing in the hall. Partly to escape the cavernous emptiness of that narrow bed against the wall, she slipped from her own one night and went to her, reached her arm about Mama's waist hidden in the nubbly robe.

"Mama, please. Please feel better. Don't cry. Somehow I think Joanie's really all right. You'll see. . . ."

For a moment, Mama leaned on her. She pushed the mass of faded blonde hair from her face with a trembling hand. A tear perched on the lower lid of each blue eye. But she thrust Jane from her.

"Get away from me." The dead voice. "Joanie's life is over and so is mine. I don't want anything. . . ."

They became inured to the fact that Mama sat motionless in the living room by day, prowled the hall by night. Papa did the shopping, taking them with him to Amsterdam Avenue where the markets had outdoor stalls, were cheaper than Broadway. There was nothing companionable about these excursions. He didn't seek their advice, merely shoved the bags of food into their arms where they waited, marooned, on the sidewalk.

Once, descending the hill to West End Avenue, all of them silent as always, they came abreast of Danny Edelman. He stopped, appeared to take in at a glance everything about their situation and, in solicitude, raised his light brown eyebrows. It was, Jane reflected, as though he were apologizing to them for the fact that he was still cared for, still possessed his childhood. They had passed on to some alien ice floe of adulthood where he'd never be able to communicate with them again. Papa grunted something, pushed Peter forward with his knee.

June, hot and humid, brought the end of school, their eleventh birthday. Nobody mentioned the date except they, exchanging the dank smiles of the criminals they were, the orphans. There was a *Thin Man* movie playing a few blocks down at the Beacon and, harvesting their savings, they joined the afternoon crowd in the air-conditioned staleness of the theater.

To savor Myrna Loy's suave unflappability, William Powell's confident poise, they stayed to see the film twice. The other feature was a stupid one, but that didn't matter, so avid were they for escape. When they came out, staggering slightly in the fetid air of Broadway, each saw how the other gave quick glances to the people coming in and going out. Perhaps Joanie . . .

The telephone call came in July. The policeman thought Peter's voice was that of the Mrs. Belmont he'd summoned. Because they were alone with Mama, because the fact of a policeman on the line was terrifying in the middle of the afternoon heat that pressed into the apartment, Peter didn't disabuse him. He laid down the phone, stared at Jane.

"It's Papa." She watched his pupils enlarge, imagined he did the same as he watched her. "He collapsed in the heat in front of some hotel on Columbus Avenue and . . . they've got him in the hotel there. . . ."

There was no need for discussion. They left Mama alone in the living room. The sun dazzled the asphalt of the sidewalks. The tar seemed to ooze and roll under their feet as they made their way over to Eighty-fifth Street and Columbus. In the lobby one policeman waited, but no Papa. The policeman came toward them, slim, narrow-shouldered, frowning. They told him who they were.

"But this isn't your business," he scolded. "Say, aren't you . . ." His severe glance recognized them.

"Yes," Peter said. "But Mama's sick. It's better for her if we try to take care of things."

"Like before, huh?" The policeman moved back to the narrow desk. It was a small damp-smelling hotel, nothing like the large ones with their imposing lobbies on Eighty-sixth Street. A pale unhealthy-looking clerk snickered briefly behind the desk but sobered quickly under the policeman's blank stare. The policeman spoke curtly into a house phone.

They must have taken Papa upstairs. That was pretty nice of them, Jane decided, tapping her foot to calm herself. The heat, the dank smell were stupefying. She noticed a long streak of dirt on Peter's arm, one on her own brown leg, and was ashamed.

The policeman snapped into the phone: "Yeah. Gotcha." He returned to them. "Listen. This ain't as simple as it looks. You gotta relative or something could come over?"

They told him to look up Uncle Ben's number at the office where he administered the business of High Hills. Then they leaned against the pale green sweating walls and waited. After a time the policeman must have taken pity on them.

"Hey, youse guys wanna Coke or something?" They brightened. "Heah. The treat's on me." He threw a couple of nickels to Peter who let them drop, had to scramble for them. The cop laughed, directed them to a corner store that had an ice chest. There they stood in the doorway, almost strangling on the sweet gurgling fizz of the drinks, and not speaking. The little woman with fat bare arms who sat behind the cash register wanted to know if it was hot enough for them. They nodded.

When they returned to the hotel, Uncle Ben had arrived, his cologne aura mingling with the smell of age and poverty in the lobby. He was shaking his head at a plump redheaded woman who had powder caked around her nose. Shaking his head and sighing. They didn't know why the woman, who wore a flowered dress that was plastered to her back by sweat and whose stockings were rolled down around her ankles, should talk so much to Uncle Ben. Unless she was the one who'd seen Papa falter out there in the heat, had helped him in?

"May as well bring the body down," the first cop said to another who had joined him.

The body. Uncle Ben noticed them and the startled evasive glances they sent him. They didn't really want to know. They didn't want to see. The second cop said to Uncle Ben:

"It's just as well your niece never saw the room anyway. Jeez, a guy his age in this heat. . . . you'd think he'd lie in a cold tub, instead . . ."

The woman interjected in a quavery voice, "Well, what do you think it was like for me?" She began to cry and they watched the mascara streak slowly down her cheeks, dotted with enlarged pores and tiny red veins.

Uncle Ben sighed again, looked as though he were about to pat her arm, let his hand with its diamond ring drop. He shook his head. His only words to them were, "This is all your mother needed."

But they were wild to escape into the pressure of the heat outside. They didn't want to see a body. Jane felt something frighteningly like pee roll down her inner thighs along with the sweat. The fetid air pressed in on her. There were cold hands at her forehead, then nothing but darkness.

When she came to, sprawled in a chair whose arms were black with grime and perspiration, she realized the noise on the sidewalk outside meant she'd been temporarily saved. The body must be out there already, with the ambulance and the added cops and the unfamiliar woman and Uncle Ben and the crowd that had gathered. Peter, holding a wet hankie to her face, stared strangely, with a quizzical half smile, at nothing.

Mama hardly reacted. It was the shock, Uncle Ben told them. The shock would have to wear off. "And God knows what next," he added, as though to himself.

That, Jane supposed, came at the funeral. It was one of those gray, airless days when the heat seemed to have absorbed the sun itself. Uncle Ben had taken care of everything. They'd ridden in a car that belonged to the funeral parlor all the way out to Long Island, where a cemetery spread its blanket of sooty headstones as far as they could see. It had never occurred to Jane that the hole for the coffin would be so deep. Or that, releasing herself from the small group Uncle Ben had mustered, Mama would suddenly, as the coffin was lowered, try to fling herself into the grave. She scrambled in the dirt, her face red and shining, while Uncle Ben grabbed and shook her.

"What am I supposed to do now?" she wailed at him. Jane wondered if the gravediggers would be angry at the way she kicked loose soil into that deep hole.

"You should have thought of that when you married him," Uncle Ben said coldly as he restrained her.

"But what do I have to live for now?" she mumbled.

Since she appeared calmer, Uncle Ben released her. Again she tried to fling herself forward. Jane saw how Peter flinched, his thin face hidden behind that new look of removed concentration.

Uncle Ben hesitated. Then he rasped: "Listen, woman. You have as much as before. Your marvelous husband didn't collapse on the street, if you want to know. He was up in that hotel room with some woman. A dame he's been sticking it to for years. When you thought he was selling insurance. . . ."

Mama became still. Peter's air of concentration was only disturbed by a slight frown between his thin dark brows. The air was heavy, wet, full of unknown meaning, only the noise of the coffin being lowered, and a lost seagull from somewhere over the Sound screeching faintly as it wheeled overhead.

Apparently, they didn't have to stay to see the hole filled in. Jane wondered for the first time if Papa were in the coffin with the pince-nez over his dead, slightly bulging eyes. She tried to recall what he'd looked like and already wasn't certain she could. Mama insisted on walking ahead of them, alone, back to the waiting cars. Jane stumbled on the gravel path and Uncle Ben, in his first gesture of kindness, took her arm.

"A widow," he said, "is just washed up on a shore. She's beached, like a whale, wherever her husband has left her. That's damned different from a woman who's chosen to live alone."

It was something about the life insurance that made Uncle Ben decide they'd have to move. Their wise Papa, he told Peter and Jane while he tapped his buffed fingernails on the arm of the Louis Quinze chair in the living room, had had everything he needed to know about insurance right there around him at his job, and what had he done? He'd borrowed on his life insurance and there wasn't a penny left. It had never occurred to Peter and Jane that there would be, but this was apparently the final trial to Uncle Ben's patience.

"Besides," he added, while Mama stared out the window toward the invisible river, "I want to spend the money on a psychiatrist, not on this apartment." For a

21

moment Jane thought he meant for himself but he shook his head toward Mama.

"Don't they only take care of crazy people?" Jane demurred. She felt stiff, as though she were made of the cardboard that used to come in Papa's shirts when he still sent them out to the laundry.

"She's a good candidate, don't you think?"

Peter and Jane exchanged glances. Were they living with a crazy woman? Surely Uncle Ben wouldn't leave them with her if she were? But then, also surely, he wouldn't wish to take them in with him. Where would they go? Jane saw a sudden scene at the bus station downtown, she and Peter separated forever, while they were sent off to different orphan asylums. Her eyes clouded, then cleared as she looked toward Mama, silent by the window.

"She's not crazy," she snapped to Uncle Ben. "She's not."

3

The place he found for them was over on the East Side. In the Eighties also, down near Lexington Avenue. It was a fourth-floor walk-up where Jane was supposed to share a room with Mama, while Peter slept in the living room-dining room next to the tiny kitchen. The bedroom windows looked down on a jumbled courtyard intersected with clotheslines and where cats leaped from islands of garbage cans in the night.

Mama, to their relief, decided she'd sleep in the living room which looked out on the street. She'd informed Peter secretly, he said, that she thought if she watched at night she might see Joanie. Mama refused to visit the doctor Uncle Ben had selected. Every month they argued about it when Uncle Ben came over to give them the monthly check and bring their bills to his accountant.

But, for Jane and Peter, life picked up. They'd both

skipped grades back at P.S. 9 and now they could enter high school. He went over to Townsend Harris while Jane traveled south and east to Julia Richman. There was something in Jane's school—seven thousand girls—called the Country School. Here a couple of hundred of the brightest students were segregated with the best teachers, and Jane was among them. For the first time she was enthusiastic about school, even Latin, but especially English. Most of the girls, however, were two years older and well-to-do; they danced the Big Apple in the bathrooms and dated Saturday nights, dancing cheek to cheek. They talked of the World's Fair where she and Peter hadn't the money to go, and of parents with whom they had no patience. Their homes were nowhere near hers. Theirs was simply a snobbery of unawareness, she told herself, as they blankly excluded her from their lives.

But Mama had lost her authority over them now. Once they'd cleaned the apartment on Saturday, done the marketing over on Third Avenue beneath the thundering trains of the el, they were free. Two important events occurred the year they turned fourteen. (Joanie would be nine now, they told each other.) Peter "had sex" and he found a way for them to get in free to Broadway shows.

The sex Peter told her about as he climbed into her bed, as always, once Mama was ensconced on the couch that folded outward in the living room. In the dim light, all was the same as when they were children. That strange, faraway concentration in Peter's dark eyes became invisible here.

The girl, he told her, was the older sister of a friend of his at school. Three of them had accompanied his friend home this afternoon to a big apartment on Fifth Avenue, a penthouse. They'd played Ping Pong and drunk from the guy's liquor closet and the sister had invited Peter to come into her room to see her foreign dolls.

"The minute we got in there, she locked the door and dropped her panties," Peter whispered. Jane stared grimly at the ceiling. "Then she took off this angora sweater and asked me if I wanted to undo her bra."

"Did you?" Peter's warm breath at her ear was suddenly irritating.

"What do *you* think?" Boastful and awed. "Biggest tits I ever saw." How many had he seen? "I thought she just wanted to—you know—pet. Like, do everything but. But after a while she asked if I had a condom...."

"What?" At her squeal, Peter laid a hand over her mouth.

"So naturally I had to say I don't use them as bookmarks in my Biology text. And she brings out this package of Trojans and tells me to put one on. And next thing I know, we're doing it. I mean: actually *doing* it!" Peter laughed softly into the darkness.

"Did you like it?" Primly polite.

"Sure." A moment's silence. Then: "Not much. I was scared shitless that thing would come off and she'd have a baby. And she made so much noise I was sure the guys could hear."

Jane was somewhat mollified. "Then what?"

"Well, then, after I got my pants back on she sent me out and called one of the other guys in. She took them all on." Peter sounded sheepish. Jane, staring at the ceiling, tried to picture the scene. Suddenly, she giggled.

"So. You're not such a hot shot after all, are you!"

Peter jabbed at her. "It was me she chose first." Then, he was giggling, too, and tickling her. They began to tell each other every dirty joke they could think of. Jane felt wet and warm down there and half wished Peter would go away so she could play with herself. That was something she didn't tell Peter about.

But the anger she'd sensed behind her own laughter astounded her. As always, she'd either lie awake a long, long time—till three, sometimes—or, if she fell asleep, come awake about then to lie staring into the darkness for hours. She'd thought when they'd moved she'd be able to sleep. But the same thoughts moved restlessly through her head. *Did* the pince-nez still rest on the bone that had once been Papa's nose? *Was* Joanie wandering alive somewhere, perhaps in the Midwest by now, perhaps suffering from amnesia and with no memory any longer of any of them? ...

As for the plays, it worked like this. They never got

to see the first act. If you didn't mind that, you mingled with the audience during intermission and joined them to push back up to the second balcony. There were always at least a couple of empty seats. Sometimes they even made it into one of the boxes, although once they were asked by a kindly usher to leave.

It was after they'd cleaned and marketed that they rode the IRT down to Forty-second Street. They scanned the newspaper while the train rocked them from side to side, took the shuttle over to Broadway, were soon pushing through the crowds. First they splurged at the Automat; each dropped three nickels in the slot for a dry cheese sandwich, for another nickel pumped the spigot for coffee. While they feasted, conversed loud and languidly in what they assumed were foreign accents of their life abroad. Then, on to the play. Few were musicals; if they were, Jane later, alone, practiced the songs and the dancing, bowing low to imaginary applause.

Besides the plays, they made certain to see movies, too, often sneaking in a side entrance. With special eagerness, they sought out the evil Marlene Dietrich. They had no phonograph but, after *Destry Rides Again,* Jane secretly bought the sheet music for "The Boys in the Back Room" and memorized it. One evening she sang it low—low so Mama wouldn't hear, low like Marlene—and did a slow dance for Peter, who clapped vigorously.

"You don't have that great a voice," he decided, "but you sure can put over a song."

So much for Miss Big-Tits, she told herself.

But it was for the plays she lived. If they weren't seated before the curtain majestically rose on the second act, it slightly spoiled things, but only slightly. The curtain was a living entity, it breathed of the secret and fabulous world behind it. If they had their own tickets, Jane thought, she'd be in her seat as soon as the theater opened, to stare at that magic tapestry that separated her from what had come to be the true reality that lay behind it. That was true reality for her since, too often now, when she scrutinized Peter and his abstracted stare, she couldn't tell what his was. He was hers, yet always slipping away from her.

In school, Jane avidly read plays. For her Junior project in English, Miss O'Brien—thirty-five? forty?—whose dainty figure in knit suits and whose languid, hooded eyes Jane studied with admiration, allowed her to undertake a study of Shaw, a comparison of his humor to that of Oscar Wilde.

"I want you to do a serious analysis, of course, but I'm happy to see you, especially, work on comedy," Miss O'Brien remarked. "It should do you good. . . . Perhaps you can find your way back to your own brand of seriousness—and not one that life has imposed on you." A mysterious little pause. "Refreshed? And renewed." The languid eyes fell, as though perhaps she'd said too much.

But it wasn't, finally, the comedy that spoke to Jane. When she came across it—Jack Tanner's speech as Don Juan, in *Man and Superman*—she read the words hastily, again slowly. Aside from Miss O'Brien, it didn't appear to her she'd ever had a mentor, a guide in her life. Now, as she copied out the monologue to carry about with her in her notebook, later in her purse, it was as though someone were actually instructing her. How to live, how to avoid existing in Hell like those Jack Tanner described. She hoped she'd remember, and believe, that *that* was what Hell was truly like, that was how it was peopled. Those who allowed themselves to become like that were the ones who'd slip down into it.

Perhaps, forewarned, she could indeed live differently. She longed for Jack Tanner's respect.

"They are not beautiful: they are only decorated. They are not clean: they are only shaved and starched. They are not dignified: they are only fashionably dressed. They are not educated: they are only college passmen." (She wondered what that meant.) "They are not religious: they are only pewrenters. They are not moral: they are only conventional." (That, she underlined.) "They are not virtuous: they are only cowardly." (That, too.) "They are not even vicious: they are only 'frail.' They are not artistic: they are only lascivious. They are not prosperous: they are only rich." (Another underlining.) "They are not loyal, they are only servile; not dutiful, only sheepish; not public spirited, only pa-

triotic; not courageous, only quarrelsome; not determined, only obstinate; not masterful, only domineering;
not self-controlled, only obtuse; not self-respecting, only
vain"; (underlining, again) "not kind, only sentimental;
not social, only gregarious; not considerate, only polite;
not intelligent, only opinionated; not progressive, only
factious; not imaginative, only superstitious; not just,
only vindictive; not generous, only propitiary." (Both of
those.) "Not disciplined, only cowed; and not truthful at
all: liars every one of them, to the very backbone of their
souls."

One evening as they did their homework, she read
the speech to Peter.

"That's good," he agreed. The thin dark brows drew
together. "But do you think *any*one can grow up and not
eventually become like that?"

"Yes," she answered stoutly. "Yes, I do."

Still, the admonitions, no matter how many times she
read them, did not, of course, stay with her all the time.
Peter saw that girl on Fifth Avenue regularly now, he
and the other boys going up to "bang" her, as he informed Jane and, suddenly, his fingers twining in her
hair as he told her about it, Jane sensed a flush that
seemed to move up her body from her toes and cover
her neck and face.

"Don't tell me anymore about it," she snapped, "I
don't want to hear." She gave Peter a shove that landed
him on the floor. When he demanded to know what had
got into her, she couldn't say, only turned her face to the
wall. He'd applauded her singing and dancing but he
was still seduced by that other. . . .

When she dreamed, it was of hands touching her,
moving along her body, a voice breathing her name. She
couldn't see the face clearly. But the eyes were dark and
shining as they stared above her with a strange faraway
abstraction that she recognized. Later, she was awake,
as always, for hours.

After all, she told herself, walking slowly home from
school in the spring sunshine, *she'd* never known any
boys but Peter. None of his friends—any more than her
own classmates—had ever even come to the apartment.
Lately, she'd been examining herself, surreptitiously al-

most, in the bathroom mirror—there was no full-length one—and now, as she walked, changing her books from one arm to the other, she saw, not the items in the shop windows, but her own figure moving past. She checked and rechecked, wondering how she really appeared to others.

She was tall, one of the tallest in her class, even if the youngest. Although her shoulders were slim, they appeared broader than they were above her small high bust. The high rib cage tapered down to an extraordinarily small waist. She always had to move over the buttons on the skirts from the thrift shop. Her legs were long, her ankles and wrists fragile. Where her black hair hung straight to her shoulders, it turned under naturally. She supposed she had what people called a heart-shaped face. The eyes were like Peter's: long, almond-shaped, dark, with thin long lashes. She wondered about her incisors. They protruded somewhat and gave her, she thought, when she smiled, a strangely wise, catlike expression. . . . But wasn't her nose too long?

Perhaps, she wondered to herself, stealing glances in the shop windows, she might be photogenic: didn't she have high cheekbones? But then, perhaps she was really almost too Oriental-looking to be truly attractive. Didn't her rear stick out too much? Was her skin olive-toned or only swarthy? Was she tall and graceful or only long and round-shouldered? She wished there were some way to know.

This year Uncle Ben informed them he had a new idea for Mama.

"After all, she isn't forty yet," he observed, shaking his head so the aura of cologne enveloped them. They were seated at the Eighty-sixth Street cafeteria near the subway. There was the clatter of trays and, at the next table, an old woman with rheumy eyes watched them. He was going, Uncle Ben told them, to ship Mama out of the city—not to High Hills, of course: she'd never fit in, a sophisticated place like that—but to a farm where she could board, July and August.

"I hope it's not the funny farm," Peter warned.

It wasn't, of course it wasn't, Uncle Ben assured them with irritation. Not only that. Now the two of them could work all summer instead of looking after her. And out of the hot city, if you please. He'd arranged it, he said.

What he'd arranged was a junior counselor job for Peter at a boys' camp. Till one of the parents discovered Peter's history, his lack of responsibility in the matter of his younger sister. Peter was sent back to live alone in the apartment. He did wangle a job as a delivery boy, he wrote Jane, and though the pay was nothing, the tips were good. There were a lot of lonely ladies in the city, he wrote her. Lucky he knew what to do.

Lonely men, too. That wasn't so great, but the tips were even larger.

He was writing because Jane was trapped with a family summering in Manasquan, over in New Jersey, at the shore. For room and board, plus five dollars a week, she cooked, washed up, made beds, dusted and vacuumed, took the six-year-old girl and four-year-old boy to the beach each day. At night she gave them their baths and read to them, while Mrs. Norris went forth to play bridge or to bowl or to the movies. Mr. Norris, when he came out weekends, was as big a slob as the children.

Jack Tanner, Jack Tanner, Jane admonished herself as the little girl pinched her to get her way and the little boy kicked her in the shins to get his. She was determined to stick it out. *These* people might not be "masterful, only domineering," but if she quit, she'd be "only vain, not self-respecting."

It was Peter's letters that intervened to save her. Mrs. Norris went through her things one Sunday afternoon in August on the screened back porch where Jane spent her sleepless nights. Peter's letters, in answer to Jane's descriptions of the family, described in vivid detail how he spent his time.

"So! *We're* not good enough for you!" Mrs. Norris waved the letters while Jane repeated in a low voice:

"May I please have those back?"

"Our kids are brats and we're animals, huh? *We're* animals? We should report this fine brother of yours to the . . . to the . . . I don't know *where* you put kids like that. A juvenile home, huh?" Her sagging bosom heaved as she appealed to her husband.

Jane recalled trying to grow fond of the children. The

furrows of blonde hair gleaming along their spines as they played in the sand had touched her. But then they'd whined so, complained so, of one another and of her.

"Mrs. Norris," she said, "your children *are* brats. But it's not their fault. They're the ones who should be sent away. From you. So they can still learn what it is to be courteous and—and loving—and human."

"Out! Out, out!" Mrs. Norris screamed. Her arms high in the air while they tore up the letters, Mrs. Norris watched her husband move forward, as though to strike Jane. Perhaps he restrained himself because the screened porches on either side of the house were filled with attentive spectators.

"Pack your things. I'll drive you back to the city with me. Though you don't deserve transportation," he snapped, and reached for her knee in the car on the way back. Jane struck his pudgy hand with the side of her palm so that he yelped.

It was only at home with Peter that she permitted herself to cry. Peter held her on his lap, their long legs intertwined, and kissed and cajoled her till she stopped. Then she held his thin dark face between her palms and kissed the eyelids, the lips salty with her tears. She felt him come alive beneath her hips and wavered, till the familiar withdrawn stare of concentration pulled him away from her, and the moment passed.

But Peter had money now; he was able to buy them theater tickets. The remainder of the summer they saw everything worth seeing. Peter bought a phonograph and Jane sang to him the songs of the musicals. Vaguely, she and Peter talked of the war in Europe. They wondered: would war spread? Would Americans ever stand, weeping, like the man in that newspaper picture when Paris fell?

The summer in the country did seem to have helped Mama. But by late March—the fifth anniversary—Mama began to wander the streets late at night and was brought home, confused, several times, by the police.

"I'm only looking for my child," she moaned. Her blue eyes were large and dry. "Why can't I look for my child?"

Her silences built up to strange brooding rages in

which she moved through the small apartment like a juggernaut, breaking things, tearing, while she groaned loudly through clenched teeth. To get through the Regents and final exams, they had to hide their schoolbooks. The night before her last test, in fourth-year Latin, Jane bolted herself into the bathroom to study while Peter grappled with the twisting, grinding damp figure that erupted beyond the door.

All the way to school on the subway, Jane trembled. Stared, trembling, at the lines from Horace and Juvenal as though she'd never seen them before. Handed in a blank paper that seemed to erase the easy triumphs of all the years in school. It hardly mattered. She wouldn't be going to the prom and she didn't bother with graduation, though she'd won the English prize. Mama wasn't aware that she and Peter were graduating. Jane knew she was a disappointment to Miss O'Brien and to her advisor because she'd refused even to apply for a college scholarship. What was the point? She and Peter would have to go to work.

But first—and at last—they were to go to High Hills.

4

Impossible, Uncle Ben said: the situation with Mama. She'd have to be sent away. For her own good. This time they knew it *was* the funny farm. This time, seated in the same cafeteria where family decisions were made, they raised no objection. And that meant—Uncle Ben's appraising glance, like his cologne, enveloped them—*they* could come to High Hills. As a caddy, Peter would be plenty busy on the eighteen-hole golf course. As for Jane: how would Jane like to help out in the theater? No pay, of course. But sewing? Carpentry? Ushering?

High Hills was a revelation. The glittering blue waters of the lake stretched out of sight behind islands but rested, as though overflowing, below the rim of the terrace that opened from the enormous dining room. Here, heavily starched white cloths were spread at every meal. Fresh flowers and ice water sparkled in the sunlight at the round tables set up for groups of ten. The help, of course, ate elsewhere, a hall abutting the hot kitchen and at long trestle tables bounded by wooden benches.

Someone—someone male—was always pulling Jane's hair at mealtimes. The lifeguard—one of ten she had her eye on—nuzzled her neck and growled, "Why do you have to be jailbait?" He went on to join the actress with the pale blonde hair whose skin was white as bleached rice paper, whose bones looked as though they'd snap like a sparrow's. Word was they had it up to seven times a night before the end of week one.

Surreptitiously, Jane examined Alec while they carried their trays along the service counters, realized this was, at last, lust. She supposed it would make others laugh, if they knew. Especially the women with whom she shared a bungalow—eight cots pushed into every available space. She hadn't forgotten the entrance one of them had made that first afternoon, dropping her gear in the doorway when she found Jane curled up, timid, on her cot. She'd shot a look of exasperated disbelief and demanded of the others, who were still unpacking:

"Oh, crap! What's this? The infant brigade?"

"Never mind her, Janie." Aurelia Anderson, the costume mistress, was twenty-four, had already shown Jane around. "Maxine's done props so long, her heart's turned into one." Later, indignant, Jane had pointed out to Aurelia:

"I *am* sixteen!"

Aurelia had dark hair, leathery skin, light brown eyes in very white orbs, very white teeth framed by heavy scarlet lips. She was somewhat overweight, with full low breasts, wore unbecoming T-shirts and shorts that revealed plump thighs, the beginnings of varicose veins. Still, she was somehow pretty; perhaps it was the air of authority that enlivened her features, gave a breathless rush to her words. At Jane's remark, she'd broken up in helpless laughter, cautioned her to keep her age a secret.

Maxine and the others either forgave Jane's youth or

dismissed it, judging from their talk. Jane listened, watching shyly sideways as her roommates tramped about naked on the pine floor and compared notes on their sexual lives. They were all old hands, it seemed, at High Hills.

But the place, the place itself! Jane—and Peter, when she ran into him—continued to marvel. All this here, all these years! The golf course rolled velvety toward the area where large summer cottages were rented by families who didn't care to live in the bungalows for transient guests. Sixteen tennis courts. Rows and rows of canoes and rowboats bobbed up and down near the dock where four college boys were kept busy doling out oars and paddles, while they selected the female guest for the night. The lifeguards, bronzed before the season had got under way, their eyes hidden behind sunglasses, unsmilingly appraised the array of breasts and hips sprawled in the deck chairs along the waterfront.

They struck at night, during the dancing, where it was part of their job, apparently, to keep the women without their husbands happy. It was a joke that the septic system would be clogged with condoms before July was out. The few days that mists rose from the lake and the hills were shrouded in fog, it was understood that the beds in the guest bungalows and staff quarters never got a rest. The women spoke exclusively, it was said, of how nonsensual their husbands were, how very sensual they were themselves.

Food was significant, too. The head chef was possibly the most important employee—"or thinks he is," Paul Talbott, the theater director, mocked. At breakfast the waiters whirled through the swinging doors with gleaming trays that bore juices, fruit, eggs, ham, sausages, steaks, chops, fish, rolls, croissants, an unending supply of silver coffeepots. There was a limitless choice at both lunch and dinner. "Just like a goddam steamship," Talbott commented over their far more limited fare at the trestle tables.

Then, there were professional instructors for sailing, riding, tennis, swimming, golf, calisthenics, dance. Also, a full complement of nightclub, dance band, theater, beauty shop, gym, gift shop, infirmary, library. Above it all, Uncle Ben administered a laughing charm they'd never known him to possess, as he chafed the regular guests and answered their complaints.

"Ben, do something for me, will you?" A woman would stop him on the path before the main building.

"Anything, darling. Within middle-class limits." Off they'd go, arm in arm.

But the guests were not the ones who mattered. The important life, the *only* life, as far as those in the theater department saw it, existed right here, always with the sound of hammering, of rehearsal, of music. There was a completely new show every weekend, with less tightly constructed presentations Tuesday evenings. Paul Talbott was a slight figure with a lean Tartar's face, small graying mustache. He looked, Jane thought, as though a tapeworm gnawed his guts—even his hair was thinning —but his vitality was awesome. She enjoyed revering him.

The splendid, the remarkable element: Jane was swept into the middle of it. There was nothing she wouldn't do in the way of work, so that she became everyone's pet, though most specifically Aurelia's. Jane, for whom this was a novel experience, reveled in her concern. One morning Betty, a pretty young dancer who shared the cabin, said to Jane as they hurried to dress, reach the front of the breakfast line:

"What's with your brother, Jane? I mean: he looks like Valentino. But what's his problem?"

"What do you mean—problem?" Jane pulled on heavy socks Aurelia had given her. The morning was chill.

"He's so—out there, somewhere. You know. Swinging on a star or something. Oh, well, if you haven't noticed . . ."

"Why don't you check it?" Aurelia snapped. "Maybe he doesn't like bulging calves."

Peter was fine, he assured her, when Jane had him to herself. Yet she wondered. That brooding, abstracted air she'd taken for granted for so long. . . . She felt herself separating from him, and was afraid. Still, when she dreamed, there were always those dark eyes above her, those familiar lips in her hair. She concentrated on adoring Alec, the lifeguard, from afar.

It didn't occur to Jane, enviously watching the performers, that she could ever join *them*. They were professionals already, relieved to have summer employment. They had talent. "Genius, to listen to some of them," Aurelia sniffed, quickly sketching a costume for a modern dancer.

But one week, toward the middle of July, it was decided that the staff would put on, for Tuesday's show, an amateur talent night. This, Aurelia predicted, would bring forth temperament, and decided Jane must join in.

"There's nothing I can do," Jane argued, timorous.

Aurelia wound up her portable phonograph, whisked a record from the sleeve of one of her short thick albums. "Can you learn words?" she challenged. "I'm going to dress you as a flapper."

Tuesday night Jane stared at her reflection in the full-length mirror backstage. *She* was behind that mysterious curtain now, the curtain as majestic and powerful here as in New York. She'd allowed Aurelia to cut her hair, twenties' style, and she appeared suddenly older, knowing, sophisticated. Aurelia had decked her out in a short waistless dress of apricot and pink chiffon with an enormous bow adorning the pleats that circled the hem. Pink silk stockings encased her legs, her feet were shod in pink satin shoes. Aurelia had coached her and now, as the music came on—Jane recalled those evenings she'd sung and danced for Peter—she didn't consider that this was herself who pranced out in front of those rows of faces in the darkness. This must surely be somebody else who made the movements to the music and sang out—"Sing *out!*" Aurelia had hissed at her just before she'd gone on—in a husky voice the words to "I Wanna Be Bad."

She was a smash. Those were cheers and stamping feet she heard out there—and from the wings, too. The band ran through it again, and Mike, the leader, gestured to her insistently to repeat. She really let herself go, strutting, slinking up to the footlights, shimmying, sideways and slow. As the words instructed, she shook her shoulders and twisted her hips. Backstage they hugged her—"So much for jailbait," Maxine snorted approvingly—and Paul Talbott appraised her quizzically while Jake, one of the male dancers, swung her around.

"I never would have known," Talbott said.

"You were sensational," Peter agreed when she joined him later. Then she was swept up by the others, they were including her at last in their late-night revels.

"Ever been skinny-dipping, love?" Aurelia's arm was around her as they moved in a crowd to the lake, swelling darkly under a full moon.

"In the Julia Richman pool?" Jane asked.

She stepped out of her shorts and halter without hesitation at the water's edge, even posed for scrutiny as her hand went up to where the long hair used to fall across her shoulders, felt—was it the flapper's shingled hairdo?—ages old as she slipped into the dark water. Hands came up around her waist as she swam out and Alec, *the* lifeguard, was holding her.

"You damn little vamp," he chuckled, his nose touching hers, drops hanging from his eyelashes, and his hands moving up beneath her armpits. "You damn little Oriental vamp. You know, in the moonlight, your cheeks have the look of a mango." While his lips brushed against them, Jane gasped against the lapping of water:

"What's a mango?"

Alec gave a short hoot. Gliding smoothly, he swam her far past the others, and guided her toward shore, onto a mossy spot beneath the pines.

He must have taken that actress here, Jane reflected. That was how he knew it so unerringly. Gently, he laid her back on the moss where she shivered in the night air, but his wet body came down over her own, covering and warming her. He was kissing her, just as she'd imagined him doing all these weeks, and Jane stared up with anticipation into his blue-green eyes, lit by the moon.

As he thrust at her she realized, almost with relief, that this was it at last. Momentarily, she wondered. Shouldn't he be doing something first? Of course, he could hardly arrive prepared, unless he had a condom stuffed in his ear. But it didn't matter. She lay quiescent beneath him, felt a long, reassuring pain as he entered her.

"So, you're a little virgin, too," he observed. "Raise that lovely plump rear and wrap your legs around my ass, innocent."

She obeyed. Everything was sliding now, their warm

wet bodies, and he inside her. She closed her eyes and saw above her Peter's face, his dark eyes shining down into hers, quickly opened her own again, tried to concentrate on Alec. But it was already over. He was kissing her neck, asking her how she was, then raising her to her feet. Swimming back, he mentioned it casually:

"Say, listen. Take care of yourself, will you? We don't want you switching from flapper songs to lullabies."

Aurelia had waited up, followed her into the bathroom. "So? You finally went and lost it at the Astor, huh?"

Jane nodded, smiling. She was shivering now and there was the faintest pink smudge on the towel when she dried herself. "He said I should take care of myself."

"That bastard!" Aurelia exploded. "He just assumed he could go ahead when he wanted it. Christ!" Aurelia disappeared, returned with the bulbous instrument Jane had noticed they each had, and used.

"Listen, fill this with warm water and stick it up you and squeeze. I just hope it doesn't sail the sperm right into your womb."

Obediently, Jane perched on the toilet and took the douche. When she squeezed, the water squirted across the floor.

"A fucking Niagara!" Aurelia fussed, and refilled the bag. "And did he even satisfy you? I mean, did he make you come? It's not good not to, you know," as Jane shook her head. "Occupied!" she snarled as someone tried the door. Then she was yanking the douche impatiently from Jane's hand to push it inside her, kneeling in front of her with concentration as she squeezed the bulb. More water shot out and Aurelia snapped:

"Sit back! Raise your legs, for God's sake!"

"You sound like Alec," Jane giggled. Suddenly, they were both laughing, the water squirting around, Aurelia helpless on the floor and Jane, legs across Aurelia's shoulders, gasping with laughter.

But, in the messhall next morning, in full view of everyone, Aurelia slapped a package of condoms into Alec's hand as he held it out for a plate of eggs.

"Slip one of those on it next time, buster," she told him loudly, "or I'll cut it off with my pinking shears."

General applause. Nearby, Jane glimpsed Peter, taut with anger. She knew a sense of triumph. She'd paid him back. Then, loss. . . .

Perhaps it was the different hairdo. Or her newly lost virginity. Jane began, brazenly as the others, to pad around the bungalow naked. She came to assume the late-night meetings with Alec, liked to be viewed as his girl. After the third time he remarked casually, as he chucked the condom:

"Where you at when we're doing it? You always look as though you're out to lunch."

Jane wondered: did she share Peter's diffidence? She couldn't explain: what went on between herself and Alec in those moments was just no big deal. She was picking a splinter from her finger where she'd been hammering on a set when the actress with the rice paper skin stopped at her side.

"I thought you were awfully vulgar the other night, Jane. And how could you let them do that to your hair?"

At that, Jane stood entranced. She hadn't realized the actress knew her name.

Paul Talbott decided to work her into the Saturday night show—the professional one—doing "Button Up Your Overcoat." For this, Talbott asked Bob, one of the young male dancers, to rehearse Jane in the Charleston.

When she came onstage this time, in a blue and green chiffon dress, blue silk stockings, green satin shoes, the audience that already knew her cheered. She sensed that Talbott had sent her out alone precisely for this ovation. Bob slinked after her, funny-sulky, wrapped in a raccoon coat. Seductively, she circled him while she sang. Then Bob swept her into a frenetic Charleston, both with the air of pouting wonderment Talbott had rehearsed them in. They sailed into a tango that swept them twice across the stage, back into the Charleston, and a frenzied finish.

The audience cheered. Bob wrapped her momentarily in the raccoon coat, then kissed her hand and left her alone onstage. Jane gazed out at these people who grinned, clapped, stamped their feet. Quite suddenly, with deep gratitude, she placed her hands over her frantically beating heart. They ate that up, as a gesture rehearsed. A flashbulb exploded. They couldn't know how grateful she was, how strange it was for her to feel loved by anyone but Peter.

Later, Aurelia obtained a copy of the picture. It showed her light-dazzled face, her hands on her heart. She might have been praying.

But, that night, a nightmare returned from the past. She was in the playground again, and Joanie in the swing. She watched herself turn away and, as she turned back, saw Joanie step down from the swing. Now! she told herself in the dream. Now, at last, she'd see how it had happened. But the dream continued, like a movie frame repeated over and over. She kept turning away— she herself now grown up as she was—and Joanie kept stepping down from the swing. Please! Please let me see, she tried to wail in the dream, but no words came. She awoke sobbing, Maxine's arms around her.

"Honey, honey, what is it? Maxine's here. Don't cry."

"Oh, so awful. So awful," Jane sobbed against her shoulder.

Aurelia was beside them. Even in the dark Jane saw how her eyes snapped with anger.

"Hey! Get back to your props. Keep your hands off her!"

"Oh." Maxine held Jane as tightly. "I didn't see the reserved sign hung on her."

"I won't have you sliming her up first chance you get."

"Better than making her into a bull dyke like you."

"Shit on toast!" From her cot, Betty emitted a groan. "Can't you call a cut? Or carry on outside, for God's sake!"

Added recommendations came from other cots. Reluctantly, Maxine arose. She shrugged her shoulders and returned to her own bed while Aurelia stroked Jane's hair.

"Okay now, honey?" she asked anxiously.

Jane nodded. She wondered if she ever really would be.

In August Peter said he needed to talk to her. They walked through the woods to a grove where they sat on pine needles and watched a bee travel along a shaft of sunlight. Jane had been doing numbers with fair regularity by now and Peter told her that he'd not only picked up a pile of dough already—"It's like the delivery boy system, only better"—but also that one of the older male guests, who ran an agency, wanted him to become a fashion model. Clothes for college boys. As Jane reached over to hug him, Peter held up his hand.

"Wait. I want *you* to go to drama school. I want to send you."

The bee hummed. From far off drifted noises from the lake. Drama school! It hadn't occurred to Jane. She hadn't even let herself think to the end of summer. They didn't know if Mama would be back with them or not. She mentioned this.

Peter nodded. "I've talked to Uncle Ben. She's been getting shock treatment." Jane shuddered. "Uncle Ben's shitting in his pants. That he might have to take us in. Us being minors still. And him our only relative. Lucky we've always looked older than our age. . . . He's willing to go on paying the rent and he thinks my plan is swell."

So they'd live alone. Their own place. And drama school. Jane lifted her gaze to the cobalt vault of sky and breathed in the pine-scented air. Was their penance really over? When she glanced back at Peter, there was that faraway gaze again. Once, long ago, he'd told her he never let himself feel anything anymore, not really. Now, as she watched, his face contorted with grief.

"Peter, my dearest darling. What is it?"

"I don't know," he whispered, staring at her. "I just —don't feel real."

That night she dreamed of swimming naked with Peter to that mossy place where she'd first gone with Alec. But, in the water, he slipped away from her arms and was lost in the darkness. She dreamed that she swam around and around in circles, calling his name, but no answer came. She was alone.

August swirled to an end. Alec, perhaps disgruntled by her lack of intense response, had returned to the actress. For Jane, it meant a bit of hurt pride, but not much. Everyone in the cabin agreed she must, indeed, enter drama school. The Neighborhood Playhouse, Maxine suggested. If she could pass the audition.

As though insulted, Aurelia snorted. "She'll pass."
Privately, Aurelia mentioned that anytime Jane wanted,
her place in the Village was open to her. "It's only a
three-room walk-up on Christopher Street. But as they
say: everything I have is yours."

How and where did Aurelia think *she* lived? Still in
a big apartment on West End Avenue? Jane thanked her,
said she'd be living with her brother.

It was difficult to leave High Hills. Harder still to
return to that squalid place on the East Side, jammed
with its fading elegant furniture, its grim memories. Of
course, they asked to see Mama. To their relief, the doctor didn't think it yet advisable. "Her moods swing too
violently still, from high to low and back," he said mysteriously, by phone.

Peter began his modeling job. The first day his picture appeared in *The New York Times*—Peter waving a
football pennant in an overcoat from Best's—they went
out to celebrate. This provided, too, courage for Jane to
audition at the Neighborhood Playhouse. Miss Jones, a
tall, equine lady with deep wrinkles on either side of
her puffy mouth, appeared initially hesitant about Jane's
age. When she understood that Jane had finished high
school, she ordered her to stand away from her desk, to
improvise. She was to pretend she was seeing her boyfriend off to war.

"Which may be a good preparation," Miss Jones
added grimly.

Before the woman's hooded gaze, Jane tried to envi-
sion Alec, raised her arms toward the shadowy image.
Nothing happened. Into his place stepped Peter, moving
inexorably away from her, unable to hear the words that
trembled from her lips.

She passed. Another celebration. And a phone call to
Aurelia.

Those autumn mornings in New York! To stride rapidly up to Lexington Avenue, await the bus, ride it to
Fifty-fourth Street, while she gazed raptly into the shop
windows with their alternations of junk and luxury, to
be jostled as she finished the trip on foot and arrived to
work with the others. It was as though she tasted in the
crisp air the cities in her future—London, Paris—with a
happy sense of déjà vu. The school's enchanting musti-

ness suggested there were more important matters to attend to here than modernity. Not only was penance paid, Jane reflected, but she must have been storing up reward a long, long time in heaven.

The night of Pearl Harbor she and Peter wandered hand in hand through Yorkville, a few blocks down. The German-Americans sang and celebrated in the streets, with their steins of beer held aloft. Apparently they had no doubt the war would end soon, Hitler, of course, the victor. To Jane it seemed alien to be alive in an actual time of war, war for her own country. Vastly depressed, they returned home, undressed silently in the dark. In the dark they gazed at one another, then away.

Shortly after Christmas, Peter told her that his boss, his mentor, was pressuring him to move in with him. They talked about it, what it would mean to Peter's life. There would be a lot of contacts, of course, a lot of luxury, too.

"But is that what you want?" Jane asked anxiously.

"You must know what I want," he told her bluntly. "If we stay on here together, it's going to happen."

Jane flushed. The next day she called Aurelia, whose response was ecstatic. It took a short time to pack. The place was sublet, furnished, till next September. For a moment Jane looked around the kitchen, wondered if she should bring any groceries. Then she realized she didn't even wish to carry from here the salt or pepper.

A taxi brought her, with her two small suitcases, past a tiny triangular park to the intersection of Christopher and Gay streets. Far off, in the distance, loomed the Empire State Building. Above her, on the fire escape of the third and top floor, whose low windows opened outward, Aurelia waved.

"Wait! I'll come and help!" she called.

Then she was on the street and hugging Jane. Leading her up the stairs. As they stepped into the small hallway, Aurelia closed the door behind them, her light brown eyes glowing. Beyond, Jane glimpsed, set out on a small table, Aurelia's ubiquitous bottle of Scotch and two glasses.

"Darling," Aurelia said as her hand closed on Jane's arm. "I promise you. You won't ever be sorry."

42

Chapter II

1

To the Neighborhood Playhouse, Jane was a despair. She rarely theorized, hung back on dissecting motivation, didn't push for center stage in the bare rooms where they worked out. Still, when Jane stepped into the role—improvisation or script—she mesmerized them. Sanford Meisner, himself, was impressed.

At the start, she'd argued with Aurelia: she must take a part-time job to pay for her upkeep. Aurelia placed a finger against Jane's lips.

"Listen, hon! I hate housekeeping. The only extra expense you are is food. You do the housework. I figure I've hired me a maid. 'Cause I do me so well."

Aurelia subsisted on free-lance work—designing for stage shows at the Roxy and Radio City Music Hall, for acts at nightclubs like the Latin Quarter, the Coconut Grove. Occasionally, Jane accompanied her to the eight-story fabric warehouse on Sixth Avenue or they went to the Metropolitan Museum, where Aurelia made notes on the hang or the color of a Renaissance robe, the design of a Greek necklace, an Egyptian headdress, while Jane admired the Turners and Monets.

Every day Jane made the double bed in the narrow room with the fire escape where they slept, straightened up around Aurelia's work in the living room—her easel, large scrapbooks of fabric samples, a dress form, sewing machine, library books on the history of costume scattered about on the couch and floor, clippings from magazines and newspapers about current plays and current people—did the kitchen work she'd been accustomed to most of her life.

There *was* another price.

Still, why consider it a price? There were actions she

43

could now permit without guilt, with almost a sense of release: every night in the wide bed she allowed Aurelia to enjoy her—Aurelia's flesh, warm and chunky, Aurelia eager to satisfy her, "which is more," Aurelia was fond of saying, "than any prick will do for you." With her, when Jane closed her eyes, there was no image of Peter above her. Aurelia demanded little in return. Often, in her arms, Jane would find herself drifting away into a movement she might use for tomorrow's workshop: to hold her arm so heavily, to let it drop so slowly to her side. . . .

"Janey-love, is that it, sweet? Happy now? You can sleep?"

"Yes, thank you," drowsily, and moving up into Aurelia's lap as she turned her back.

There were many friends in the evenings when Jane returned from whatever play she'd seen. There was something to be learned from production. Coming in, she offered to toast cheese sandwiches to go with the drinks spread out on the floor where Aurelia's friends sprawled—some women Aurelia's age, several quite a bit older, a few homosexuals—and she saw how Aurelia bristled with pride while Jane passed under review. One of the women said, one evening:

"With this rotten war, you know, we're all going to be old maids."

"A lot she cares," a youth rejoined, indicating Aurelia. "She's got her honey to keep her warm."

Many young men at the Neighborhood Playhouse observed they were only marking time before they were called up. The streets had begun to fill with those in uniform. Meanwhile, Jane carried *The New York Times* every day because, several times a week, there was Peter, debonair, lounging in front of the ivy-covered buildings of Columbia, or handing a girl into a horse-drawn carriage in front of the fountain at the Plaza, and dressed in clothes from Best's or Altman's or Lord and Taylor's. He met her and Aurelia for spaghetti on Eighth Street.

Amused, he told them: "They say I have the understated college-boy look."

"With the typical college boy's curriculum," Aurelia commented. She broke off an end of French bread.

44

"How is it—with him?" Jane found it difficult to mention the name of the man Peter lived with. Peter shrugged.

"You can learn to live on caviar." He glanced side-long at Jane. "And other things. Right?"

Jane flushed. Aurelia went on chewing.

Jane wondered, as summer approached, whether they'd return to High Hills. But one day Aurelia awaited her, triumphant, at the head of the stairs as Jane appeared with groceries. She took the bags from Jane's arms, led her into the living room, knelt in front of the one armchair where she sat Jane down.

"I've had an offer to do the costumes for a play opening at the Village Theatre in September. They pay Equity salary and I've wangled a tiny part for you. You won't mind summer in the city, will you, love?"

The theater was half the size of the one at High Hills. While it underwent redecoration, rehearsals were held in a hot, airless loft near Second Avenue. The part *was* tiny—a walk-on, as a maid—but the play would be reviewed, the cast was Equity. Just before their seventeenth birthday in June, Jane met Peter at Chock Full O'Nuts. They leaned against the crowded counter while they consumed cream cheese and date-nut-bread sandwiches with orange juice. Not many investors, Peter told her, proud of her, had such quick success with their stock as he'd had. Then:

"Look. I hope this won't let you down. But I'm cutting out. As soon as I turn seventeen, I'm enlisting."

Jane's knees turned weak. She laid down the remnant of her sandwich. "Why?"

"If I enlist, I get my choice of service. And if I lie about my age." His gaze, always remote, wandered from her distraught face. "Besides, I've had it. Up to here. He demands too much."

She didn't want to hear, didn't want to know what the mentor demanded. The noise around her clogged her ears and Jane recalled her audition, saw herself raise her arms toward Peter to say goodbye. Her lips felt numb.

"I don't want you to go."

He brought his face close to her own. "If you love me, you don't want me to stay."

Before he left, they went to visit Mama.

It had only been a year. The hospital near the East River was high, white, impressive. The halls were air-conditioned, the elevators soundless. As they followed the nurse's squeaking rubber soles over the asphalt-tiled hall, they briefly held hands as they used to do, barely aware of the fumbling contact. For a moment of terror, Jane felt a raw wind at her back. She and Peter were scrambling up the hill from the park, she could hear the melancholy cry of a tug on the river, their eyes were scanning the dusty streets for that small figure. Somewhere behind them, Danny Edelman's voice tried to reassure them.

Then they saw Mama in the lounge on one of the green plastic couches.

She'd grown enormous. Her blonde hair was even more faded and streaked now with gray, the face florid, shining. She appeared to be waiting for them, waiting to pounce on them, to devour them. It occurred to Jane, just for a second, before she was flooded with pity, that for a child to love this mother was to be like those fish or chicken that smiled from billboards and entreated you to cook and eat them.

The visit began well enough. Mama was remarkably calm. Was that medication? Jane tried not to imagine this enormous bulk laid out on a table, nurses applying ointment to her temples, attendants holding her down as her body flailed in convulsions. She tried not to see those blue eyes bright with terror as they shone, now, bright with almost palpable joy.

"Nobody here would believe I have two such beautiful children," she gushed. "I keep asking Uncle Ben for pictures so I can show people. But he never gives me any." Did they exist? Jane wondered. "I didn't remember myself—with what I've been through—how beautiful you two were."

Peter took her hand. "Has it been very terrible, Mama?"

"Oh, they're good to me here," Mama insisted. "They better be. They need me. It's not terrible for *me*. It's only seeing the others. The way they suffer. The way they make them suffer. . . ."

Jane glanced quickly away from the shining face. It

glistened with perspiration as though a terrible inner heat consumed her. On the East River, a freighter glided slowly by.

"But do they help you, Mama?" Peter asked.

"Help?" Mama took her hand from his. "I'm not the one who needs help. I wouldn't stay here a minute if I wouldn't feel too guilty about leaving the others. They're the ones need help. They need *me*. . . ."

"Well, but, Mama," Jane began.

"You think I'm here as a patient?" Mama's laugh was short, impatient. "Maybe that's how I first came. I was a little upset when I got here. I remember how you treated me," she told Peter, her bright eyes watching him with the stare of a blind woman. "Fighting me. Running me out of the house. . . ."

"I didn't," Peter put in, but her voice rose.

"So I was willing—for the sake of you children—to come here for a while. Instead of spending all my time taking care of two ungrateful kids. I found a place I could be useful."

"Yes, Mama?" Peter urged now. "What do you do?"

"What do you mean, what do I do?" At the placating note in Peter's voice, she swelled. "If I tried to keep track of everything I do all day and night, I wouldn't have a chance to breathe. . . . Help with the shock treatments. Empty bedpans. Wash the floors nights. Write letters for patients. Figure out their treatments. . . ."

"How do you do that, Mama?" Peter's voice was toneless. Jane sat by, chill, stupefied.

Mama leaned in closer to whisper. "You see those electric sockets in the wall? I get messages from them. They tell me what to do. . . . And how to fight off the doctor when he tries to fuck me. He can do that, you know." She leaned back, sly. "Just with his eyes, he can do that. Of course, not one letter I've written to the White House has got me an answer. Not even a form reply." Her voice rose again. "But I never really expected that warmonger to take time off. . . . You know we're at war, I suppose?" she interrupted herself, conversationally.

"Yes, Mama. That's one of the reasons," Peter began. But Mama raced on, her words running into one another.

"I have a telephone directory hidden in my room

with the names of all the traitors in the country. You think we're at war with Germany, don't you? Really it's Mexico. Only nobody knows. I've been trying to learn Spanish—secretly, of course: *por favor*," she simpered, and laughed at their startled faces, "because when they let the cat out of the bag, they'll need someone like me who can—what's the word?—infiltrate?"

"Yes, Mama," Peter said. "That's the word."

"And then, someone like me, someone without family to worry about, that's the kind of person they can send into the most secret places to find things out. Because what do I have to lose? I mean," and Mama's arms flailed the air, "I've lost everything already, haven't I? What more can happen to me? Only," and now the bright eyes clouded, she was suddenly Mama as she used to be on West End Avenue, sad and quiet and gentle, back even when Emmy had cared for them, "only I can't remember what it is I lost. If only I could remember, it would really help me a lot." She scrutinized their faces. "You don't remember, by any chance, do you? Do you have any idea what it could have been?"

2

For their seventeenth birthday, Aurelia made a party— their first—but it was rather a forlorn affair. Even the calico kitten she brought out in a box decked with crepe paper only evoked from Jane a bleak smile. Peter would be gone tomorrow. As she fixed her gaze on him, Peter leaned across the table, covered her hand.

"Hey, whatever happened to Jack Tanner?" he admonished.

"Who's he?" Aurelia demanded quickly. Her ice cream spoon hovered in midair over the slice of birthday cake.

" 'They are not disciplined, they are only cowed,' "

Jane murmured obediently. Peter explained to Aurelia, who nodded.

"You mean, that's how I keep her in line?"

"That's how," Peter said. "It's as simple as that."

Then he was gone. In deference to the conversation, Jane named the kitten Jack Tanner. The summer punched in, punishing. When the air cooled, Jane and Aurelia sat out on the fire escape with their drinks. Aurelia often went inside to work while Jane continued outside, reading plays. In the breathless heat there was constant bickering at the rehearsal loft and, when they moved into the theater, tantrums, rebellion against the director.

The play opened in September to reviews that praised Aurelia's work. She bought a scrapbook for Jane, pasted in the clippings, though Jane's name appeared only in the cast of characters. "How do you think Bernhardt started?" Aurelia wanted to know.

Before Thanksgiving, the play folded. Winter dragged on. The skies were endlessly gray, the streets filled with black slush and ice. Between classes, Jane trudged to agencies to line up something—anything—in summer stock. The answer was always to come back at some nebulous "later." In February, there was a visit to see Peter off from Easton, Pennsylvania, before he left for a camp in Louisiana. He'd opted for the Air Force, was training as a bombardier, with the fib about his age would become a second lieutenant before shipping overseas, still a year from now. Perhaps the war would be over by then? Jane wondered aloud to Aurelia.

Pityingly, Aurelia laughed.

She pierced Jane's ears, gave her a pair of hand-wrought silver earrings, each a tiny hand containing a pearl. Jane attended the Stage Door Canteen and USO dances, talked to soldiers and sailors sanguine with talk of easy victory, parried their accusations of hindering the war effort when she wouldn't sleep with them. The nightmares were growing worse again. The dream about the swing returned. She was caught in that stuck frame where she revolved, stood transfixed, saw the small figure step down, turned, always turned too late and missed what had happened next. Aurelia comforted her.

Then, as a false spring rustled into the city, as the wind warmed into gentle breezes in March, she was handed a part on Broadway. A very small part, one for which there hadn't been an understudy. The girl who played her was leaving to marry her soldier, accompany him to camp. The director had contacted the Neighborhood Playhouse. Sandy Meisner had recommended Jane.

Jane wandered backstage, the first Broadway backstage she'd ever walked on, and wondered if the audience could ever understand how large a world existed here, behind the silent, rustling velvet curtain that separated them, out there, from the reality she'd always known existed here. She played the high school sister of a young girl whose husband has gone off to war. Her hair, grown long again, was tied back in a ponytail and she mostly ran onstage in skirt, sweater and saddle shoes to drop innocuous remarks between important entrances and exits.

One night, as she removed her makeup in the crowded room set aside for those with small parts, someone handed Jane a note.

"May I see you? Danny Edelman."

For a moment, there was reluctance. Jane saw herself and Peter carrying the groceries with Papa as they descended the hill to West End Avenue, saw Danny approach, hesitate, the pitying awareness of their lost childhood in his eyes. Then, she chided herself, returned a short note of assent. If nothing else, Danny was a link to Peter.

Jane emerged into the damp air of the March night and looked about. Several soldiers stood at the stage door, but one—a second lieutenant in the Air Corps—immediately separated himself from the others and came toward her.

She would have recognized him anywhere. The light brown curly hair, the wide-set golden eyes, the long, straight nose of Michelangelo's Moses. Maturity had brought into prominence the bones in the bronzed cheeks, the tender curve of the wide, generous mouth. He'd been a good-looking boy, she'd always thought. Like his eyes, he was a golden one, now.

"Jane! It really is you!" Danny took her hands.

"I never thought I'd be glad to see you again," she confessed. This was, she knew, hardly tactful. She wondered if he realized his hands were crushing hers as he stared down at her.

"But you are? You don't mind?"

"You mean: does it reawaken memories?" Wryly, Jane smiled. "You don't have to worry about that. Some memories are always there." Seven years ago this month, she added silently.

"She was never found, was she?" His low voice, his gaze expressed concern.

Jane shook her head. The main actors emerged from the stage door, she and Danny were jostled aside. She touched the bars on his uniform.

"Peter's in the Air Force, too. Training to be a bombardier. Did you enlist?"

"Yes. Going over in a week. I'm a pilot."

She remembered he'd been older than they. As they began to walk, a light drizzle touching their faces, he drew her arm through his. He told her he'd had a year and a half at Columbia, wanted to be a playwright. He, too, was in love with theater.

"I never thought I'd drop in on a play and see you up there onstage. I didn't even notice your name before the first act. But I recognized you right away." He paused briefly under the streetlight and studied her. "You always had the most perfectly articulated lips, even as a child. And that certain wistful air. . . ."

Jane smiled. "You noticed things like that? Back when you and Peter played ball?"

"I always noticed you." They walked on. "Maybe when this is over, I'll write a play. And you'll be the star."

"Is that a date?"

"You can count on it."

He was staying with his parents, still over on West End Avenue. But he had a friend, with a place of his own. It was at Lindy's they understood they didn't care to eat. They contemplated the strawberry shortcake, covered with heavy cream and strawberry syrup, then each other. The potency of her own desire surprised Jane.

When Danny excused himself to telephone, she watched him thread his way between the crowded tables and felt excitement mount in her at sight of his tall graceful figure.

The friend's place was up on Ninetieth Street and Broadway. He'd graciously stepped out for the night. In the cluttered bedroom, as Danny moved to take her in his arms, Jane stopped him.

"Don't you have a girl friend?" she asked curiously.

"Yes. She's at a Bar Mitzvah dance tonight. We were supposed to get married after the war."

"Oh?" She rested in his arms, secure in what he'd say next. He said it.

"Guess I'd better write her a Dear John letter in the morning."

But later, lying against his side, her face on his chest, his fingers stroking her bare shoulder and arm, Jane refused to say she loved him. It was only to herself she could admit there was something about this that was like coming home. Peter himself had hung in abeyance while they made love. Perhaps it was because Danny was almost a part of a triangle, one they'd made together that day seven years ago. And Peter *was* her, a part of her. Danny lifted her face to his, kissed her long and ardently.

"So you don't love me yet. I'll love you enough for both of us. Until you know what you feel."

She saw him all day and every night after the play until he left. Aurelia wanted to know why she was doing this to herself, letting herself get hurt, becoming involved with someone just before he was due to go over. Was this trip necessary? she demanded.

"When you talk like that, you make me think that anyone who goes over in the Air Force is never coming back," Jane flared. It was the closest they'd ever come to a fight.

Still, that last evening at Penn Station, Jane wondered if Aurelia hadn't been correct. She nestled into Danny's arms, opened her lips to drink in the smell of his mouth. He was warm, so warm, he lit her from within.

"Can't you say it?" he whispered. "Don't you know you love me?"

Jane shook her head. "You have to come back for me to say it."

The golden eyes were alight. "Don't worry. I'm not going to disappear. I'm coming back to you."

Then, he, too, was gone. She was just settling into the same melancholy as before when Paul Talbott, the director from High Hills, met her as she came out of the Neighborhood Playhouse.

"I have a new play," he said. "I want you to be in it."

Here Be Monsters, he explained as they sat at the tray tables over sandwiches at Hamburger Heaven, was by a new playwright, a fellow barely thirty, by the name of James Hooper. It was the biggest chance Talbott himself had had, and Hooper, too.

"As soon as I read it, I remembered you at High Hills. I knew you had to be the girl. . . . I checked you out in this lemon, by the way." Talbott's thin face, with its iron-gray mustache, was tense with its usual controlled calm. Jane sensed the suppressed excitement.

The part was a small but pivotal one, he explained. The title: that came from ancient maps that showed the known world and where the seas ended. Beyond that was always printed: "Here Be Monsters." The play concerned a girl of seventeen who has taken care of the children of a young doctor and his wife. Since the age of fourteen, she's had an affair with the doctor, a fact just discovered. A protracted battle has been drawn between the doctor and his wife, who continue to live together while the affair continues. As they wrangle with one another, the girl's mother defends her daughter's actions. It becomes evident she is enjoying this all vicariously, is herself attracted to the doctor.

"But you're the catalyst that turns on all their sicknesses." Talbott sipped his coffee. "You're going to provide just the quality of wanton innocence we need."

Rehearsals began immediately, this time in a large empty warehouse over Broadway. They had April to prepare, would open for two weeks in Philadelphia May first, at the Booth Theatre across from Sardi's May fifteenth. That first day in the rehearsal hall, Talbott introduced Jane to Harold Channing who played the doctor, to Sybil Fox who played his wife, to Laura Cottman who would be Jane's mother. They were all well-established names. It was Talbott, James Hooper, and herself who would be on trial, Jane saw, as she shook hands nervously with the producer, his assistant, the general manager, the production stage manager. While she signed Social Security and Actor's Equity forms, she was aware that the four men eyed her somewhat askance. She heard one ask, "But who *is* she?," saw Talbott, speaking rapidly, explain.

Aurelia had landed the costuming for a play opening at the St. James up the street, came in with its star, Cynthia Blackwood, the day they moved into the Booth for the last week of rehearsal. Cynthia, complacently notorious, clad in mannish slacks and shirt, with a man's fedora on her golden tousled hair—shades of Marlene Dietrich—patted Jane's fanny afterward and commented briefly, over the cigarette dangling from her lips:

"Nice work, baby. I see what your pal here's been mouthing about."

But it wasn't nice work.

By now Jane had been released from the other play. She should have been strong, confident. But Jane sensed herself waiting for something to happen inside her. Although everyone appeared mildly pleased with her, Jane herself had not yet realized a solid handle on the role and suddenly, a few days before Philadelphia, she began to come apart. A rising terror immobilized her thoughts, thickened her tongue onstage, stiffened her body. She saw how the others, at the start tolerant and helpful, turned toward her in amazement, finally away in something like panic. Talbott took her aside.

"Look, are you having your period or something?"

She heard the controlled desperation and shook her head. Her throat kept closing up.

When Aurelia came to watch, that last day before Philadelphia, Jane saw the corroboration of her own fears in Aurelia's ashen face. Backstage Aurelia gripped her shoulders and insisted heartily: "You were fine, love. Just go on out there in the boondocks and break a leg." Then she turned away and lit a cigarette, rare for her.

In the boondocks, they weren't cruel. Both the *In-*

quirer and the *Bulletin* issued mild reviews, one always happy to see three veterans of the theater "who can hardly give less than a good performance," the other moderately interested in the "novel interlacing of time and space conceived by the new playwright, James Hooper." But the review went on: "There's something missing at the heart of this play and it may be the lack of focus in the person of the little teen-ager around whom the whole storm centers. One wonders, at the end, what the turmoil was really all about."

Jane marched into Talbott's hotel room in the morning.

"I want you to replace me." The mirror opposite revealed her, pale, dry-eyed. The stubborn thrust of Talbott's jaw, despite the weariness on his face, prompted her. "Not for you. Or the play. Or the others. I can't go on." Her voice trailed into a whisper. "I'm too ashamed . . ."

"I can't replace you now," he rasped. Which meant: tacitly, he agreed. "This is still a try-out. You were doing fine till a couple of weeks ago. We'll iron it out."

But the ride back on the train to New York was funereal. Aurelia's false cheer only served to turn Jane sulky. By opening night—the streets a confusion of people, cabs, limousines—when Aurelia delivered her backstage, Jane told her in a hollow voice:

"Please. Do me a favor. Don't tell me to break a leg. And don't try to congratulate me after."

She stood in the wings then, hidden by the stage tormentor at stage right, before the curtain rose. She remembered herself romanticizing this so-called reality behind it. She wanted now only to get it over. The play took place in a time frame of sorts and, as the houselights darkened, she watched the curtain rise on Sybil Fox, the wife, who stood at the long windows of her "charmingly furnished" suburban living room. Sunlight slanted through the glass panes and a coffee service stood on the low table before the couch, on which sections of the Sunday *Times* were spread. Sybil listened tensely to the sounds of a car parking outside, footsteps coming up the walk. The doorbell chimed, she stiffened (count to three), then opened the door to Laura, the mother. Both women were fashionably dressed. Sybil plunged immediately into speech.

"I realize this is a new one on an old situation. But then, for me, the situation itself is rather a novel one."

"I've hardly had much practice at it myself," Laura countered.

"Haven't you? I wondered. Do sit down, won't you?"

Jane watched, her throat closed. The "situation" was quickly revealed. The doctor's wife appealed to the mother of her husband's mistress to call the girl off. The mother refused to intervene. She admired her daughter's courage, her daughter's taste.

"*Your* taste," she pointed out.

At stage left, the doctor, suave, good-looking, came slowly down the steps from upstairs. The three-way battle was joined. Jane listened to the familiar words, to the faint rustles from the darkness beyond the stage, a muffled cough. Her fingers were icy. She would enter soon: the uninvited guest her mother had brought along.

Suddenly, she saw them, those three adults who bickered with one another about their lives, about her. A slow, murky tide of resentment began to mount in her, to thrust against the constriction in her throat. Who did they think they were? Like all adults! All the ones who'd pushed her and Peter around all those long, dreary years! Peter wasn't beside her now, she knew that. Yet she sensed his presence somewhere here in the wings, resenting them with her.

" 'They are not moral, only conventional,' " he seemed to remind her, in the words of Jack Tanner. Jane's vision, that had appeared dimmed these past weeks, fogged in, began to clear. She narrowed her eyes, felt her lips twist in a cold, controlled rage. Her cue was coming. She moved quietly around to the doorway and lifted her chin. She suddenly couldn't wait.

Between acts nobody in the cast said anything, except with their eyes. Paul Talbott and James Hooper stood in the rear of the auditorium, would mingle with the audience to get feedback. Jane was receiving hers in the intensity of the listening out there as she spoke her lines, the casting back of light onstage by the others to her new illumination. When the curtain fell, when they lined up for their calls, Jane saw Malloy, up on the light grid, grinning down at her while he held his index finger to his thumb in congratulation. They stood together, the four of them, bowing to the applause, then each of them stepped forward. The applause continued, vigorous, generous. The three veterans handed Jane forward to the apron. From here and there she heard them: cheers.

In her dressing room Jane could deliver from their green tissue paper the flowers Peter had sent and that she'd been too humiliated to handle before. Uncle Ben appeared, bearing his air of surprise about him like his aura of cologne. There was a cable from England, from Danny:

"They're going to love you. Almost as much as I do."

Across the street at Sardi's, Talbott—looking drained—wanted to know what had come over her. Harold and Sybil insisted they'd always known she'd finally come through.

"I must say," Laura drawled. "That's more than I did."

People kept coming to their table. James Hooper, lean, teeth stained by tobacco, was sweating, kept picking up people's champagne glasses, drinking sloppily while nodding in agreement to their praise. At one point Jane ran upstairs to the ladies' room to be alone in a booth, to catch up with herself. When she emerged, women stood before the mirrors and helped themselves lavishly to the cosmetics and perfumes while their reflected faces beamed felicitations on hers. By the time she rejoined the others, the papers had arrived.

They'd all triumphed. Jane tried to read the words that singled her out, had to permit Aurelia to chant them aloud:

"This is a new young presence to watch. . . ." "The director and author of this play have found themselves a wisp of magic in the new young actress, Jane Belmont . . ." "The authority with which Jane Belmont, the same age as the character she portrays, pits herself against the veterans onstage is something I urge you to hurry over to the Booth to see." Walter Winchell had written: "I wouldn't want to light a match if I was up there on stage with little Miss Jane Belmont. The scene is ready to explode, as is, every second she's out front."

Best of all, in the *Times*: ". . . her sense of control, of airy calm insolence, the manner in which she waits just for a moment and then pronounces: 'Regret? I'm too young to know regret.' *Here Be Monsters* should become a classic on the strength of the way young Miss Belmont renders that line alone. . . ."

3

Next morning the phone rang incessantly. Aurelia screened the calls. Agents wished to represent Miss Belmont. Would she please return the call? Someone from *Mademoiselle* would like to set up an interview. Would she please return the call? Peter, from Orlando, Florida, where he'd just been transferred. He'd work a weekend pass for their eighteenth birthday. Did Jane think she could wangle him a seat?

"Now listen, love." Aurelia perched on the side of the tub where Jane lay soaking and consuming her fourth cup of black coffee. "You have to eat. You want to get out on that stage tonight and pass out?"

"It wasn't just a fluke, was it? You think I'll bring it off again?"

"You'll be even better tonight. Let me wash your hair and feed you. Then you're taking a nap."

After the performance that evening, Aurelia waited for her with Cynthia Blackwood who sported, along with her man's clothes, an extremely long gold cigarette holder. She wanted to know if Jane preferred to soak up a little more well-deserved adulation at Sardi's or go on up to Harlem for some jazz.

"Because you're never going to go right to sleep after a performance, you know, darling, don't you?" Cynthia's hand caressed the inner flesh of Jane's upper arm. Jane saw Aurelia watching.

"She never sleeps anyway." Aurelia looked away.

"Oh? What does the love do when she's not sleeping then?" Cynthia asked. They were in a taxi by now, Cynthia between them, and her other arm went around Aurelia's shoulders.

Suddenly, Jane understood that during this time of her own self-absorption, Aurelia had formed a link with someone else. She couldn't, considering how little she'd always given in return, begrudge Aurelia this. But she slipped her arm loose from Cynthia's fingers. *That* they didn't need between them, too.

The reviews kept coming, from weeklies and monthlies now. *Variety* announced: "Youngster Stamp on Vamp." *The New Yorker,* analyzing the erotic quality of Jane's performance, stated that her unique characteristic onstage consisted of the ability to be absolutely still and command attention, even while the swirl of others' talk went on about her. Fan mail and stage-door Johnnies materialized. Danny, who wrote regularly, wanted to know if such a great star would still be available for the play he was planning. On their birthday, Peter sat in the first row, slim and elegantly beautiful in his uniform, his dark eyes shining up at her as she stood onstage. Sybil, the wife, poured herself a drink, asked:

"Tell me. When did you first decide you were in love with him?"

Jane, after a pause: "When he touched me."

"And? If he hadn't touched you?"

Jane turned slightly, something she didn't ordinarily do. She gazed down past the footlights at Peter. "I would still have loved him. You don't understand. . . . He doesn't have to be anywhere near me and my skin burns for his touch." She saw Peter frown. "Do you think I'm ever going to give him up?"

Then Peter was gone again. He wrote that Orlando was full of flying cockroaches, it rained and thundered every afternoon. They had a saying here: if you ordered a slice of pie in a restaurant, you hit the pie three times with a fork. If the cockroach didn't come out, you didn't eat the pie. The bug was still inside.

They were getting roaches, on Christopher Street, because of the heat, a new tenant below. Aurelia suggested it was time for them to move. They made enough money between them now. She could have a room of her own to work in and they'd have a real living room to entertain all the high muck-a-mucks that wanted to come by.

"Do you still want to live together?" Jane asked. They'd never discussed Cynthia. Aurelia flushed.

"Do *you?* I love you, sweetheart. I thought you were sure of that."

Aurelia worried on moving day about the birds accustomed to the crumbs on the fire escape. But they'd found a big, airy apartment on the second floor near Sheridan Square. Jack Tanner, by now a large and handsome cat, trotted quick and low to the ground from wall to wall as though, if his paws touched the floors lightly enough, he wouldn't be committing himself. The four rooms were large, with long low windows. Still, with Aurelia using one room for her studio, there was only a single bedroom.

"We *can* fit another bed in here," Jane suggested, as they moved the furniture about.

Aurelia straightened. "If that's what you want, hon." She appeared so hurt that Jane let the matter ride.

The summer passed. With fall, there was even greater demand for tickets to *Here Be Monsters*. Jane still attended the Neighborhood Playhouse, had little free time. But as the day grew closer for Peter's last furlough before going overseas, that dream of him swimming beside her, being lost in the water, recurred more often. Just before Christmas he called to say his leave had been canceled. They were all to be shipped over in a week. Could she come down to say goodbye?

In winter, Orlando glistened with perpetual color and breeze. The sky was always blue like this, day after day, Peter told her at the airport. She'd never seen palm trees before—had never flown before—and didn't know the names of the flowers. Peter introduced her to his friends. They wanted to know why a brother should keep such a sister to himself, tagged along that first evening as they went out to drink and dance. There was a good deal of laughter. Somebody noticed that Jane and Peter didn't laugh.

"Jeez, I wish I had a sweetheart looked at me the

way your sister looks at you," one soldier complained to Peter. "You sure you're twins? I mean—she's not really your girl, is she?"

When they danced, Jane clung to Peter, sensed the fragility of his body, the bones, the flesh so vulnerable. "Isn't there a way of getting out of going?" The orchestra played "I'll Never Smile Again."

Peter gave his slow, distant grin. He held her closer.

It was the second night—the last night—that they locked themselves into her hotel room with a bottle of Scotch and got smashed.

It began soberly enough: reviewing the past, the days before Joanie disappeared, the day it had happened. They wept, drying one another's tears. The move, and how they used to sneak into theaters. High Hills. The year he'd modeled clothes. Her success. His training. She told him about Danny. Peter appeared quizzical, lying back, his arms behind his head while she sat cross-legged on the bed beside him.

Drinking, they began to go over all their favorite movies, from *Flying Down to Rio* on up. They quoted lines and the other had to guess who. Jane sipped more Scotch as Peter imitated Humphrey Bogart in *Casablanca*. She laughed. She set down her glass and spread her arms.

" 'I cannot live without my life. I cannot die without my soul.' "

"*Wuthering Heights.*"

She was laughing. Then why was she suddenly crying, clinging to him, the walls streaming upward as she repeated over and over: " 'I cannot live without my life! I cannot die without my soul!' "

"Hey. Hey, Janie! Come on. None of this. . . ."

She couldn't stop weeping. He held her to him. Then she was kissing him, kissing him as she'd never kissed Danny or Alec or anyone. How could she have supposed Danny could take his place? Peter was letting her, was kissing her back, they were twined around one another as they used to be when they were young, but now her hands had undone his shirt, had sought the smooth skin of his chest, her mouth tasting her own tears and his lips at once. Then he was pushing her off.

61

"Why not?" she cried. "Why not?"

"Because, if we do, it's as though we're saying good-bye forever. As though I'm never coming back. And I am."

"You are? You promise you are?"

He promised. They lay still then, side by side, his arm beneath her neck and his fingers stroking her forehead. Somewhere in the distance a church bell gonged two. When Jane awoke, he'd gone.

His letters began to arrive. It wasn't long before Peter reported that he'd run into Danny. Danny was evidently pretty serious about her. Also about clocking through his forty missions before furlough. And about writing plays. Nice combination that would make: an actress and a playwright. Jane read the letter to Aurelia, who sat on the floor of her studio while she matched swatches of brilliant cloth. She was working on a production of *Twelfth Night*.

"Your brother's quite the matchmaker, isn't he?" Aurelia commented.

Danny's letters about Peter smacked of a family feeling that Jane also resented. When Cynthia brought Natalie Young—the equally notorious Natalie Young of the man's voice and the relative on the Supreme Court who refused to see her plays—Jane danced with her, cheek to cheek, at the Village Hop, permitted herself to be fondled. There would be nothing settled about her life, she told herself with something like venom. Not until Peter came back. A reproving item appeared in Winchell's column:

"Why, when our boys in uniform—who are all real men—and who need all the morale-boosting they can get—does a classy number like Jane Belmont spend her time dancing with dames?"

One Saturday evening in spring, before the performance—the play would soon end its run—Sid Arkoff, the agent Jane had settled on, ambled into her dressing room. He was tall, angular, a long, mournful face with watery blue eyes, expressive, scruffy eyebrows.

"Listen, there's somebody wants to meet you. You free for Sardi's later?"

"I can be. Who is it?" She was applying mascara, part of the scant makeup she wore onstage.

"Some guy wants to sink money in a play. I don't know. Maybe for tax purposes. Maybe he wants a name for culture. God knows he could use it."

"Why? Who is he?" She stood, waiting to discard her robe, slip on the skirt and sweater she wore in the first act.

"You never heard of him. Name's Salvatore Celucci. I think he made his money in Prohibition."

"He's that old?"

Sid Arkoff winced. "Yeah. Like all us dinosaurs. . . . Ten to one, he's into the black market now."

Jane shrugged. "Okay. Call for me."

Sardi's, as always, was mobbed. Sid spoke to the headwaiter who bowed, awarded a special paternal smile to Jane before he led the way to a round table directly in the center. The table was dominated by a large, barrel-chested man who, when he stood for introductions, looked as though he were a thick, waistless slab of cement from his shoulders to his hips. The hair was abundant, black, parted in the middle, and pasted down with grease. The brown eyes snapped with attention and the jowls shook with pleasure as he gravely took Jane's hand. He was altogether a heavy man in a dark suit—despite the weather—and surrounded, she realized with amusement, "just like in the movies," by three excessively sober companions. Jane was enchanted.

"Are they your bodyguards?"

The men looked aggrieved, like children whose hiding place has been discovered.

"They travel around with me," Celucci told her solemnly. The diamond rings on his fingers flashed as he motioned to the waiter for drinks. There was the usual momentary impasse about the fact that Jane could only order ginger ale. "I suppose you're wondering—how did Sal Celucci latch on to you?"

"I never heard of you before tonight."

It was Celucci's turn to appear pained. He directed a long stare toward Sid Arkoff, who ducked his head toward his drink.

"In my opinion," Sal pronounced heavily, his jowls shaking, "you are a very hot little number. I called your friend here a few days ago to talk business. He steered me to this play you do. You think I didn't see you yet?

Let me tell you: I sat there and I was transfixed. Mind you, it don't please me to see a young girl like you in a play with this kind of morals. But what you done up there!" He shook his head, releasing a spray of scent, much like Uncle Ben.

Jane thanked him. Peeping sideways, she watched the pleasure with which he assumed authority in ordering for everyone. Salvatore Celucci. She savored the name, rolled its bandit sound over her tongue, with her drink. It smacked, as he did, of assurance, power. Suddenly, as though his back didn't bend, he leaned stiffly toward her.

"Say, now. What is it with you? I hear you live with some dame. You go out dancing with her and some other dames. But you also got a boyfriend, right? So what is it? You swing from guys to dames and back?" Indignant, Jane opened her lips. "Listen. You don't got dough to live by yourself? Let me set you up. It would be my pleasure." Again, Jane attempted to speak. Sal held up his hand, sparkling with rings. "Don't ask me how I know about you. I know. When I consider investing my cash, I find out about the merchandise. . . ."

"Sal," Sid Arkoff protested. "This isn't merchandise."

Celucci considered him a moment. He nodded, shaking his jowls. "You got me. To call a girl with the classiest nostrils I ever seen merchandise is not polite." He turned to Jane. "In my opinion, this is a great country. I seen what Winchell wrote about you. I don't say you gotta dance with all these roughnecks out there. I only say, *if* you're gonna dance, why dames?"

"Mr. Celucci," she began, but he covered her hand with his massive one.

"Please. To my friends, it's Sal. And we gonna be friends." He almost smiled. "Maybe you don't think so right now. But you look up today's date and you write it down. You write down: this was the day you met Sal Celucci and he became your friend. Now. Let's eat."

While he did so, Celucci evidently didn't believe in talk. To Sid, about to speak of some play, Celucci—bent over his plate—held up an arresting hand. The three bodyguards munched in silence, one of them prinking his little finger while he sopped up gravy with a roll. When people paused to speak to Jane, Celucci lifted his heavy head, frowned above the napkin tucked below his double chin. When they left, he continued to eat.

It was over coffee and his cigar that he suggested Jane come out to spend the night and Sunday at his home in the country. "I want you should see this place. I know you don't gotta get back to your play till Tuesday. And you got big rings under your eyes. You come out there, rest up, Sid drives out tomorrow afternoon, we talk business. How about it?"

Jane's first impulse was to answer as Aurelia would have. Was he willing to back a play or not? Crap or get off the pot. Stalling, she asked: "Where is this place in the country?"

"Scarsdale," he told her, soberly.

Jane met the stolid stare. Suddenly, she giggled. Scarsdale? Then she saw the surprised hurt on his face, the wary amazement of his companions. She set her mouth to keep the lips from twitching.

"I'm sorry. I don't know what came over me. But I don't have anything with me. . . ."

"It's up to you. We can run down to the Village, pick up your stuff, what you want. Or we drop over to the Astor, I buy you what you need."

Sid shrugged assent. Jane was too intrigued to say no. Outside, Sid headed into the thinning crowd while they drove down to the Village. For Aurelia, not yet in, Jane left an ambiguous note. Then she climbed back into the Cadillac limousine beside Sal. One of his companions drove an identical car ahead of them, one behind, while the third sat beside the chauffeur in front. As the heavy vehicle slid out into the traffic by the river, Jane wondered how they managed with the gas rationing. Then it occurred to her. Sal's black market dealings were probably in gas.

She had a sudden wild fantasy. He was taking her to Joanie—not thirteen as Joanie would have been now— but still small and blond, still a little girl. She closed her eyes. Sal's gravelly voice intruded.

"I seen you wuz knocked out. You're a gallant little fighter. You had plenty in life to make you tired."

Bewildered, Jane opened her eyes. He nodded, again covered her hand with his. "Sure. I know all about you. Some life you been through. Some life. And cops messing you up, too. But you're gutsy. I like guts. I'm going to fix all that."

It was almost three when they reached his house. His estate. He had one of the bodyguards go ahead, turn on all the lights, so the place was ablaze. They entered a large hall with a fireplace and Sal led her from room to room, watching almost childlike for her reactions. His fervor reminded her of Gatsby. There were terraces on three sides, balconies upstairs. From the second floor, he pointed out the stream with its Japanese bridges and weeping willows. Beyond that, to the left, a giant aviary.

"You wanna guess how many birds I got out there?" he challenged.

"Fifty?" Jane was rocking with fatigue.

She'd made him happy. "Almost a hunnert. . . . One more thing I gotta show you. Then you gonna hit the hay."

He led her back downstairs and out into the sweet-smelling air. Past a long swimming pool, still empty. Where the grass ended at a wood stood a large cage attached to a small brick structure. Jane thought at first it was a short man in costume jumping up and down inside the cage. Then she saw that it was a chimpanzee.

Frank, one of the bodyguards, had followed them and now she noted that he cautiously carried a mug of beer. Sal, watching her from the corner of his eye, carefully opened the small door and handed in the beer.

"Hey, Bonzo! Whadda you say? I want you to meet my new friend, Miss Jane Belmont."

The chimp took the beer mug in both paws and held it aloft in salute. Next, he reached one paw through the bars for her hand. She gave it into his hot, leathery grasp. The chimp guzzled the beer while Jane heard Sal Celucci laugh for the first time.

"You gonna sleep like a house afire now," he assured her. He placed his heavy arm across her shoulders and guided her back to the glittering house. "Bonzo says hello, how are you, to somebody I interduce, all their troubles are over."

Jane did indeed tumble into a deep sleep of vague dreaming, only to awaken before six. For some moments she lay in the wide bed, the satin quilt slipping toward the floor, and stared at the heavy drapes that framed the windows. Below the Venetian blinds, a slit of sunlight had slipped like a letter. What was she doing in this stranger's house? She was frightened, lonely. She saw how ephemeral was the security Aurelia had created around her.

Hugging the quilt about her, Jane went to the window seat, raised the blinds. Below stretched the grassy slope that descended to the stream, with the aviary beyond. Forsythia bloomed, trembling slightly in the early morning breeze. She wondered if Bonzo were asleep or lonely, too. She wondered if, at this moment, Peter were flying somewhere, in danger, and she realized her dreams had been of him, of terrible peril from which she hadn't been able to save him. She wouldn't, if anything happened to Peter, forgive the world. She leaned her forehead against the window, suddenly rose, cast off the quilt, pulled on her crinkly taffeta robe over the thin nylon gown and—she'd forgotten her slippers—went to the door.

Outside the grass was wet beneath her feet and cold, but already the sun was warming. She moved indecisively toward Bonzo's cage, past the empty swimming pool. It occurred to her she hadn't been in a country setting since High Hills: the play of light and shadow in the woods beyond reminded her of that summer. Yes, the cage was empty, Bonzo passing the sleep of the just inside. As she turned slightly, Jane saw the lounging figure of Dino, another bodyguard, as he lit a cigarette near the house. He was watching her.

It was a matter of moments before Celucci himself appeared, padding massively toward her in a purple brocade robe from which emerged silk pajamas. His feet stamped through the wet grass in suede slippers. As he drew near, his dark eyes snapping with curiosity—or concern—her own sophistication at Sardi's evaporated. Jane felt slight and silly. He told her, as he steered himself over:

"You look about six years old. I can't believe that was you on that stage. . . . Why aren't you asleep?"

Shamefaced, Jane shrugged. Celucci reached out his big square hand and held her chin to scrutinize her.

"You worried? You worried maybe about your brother?" As her eyes widened in surprise, he nodded. "Too bad you didden know Sal Celucci in time. I could've wangled him a desk job in Washington."

Jane shook her head. "He wanted to go. He believes in the war. . . . And maybe he wanted to get away from me," she added, so low she wasn't certain he'd heard. Had Peter? Had Peter wanted to escape her?

Sal frowned. "Whadda you say a thing like that for? He should be home taking care of you, not flying around there somewhere. . . ."

She couldn't restrain some amusement. "He's not on a pleasure trip. And he's not my father, you know. He's my twin."

Sal puzzled over that. "Funny business, twins." Then: "Listen. We neither of us is getting back to sleep. I'm now gonna surprise you with the best French toast you ever ate." He lifted his chin pugnaciously. "You think I live like this, I don't know how to work in my own kitchen? You'll see. . . ." He was steering her back over the sparkling grass to the house. Dino slipped in ahead of them. From the kitchen, Jane glimpsed him bent over a racing form at the elegant table in the dining room.

The French toast, thick, crusty, smeared with sweet butter, dripping with syrup, *was* superlative. Then Sal sent her up to bathe and dress. When Jane returned downstairs, he was waiting to show her the place in daylight. In what he dubbed the "Chinese room," Jane curled up on the red brocade couch, found herself wondering again: what was she doing with this stranger?

As before, Celucci appeared to read her thoughts. "Hey, wanna have some fun?"

Jane stiffened. She should have known. But in front of his henchmen? Frank and Dino hovered beyond the doorway with the *Daily News* and the *Journal-American*. Celucci unlocked a teakwood cabinet, portentously carried forth a tiny silver dish, a tiny silver spoon.

"You go by that song?" he asked. "You think you get no kick from cocaine? Well, little girl, you gonna. . . ."

He let himself down on the couch beside her. "Ordinarily, I woulden offer this stuff to a kid like you. But then, I also am not gonna let you develop a habit, am I? I just wanna see some sparkle in those eyes."

He instructed her how to use the tiny spoon at her nostrils, how to inhale the less than half a gram he'd let her have. The newspapers rustled in the other room. A large dog entered, plopped down before the fireplace. Sal helped himself after her. Jane was still tense but, when he rose to stash the equipment away, she closed her eyes and waited.

The euphoria came gently, lifting her from the couch so that she sensed herself floating in air two feet above it. The sunlight dazzled the mullioned windows and the dog appeared to smile at her as he slowly and rhythmically thumped his tail. Sal sat away from her and she saw him watching her through the smoky haze of a cigar.

It was rather like being high, she decided, only better. She wondered why Sal should be so good to her and a flutter of tenderness stirred in her lower abdomen. When she thought of it, why should Aurelia? All the people in the cast? *All* the people who'd helped her over the years. She should be more aware, she reflected, with that spreading tenderness, of the solicitude people poured forth on her. She wanted to tell Sal this but she was almost flying now, too far to speak. Possibly, with his intuition of her thoughts, he knew what was going on in her mind, and she smiled dreamily down on him.

By the time Sid Arkoff arrived, Jane was alert, sensitive to all the colors in the room, to Sid's questioning face, to Sal's impassive one. Administering a tray of coffee, she told Sid he must call Paul Talbott, sound him out about directing *Pygmalion,* with her as Eliza Doolittle. Sal held up his hand.

"What's this Pig Mallion?" Briefly, Jane explained. Sal didn't appear happy. "A foreign play? There's nothing American?" Sid was already handing her the phone.

"*Pygmalion?*" Paul asked lazily. "With American accents?"

Momentarily, she was dashed. "It wouldn't work?"

Sal turned pugnacious. "This guy don't wanna do what you want—we get somebody else. . . ."

Jane shook her head. "Can't we use New York-ese for Cockney? And high New England for Professor Higgins?"

"That *could* be a gimmick." When Paul heard where she was, who the backer might be, there was a slight squeal at the other end of the line. "Salvatore Celucci! Backing *Pygmalion!* This I must be in on. . . ."

By the time the third bodyguard, whose name was Joe, was driving her back to the Village (proudly, he offered a peek at the submachine gun stashed below the dashboard), the deal was tentatively set. There'd have to be a business meeting, of course—Celucci, Talbott, Arkoff. She was not to worry. She was to prepare her transformation into an American Eliza.

4

Those next weeks, as April moved into May, Jane saw Celucci regularly. Sometimes at his place, mainly in the city. In Scarsdale, Sal always fed her his French toast, the half gram of cocaine. Each provided its specific comfort. Later, Jane wandered the grounds, blazing and fragrant with azaleas and lilac.

Her evenings of dancing with Cynthia, Natalie, and Aurelia she confined to only once a week. She'd wanted Aurelia and Celucci to meet, arranged it early in May, at Lindy's, after a performance. Immediately, Jane saw it wouldn't work. They were like two parents, squaring off for a custody battle.

Meanwhile, her nights were still difficult, sleepless or filled with nightmares. One Monday evening toward the end of the month, as she sat on the floor reading the old fable of Pygmalion and Galatea aloud to Aurelia, who was stitching a piece of cloth, she paused when the news came on the radio. She felt a spasm of terror cross her face and saw how Aurelia watched her.

"You know . . ." Aurelia laid down the material. "Maybe you should see a psychiatrist. It might help."

"Help what?" Jane demanded, defensively.

"Do I have to tell you?" Aurelia's tone of kindness was maddening. "Maybe you could work out some of this awful panic about Peter, for one thing. . . ."

"You mean my panic isn't natural?"

Aurelia smiled. "Who am I to talk about natural? I just mean: well, maybe that's why you're letting yourself be taken up by a hood like this Celucci. I mean, after all, the guy's a racketeer. . . ."

"He's like a father to me. What's wrong with that?"

"I'd think—knowing he's in the black market—you'd be ashamed. Peter fighting over there and this gangster sabotaging the war effort over here."

Jane threw down the book. "You always have it in for any guy I happen to like. First it was Alec. Then Danny. Sal Celucci's at least forty. The only guys you want me to associate with are queers like Cynthia and Natalie— and you . . ."

Aurelia bent her head over her work. Jane stared at the plump, sagging shoulders. Then she was on her knees before her, fumbling for Aurelia's hands.

"I'm sorry, I'm sorry! I didn't mean that. Tell me you won't remember I ever said that!"

Aurelia allowed her to clasp her. She patted Jane's cheek. "Forget it, honey. You know what they say. . . . Love is hell. . . ."

June sixth arrived, hot, hazy, overcast, the sky swollen with gray heat. Jane had been thinking that this— their upcoming nineteenth—would be the first birthday she and Peter would spend apart. Then the news came over the radio. People were screaming in the streets. She thought for a moment the war had ended.

It was D Day. The Allies had invaded France. There were conflicting reports, reports of terrible destruction, of victories violently wrested. After that, each day that passed increased the brooding sense of danger in which she moved. Every day that closed in on the war, that brought its end nearer, suggested a possible trap from which it would be Peter who wouldn't escape.

A letter from him said he still couldn't comprehend the destruction London had withstood, the will of the English people. But now the tide had turned. The Nazis would go on fighting, but now they couldn't win. . . . A letter from Danny: two more missions to go.

It was late Wednesday morning. Jane was drinking her second cup of coffee over *The New York Times*, after the large breakfast she always ate on matinee days. Soon she'd bathe and dress, make her way to the theater. The phone rang and she removed Jack Tanner, protesting, from her lap, stepped into the living room. Through the low open windows drifted the voices of children at play on the hot sidewalks.

"May I please speak to Miss Jane Belmont?" It was a male voice. She wondered if this were another talent scout from Hollywood, like the one she'd turned down, with the allure of *Pygmalion* before her.

"Speaking."

"This is Dr. Ferguson, over at the hospital."

Jane tensed. She'd seen Mama only last week. "Yes?"

"Are you alone?"

"Yes. What is it?"

"I'd rather you weren't alone. I'm afraid there's some rather bad news."

"What? Tell me!" The air in the room was hot, close.

"Your mother received a telegram a short time ago. From the War Office. . . ."

There was a sudden roaring in her ears, like a subway train passing through her head. Jane gripped the phone. She heard her own sound, a pleading mew of inquiry, a plea for mercy.

"It's your brother. Shall I read it to you? 'The Department of War regrets to inform you that your son, Peter Belmont, was killed in action in a mission over Germany. . . .' "

The phone dropped from Jane's hand as the brutal fist, making her grunt aloud, crashed into her stomach. The roaring in her ears became stupendous. She replaced the phone in its cradle and turned, staggering slightly. She began to stumble, holding to the furniture, and moving as though drunk, as though underwater, toward the bedroom. As though underwater, yes . . . his body slipping away from her and she swimming in the darkness and never able to find him. She heard loud struggling gasps as though someone were drowning.

72

Then she was in the bedroom, vomit pouring out of her onto the short nightgown, over her legs and feet. She kept reaching for something, for a piece of furniture to hold to, for air. Another terrifying sound arose, a swishing through the room.

It started at the far corner behind her and she was aware of its approach through the air, aware of the pain as it knocked her in the back and, with the force of the impact, sailed off again, swishing through the air, cutting it with a rushing boom. It was a gigantic wooden swing, she understood, as it came sailing back toward her and she lurched, trying to get out of its way, but it hurtled, in time with the beating thud in her ears that must be her blood, and again it knocked against her back, again swirled invisibly back through the room to prepare its return assault through the stifling air.

Jane heard herself scream and it terrified her, enabled her to concentrate on the inhuman sound, almost to forget what had caused it. She staggered toward the bed and screamed so that all other sounds were blotted out, the sound of the rushing swing last of all, until her voice cracked and she could barely moan. Hot hands were on her forehead, pushing her down, the roar through her head of the subway train was a noiseless thunder, and she sank, sank for hours, through layers of searing heat that suffocated and rescued her all at once.

. . . But there were voices now. Loud voices. What was happening? Voices on the stairs and the front door slamming heavily. Whose voice cried out:

"I'm telling you she knows. The doctor told her uncle he spoke to her personally. That's why her uncle called me. Thank God you were able to get here. . . ."

And another voice: "So where is she?" Heavy footsteps pounded through the other rooms while she listened. She couldn't understand why everything was so dark, why she couldn't move, why there was this pressure on her head. The footsteps were all around her now. She wanted to call out. Why couldn't they see her? Then that first voice—of course, it was Aurelia—moaned:

"Oh God, the vomit . . . where is she?" Jane watched shoes flashing by toward the bathroom, the shoes turning, again that voice, but descending into a tone she'd never heard before, at least an octave lower.

"Oh, my God. Sal, look at her. Look where she is!"

She was being dragged out now, out from under the bed where she didn't remember crawling. She was smeared with dust, with vomit, a rag doll that tried to fight their arms, helpless to their ministrations, a figure that grunted protest against the consciousness into which they were dragging her back.

So it was true then, all true. She flailed helplessly against them, helpless without a voice, but she suddenly sensed that it had returned to her. She heard it rise, loud and strident, heard somebody—this self she had to escape—as she howled.

Chapter III

1

There was a letter from Danny.

"My darling: For what it may be worth, Peter never knew what happened. We flew the same mission that night. I saw his plane explode. . . . You know he loved you most awesomely. He said once he'd promised you he'd come back. I wonder if he ever believed that. If only I could be with you. But I will be, very soon. . . ."

The letter dropped from her hand. She didn't finish reading it. Nor the ones the following days. Each so staunch an effort to infuse love, strength into this receptacle she'd become.

But Jane didn't weep. Nor did she consider that she mourned, for she carried death within her now. The alien force had intruded, taken over. For Peter there had been an ending, for her it was a beginning. The world was grown too vast, too barren to wander in. In her mind, an image of the planet spun away from under her feet, sand blowing upward from endless deserts. The love of others was not enough. The essential part of her was gone forever, had left a vacuum within and outside her. To fill that vacuum, death had raised itself up from where it crouched, waiting always, and had moved inside.

The fragment that linked her to others now watched them with something akin to pity as they tried to help. For their sakes, she allowed Aurelia to move her to Sal's place in Scarsdale. Aurelia, brown eyes shining with helpless guilt, was unnecessarily frightened at leaving her alone. Jane would have liked to reassure her. But her own best gratitude was simply to permit Aurelia to shift her about like this rag doll she'd become.

Only once, she struck out: when Aurelia, bearing Danny's letter, asked if she wouldn't like Jack Tanner brought out, too. Sal would never mind.

"But the cat doesn't belong here," Jane said. "It's all right for me. I do. You said if I had anything to do with Sal, I was hurting—the war effort. Remember?" Within the anesthetic that encased her, the glimpse of pain on Aurelia's face was comfort.

Sal—quickly laying aside at her frozen stare the grandiose diamond he'd bought for her nineteenth birthday —made certain she was never alone. Silent, watchful, he hung there, severely brooding. When he was himself mysteriously gone, there was always Frank, bulging eyes stolidly jolly as he stood sentinel over her. There was, too, William, the cook. Tall, stately, very black— despite Sal's reiterated aversion to "spades"—William came only weekdays, cooked for her everything Sal remembered she'd always liked. Lobster, mushrooms, asparagus, charlotte russe. Silently, William removed them, uneaten, from the table. Her abdomen was empty, hollow, her throat closed, her fingers cold, numb.

Uncle Ben visited, quite early on. Mama had taken it, all things considered—what things?—quite well. Undoubtedly, there'd been a setback. But . . .

Then, there was Peter's life insurance. Ten thousand dollars. He'd named Jane his beneficiary. Would Jane like him to invest it for her? Jane stared. The closed throat forced back her feeble anger. Sal, from his end of the couch, motioned with his sleekly greased head to Uncle Ben. In the other room, through the strange cottony feeling in her ears, Jane heard their voices, Sal's rumbling, authoritative, Uncle Ben's haughty, but willing to listen.

"In my opinion, you should invest this money, just hold it for her. To her now, in her present condition, it's blood money, see? She's ready to use it, you have it for her."

Their voices drifted off as Jane turned back into herself. She was still having to shut doors, one after the other, that opened into the past. At this moment she'd floated for just a short space into that time when they'd danced together, she and Peter. She'd sensed his body fragile and vulnerable against her. The music had played "I'll Never Smile Again." . . . The door shut. That body was nowhere now, scattered like Osiris across the land, not even a burial place. There was only loss.

Abruptly, Danny's letters stopped. One day Jane called his parents, spoke his name. At a woman's hoarse demand to know who this was, she remembered the tightly corseted little person in the apartment on West End Avenue the night of Joanie's disappearance.

"Just a friend," Jane said. "From Columbia."

A strange rasping sound at the other end. "He's missing in action. We got word a week ago. His last mission, you understand? And now they tell me my son is missing. . . . Who did you say this was?"

Jane's numbed heart appeared to halt completely, to stop at last. She hadn't cared enough—was that it?—to prevent this further loss. Was it her guilty omission that had done this, too? She dropped the phone back into its cradle. For a moment only, it appeared as though the tears might come at last. Missing meant gone. She'd learned that well enough. Early enough. The vast world stretched around her, but again she didn't weep.

She didn't even dream, no nightmares anymore. Every night she lay stiffly awake on her back, staring into the dark, not dwelling on the past, not reflecting on a future, till the birds stirred in the aviary. To their clamor, she fell into numbing sleep for two, three, sometimes four hours. To awake was like being dragged out from under the bed where they'd found her. Being dragged out into this semblance of obedience in which she did as she was told, although completely turned away. It was as though whatever scenes of life they tried to show her—Aurelia, Sal, Paul, Sid Arkoff, Cynthia Blackwood, the members of the cast who visited once or twice, and who seemed to her either to be very far away or shadowy, small—she was like a camera focused off center.

There was a price to life, to love, and the price was too high. That was what Jane felt in her chest, in her throat: a part of that price.

Occasionally, Aurelia came for her, brought her into the city for afternoons, evenings, when she could devote herself completely. But the towers of New York were menacing, the shafts of sunlight that poured between them served only to accentuate the thick shadows that spread in stagnant rivers on its suddenly foreign streets. Those streets were crowded with servicemen, some returning, some just on their way, as the Allied forces fought through France. At every street corner far ahead and just out of reach, there seemed to be a familiar figure in uniform, lithe, elegant, turning out of sight and lost. They walked past restaurants and, behind the windows, it would seem as though Jane had glimpsed him. But when she forced Aurelia to stop so she could gaze inside, it was always a stranger. Or her own reflection, which now often bore the faraway concentration of *that* face. Had he been focused, even then, in those past years, on the blankness that lay ahead?

Sal did, in this strange glittering summer, become her anchor. Sometimes there were business meetings at the house; from the solarium, Jane heard unfamiliar voices raised in husky agitation, Sal's in glacial command. She gazed out at the flowers while she waited for him to finish. Occasionally, through a morning mist, it seemed to her that she saw that lost figure far off among the trees but if she moved, it vanished. When Sal emerged alone, she trailed after him. She watched as he floated in the pool in stiff consecration to the sun, arms rigidly at his sides, but didn't join him.

One day, simply to please him—she'd do anything he wanted except enter back into life—Jane accompanied him to South Philadelphia where he'd been born, where his mother and married sisters lived. She could see, when he walked her through the Italian Market and boasted of her as an actress, that they thought him a liar. This wan, apathetic creature on his arm? His mother was stout, white-haired, tiny dark wisps growing from her chin. When age had unsexed Sal, he would resemble her. She embraced Jane, brought out soup, Italian bread, manicotti. To Sal, opening a bottle of wine in the kitchen, Jane heard her say:

"So you finally let me see one of your women? What is this: with a child?"

And Sal: "This ain't one of *them*. Them I don't bring near you, you don't know that yet? . . . This *is* my child."

That night, back in Scarsdale, when she couldn't sleep, Jane came to his room. She passed the silent dog and, before she'd closed the bedroom door behind her, glimpsed Dino appearing as guard in the hallway. His stolid glance passed her on. At the side of Sal's bed she watched him sleep with the same massive attention he paid to life. In the morning, when he found her curled up on the floor beside his bed, he said only:

"So? So now we do what we should have done before."

Her bed was moved in, across the room from his.

The days continued to pass. While the autumn leaves drifted slowly past the damp windows, Jane would pull on her robe, descend the stairs, walk to the dining room windows to watch the sun glisten or the rain bounce off the flagstoned terrace. From the hallway she heard Frank stir to his feet, William's radio tuned softly to the religious music he favored.

One morning she woke to a pervasive weakness, a strange stiffness in her neck, barely responded when Aurelia called. As William cleared the dinner table that evening, she told Sal she thought she'd go directly up to bed, just for a little while. Her head had begun to ache so that her vision blurred. Sal, breaking his dinnertime silence as he lit a cigar, ordered:

"Okay, you take aspirin. But I'm coming to get you up in an hour. In my opinion, you sleep too much now, you gonna be up *all* night, not just part of it."

Docile as ever, Jane nodded. She swallowed the aspirin, stumbled in the gathering dusk of early October to her bed. Once there, a new explosion of pain forced itself into her head, as though her brain had exploded within the skull. Had *his* brain exploded? Had he really not known anything before that shining light was out forever? The effort swiftly to close that door brought new more massive pain and Jane offered herself up to it, sought it like oxygen. At last everything else was finally and completely shut out.

When Sal came to her, she could only mumble. His figure was a shadow as he stalked to the phone. She was hazily aware of him barking orders, questions. The pain appeared to shift, to rear, to roll in on her like a tank, and she plummeted beneath it. Again, she heard Sal, now rasping threats into the phone. Time hung in abeyance, each second trembling after the next while she sank under more layers of anguish. It occurred to her this must be a cerebral hemorrhage, wondered if there were a way she could crawl past Sal onto some highway, where a truck could roll over her as the pain rolled now.

An unfamiliar hand lay on her forehead, a voice told her to lift her head, touch her chin to her chest. She couldn't. The new voice told something to Sal that caused him to cry out.

"Whatya mean? How is it meningitis?" It seemed to her there was a brief scuffle, then Sal leaned above her. She tried to focus her eyes. In the lamplight, his heavy face was strangely mottled. "Lissen, little sweetheart, we're running you over to the hospital. I don't know what's with this nut, but may as well do what he says."

Gently, Sal swept her into his arms. Jane tucked that ball of pain against his chest, was dimly aware of a strange, whimpering sound, either his or her own.

They were in the car then, it was as though its swift flight tried to speed ahead of this demon that had got hold of her. But nothing could outrun it. Sal had laid her out on a white bed, they'd made him leave, they were undressing her, strange hands were putting her into a hospital gown. Many hands were on her now, many low voices surrounded her. A machine had been wheeled up to where she lay, shuddering with fever and pain.

"This may be somewhat uncomfortable, Miss Belmont," the doctor said. "But we have to do a spinal tap to make sure of our next step. Nurse, turn her on her stomach and hold her down. You, too, nurse."

The women's voices sounded softly, little bells of condolence and praise. "My, what a good girl you are. Have you ever seen such a brave girl?" Not knowing she welcomed this digging, this boring into her bone, this new torment.

It was over. They were giving her an injection, covering her with many blankets, telling she'd sleep. Her eyes closed and it was as though a heavy elevator freighted with cement descended furiously on her head. She gave herself as to a lover. Soon, she, too—like Danny, like Peter . . .

But the doctor had been correct. Through the haze of pain, the injections began to alleviate enough of it for Jane to understand what he said. There was really nothing to worry about, this form—lymphocytic meningitis—was rarely fatal. His voice was muffled behind the gauze mask, as were those of the nurses who tended her. It was a shame, she heard them tell one another, that she had no parent to visit her, no husband. No others allowed, total isolation. In the mornings she woke to less pain, was able to be spoon-fed cereal, a bit of fruit. The nurses sponged her, gently combed her hair.

Then, in the afternoons, the pain slouched in on her again. By evening and into the night, she was again forced down and down into that suffocation of everything but the agony in her head. The doctor had given no solace. This was rarely fatal.

It was in the hospital that at last she began again to dream. In the early hours near dawn, when she was finally released into sleep, the apparition came to stand just beyond the window and, though she'd never seen it before, she recognized what it was. Massive, shapeless, silent, and faceless beneath the hood, it hovered beyond her reach, implacable, cold, unmoving. It had taken everything but still it refused to encase her within its robes.

Only once, when her fever mounted, the figure was replaced by a great green and grayly shining sea, lashed by waves. Jane dreamed she was in a boat tied to a creaking wooden pier. All night long, the rope that tied her craft strained and pulled while she watched it unravel strand by strand, and hoped. When she awoke, the noise of that sea was still in her ears but the fever had disappeared.

She had lost again.

It was ten days before they allowed Sal to come for her, bring her home. Aurelia waited in the hospital lobby. To Jane, it appeared that all three of them had been severely chastened. Aurelia, dark circles below her eyes, clucked behind the wheelchair as they emerged into the windy sunshine of November. Sal, dark eyes snapping, complained bitterly of hospitals and their rules. Nurses followed, carrying flowers, plants. Jane watched the buildings, the traffic, the countryside as they sped toward Scarsdale.

She'd been forced to return to the world.

2

For some weeks it was a struggle merely to regain simple reflexes. She tried to write thank-you notes but the lines trailed off the page as her fingers lost their grip on the pen. Slowly, she began to be able to turn her head again, instead of her whole body. Sal took her for walks around the estate, matched his solid tread to her feeble one. As she seemed to have recovered, as the snow began to fall and the public hopes for the end of the European war turned to horror with the Battle of the Bulge, Jane came down with other ills she'd never known before. Over Christmas, it was an ear infection. In January, tonsillitis. In February, flu.

Always dreams now, dreams that accompanied fever, dreams with only sleep. *He* came to her in every guise. He stood before her, a child in that fetid hotel lobby, a long streak of dirt on his thin arm while the policemen gathered around them. He held her in his arms in bed and told her about that girl in the penthouse on Fifth Avenue. He sat in the pine grove at High Hills while a bee hummed on a shaft of sunlight and he spoke about sending her to drama school. He smiled to her from the pages of *The New York Times* as he lounged near the fountain before the Plaza Hotel. He gazed up at her from the darkness of the theater as she spoke to him from the stage. He held her body away from him as he promised her he'd come back.

Someday, in some guise, she believed he would. Sometimes she dreamed that she herself passed before endless mirrors which reflected unfamiliar rooms but not her image. . . . Always this hollowness in her chest, this constriction in her throat.

It was April before she was well enough to take long walks by herself, even to help Giorgio, the gardener, as he worked in the flowerbeds. She found a certain release in his ordering her about, there was solace in the feel of the damp earth in her hands, the sun warming her back as she knelt there. A small, wizened Italian, with no interests but his flowers and sports events, Giorgio decided she must have a small plot of her own, helped her to set it out, brought her seeds and flats, instructed her with the severity of a teacher from P.S. 9.

It was while she worked there, one morning in May —ten days after Germany's surrender—that Jane became aware of a figure other than Frank or Dino advancing from a distance. Perched back on her heels, Jane held her hand above her eyes to shield them from the sun, saw that it was a man in uniform.

For a moment her heart seemed to rise, then stop.

No, it was not that slim, graceful form that had eluded her in those morning mists for so long, that had escaped her in the city streets, that came to her now at night. As she watched, she saw that it was Danny Edelman who came slowly toward her, and that he was real.

Jane rose to her feet. It was Danny, his golden eyes, his ruddy cheeks, his hands outstretched. In the next moment, he'd clasped her to him, no word spoken, his hands in her hair, his lips covering her face with kisses, his warmth penetrating her body which she'd thought even the sun could barely warm again. He was speaking between the kisses. But his words were a meaningless shower, tumbling over her like fragmented light.

"You thought I was dead. Or missing. Didn't you? My parents said somebody called. A woman who wouldn't leave her name. I was shot down . . . my last mission. . . . But I was hiding out in Holland, fighting with the Underground. . . . I did get word out—we had our contacts in London—I wrote them to let you know. But they didn't. I'll never forgive them for that. . . ."

"Don't. Don't." Jane held trembling fingers to his warm cheek, hollow now and thin. How could he blame them? Why would they share their sorrow—or their joy —with her? She knew what she must seem like to them, from the past.

Danny caught her hand to his lips. "Why did I trust them? It was you, only you, I should have got word to. My darling one, how are you? Tell me," and he held her face in his hands, looked into it with a love and concern unbearable to her. She tried to turn aside and he began: "Peter . . ."

"Don't!" Her hand shot out, the quick gesture of the person with a wound who stops another from touching it.

His lips narrowed as he gripped her shoulders. "Yes, she told me. Aurelia said you don't speak of him—you won't allow it. . . ."

She tried to turn from him but he held her, his hands hurting. It occurred to Jane for the first time in months how she must appear. Bony. Her arms so thin the veins showed through the faintly tan skin. Her hair hung lank down her back, pinned carelessly away from her face with bobby pins. She tried not to look at herself ever, but she knew there were dark circles under her luster-less eyes, that the glow of which critics had spoken had disappeared. She'd been only a temporary comet that had flashed across the sky of others. She was gone now, into some other space. Didn't Danny see? Why had he come to her? Why did he enfold her again in his arms, clasp these bones so tightly to him?

"How could my parents do that to us?" he muttered again. "Why did they have to extend any of the pain in this world?"

Her eyes were dry, unblinking, her face against the rough texture of his uniform. "Maybe parents have to hurt us: we hurt and disappoint them so. . . ."

Danny made an impatient sound. "Listen. All the old laws of human relationships are turned upside down. So don't say that. The world is going to discover such horrors, such things that were only hinted at before, that nothing can ever be the same again." At the strangeness of his voice, Jane stepped back from him but he still held her. His golden eyes blazed down at her, yet as though he no longer saw her. "I got into Germany before I left. We went in there, into that country. And we saw Hell. Nothing, not even the pictures you and the rest of the world will see can even suggest that Hell. I don't know, after this, how anyone will ever believe that worse can exist anywhere in an afterworld. Hell was here. . . . Jane, Peter didn't die for nothing. Among other things, he did help to save this remnant."

She looked at him and away. He knew, didn't he, that Peter had promised to come back?

"Jane, I don't know this guy, this Celucci. But I'm grateful for whatever he's done. But *I'm* back now. Let *me* take care of you. I mean to do great things. I told you: I was working on a play. . . . And since I've seen what I saw, I know how to finish and improve it. I want you for that play, Jane. You've got to come back to the city—and to me. To life. . . ."

Politely, Jane smiled. "What's the name of your play?" She was backing away from him, brushing the dirt from her skirt, playing for time.

"*Zeal for Thy House.* It's from a Psalm: 'Zeal for Thy house has consumed me.' About the price the Jews paid for their identity. And how that remnant must now have a land of its own. . . . Jane, you have to do the girl. I wrote it with you in mind. Will you read it?"

Now that he was no longer so concentrated on her, Jane moved away from Danny, began to walk slowly along the gravel path between the flowerbeds. Frank hovered in the distance. For only a second she wondered if Frank, too, saw this importunate stranger from the past, if Danny were indeed real.

But apparitions made no demands like these; apparitions shimmered in mist and darkness, in dreams. Her heart began a slow thudding and her arms were suddenly covered with chill. She turned and looked back at Danny as he followed her—a reversal of Orpheus and Eurydice—and she sensed how her face was full of wonder.

"But you're alive! You're really alive!" she said, now actually believing it.

"Yes, I'm alive! And so are you. For better or worse, we're alive. And we have each other. We have life, precious life. Don't throw it away from you, Jane. Don't!" He had her in his arms again and for the first time since that day in June, she sensed something rising from the hollowness in her chest.

It was some essence that had refused then to accept what had happened, that struggled continually to assert itself, to insist that what had always been could not be taken from her, that she would not let it be true. It rose again but now she knew that it was indeed all true, that it had indeed all happened. For the first time since that day in June, her throat opened, but she pushed down the strangling sob that struggled to tear out of it, fought back the tears that always refused to come. She would not mourn.

Something new, something cold and strange coiled up in her. A promise had been made and broken. *He* had made that vow when he hadn't the right to make it, and then it had been broken.

But Danny, too, had said that he'd come back, and he had. Joanie had also disappeared long ago, but Fate had yielded in its harshness, had allowed Danny to keep his word. What, after all, did she owe anymore to the one who'd broken her heart and her life? This new, this implacable hostility was like an armor that grew from within. It enabled her to focus at last on Danny's face, his wide-set eyes, the thrust of the cheekbones in his thin face, the nervous intensity of his gaze, the glint of sunshine in his hair. It was as though she were opening one of those doors, looking within and locking it, to step outside. Locking that Other firmly behind them where he'd taken himself. Let him stay there, forever, then.

"Yes," she told Danny. "I'll come with you. Whatever you say."

He had to return at first to camp, for reassignment. Which would be New York. He'd come back, he told her, in two days. When Sal entered the Chinese room that afternoon where Jane sat in blank wonder, he said immediately:

"I hear this Edelman is back. You like this guy? I mean, you really like him?"

For answer, she turned her face up to him. He understood that something had at last happened, probably mistook it for joy. Sighing heavily, Sal sank down beside her on the couch.

"So. It's a good thing. Somebody comes back from the dead, after all. A playmate, even, from childhood."

She had to smile. "Somebody was in on everything you been through, from the start. And a good American. Goes over a second Looie, comes back a captain." She hadn't even noticed. "What more can we ask?"

"There is something." She hesitated. "I didn't want it before because . . . I can't go to him like this." Like this robot, she meant. "Sal, give me something."

The dark eyes widened, snapped with attention. Sal nodded. He went to the gleaming cabinet, unlocked it, brought out the little dish, the miniature spoons, carefully measured out a portion for each of them. Jane took hers into trembling hands and brought it to her nose as he'd taught her in what seemed another lifetime. Deeply, she inhaled, held her pinkie to her nose, waited. For some moments, in disappointment, she wondered if it had lost its power.

The rush came and, as that strange, erotic sensation stirred in her abdomen, Jane felt the depression, like a choked ice floe, slowly dislodge. She heard the grinding noise of that movement in the half light of her polar universe and gave herself up to it. Briefly, she saw an image of flowers bent in the rain, their stalks seemingly broken. As the euphoria lifted her, their stalks slowly straightened. Part of her struggled against that image, tried to deny it.

Then she was flying, flying above all pain.

3

Danny was assigned for the duration to the Hotel New Yorker. It was a simple matter, he said, to live outside. He'd accumulated close to a year's back pay, quickly found them an apartment on Fifty-fifth Street, between Sixth and Seventh avenues. Bedroom, living room, kitchen, in a rather shabby building that nevertheless had a doorman, even elevator men. Jane hadn't lived in such a building since West End Avenue. The superintendent understood, of course, that they were married. Which Danny begged her to make true. Which Jane refused. Did he think that would cause her to respond more, in bed? While the apartment was painted, Danny came for her, walked with her in the late spring sunshine through the new neighborhood.

"We can stroll over to the theater district for our morning coffee," he said, tucking her arm under his. "I'll fatten you up on pastrami sandwiches at the Stage Delicatessen. We'll take the Sunday *Times* over to Central Park. Then we'll drop in at the Plaza for tea. A movie house next door, City Center across the street, Carnegie Hall two blocks away. And Broadway. Broadway and all the theaters at our feet."

Moving in, Jane didn't know if it was Danny—his elation, his zest—or her new secret armor against that Other, or the covert supply of cocaine with which Sal sent her on her way, that enabled her again to imitate sociability. She allowed Aurelia to convey her to Elizabeth Arden's to style her hair, to escort her to Bonwit's and Lord and Taylor's for summer dresses, to a wholesale house for lush material for drapes, to Macy's for Russell Wright dishes.

Danny installed a minimum of furniture, said she must do the rest. A big bed rested on cement blocks in the room where his typewriter sat amid the pages of his play. A couple of secondhand couches in the living room, a plain wooden table at the sunny window where they ate, planks separated by bricks for bookshelves. Also, an upright piano. It was, after Sal's, all quite lovely and Spartan.

At Aurelia's suggestion, Jane rode down to the Margaret Sanger Clinic, had herself fitted with a diaphragm. In bed, Danny slept nude but she didn't: no impulses, no accidents.

With Danny, Jane went at last to visit Mama. A new doctor on the case advised against mention of Peter. Mrs. Belmont was doing rather well these days, he said. A combination of group therapy—a new process learned from treatment of soldiers—and something he termed a token economy. Mama confided that this doctor was in love with her.

"After all," she added as she pushed back newly tinted blonde hair, "I'm still a young woman. I mean: I'm not yet all that old." There was guarded lechery in the beam she turned on Danny.

When Danny refused to bring Jane to his own parents on West End Avenue—"They're so scared I'll marry my *shiksa*"—the Edelmans dropped in one evening, unannounced. Jane had just washed her hair, WQXR played Schubert's Eighth Symphony, Danny puttered in the kitchen where he never appeared able to become used to the wonders of American food again— any food, he said, after the scavenging and famine of that last winter of the war in Holland. Faced with the little couple, he balder and still perspiring with embarrassment, she plumper and more tightly corseted, Jane felt only pity, frowned at Danny's uncharacteristic coldness.

"Danny, run down to the Stage and pick up some Danish," Jane implored. "I'll put on some coffee."

"Don't bother, don't bother." The Edelmans protested in chorus. Their parental scrutiny took in the sparse furniture, the painting Aurelia had given as a housewarming gift, Jack Tanner who leaped, large and handsome, across the piano keys. When Danny left, Jane offered to show them the rest of the apartment. At the bedroom door, the bed assumed a sudden blatancy, and Jane flushed. Sensing their equal outrage at the clutter of discarded clothes and of lechery, Jane gestured nervously toward the desk.

"That's where Danny works."

"Does he?" Mr. Edelman's features drooped, mournful. "He was so brilliant. Top of his class at Columbia. Now—what's the chance of him ever going back? He's just going to loaf, do nothing?"

"He *is* still in the Air Force," Jane pointed out. She led them away from the offending room.

"But what are his plans?" Mrs. Edelman sat forward on one of the couches. How odd: Danny's golden eyes in that plump, pancaked face. "He's too young to get married. You know that, don't you?"

"Just because we're living together doesn't mean we're ever going to marry." Jane held her voice steady. She remembered trembling before them that night, ten years ago, over her glass of milk.

Mr. Edelman clucked, shook his head in shocked dismay. His wife continued her pursuit.

"And if something happens? You get pregnant, maybe? I'll be open with you. Why does he have to take up with a gentile when so many Jews have died? He'll only get hurt. Does he want the Jews to disappear from this earth completely? Doesn't he care?"

"If you read his play—if it's produced—you'll see how much he cares."

Mr. Edelman bridled. "Sure. What are the chances of that? A twenty-two-year-old boy doesn't come out of the war and have a play on Broadway."

"Of course," Mrs. Edelman put in, smoothing the dress over her plump thighs, "I guess he figures you can help him with that. You know everybody, don't you? Tell me: you still go dancing with those actresses that dress like men? Like Walter Winchell wrote about? . . . And your sister—was she ever found?"

Anger brought a rush of color to Jane's cheeks. But mention of loss only carried with it the pain of that other deeper loss, and she was silent. Danny returned. His quick eyes took in the scene. Now it was as though, having been permitted to inject their poison, his parents were mollified. While Jane set out the coffee and pastry, they spoke of relatives, of Roosevelt's death, of cousins still fighting in the Pacific. With murmurs about Danny and Jane joining them for Sunday dinner sometime soon, they left. Danny turned to her as the door closed on them.

"What did they say? What happened while I was out?"

"Nothing." Jane went to the table to collect the dishes. He blocked her way.

"You think I can't see in your face what they said? You know, the reason you were probably so good on-stage is that you were always so open. To your own emotions. Aren't you ever going to let that happen again?"

"Maybe not." After Danny went to sleep she didn't have to lie in the dark, awake. She could lock herself in the bathroom, give herself up to cocaine.

"You won't open yourself to me, will you? You won't

give all of yourself, even the hurt. You never give all of yourself, do you? Have you ever?"

Perhaps he thought there was still pain, still mourning. He didn't know it had changed to implacable hostility toward the one who'd so made her suffer. "Maybe not. Maybe there's not that much to give. Did you ever think of that?"

"That smacks of self-pity. Well, I'm not going to let their coming make us fight. . . . Are you going to do the play?"

Zeal for Thy House, unpolished still, was indeed fine. Too fine, she'd already told Danny, for her to risk ruining it. There were others, other really good actresses, who could do it justice. She'd now turned twenty, she'd only been a flash in the pan, an early bloomer with nothing left to give. Aurelia, reading the play, fought against her, too—brave enough again—for the first time. Sal, led to the scent, insisted he be given the chance to invest his money at last: he'd be proud to back a play by a young American hero, not some mick vegetarian. Danny wouldn't have to know: Sal saw where a clean-cut young American hero might be reluctant to use his money. Sid Arkoff came gingerly around: if the play were about Jews on the run, Jane certainly looked the part. Why didn't he contact Paul Talbott?

They were closing in on her when she'd already made this large concession, it appeared to her, of coming back this far into life. Talbott, reading the play, grew as excited as when he'd had *Here Be Monsters* in his hands. The time was right for this play, he argued. Before people tired of confronting the war, what had happened to the Jews. The part was right for *her:* he understood what Danny meant about writing it for her. He came to the apartment when Danny was off shift, labored with him on final touches, told him what would work, what wouldn't. Aurelia could do the costumes. There were children to audition. Come on, come on: they were all baying at her heels.

Still, Jane hung back. She hadn't even entered a theater for a year. . . .

Now Jane looked up at Danny and he turned away from her to pour a drink. She sensed he'd temporarily moved far away, for she'd come to recognize the wooden expression that transformed his face at times. He was transfixed, she understood, before those inner images of Hell he'd seen, pictures of which appeared in all the papers these days. Those acres, those mountains of in-human-seeming corpses, those ovens, those ditches, those faces that, just barely rescued, stared back at the lenses of the world's cameras and that seemed forever set apart, that would always be staring back at death. There was a scene in the play that recaptured an early photograph of Jews being rounded up. A boy of perhaps ten, a cap on his head, stared at a world that would never see him again. Reluctantly, Jane heard some of the lines in her head. Zeal for Thy house has consumed me. . . .

She didn't want to go further into feeling, into passion. She had come this far. No further.

It was several days later that, walking along Broadway in the afternoon heat, Danny led her west up Forty-fourth Street, presumably at her grudging assent to buy tickets at last for a couple of plays. At the Majestic, they passed the line gathered at the box office for the previews. Suddenly, Danny was opening the door that led inside, a door uncannily not locked.

"We can't go in here," Jane protested. But Danny pushed her ahead of him, led her into the darkened theater, down the carpeted aisle.

The theater was hushed. A gray-haired man in a turquoise T-shirt pushed a bucket on its rolling stand across the stage as he slid the mop silently back and forth across the dark wood. Behind him, head tilted toward the array of overhead lights, a younger man pulled a cherry picker across the stage. Drawn to each side, the red velvet curtains rustled slightly. In their old mysterious way, they breathed. The thrill is gone, Jane tried to tell herself, knowing that Danny watched her, waiting, and yet—was it possible?—she lied. The curtains breathed. He whom she had now cast aside, no longer breathed, but they did. And she . . .

Slowly, Jane moved forward. Life might not be anywhere anymore, not even in Danny's urgent arms. But it was unbelievably here still, upon that stage, waiting to be born. It had, she supposed, always been.

92

The day all the contracts were signed—the same week the war ended—they went to "21." Milton Kaufmann, the producer fronting for Sal—Danny *didn't* know—was well enough recognized to get them past the downstairs seating area to the brighter front dining room upstairs, where Kaufmann, Paul Talbott, and Aurelia waited. There were drinks all around—"Congratulations, sweet. You weren't asked your age," Aurelia said —and Kaufmann advised they stick to the simplest dishes. The steak tartare, he insisted, was the best in the city. Danny lifted his wineglass toward Jane.

"Now our fortunes swing up. May they never swing back."

Before they left, Aurelia took her aside in the ladies' room, held Jane's chin firmly in her hand as she gazed at her. "You're beginning to look like my girl again. Even if you aren't. I suppose I don't have to say I still love you. I don't mind stepping aside for Danny the way I would for a gal. . . . Just remember. Any time you need me or want me . . ."

Rehearsals began in that empty warehouse over Broadway. The opening would be right here in New York at the start of October, at the Martin Beck. No out-of-town try-outs. This was where it belonged, Paul said.

Jane had to study mirrors now. To look closely was to see a familiar but almost unknown face. Her dark hair was shining and lustrous again, the arched brows thin, unplucked. The almond-shaped eyes, whose slant used to worry her so, appeared to her at times to be opaque, sealing off the world, at others to hold such depths that anyone's gaze into them would sink forever before reaching whatever it was they seemed to hold. There were now hollows under the cheekbones in the heart-shaped face, and she saw, objectively, what Danny meant when he spoke of her finely articulated lips—or Sal, of her nostrils. Her face, she reflected dispassionately, was a fine instrument for expressing emotion. Her body, her limbs, long and lithe—like his, who was now gone—projected both strength and fragility. She began, as though to tune this instrument again, to exercise, to run through vocal practice, to dance.

She, too, sat in with Talbott and Danny on the auditions for the two male leads. One would play her brother. Early in Hitler's regime, they'd been adopted by a German family friendly with their parents, who'd been taken away, and had been brought up with their son. With the advent of war, the family had denounced them, denounced their son's friendship for the brother, his love for the girl. Rounding up orphaned Jewish children, the three escape across the border into Holland. Cornered by German troops, the German lover is killed, she wounded. At the moment of joining with the Dutch Underground, she dies. Her brother goes on to fight, determined that if he and any remnant survive, they will struggle for a homeland of their own.

It had been comparably easy to choose the German lover. To Jane, none of the young actors appeared right for the role of the brother. One day Danny confronted her obstinacy.

"You know what you're doing? You're saying anyone can do for your lover. Let's forget what that says about me. But nobody can take *his* place—the one that was Peter when I was writing." Jane stiffened. "But they aren't us anymore. They've become themselves, separate people, don't you see? Remember, in the play at least, you love your sweetheart as much as, if not more than, your brother. It's only a play."

In his hurt and anger, he didn't yet know that other love was gone. Jane gazed dispassionately then upon the dark, thin young actor—Anthony Brahm—and gave her nod. He was, like them all, only litmus paper, would be changed to fiction by the lines, the movements of the play. He—none of them—were as real as the fictional reality of the play itself.

During rehearsals, many of the cast, moved by their lines, wept. Talbott encouraged group expression. "I want the action to bring out the essence of the proscenium stage. Every scene has to jolt those people out there so their vision is dazzled, they'll never lose those images. This has to be a true theater of confrontation."

Confrontation was what Anthony Brahm was after, the last week before the opening. They'd gone over it many times—the final scene in which he dragged her, wounded, down the steps into the basement where the children were hidden. There were still noises of carpentry backstage. The stage itself was hot. Their sweat mingled as he pressed his face against hers. To Jane, the constant replaying, the discomfort began to churn up in her—rather than weariness—all the lovely old sense of dedication, of exalted but controlled sensuality she had used to associate with strong theater work at the Neighborhood Playhouse. It was like being able to sing at full voice again in violent sunshine, after only whispering in darkness. Wiping her face with the T-shirt she wore for rehearsals, she smiled almost dreamily on Anthony as they mounted the steps for another run-through. She realized what she was doing, turned on him the usual blank stare she reserved for him when they weren't acting.

Anthony followed her to her dressing room. As he closed the door behind him, Jane stared.

"Can't wait to get my sweat off you, can you?" His dark eyes snapped. "You've been handing me this dog treatment ever since we started. Just because you were in a hit before doesn't give you the right to high-hat me. And just because you happen to be laying the playwright. . . . I hear you're not above spreading your legs for the real backer of this show, too. A gangster. But my sweat isn't good enough." He was quivering with rage.

It was hardly his business she'd had exactly two men in her life. "Your sweat, as it happens, it almost the only thing about you that *is* good enough."

"Listen!" He seized her, pressed her against his hard chest. "I'm supposed to be your brother, damn it. You're supposed to love me. You think . . ."

Jane pushed him off. Her dark hair fell across her eyes and she swept it back. "I'll be responsible for giving a good imitation of a sister's love for her brother. I haven't heard Paul complain. . . ."

"Sure." He pulled her back to him. "You probably give it to him, too, for all I know. What is it you have against me? Huh?"

Jane stared into those blazing eyes and a different anger flowed along her frame, through her joints, to freeze her face and heart in a new way. She heard her own voice wailing that night long ago: "Why not? Why not?" and *that* voice's answer: "Because if we do, it's as though we're saying goodbye forever. As though I'm never coming back. And I am."

"You want to be my brother?" She breathed the words into this face above her. "You want me to show you how I can love?" She saw the fury turn to consternation and that to disbelief. As her hands crept up the bare skin under his shirt, his own hands fumbled in her hair and brought her mouth to his. They were backing to the small couch, he mumbling phrases of surprise, of gratitude as he lifted her cotton skirt above her thighs. Callow youth! she thought, as he took her. But he didn't really matter. He thought it was he who'd triumphed. He couldn't know the bitter victory she tasted in her mouth when it was over, he couldn't understand the wryness of the smile with which she sent him off.

She'd had her way, at last.

Dress rehearsal served also as preview. Jane's name was in lights now for the first time on the marquee, though her write-up in the *Playbill* was, of necessity, fairly short. She'd separated herself from all of them, had made herself into a prism through which shone the girl in the play. Her emotions were under control while Paul and Danny argued about the variable speed of the second act curtain, while Anthony insisted that the lighting from the first balcony rail shone directly in his eyes when he spoke his last eloquent lines. He was strangely pious toward her now while she felt only professional detachment. This would be the first time they'd do the play from start to finish as it would roll on opening night.

It flowed, it all worked beautifully. Hypnotized by his role, Anthony caught Jane's hand backstage after Act One, murmured: "Sister! My sister!" before taking his place onstage for Act Two. Jane's heart seemed to have slowed at his words, her eyes momentarily dimmed. There was a slight tremor in her legs as she watched him from where she stood at the stage tormentor. His breath, his words were still in her ears.

She tensed, made her entrance down the basement steps. Anthony struggled with her to convince them both she wouldn't die. The children were huddled to one side behind the temporarily opaque scrim. Anthony pulled himself up to a small window at street level to watch for danger. Jane moved from the cot where he'd laid her, sank to her knees, crawled to the point where he turned to meet her, to catch her in his arms.

Jane spoke her lines of apology, encouragement, farewell. Gazing at him as she was supposed to do, she saw, as through a haze—the haze of death?—his anguish. Her own deepest penetration of their relationship in the play, one she'd half-consciously held in abeyance till now, would no longer remain submerged.

These were now, as they hadn't been in the dressing room at all, those dark familiar eyes from the past that had looked into her own so many times in so many ways, in life, in dreams. They were no longer Anthony's eyes, after all, that she stared into but those others she'd never see again. The anguish she saw, that she recognized, transported her to that flaming moment when Peter, himself, must have tried to say goodbye.

Something broke, at last, inside her. Almost mechanically, she spoke her last few words. For the first time there came with them slow hot tears. Improvising, thinking it was the play itself that had moved her, Anthony bent to kiss her and his own eyes filled. He carried her supposedly lifeless body to the cot, gently laid her down. The light came on, illuminating the children behind the scrim. Anthony moved to the apron, clicked his rifle as he spoke his closing lines. Jane lay still. All that hatred she'd nurtured, she'd clung to, dissolved. She was completely open now.

For the first time in over a year she could say the name. The pain flowed over and through her. Peter, my darling, you are really dead. My love is wrapped around you.

The ovation was tremendous. Danny, hailed onstage and handing Jane flowers, gazed at her curiously, at her makeup streaked with tears. Let him think it was the play that had happened to her. What had was too private for her to share.

Except with Peter, whose name she could say at last. She was still, of course—would always be—holding up a shield between her and life. But she could say his name. To Danny, as they walked home up Broadway, she commented, with an attempt at casualness: "Too bad Peter couldn't have been here." She saw his pensive eyes widen, taking that in.

That night, she dreamed differently of Peter. He walked away from her through a mist lit from above by streaks of sunlight. In his arms, he carried Joanie.

4

On opening night, when the papers arrived at Sardi's, Jane bent forward to hear: it was Danny's name she waited for. This must be Danny's night. The critics did come through.

"Twenty-three-year-old Dan Edelman has scored a personal triumph in his masterful representation of the particular and the universal. . . ." "The energy of language in young Edelman's first play is astonishing and signals the advent of a strong new voice in the theater. . . ." "What it has taken hundreds of pictures and millions of words to bring home to a stricken world, Dan Edelman has accomplished in two hours of passionate drama. . . ."

They hadn't overlooked her. "Jane Belmont's peculiar haunting quality of mystery and loss. . . ." "She is still the leggy colt that enchanted us in *Here Be Monsters,* but Jane Belmont has grown up. She has a very personal way of conveying the anguish of life, of teaching us something we can never forget. . . ." "The timing, the eloquence of gesture in Jane Belmont's performance. . . . Not since Merle Oberon have we seen this type of exotic beauty, illuminated here by a singular intelligence and vulnerability. . . ."

At least three critics prophesied that the play and she would win the Tony Awards. They admonished readers to reach the box office early.

Danny, discharged from the Air Force, dressed in old pants and sweaters, his hair grown long and curly again, resembled closely the Danny of their childhood. Saturday matinees he went to the home football games at Columbia, other afternoons played soccer up at Morningside Heights. He gave interviews now, sometimes with her, sometimes alone: Rising-young-playwright-says sort of thing, over drinks at the Algonquin lobby, or Sunday brunch at the Plaza. Sometimes, but not always, he accompanied Paul Talbott to a performance. Talbott returned every two weeks to check on what he termed "loosening" in anyone's part—Anthony's, in particular —to enlarge on his role. Every night, Danny met her at the stage door and they walked home, arms around each other, along Broadway. Often they stopped in at Lindy's or the Stage.

With his severance pay, Danny had bought a 1938 green Plymouth convertible and, before the autumn foliage was gone, they drove into the country for a Sunday picnic. He'd decided, Danny said, to use the G.I. Bill, return to Columbia to study world drama. He'd take an extra load, attend summer session, graduate the following June. Why, Jane wondered, didn't he just read Aristotle's *Poetics*, study acting at the Neighborhood Playhouse? They were drawing down enough, between them, from the Martin Beck. Comfort was no problem.

"But if you marry me, the G.I. Bill goes from seventy-five to a hundred and five!" He grinned. "Besides, I need the B.A. for security. For the kids."

Jane gave him her sidelong glance. As she had before, she shook her head. They were lying on an old plaid blanket, a bag of chocolate Indian babies between them. ("I like to eat their heads first, so they don't feel the pain," she'd said. Danny had countered: "I eat the feet first. So they won't run away.")

"I don't want us to marry. I don't ever want to marry." She hesitated. It was still novel to speak that name. There was still that quick pang in her belly. "Peter and I decided that long ago. It was one of the promises we made each other when we were little."

"Promises?" His eyes were mocking, amused.

"Besides, I have to decide about myself. Do I want to use another person to live—or do I want to use myself?"

99

"Does it have to be mutually exclusive?"

"Maybe. Anyway, I don't feel I can really give you anything. In the long run. It's not fair to you."

"Can? Or want to? And why not let me be the judge of that? I get what I want. Almost. . . . There's nothing I *do* want, really, aside from theater, except you." His voice roughened as he leaned above her. "I can never look at you enough. There's a gentleness in you that turns me weak. The shape of your lips is part of my imagery. The skin of your arms. I'm in love with your hands, your fingers." He kissed them. "I move in your aura. I don't want—I can't imagine—any life without you." He kissed her, her cheeks, eyelids, lips. "You're my ivory goddess. I can never get enough of you." He buried his face in her neck and his hands went under her jacket, her sweater, to caress her breasts.

As he made love to her, Jane lay back, her hands in his curly hair, but her eyes watching the heavy drifting clouds, swollen with rain. She wished, for his sake, she could feel something more—anything—when they made love. She wondered if she ever would.

The play was constantly sold out and, in the spring, *Zeal for Thy House* did win the Tony for Best Play, Paul Talbott for direction, Sean Flaherty for lighting. Jane was nominated for Best Actress, lost out to a fading grande dame of the stage. To have been nominated was marvel enough. That Danny had won somewhat eased her guilt for what she didn't give him.

There were many parties now, many late afternoon teas at the Algonquin, sorties to the Village and up to Harlem. Parties where Katherine Cornell, the Lunts, Helen Hayes came up to congratulate them. But also, there were evenings with Danny studying, afternoons with him at class when Jane was alone, could putter about the apartment, clean, cook. There was a coin-operated laundry around the corner on Seventh Avenue. Jane would take their things a couple of times a week, drop in, while the machines were going, at the Horn and Hardart's on the corner for coffee, watch faces, hands, for expressions, gesture. She wore no makeup but a thin pancake to protect her skin from the city grime, but occasionally someone—at the launderette, at the counter —would approach her, speak in excitement, awe.

"Aren't you the one in that play? . . . I saw you in *Zeal for Thy House.* . . . Aren't you Jane Belmont? . . . I think you're magnificent! You're so beautiful!" They'd ask for her autograph. Obliging, Jane always felt herself pale a bit, from embarrassment mingled with gratitude.

Danny's seriousness about his studies amused her. Nobody else of his age, Jane pointed out, would work for grades when Paramount and Warner's had approached him for rights to the play. From him, she hid the hurt the talent scouts had dealt her when they said she wasn't right for the film role. What that amounted to, Sid Arkoff bluntly explained, was their usual timidity in the face of Winchell's past columns, the gossip that roiled beneath the surface affection of the theater world about her and Sal, about her living with Danny. Word came from Hollywood that the head office didn't want the girl to die at the end, and Danny halted the conferences.

Meanwhile, she, Aurelia, and Cynthia Blackwood— going down to the Village as in the old days—laughed at the sanctimonious morality that covered like thin gauze the world of showbiz. Jane was a little high as she drank the liquor Cynthia smuggled into her glass at regular intervals—"I'll be glad when you *do* reach your majority"—applauded vigorously the colored folksinger they'd come to hear. His name was Scott Williams. In this, his first appearance in anything like the big time, he alternated a sweet melancholy with youthful delight in his songs. When he'd finished, he laid aside his guitar, came to their table, asked Jane to dance.

"They say you're an actress, up on Broadway. That right?" He was slight, lean, with a deep hollow in each thin chocolate cheek. A mustache drooped over the full upper lip that extended slightly above the lower one. His somewhat protruding eyes were light brown, curious, lit as though by a constant secret joy. He held Jane carefully away from him. "Hope you don't mind my taking this liberty. Asking you out on the floor."

"Why should I mind? I'd like to give you tickets to my play." Jane moved in closer to dance. Scott Williams moved her back.

"Along with the Saturday matinee crowd from Westchester? Folks might ask to have their seat changed!"

He smiled, testing, teasing. "Then, they might just be the kind gets a kick outa tasting forbidden fruit. Right?"

"You think that's what I'm doing now."

"Well . . ." He grinned widely. "This *could* just be what they call amazing grace." When he'd led her back to her table, reappeared for his second performance, he concluded with that hymn, looking toward her in the semidarkness from his spotlit circle:

"Amazing grace: how sweet the sound,
That saved a wretch like me;
I once was lost but now am found,
Was blind, but now I see. . . ."

Cynthia Blackwood stared. "Darling, I think you've made a conquest."

Next morning, early, the phone rang. It was Sal.

"What's this I hear about you dancing with a spade?" There was no greeting.

"Don't talk to me like that," Jane warned. Jack Tanner shifted on her feet. Danny, setting down a cup of coffee at the bedside table, glanced toward her curiously. "Don't use that language. And don't have me followed."

"I got my rights," Sal intoned. "Just 'cause you don't live here no more don't mean I got no rights in your life. In my opinion . . ."

"Sal, what I feel for you has never had anything to do with your opinions. Now. Do you want to come to dinner Sunday? Or do you want to say something else that will make me hang up on you?"

He came to dinner Sunday. Asked, over coffee, when she was going to go ahead and marry this fellow. Danny concurred. Jane sensed her own flush of annoyance. But she accompanied them downstairs to see what Sal insisted was the first Caddy limousine off the assembly line since the war. While he and Danny circled the car, Dino jerked his head toward her, winked, showed her the submachine gun in its new casing below the dash. Danny had once mentioned talk about Sal being investigated. Jane shook her head resignedly. She believed

Sal inhabited a world of imaginary dragons that made him happy. Sal came up behind her and Dino flopped innocently back against the seat. Not quickly enough.

"Whatta ya think you're doin', smart ass?" Sal roared. Two children playing at the stone lions that stood guard beside the entrance to the lobby paused. "I ever tell you to show off anything? You want me to lay your ears back?"

"I wasn't doin' nothin'," Dino mumbled.

Sal lifted his elbow in swift challenge, as though to attack. Instead he glanced somberly back toward Jane. "You didden see nothin', did ya?"

Jane agreed. Of course not.

Upstairs, she arranged to have two tickets sent to the young folksinger for the Wednesday matinee. When she came out the stage door Scott waited, at the fringe of the crowd gathered for autographs, with a mulatto man she'd noticed at the Vanguard. Scott was, she realized in daylight, younger than he'd first appeared. The drooping mustache, those vertical hollows in his thin cheeks lent maturity. He introduced his friend—rather stern, heavyset and bespectacled—as Clyde Simpson. Then he smiled his lazy, joyful smile.

"You were a lovely thing up there. Yeah. Amazing grace. . . ."

"If I was a Jew, baby," Clyde offered, "I'd be back there, Hell or high water. I'd gun down every damn bastard killed anyone belonged to me." A muscle twitched at his jaw, his hands curled into fists that jabbed the air. "An eye for an eye."

The play, Jane noted, had really got to Clyde. As they began to walk toward Broadway, people turned to stare. What, Jane wondered as she shook hands at the BMT that would take them back to the Village, would Sal have said about *two* spades?

As though to reassure him he was still important to her life, she allowed Sal to give her—the second anniversary of Peter's death—a twenty-first birthday party, an extravagant affair on a Sunday evening in Scarsdale. This time Sal insisted she accept the ring he'd purchased two years before—three rows of one-half carat diamonds set around a larger one. Danny had already given her, beautifully framed, a Degas lithograph. Aurelia had sewn the glittering red gown she wore.

Sal had ordered one tent for the bar, another for cooking, a third enormous one for dinner, with canopies and hardwood decks that ran between them. The pool had been laid over by a dance floor where, at one end, an orchestra played on a dais. The florists, Aurelia speculated, must have realized two thousand dollars on the poles covered with roses. Beluga caviar, truffles, champagne. No press: Sal still saw himself, almost comically, as protective of Jane's reputation. The one reporter who sneaked in had his camera smashed. The women were given tiny flaçons of Chanel No. 5, the men gold cuff links. Bonzo became extremely agitated, drank too much beer, had to be locked in his house.

"This outdoes any Bar Mitzvah I've seen," Danny remarked. Jane sensed his annoyance, reinforced by the ring on her finger. On the way back to the city, he mentioned it.

"It's okay to remain friends with Sal—God knows he did enough for you when you needed him. But do you have to accept material things, bought with blood money?"

"It *is* vulgar. I'll never wear it except when I'm with him."

"Has it ever occurred to you to wonder where his money comes from? Up to a point, he's funny. But every once in a while, I hear things that make my flesh crawl."

"Then don't let *me* hear them," Jane flashed. "I don't want to know."

Danny sent her a look as he swung the car down the empty early morning streets. "Right. . . . Who'd want to know a hit guy?" Quickly, he reached out to squeeze her clenched fist. "Sorry. I didn't mean to ruin your evening, my sweet."

But ruin it, he did. Tired as they were, they made love and then Danny had to wonder aloud if marriage would release her, allow her to meet his passion with her own. "Is that it?" he asked. His eyes widened at her sudden fury.

"You're stupid!" Jane flung herself from the bed, pulled on her kimono, started for the kitchen for a drink.

"Well, there has to be *some* reason." Danny followed her. "You just won't connect. You're always holding off."

"Get another girl then." Her hands shook as she reached for the ice trays. Danny took one from her, brought out the bottle and glasses, poured them each a drink.

"Don't think other women wouldn't have me."

"Don't think I haven't noticed."

"I don't want another girl. Damn it! I'd rather have you—even an image of you, like outside on the poster at the theater—than any other breathing female anywhere. The trouble is, you know that!"

"Number one. Marriage. I've told you. I don't want it. Number two. Sex. I can live without it. I'd be just as happy to share this play with you and share our lives as we do, without ever having sex. I only do it for you."

Danny flinched. "Thanks." Seated at the kitchen table, he swirled the ice in his glass. "I know you'd just as soon treat me like a brother. Tell me." He stared up at her where she stood, one arm akimbo, her drink trembling in her right hand. "Are you going to spend your life reconstituting your family?"

Jane's fingers turned cold. "What do you mean?"

"It's pretty obvious, isn't it? Sal's become your father, hasn't he? Aurelia's your mother. I guess you still have to find your sister. And you want me to be your brother." He watched as she inhaled sharply. "But I can't be. I won't be. I want to be your new family. Or nothing."

She waited, as though for the echo of his voice to dissipate. "I guess it will have to be nothing, won't it?" Her voice was tight. She walked to the living room windows, looked out at the lights still twinkling toward Broadway in the dawn. In his apartment across the court-yard, the pianist from the Philharmonic was marking pages of music.

"You know I didn't mean that," Danny said. "I could never mean that about wanting nothing. I just got through telling you—I've always told you—I'll take you anyway you care to have me."

"Maybe I *don't* care." A part of her said dully: don't do this to him. Don't do this to yourself. Another found a strange joy in the pain they both felt. "I think it's time we had a rest from one another. I think it's time I got out of here. After all, I've reached that much-vaunted majority. I don't need a guardian."

"Jane, Jane!" He moved to take her in his arms. She eluded him. "What are you doing? This is just a lovers' quarrel. We're both punchy with sleep. You're not going to do anything drastic because of this. . . ."

"It's not a lovers' quarrel," she said, with that strange awful joy. "It's a sibling quarrel, remember? I'm getting out today. Aurelia will take me in. My mother. Remember?"

Danny forced her around to face him. "You know, we never forgive those we've wronged. I don't want you to place me in that territory."

"Don't make stage dialogue." Her eyes, dry, hot, blazed back at him.

"Okay. Happy birthday. I have to be in class early. Let's forget this. Let's go to the Stage tonight, take in a movie. Thank the Lord you don't have a performance."

"Um." She let him precede her to bed. He'd see. She'd given it a year, hadn't she? Grieving already, she imagined his face this evening when he returned, found her really gone. She could also, she told herself, disappear from people's lives. It didn't always have to be what happened to her.

5

"I guess I was always waiting," Aurelia said when Jane arrived, unannounced, with one large suitcase, a cardboard box that held the cat pan and dish, and Jack Tanner. "I'm ashamed that I've been waiting." Over drinks, Aurelia confided that Hollywood had been after her for some time. "I guess I just couldn't leave. Leave you."

Jane hesitated, moving bits of cheese on the dish between them. "But I'll sleep out here on the couch. Okay?"

Something not quite a blink passed across Aurelia's eyes. She smiled. "Did you think I was only after your body?"

Jane smiled back. "I won't be interfering—with anything you've got going?" She thought of Cynthia Blackwood.

"New York's a big place, sweetie. I guess this one's large enough for you and me."

Danny called, of course. And presented himself at the door. Jane, placing her hand on his chest, shook her head.

"I'm not angry. *You* have every right to be. But there's nothing to talk about. Really. This is a decision I had to make. That evening just triggered it. And please: can't we not be friends? At least for a while?" At his eyes, his face, she remembered his words: we never forgive those we've wronged. . . . Was it such a sin to flee commitment?

She spent the summer going about a great deal with Aurelia and Cynthia and Natalie Young, who'd just returned from a stint at a sanitarium. "She reminds me of a piranha—the way she looks at you," Aurelia commented, one evening.

"Don't worry. I'm in quite a celibate mood."

This she had to impress on the *Herald Tribune* reporter who launched a siege on her and who gave up with some remark about *The Well of Loneliness.* On a producer who wanted to build a musical comedy around her. On the other who pitched his seduction with: "You wanna play Juliet? You got it."

She returned, more or less, to the life she'd led before *Here Be Monsters:* the lessons, gymnasium, theater. She spent a good deal of time walking, observing people. But not near Fifty-fifth Street. Not to avoid Danny but herself. It was painful enough to spot him sometimes in the audience at *Zeal,* almost painful, at times, to speak his lines.

For the Halloween Beaux Arts Ball at the Manhattan Art League, Aurelia decided to dress Jane as Cleopatra. Would Jane have the nerve to wear a gauze top with an asp circling one breast, both nipples bare beneath? The skirt would be brocade, slit up the sides, a low belt held by an amulet.

Jane shrugged. "Why not? It'll be a break from the rags I wear in the play."

She wasn't, after all, the most daring. A young dancer from a new musical appeared as Venus rising from the sea and draped only in sequined gossamer. There were quite a few bare buttocks among the men. Jane hadn't counted on Danny showing up. Dressed as Ghenghis Khan, he cut in on her.

"What's with the bare tits routine? Is this your new *persona*?"

"I said I don't need a guardian. Are you going to dance? Or lecture?"

He held her away from him a moment. "You're very beautiful. But, as a matter of fact, neither." He stalked off. Almost immediately, a Harlequin's arms enfolded her.

"It's been a long time," a bright voice said. She realized it was Scott.

"Where have you been?" She nestled in close. Her heartbeat of anger and hurt might be visible.

"Touring. Cut a couple of records. Just got back last week. I was wondering if I'd run into you again." The music was so loud, he had to speak directly into her ear. His mustache was soft against her cheek.

"You could have looked me up."

"I wasn't sure you'd like that."

"You mean, *you* like to play hard to get." She wondered if her remark were wise. It might be far more complicated to convince a colored man she simply didn't want to go to bed with anyone.

But she left with him. With him and a large crowd going down to the Village. It was only when they'd arrived at McDougall's that he suggested they ditch the others, she come up to his room on Charles Street, hear his records.

"I don't mean like my etchings. If you're interested." He peeped beneath the bangs Aurelia had given her.

"Of course I am." In the walk-up, it was cold and she held the Kashmiri shawl about her—another gift from Aurelia. "Is 'Amazing Grace' one of them?"

Scott smiled. "Don't you know it?"

108

While the records played, Scott made coffee over a two-burner stove set on a wooden crate, changed into faded dungarees. "The Harlequin, you know, was really the devil in the Middle Ages. Death and all those bad ole things. I sure don't want to come on at you that way."

"Cleopatra wasn't exactly good news for the man in her life." Jane was a little high, regretted saying so much, then didn't. "I don't want to be bad news for you."

She was in his arms then, on the sagging bed he used for a couch. It was surprising how warm and comforting it was to be there. His lips were sweet, his kisses tender, urgent. Later, lying against his smooth, gleaming dark skin, she remembered eating those chocolate Indian babies with Danny. She didn't think she should mention this to Scott. She knew him in the Biblical sense, but not well enough for that. She did say:

"Our bodies are beautiful together, aren't they? Yours like chocolate. . . ."

"And yours like cream," he finished, and kissed her. Holding her away from him, he scrutinized her. "Back in Maryland, where I come from, I gotta stand at the end of the counter at People's Drugstore in Fritchieville— that's what we call the town—just to pick up coffee and a doughnut. *Would* you be willing to tell me if you're doing this just for kicks? I mean: 'cause even without my costume, I'm dark and I'm the devil?"

"Even without your costume, *especially* without your costume, you're dark and you're beautiful." She brushed her lips over his eyelids.

" 'How sweet the sound. . . .' "

Charles Street was close enough to Sheridan Square for them to see one another easily during the day. Scott had a solid contract at the Village Box and often got out later than Jane did. Sometimes he picked her up at Sheridan Square, sometimes he waited for her on Charles Street, sometimes they met at the Village Box or another nightspot. What they had together was a quality of innocent joy she hadn't known since long ago with Peter. In early spring they strolled through Central Park, one day visited the zoo and rode the merry-go-round. After, they chased each other on the boulders nearby and beneath the trees further uptown in the park. Jane suggested they pretend they were escaping from pirates. Scott won out with the idea they make believe they were runaway slaves.

"How come you got no ball and chain on yo' feet, boy?" Jane challenged as they pushed their way up the rocks.

"White massa lady up the big house—she fancied me, coulden have her way with me, she done took off my lil ole ball and chain, right off!"

There was rarely difficulty in the evening. It was when they were in the park or strolled along Eighth Street during the day that people turned to stare, women to cluck in distaste. One morning, Scott showed her a piece of paper that had come in the mail. On it were pasted words cut from a newspaper and reassembled:

"This is a warning. Get your nigger hands off that white girl."

Jane felt sick. "It could be. . . . No! Even Sal wouldn't do that." Since she'd left Danny, Sal had called —busy with lawyers in Washington—only once. To tell her she was making herself into filth. At which she'd hung up. One day it had seemed to her she'd spotted a black Cadillac limousine turn the corner slowly ahead of them at Charles Street, decided then she'd been mistaken. Dino or Frank still delivered a ration of cocaine at Sheridan Square; that was all.

Now, as Scott questioned her, she told him reluctantly about Sal. "But I think he knows better than to intrude on me again. And I just don't think that's his style."

Occasionally, Scott's friend, Clyde Simpson, joined them. Once, after he'd left, Jane commented: "*I* wouldn't be surprised to get a note from *him*. 'Get your honkie hands off that colored boy.' "

Scott tousled her hair. "Guess he's afraid I'm gonna end up like Icarus. Flying too close to the sun."

"Some sun. . . . He doesn't trust me."

"*I* do." He smoothed her hair and gave her his sweet smile of joy. It was strange: the dreamy quality of Scott's eyes. Danny's gaze had always been so direct. Jane reflected a moment.

110

"The color business? Oh, yes. We can both trust me on that. It's just in general I wonder if anyone should ever trust me at all." She refused to elaborate.

A second note arrived. "This is the last warning. Get lost, nigger." Jane wondered if it would help to notify the police.

"What could *they* do? Nothing that keeps me from being up Shit Creek if this redneck decides to act." Scott, lolling on the decrepit couch, looked amused. But worried, too. Jane flung the paper down, came to him in a loud rustle of taffeta skirt—the new long look with the crinoline petticoat beneath. She crushed his lean body against hers.

"I won't let anything happen to you," she vowed. "This isn't the South." She sat, studied him. "If you're at all scared—I mean, if you're at all uneasy—I'll leave you alone. You're too important to me to take any chances."

"Just try it. My little ole Amazing Grace." Scott buried his face in her neck. She held his head against her breast, dug her fingers into the soft curly mop of hair. He emitted a deep groan. Solicitously, she laid her lips against the thick curls. "What is it?"

"I just gotta have us some big fat eclairs from the bakery downstairs. And two big glasses of chocolate milk."

It was a week later the doorbell rang very early at Sheridan Square. Aurelia called sleepily from the bedroom: "Who in Hell is that, at this hour, for God's sake?"

Jane, struggling to come awake, went to the door. It was Clyde Simpson. There was a strange flush under his beige skin as he pushed his way in past her. At the look of hatred in his eyes, it occurred to Jane that perhaps it *was* he who'd sent those notes. Simultaneous with that thought, she was aware of a familiar protective armor that hardened within her. Clyde was fighting for breath. He smacked one fist into the other hand, then whirled on her.

"Well, you did it. They got him. While you were sleeping the sleep of the just and the innocent, you know where Scott was? Do you care? Huh?"

Aurelia hurried in, tying her robe about her. There

111

was a strange sensation as of cold water spurting from Jane's ears, as though that would prevent her from hearing. And, far down in some barely accessible reach of her consciousness, the faintest sound of a wooden swing came toward her. She thought she'd said something, framed a question, realized her lips hadn't moved.

"He was gunned down. A couple of hours ago. Walking along Charles Street. People on the block said they heard the skid of tires from what must have been a real heavy car. Somebody used a submachine gun on the poor bastard. Right in the back. He never had a chance. I guess he never knew what hit him." Clyde brought his sweating face close to hers.

"But *you* know. Don't you, you white bitch? You had to have a nigger plaything. *You* know who it was. Scott told me about those notes. He *said* you thought at first it was your bigshot gangster pal. But what did that mean to *you*? Huh? It wasn't worth your doing anything about it, was it? After all, you were just having yourself a few kicks, weren't you? You . . ."

"That'll be just about enough." Aurelia interposed herself between them. Jane saw her dig her hands into Clyde's stomach, shove him away. Clyde emitted a choked sob, then straightened. Over Aurelia's head he turned on Jane the stare of an Old Testament prophet.

"You gonna do something about this or not? You know who it was. There's no way anyone else can pin it on the bastard. What are you gonna *do*?" His voice sank to a whisper. "Remember the day we met? What I said about anyone did anything to somebody belonged to me? That boy belonged to me. He was like family. You don't do what's right, some day this will all come back on you."

Aurelia propelled him, finally, out the door. For one confused moment, Jane saw Joanie's body crumpled like a rag doll's beneath a park bench. Then this changed. It was Scott's slight form that lay facedown in his own blood in the early hours on Charles Street. But his face, his sweet eyes, his eager smile—surely those still awaited her upstairs in the dingy room where they'd laughed, sung, made love? She kept trying to speak, to say something to Aurelia, but that faint sound of the wooden swing terrified her. She allowed Aurelia to hold her, guide her into the kitchen where Aurelia sat her down, made coffee, crooned comfort. By the time the police came, Aurelia had her dressed.

Yes, Jane admitted from numb lips, there'd been two anonymous notes. No, she said, seeing the contempt on their faces, she didn't know who'd sent them. What had they done with Scott's body? A friend of the deceased —one Clyde Simpson—was claiming the body, planned to take it south for the funeral. Could she see him? Jane asked. Oh, they advised her, they wouldn't do that if they were her. This friend was taking care of everything.

Aurelia's eyes were all dark pupil. "Will there be an inquest? Will she have to be there?"

The cops' stares were cool. "Nothing you have to bother about." Beneath the words, gestures, Jane sensed what was uppermost in Aurelia's mind: not what had happened to Scott, but what must not happen again to her, Jane. The balance struck must not again be shattered. A familiar impersonal pity for Aurelia touched her. If she had nothing else to say then, the cops decided, they'd be on their way.

Except that one of them, reminding her of the policeman who'd questioned her separately the night of Joanie's disappearance, added, just as he was leaving: "Why doesn't a good-looking dame like you, who's got it made, stick to her own kind? See what mixing with colors can get you?"

Aurelia wanted her to lie down. Aurelia wanted her to come with her to the warehouse on Eighth Avenue to look at cloth. Aurelia offered to go with her to Charles Street.

"No," Jane said. "I have to go out. Alone. Please."

She took the train out to Scarsdale, hailed a taxi to Sal's place. The forsythia and daffodils were in bloom again. Across the stream, the birds cried out from the aviary. This was where she'd mourned all those days and months that other death. She'd walked these paths, had lain in the chair in the solarium, had followed Giorgio as he tended the gardens, had watched Sal drift, faceup, in the pool, had slept in a bed by his side while she'd mourned and never admitted to herself that that was what that half life had been. She heard Sal's voice: This *is* my child. . . . and Danny's: Sal's become your father, hasn't he? . . . Her cold heart seemed to stop, to quiver.

William, surprised, admitted her. Frank appeared, sent her his jolly look from behind his spectacles.

"Is Sal home?" She was grateful for the numbness. Only her legs trembled.

Frank hesitated. Dino appeared, standing at the other side of the doorway where Frank lounged. Dino, who had always combined with his sinister air a certain deference toward her—her "classiness," she'd inferred —now narrowed his eyes and lips, peered at her and slightly away. . . . Who'd want to know a hit guy? Danny had asked.

"What does she want?" Dino asked of Frank.

"I want to see Sal." Jane walked toward them. She saw how Dino raised his arm to thwart her, how his right hand went to his pocket. Her own hand shot out, pushed against his face. She stepped between them, walked— they following in what must have been amazement—to the Chinese room. Sal rose up in the shadows as she entered.

"Well! So you finally come back to see your old pal!" The tone was avuncular, so smooth that for a moment she wavered. Then:

"What have you done? Tell me, Sal. What have you done?"

Sal spread his hands. "What's this? Whatsa matter? Sit down and tell me whatsa matter?"

Her legs trembled. "It *was* you, wasn't it? It was you who sent those notes. And you who had him killed. Who did it? Dino?"

Sal, his heavy head tilted to one side in exasperation, came toward her. "Did what? What did Dino do? He's been right here with me since we got back from Washington. A coupla hours ago. So whatta you saying he done?"

"He killed Scott Williams. At your orders. Don't try . . ."

Sal held up the hand flashing with rings. "Now, waita minute. Just waita minute. Something happen to this

114

spade you been runnin' around with? First thing I know. Honest to God. He's dead?" The eyes tried hard to narrow in sorrow. "Oh, that's bad. That's bad." The heavy head shook, portentous commiseration.

"You know he's dead. You always know everything about me." She was aware of Frank and Dino behind her. The trembling in her legs forced Jane to sink on that red couch where Sal had so often ministered to her with the tiny dish and spoon. "Oh, Sal. Make me believe it wasn't you. How can I live, thinking it was you?"

"Well, you got no problem then, little girl." Sal let himself down beside her, tried to take her hand, but she shrank away from him. "You know what I think about you runnin' around with spades. But you think I'd kill somebody for that? Specially if I thought I was gonna hurt *you* in any way? That what you think?"

Jane forced herself to meet those dark accusing eyes. This *is* my child, he'd said. But, in the doorway, Dino seemed to have snickered. Danny had said: Every once in a while I hear things that make my flesh crawl. . . . Dino had shown her the submachine gun in the new Cadillac. She heard Scott's voice: I once was lost but now am found. . . . Scott! The tears, crippling, weakening, threatened, the tearing sobs. She stood again, looked about her as though some veil separated her from them. She tried to steady her voice.

"I'll probably never know, Sal, will I? But as long as I think even for a minute, it was you who did this . . ." Her breath caught, she had to stop for a moment. "I never want to see you or hear from you again. And if I ever prove that it was you, I'll go after you. Believe me." She remembered, dug into her purse, brought out the diamond ring. For a moment, it glittered on her palm between them while Sal breathed heavily over her. She turned, threw it toward Dino. She knew that Dino's fuse was short.

"Here, Dino," she said clearly. "Stick that up your ass."

She waited for the blow, the shot that didn't come. Not till she reached Sheridan Square where Aurelia, damp with concern, awaited her, did she cry. Aurelia called Paul to alert the understudy and they walked then, up and down the streets. of the Village, Aurelia's arm about her, while Jane wept, not caring about the passersby, caring about nothing now but Scott, what their brief interlude had cost him. When they returned to the house, she kept Aurelia awake, talking, talking about what Scott had been like, what they'd done and said together.

When at last she allowed Aurelia to lay her down in the bedroom, she closed her eyes and saw an image of Peter, one arm holding Joanie, standing in mist high overhead, his other arm reaching out toward Scott who traveled slowly toward him. But there was a cold rim of horror around her heart. She couldn't protect those she loved. Scott's eyes were turned toward her, his smile forever frozen, and she never saw their hands meet, his and Peter's.

Later, Aurelia woke her from a nightmare. That old one had returned. The swing moving slow and empty while she turned and turned again, always too late to see.

6

There were photos in the *Daily News* of Scott's body sprawled on the sidewalk. It was said he sometimes liked to stroll in the early morning hours. There was one other visit from the police, Aurelia watching Jane, willing her—she knew—to say nothing of what she might suspect. She *didn't* know, after all. No matter what Clyde might think. Also, it would have been the simplest matter by now for Dino to chuck the gun from the Cadillac. There was a note from Danny. She didn't reply. She couldn't play Scott's records, couldn't hear him sing "Careless Love." Or *their* song. "I once was lost but now am found. . . ."

Life, she'd discovered, was loss. She saw continually his eyes turned in shocked sorrow toward her, the smile frozen on his lips, the hand that would never quite reach Peter's.

Some weeks later came an envelope with a Maryland postmark. In it, photographs. One, a group of colored people standing around a gravestone. The other, a closeup of that stone:

SCOTT WILLIAMS
1922–1947
Amazing Grace: How Sweet
The Sound

For some hours Jane sat immobile, the photographs in each cold hand. Lear's line came faintly to her mind. *Never, never, never, never, never.* Her heart, not her eyes, dripped tears.

By summer, Talbott had arranged to take *Zeal* on the road. "You've never been in stock. You've never been on tour," he argued.

But Jane was adamant. She wanted out. She'd been suffering in silence the lack of cocaine by which Sal made his absence felt. If the deprivation gave her more sleep, it brought with that sleep more dreams. Suddenly, these were always of Joanie, whose face she saw at last, strangely adult, taunting, accusatory. I am going to meet you yet someday, that face appeared to say. Then I'll repay you for what you did.

Meanwhile, John Wilding, one of the grand old princes of the theater, had been in touch with her to do *The Wild Duck.* As Hedwig, she'd again be obliged to die. But this would be her first experience with a classic, with another director. There'd be no problem, Wilding assured her, in her convincing an audience that she was fourteen. While the production was still in its planning stages, he encouraged her to accept an offer from the NBC "Theatre Series," now getting established on the comparatively new medium of television.

"Experience," Wilding instructed her, "is everything."

He *hadn't* mentioned—impossibly didn't know?— that the author of the television play was Dan Edelman. She was alone in a small shabby office at 30 Rockefeller

Plaza, bent over the script and holding an unlit cigarette —she'd recently taken up the habit—when a lighter came between her and the pages, and there was Danny himself. The golden eyes were slightly mocking at how they'd found one another.

"I didn't know you were into all this." Vaguely, Jane waved the cigarette to indicate the surprisingly unglamorous setting of NBC.

"They let me work on this as my senior project for graduation." He seated himself in the worn swivel chair beside her.

"So you have your much coveted degree?"

"I have. And now all the same problems of career as before."

It occurred to Jane they'd always been like two intense children. Now, like sparring strangers. She inhaled once more, stubbed out the cigarette. "Well. I'll read this with more than personal interest."

"I hope so." He gave a slight bow. "If you decide to do it, I'll watch with the same. . . . To my shame, I admit I fell into the habit of seeing you as I wrote." Something quivered there for a moment behind the golden eyes, was quickly hidden from her. "Would it be out of the question for the author to ask the star to join him for a drink? After you've read the script, of course. You turn it down, the invitation's off."

"I see you still believe in setting your own terms."

"Yes," Danny said. "I do."

He left her alone, then, to read. It was a different voice in this play, crisper, more objective than that in *Zeal*. But the talent for sentiment without sentimentality was still there. There were good scenes, the telling "energy of language" for which Danny had been praised in the past. She was talking to the vice-president, Prime Time Programming, when Danny returned. The producer suggested they all visit to the top of the RCA building for drinks. He noted Danny's hesitation, her face, and grinned.

"Oh, look. I don't want to be a third leg. Why don't you two youngsters take the middle bank of elevators on up?" He bit the bullet: "And charge your drinks to the studio."

The city floated in late summer smog below them.

118

Jane commented, after the waiter had taken their order: "I'm surprised you haven't gotten away, this time of year."

"I wanted to see the deal closed. As a matter of fact, I'm leaving this weekend. Two weeks on Cape Cod." Very casually: "Why don't you come along? It's a house in Wellfleet. You'd have your own room. All the privacy you want. If you want it. . . ."

She rather liked this new not-so-vulnerable Danny. "And if I don't?"

"That could be taken care of." He looked her in the eye. "I hear that sun, sand, and sex make a good trio."

"I'd only have a week—before rehearsals for your play." The waiter had brought their drinks. She lifted hers. "To it." She hesitated a moment. "And Wellfleet."

While they drove north, Danny chatted easily of friends, theater, current events. He still lived on Fifty-fifth Street. Then he spoke of Palestine, of the Jews' struggle to become a nation again, Britain's threats to their existence, the refugees trying to reach its shores. "I often think that's where I should be," he said, as they swung into the pine barrens that lined the highway leading to Wellfleet.

"War again?" Jane protested. "Didn't you have enough?"

"Oh," he said, almost carelessly, as he switched on the headlights. "The Jews are overrepresented in the arts and underrepresented in wars. Let's say I could easily be taken over by that character in *Zeal*."

They drove in silence till they reached the house, a wood and glass structure erected by an older friend of his. They dropped off their bags, drove to a small plain restaurant on the waterfront, a place that sold books in the back room. It was high tide and a few boats, their running lights on, sailed slowly back toward harbor.

"Can we do that?" Jane asked. "Can we sail?"

"My friend left me the keys to the cuddy of his day sailer."

"You *have* learned a lot, haven't you?"

He lifted his glass to her. "Let's hope. . . . We can do anything and everything you want. And nothing that you don't."

This Danny underlined by ostentatiously ushering

her into the larger of the two bedrooms when they returned. And saying: "I'm beat. I'll make our coffee in the morning. You'll like the water here. Purest well water you'll ever find." Casually, he shut the door on her.

It was after four when Jane awoke, wondering if that were a mourning dove she heard. The house was surrounded by pines and, kneeling up in bed, she gazed out, saw squirrels and chipmunks already busy, heard another call that might be a bobwhite. The tops of the trees were already touched by sunlight and through the open window their fragrance came to her. The door slowly opened and Danny stood there. He must have remembered the hour she so often came awake. The new toughness didn't quite camouflage the old light of tenderness in his eyes, on his lips. Jane hesitated, turned to him, held out her arms.

The trio was, as he'd said, quite magical. They marveled, as they played in the waves, at the comparatively uncrowded beach. That first day they both had too much sun and, lying beneath the white golden dunes, groaned with pain while they made love, laughed at their groans. They sailed, ate lobster, walked across the dunes of Truro to the beach, swam in the spring-fed ponds that dotted Wellfleet. The town was very small, very New England, and, as they lay entwined in bed, they could hear the chimes of the church. When it was time for her to leave, Jane agreed: she'd move back to Fifty-fifth Street.

"You're very patient with me," she told Aurelia as she packed.

Aurelia's brown eyes gleamed. "Sweetie, I've always had time. For the waiting game."

When Danny rejoined her, his play was ready for the cameras. Jane was continually amazed at the lack of elegance at 30 Rock, as it was known—the shabby furniture, the hallway walls covered by linoleum. Even the regular stars worked in cramped cubicles, dimly lit. But the production facilities were good and it was exciting to learn how to act for this new medium. If one were to rise from a chair, one signaled with the hips so the cameramen would be ready. There were ways to dodge hitting one's head on the overhead microphone. There were all the hand signals from the floor manager when the cameras would actually roll: the rotated hand clockwise with extended forefinger to accelerate, the stretched imaginary rubber band to slow down, the fingers held up to indicate minutes remaining. Above all, there was the emoting toward that living-room audience hidden within the cameras, beyond the real one. It was a challenge Jane enjoyed.

Later, they went to dinner at the home of a young couple from Columbia, the couple visibly abashed and honored to analyze the performance. It was with them, Jane learned, that Danny spent time polishing his Hebrew, a subject he hadn't touched, he confessed, since his Bar Mitzvah. He was working on a new play again but she was aware, as rehearsals began for *The Wild Duck*, how he followed the news about Palestine. He doubted the potency of the newly founded United Nations to resolve the conflict. Jane held back from argument. There was enough, she soon found, to divide them.

Not her refusal to give up the friends she'd relied on for so long in the past, though he couldn't abide them— Cynthia, Natalie, others. It became, too soon, the old battle: his desire to possess her in a way that could not be. She'd thought he'd changed, but it had been only superficial.

"Were you able to respond any differently to your folksinger?" he challenged one night.

"He never asked me to," she flashed back. "And don't question me about Scott Williams. What we had has nothing to do with you."

"Yes. Everything in neat compartments. It would be a relief if *you'd* show curiosity about *me*. Like, did I have anyone to take your place while you were gone. . . ."

"Is that something you feel you have to tell me?" She knew her calm to be maddening, as she poured black coffee for them.

"I wouldn't want you fainting from ennui."

"Yes, frankly I can think of more stimulating subjects. Like: why don't you leave me alone and get on with your work?"

Danny watched her over his coffee cup. "Ah yes,

121

work." His hand shot out, gripped hers. "Don't you know work *is* everything? But only together with love. Those two—that's the key to paradise, Jane: the entrance of the gods into Valhalla. Janie, Janie. Give up. Give in. I love you. Let's get married. Let's have kids. Let's . . ."

She retrieved her hand. "Now it *is* ennui. I'm having a shower and going to bed." She could hate her cruelty, she told herself, sometime later.

The Wild Duck opened to wide esteem, the greater portion divided between John Wilding and Ibsen, but a gratifying share for her. Jane found herself taken up by a new segment of the theater world, the more rarefied one of established and serious stars. As though in deference to her new triumph, Danny appeared for a time quiescent. But by spring—his own play in the hands of a producer—he was at it again. They were always skirting each other now, animals circling for the assault. The worst times were after they made love. One night, Danny lay away from her afterward, suddenly turned back and gripped her bare shoulders.

"Is it me? Is it that you just don't cotton to me at all?"

"There was only one man I ever really wanted." She spoke into the dark. "It has nothing to do with you—or anyone."

"What happened? He wouldn't have you? Or you held out and lost your chance? Or what?"

"Maybe some of all of that. . . . But he's dead a long time now."

Danny released her. Jane moved slowly into her kimono, set her feet into her slippers. She heard his quick intake of breath.

"Are you saying what I think you're saying?"

"You figure it out." She moved out of the room. He followed her. Again, he turned her toward him.

"Are the living always going to have to pay for the dead? Are you going to let something you felt as a child fixate you forever?"

"I wasn't a child." She met his serious gaze. "And it's not a matter of 'let.' It's the way I am. Apparently, you can't accept that. The way I am. That's what ruins it between us."

122

"I said it before. You're going to spend your life reconstituting your family. But I can't be your brother. Aurelia as your mother, I don't mind. Where you're going to find your sister, I don't know. The fact you ever let a hood like Sal become your father. . . ."

She swept his hands away from her. "What there was with Sal is over. But while it went on, you didn't mind it all that much."

"Didn't I? I only tolerated it—what you took from him—because I knew you needed whatever it was he gave you. . . ."

She wavered, remembered Sal's dark, accusing eyes that last day. Then: "You took, too, my darling. You weren't above that, you know."

"What do you mean? I know he wanted to put money into *Zeal*. But I'd rather not have had it on the boards than take from him. . . ."

"My poor Danny!" Jane hesitated only a moment. "Where did you *think* the money came from for a twenty-two-year-old Air Force captain's first play?"

"Milton Kaufmann. He produced it." She saw the uncertainty flicker in his eyes.

"Producers," she told him, "don't *have* money. They *get* money. Where did you think Milton Kaufmann got his?"

Danny stared. His face sickened. "Oh, Christ." He turned away, then back. "I was quite innocent in my way, wasn't I?"

"You all of you coddled me, I know. But you were coddled, as well." She walked away from him, took a cigarette from the coffee table. It was as though, when she lit it, she'd be lighting the bridge between them, burning it forever.

Danny meditated. "I don't suppose I could ever repay that bastard. Not with the interest it would entail. . . . Well, one silver lining to all that gold: it's a small consolation to know you ever felt protective toward me."

"Don't overrate me." Jane faced him, exhaled smoke. "I let Anthony Brahm fuck me. Before *Zeal* opened."

Danny winced, reached for a weak grin. "I'll bet. You couldn't stand the prick."

"Not really. It just seemed a good idea at the time. It did win him over."

He was silent a moment. "You're serious?"

"I'm serious." She waved the smoke away from her face. "Another thing you never knew about Sal. All the time I lived here before, he was supplying me with cocaine. So don't overrate me. None of this, I'm sure, qualifies me to be the mother of your children."

Danny walked across to the dark windows. He leaned his head back and stared, wide-eyed, at the ceiling. Walked back. "I suppose there can only be one reason you're telling me all this. There *is* a simpler way. Good drama should always be short and to the point. Your dialogue could have been cut way down, couldn't it?"

The cigarette burned her fingers. "To what?"

"Just a word. Goodbye."

Danny moved past her to the bedroom. Jane heard the closet door open, the smack of the suitcase onto the bed, the sound of bureau drawers. Even now, she understood there were other lines she could speak. She could make him stay. But she stubbed out the cigarette, forced back the hot tears that threatened, lit another. It is a far better thing that I do, she told herself. . . . She couldn't yet face the truth of it: that this time it was Danny who was leaving *her*. For him to take this step meant, she knew, forever. The child long buried within her whimpered at being abandoned. The woman she was stood frozen, immobilized, with the love she could not hand over.

This time, she kept the apartment. As she told Aurelia, with grim humor, over lunch at the Russian Tea Room: "I think I should stop appearing and reappearing in your life like the Cheshire Cat. I've never lived on my own. Let's see if I can make it."

And Aurelia: "Fine. Just: what do you ever want to fool with men for?"

She didn't mention to Aurelia how dreadful the nights were. The sleepless ones and the ones with dreams in which Joanie appeared to menace her. Danny, even in his sleep, had held her at those moments. She lay awake, after those dreams, aware of the silence, the emptiness beside her.

It was the producer who turned down Danny's play who told her. He'd liked the play, he said, but he couldn't take a chance. In the past fall the Attorney General's List had appeared and Danny's name, it seemed, was on it. Apparently, he'd attended some meetings, subscribed to some magazines. With this rejection, the producer said, Danny must have come to a decision. He'd gone off to fight in the war that had finally erupted in the Middle East. A madman, said the producer. Throwing everything away.

Reading the papers, Jane tried to imagine Danny in the hot desert, a gun again in his hands. She fought off the dread, the guilt. He'd been homed in on that land before she'd returned to him, she argued with the censor within. It hadn't been her words that had driven him there. When the state of Israel emerged at last from the flames and she knew—from his friends—that Danny was safe, she told herself that perhaps he'd found the true haven she hadn't given him. As though in flight, she agreed with John Wilding that they should consider taking *The Wild Duck* on the road.

It was after a Wednesday matinee that the stage manager came to her dressing room, told her a group of debs from Philadelphia wished to speak to her out front on business. Jane slipped on her street clothes, walked to the wings, emerged through a stage door into the partially darkened auditorium. There were three of them but one, the apparent spokeswoman, turned as Jane appeared. She wore a pale green linen dress with a thin cashmere cardigan over her slim shoulders. A joke of Aurelia's surfaced: A Peck-and-Impeckable type.

"It's good of you to see us. I'm Claire Hamilton and these are my friends, Susan Russell and Polly Stewart." The words were polite but the voice languid, supercilious. She didn't bother to praise Jane's performance as the others did. Intrigued, half amused by the insolent poise, Jane regarded the young woman.

It occurred to her that Claire Hamilton bore herself with the brash arrogance of one who has not yet been zapped, had it socked to them by Fate. Claire was explaining: she and the others hoped they might prevail on Jane to bring *The Wild Duck* to Philadelphia. For a couple of benefit performances.

". . . and of course a longer run. If you like."

The girl couldn't have been, despite her manner, her elegant clothes, more than eighteen or nineteen, Jane decided. Joanie's age, by now. Her coloring was so fair it bordered on albino, the flaxen hair waving to her shoulders, the skin like the softest of white rose petals, the eyes flat, pale blue. Her forehead was curiously long, rounded, the cheeks flat, the nose rather long but delicate, the lips—barely touched by color—small, almost prim, almost redolent of easy scorn. Claire Hamilton finally noticed that Jane was staring. She stopped, returned her look.

It was then as though the two others, far less assured except by whatever it was that position and money gave, weren't even there. The prim little mouth paused, the lips half parted, and the pale blue eyes glanced directly into Jane's. As she allowed herself to meet that look, for the first time Jane understood how Aurelia must feel about her. It was as though, in all innocence, she'd always been moving toward this moment.

There was still time to turn away. But she knew she wouldn't. She'd thought all along she'd moved through her life like a sleepwalker. Now, she stepped forward onto this ground she would claim, with full knowledge, as her own. By doing this, she told herself, she accepted at last that it was she who had made, after all, all her choices.

Chapter IV

1

In Philadelphia, the cast put up at the Warwick at Seventeenth and Locust. Jane, unpacking after the early Saturday morning train trip, recalled those desperate hours with Paul Talbott in this same hotel, when she'd tried to extricate herself from *Here Be Monsters*. Was that five years past, or another life? The last time she'd visited this city she'd hung, a wan, pathetic creature, on Sal Celucci's arm, as they'd walked through the Italian Market. She wondered if Sal's mother were still alive. *This is my child. . . .* Since then, there'd been Danny. And Scott . . .

The night before leaving from Penn Station, she'd dreamed again of the swing. For the first time, Joanie's figure, turned away from her, had sat in it. As the swing slowly revolved, the face revealed was Claire's. . . . Claire Hamilton, they'd learned, hailed from the Hamilton candy fortune family. She'd invited the troupe to a party at their townhouse at South Washington Square after the opening that evening. To Jane, in New York, she'd sent a personal note:

"Come to lunch your first afternoon. Or do you have to rehearse?"

The diffident afterthought caused Jane to smile. She'd written back: "Yes. Why don't you come? Perhaps we can meet after?"

Now, laying out her things in the dressing room at the Walnut Theatre, Jane wondered if the girl would be curious enough to visit her backstage. Part of Claire's appeal, Jane had decided, was her air of being completely out for her own enjoyment, unself-consciously, with no apology, like a child. Because she was not a child, an aura of danger floated about her. Claire would

127

not be easily impressed, wouldn't understand—wouldn't care to—what acting, theater meant to Jane. Seeing as if through those dispassionate pale blue eyes, Jane recognized how ritualized had become the decoration of any dressing room assigned her, how almost cabalistic the array she set out: the special robe, special brushes, combs, towels. Her tubes and sticks of makeup, the lotions and creams she laid out in a definite order.

All of this underlined the sense she had of holding herself like a special vessel for each performance, waking in the morning for it, drawing toward it every hour, gathering herself into it. When there was a break—Sunday and Monday evenings—she ordinarily went to bed on Monday night with a small bleak sense of dread, her breathing shallow, wondering if she'd awaken Tuesday to that ability to dedicate herself again.

Then, no matter how she spent the day—dance lessons, voice, gym—there was always beneath it that mingled wonder and fear: would she be able to make it, to reach for it again: her craft, to create those new moments that had never lived before in exactly that way?

Not unexpectedly, Claire did not appear at rehearsal till Jane had gone through Hedwig's death. The stage manager brought another monogrammed note to her dressing room. "My car's outside. How about tea at my place?"

John Wilding assembled the cast onstage for last-minute instructions. Jane, changed into a cool Balmain frock, saw Claire, one hand impatiently on her slim hip, at the shadowy rear of the theater. When she nodded, Claire shifted her stance slightly, moved toward the front doors. No, the girl hadn't thought of a visit backstage.

She drove a red MG, now parked in the towaway zone before the Walnut. The long pale fingers of her left hand were enmeshed in the flaxen hair, her gaze fixed on the traffic as she swung down toward Pine Street, the prim lips rather wantonly pursed in a small smile.

"I couldn't make it to rehearsal. I had to find some shoes." Her slim foot pressed lightly on the gas pedal, then hard as she shot around a slower car ahead. "It's difficult: I have such a high instep," she added, with evident self-love. She slid that special glance toward Jane, that sly watching regard she'd returned her that afternoon in New York, the little mouth half open, like a cat's. It was as though Claire sensed the mysterious power she exerted over Jane, the strength of the delicate web she seemed able to hang in, almost motionless, while Jane moved toward her.

Claire parked before a four-story townhouse. In the summer heat, the trees in the small park opposite drooped limp and dusty. Her parents, she explained, were away in Europe. Jane wondered aloud, as they crossed the cobblestones to the steps, that Claire herself wasn't. Away, that is.

"Oh, tomorrow I'll take you out to our country place," Claire announced carelessly. "I don't stay out there because my brother's all over it." She led the way inside, cast gloves and bag on the hall table, opened doors into a square room with deeply recessed windows, pegged floors, gleaming andirons at the fireplace. Tea was laid out on a low table between masses of flowers. Claire went on: "I may still get away for a while—probably Newport in a week or so. *He's* content to stay there all the time." She bent above the tea tray. "He's my twin."

Jane inhaled quickly. "I had a twin brother, too."

"Had?" Claire's fingers were as pale as the milk she offered with the teacup. "What happened? A divorce?"

"He died in the war."

"Oh." Claire paused, as though to decide whether this merited comment. Then, mockingly: "No army would take Bill. The male of the species is always weaker. Isn't that so?" She offered cakes.

For a moment Peter appeared to lurk in the shadowy hallway. As sometimes still happened, the planet whirled away from beneath Jane's feet, a vast, empty desert that spun from it gusts of sand. She forced her concentration toward the figure beside her, chin tilted to register contempt as she continued: "He's always hiding out there in that great drafty place. He's weird." The small even teeth bit down on a square of cake. Her eyes met Jane's. "Tell me. When you're not acting. What do *you* do for kicks?"

Jane smiled. "Have tea with cocky young society girls."

Claire blinked. She wasn't invulnerable. "Do you really?"

Jane relented. "I honestly can't think when I spend much time with anyone not connected with theater. . . ."

"So this *is* different?"

Jane studied the pearly skin that had momentarily turned chalky. She set down her cup. "How old are you? Eighteen? Nineteen?"

"Nineteen. In September." The wings were fluttering again. "How about you?"

"Twenty-three." She felt years older than Claire. She hesitated. "Yes. This *is* different."

The little smile returned. "I saw you looking at me in the theater that day. Why did you look at me like that?"

"Maybe I'm here to find out why myself." Jane felt she'd said too much. She rose. "Can you drive me back or shall I take a cab? I have to rest and wash my hair before the performance."

At the party that evening, Claire—perhaps for the benefit of Susan Russell and Polly Stewart, who *were* impressed by the company in which they found themselves—assumed a rather proprietary air toward Jane. For the moment. Tomorrow, Jane sensed, it might be a racehorse, a new car. The girls were discussing the past year at Miss Chapin's. "That's a private school, in New York," Susan put in, for Jane's possible edification.

"But the two of you are going back. I'm not." Claire's friends rounded on her.

"Since when?"

"Oh, I'll *be* in New York. Only I've had it with being told what to do." Claire spoke toward Jane. "I'm going to live on my own."

"Do your parents know?"

"All in good time." Later, Claire reminded Jane. "Remember, I'll be picking you up about two. To take you to our country place."

"How far?"

"About an hour and fifteen minutes, northeast of here. The way I drive." Claire exhibited her small, self-satisfied smile.

130

Forewarned, Jane wrapped a silk scarf about her hair. The heat still hung oppressively above the city, but as they passed the Art Museum and wound along the river where college boys were sculling, they picked up a deceptive breeze from the speed with which Claire drove.

"They're from Penn." She indicated the boats. "That's where my brother goes. My father thinks if he forces Bill to get a degree in Business Administration, he'll be able to shine—dimly, of course—in the front office." Her sniff expressed derision.

Then they were driving through suburbs and into open country, the roar of the engine making it difficult to talk. When they passed a small cluster of stores— grocery, bank, antique shop, post office—Claire announced: "This is it. New Cardiff. . . ."

She swung the car down a side road. A sign on a low stone wall proclaimed: Hamilton. They passed a row of two-family wooden structures, a larger house, barns, stable, swing and slide set. Masses of maples and oaks arched above them. Then the view cleared before fields that swept up and down gentle inclines. A stream wound out of sight. Claire waved a hand carelessly. "This is all part of it." Around another curve, and Jane said, "Oh!"

To their right, on a hill hidden till now, stood a medieval castle. No special plan, asymmetrical design, just your ordinary modified Romanesque-Gothic pile, Jane reflected. Rounded turrets, battlements, narrow openings from which archers might defend themselves, long windows in the central curved section that must span at least two floors. A tower with a high peaked roof—arches three to four stories high surrounded it—was encircled by balconies and rose above a chimney that must give vent to a minimum of eight fireplaces. An attached chapel with long stained-glass windows. All in a rosy fieldstone, topped by dark green slate roofs. Claire had halted the car at the bottom of the driveway, was watching her. Jane spread her hands.

"This is your 'country place'?"

Claire's prim little mouth twitched at the corners. "Yes. You like? . . . Granddaddy Hamilton had the family castle in Wales sort of replicated. When Grandmommy Hamilton handed him the chocolate recipe from Switzerland."

Jane gazed on. "Fantastically realistic set. Who did the lighting?" She had an image of a small fair girl scuttling through stone corridors, another of herself and Peter in the back room of the apartment overlooking the garbage cans. Claire said:

"Glad you approve." She started the car up the winding driveway. A pond came into view, swans dutifully gliding across its surface. As though to complete the picture, a horse and rider trotted slowly toward them. Jane unwound the scarf, let her hair fall loosely across her shoulders.

"Oh." Claire's smile was derisive. "Here comes Beowulf."

Bill Hamilton eerily resembled Claire. The same almost albino coloring, the same almost flaxen hair. Exactly her features. But not—as he pulled the horse up, dismounted—the same pale eyes. His were a very deep blue, startling in their alabaster background. His expression, too, altered the resemblance, being so diffident, shy, as did his careless dress—Levi's, a T-shirt. He might have been three years younger than Claire, a boy not yet out of high school.

"This is my brother, Bill," Claire announced languidly. "Bill, this is Jane Belmont. She's in town to do a play."

Bill started to extend a hand, shrugged, slid it in his pocket. "Hi. I know. Don't you think I read the papers?"

"Where you're concerned, I don't think." Claire looked away.

Politely, Jane put in: "I wish you'd come last night."

Bill's feet scuffled the gravel while his eyes turned from her, searched the horizon where clouds were massing. "Um. Yeah. . . . Well, I'll be seeing you. Glad to've met you." He touched two fingers to his forehead, sauntered back to the horse that chewed impatiently at its bit, remounted. Claire, watching him trot off, shook her head.

Then she drove on, brought the car into a garage between a Jaguar—"That's Bill's"—and a Rolls— "That's my parents'; they keep the plane at the factory." Together, they crossed the wide stone terraces with enormous flowerpots as sentinels, through an archway, and into the castle.

Here it was cool. Their footsteps echoed along the stone floors. In certain high-ceilinged rooms their voices rang out strangely hollow. Tapestries muted the sound in others and there were smaller areas, with thick rugs and stained-glass windows, that appeared almost habitable. The chapel turned out to be the living room.

"But can you imagine *living* here?" Claire asked.

Jane couldn't. Until Claire led her up the wide stone stairs to her bedroom with its view over the treetops and the sweep of fields below. On the other side, the terraced grounds dropped away toward other fields, other hills, beyond what Jane now saw were the manager's and servants' quarters they'd first passed. Here were *some* signs of life: a small kitchen, a long-disused playroom with a circular hopscotch still faintly outlined in chalk on the rough wooden floor. A modest library, unlike the forbidding one downstairs, a small piano in one corner, rather than the Steinway grand below. But still . . .

Claire led the way down again to another wing and a ballroom—"just like in the movies"—straight out of MGM. Jane wandered across the parquet floor, turned back toward Claire, and held out her hands. Claire's pale eyes widened, then gleamed. She placed her hands in Jane's who led them, whirling, around the enormous room in a schottische, a polka, finally a tango. Bill, holding a tray, appeared.

With the almost white hair slicked back, his resemblance to Claire was even plainer. Except for the flicker of apprehension in his eyes.

"I thought you'd like mint juleps," he explained. His shoes clacked on the wooden floor. "I mean: would you?"

At Claire's sigh, Jane moved forward almost protectively. "How splendid!" Claire walked away from them to the long windows. While Jane sipped from her long glass, Bill examined her with a child's curiosity over the rim of his own. Into the uneasy silence, Jane said: "Do you like theater, Bill? I can have the box office hold a couple of tickets for you."

"Oh." His stare broke off. "I guess that would be nice. Okay." He never glanced toward Claire who paced before the French doors that led to one of the terraces.

It was as though she were forcing Jane to choose between them. Bill took the initiative. He laid the tray on the floor.

"Well. I'll leave this for you. So long." As abruptly as he'd appeared, he was gone. Two evenings later, Jane noticed him in the fifth row, alone. He didn't come backstage nor did he send a note of thanks. By the time Claire, burdened with packages from Nan Duskin's, met her for lunch, the matter had slipped Jane's mind. Claire was off, she explained, to Newport. Her air of attending now almost as a social duty put Jane off. Then, Claire lowered her head. Holding her cup in both pale hands, she murmured:

"But I'll be seeing you in New York. After you finish the tour."

2

They brought the play to Baltimore and Washington, in the grip of the heat wave that had descended on the eastern seaboard. Jane imagined Claire in the sparkling water off Newport, wondered how she protected that white skin from the sun. Returning to New York as the heat broke, Jane accepted for the first time how much she needed this city, its glitter, the sweep of its avenues, the constant muffled roar of the traffic, cars sliding in and out as they deposited people with an air of concentration on their faces, of purpose, of belonging.

It occurred to her as she walked into the stuffy apartment and saw it through Claire's eyes how shabby it really was, how good it would be to make a step, herself, toward really belonging, too. Jack Tanner, cared for her in her absence by a neighbor, came whining toward her. She scooped him up, held his moist nose to hers.

"Jack," she said, "what would you say to a house of our very own?"

Full of personal concerns, Jack Tanner emitted a low cry. Holding him, Jane crossed to the phone, called

Uncle Ben. There were a few perfunctory words about Mama. Then:

"I wanted to know," she began. "Is there enough in that insurance policy—you know the one I mean—to cover the down payment for a house?"

"You have one in mind?"

"I haven't even looked. I'm thinking of a brownstone. Do I have a right—financially—to look?"

"Just a minute." Muted conversation. Finally: "Why don't I send my accountant over? Name's Walter Raney. He should handle this."

Walter Raney was a quietly attired young man in his thirties, a round face and dark mustache that made him resemble Dewey—the probable next president. He sat before her, spread his papers out. He had very serious brown eyes, very serious words.

"Your uncle invested that policy for you. It's done rather well over these years. I'd say you now have negotiable close to fifty thousand dollars."

In exchange for Peter. . . . "I imagined something like fifteen."

Pleased, Raney bowed his head. "We do our best. . . . Your uncle mentioned a brownstone. You'll manage more than a down payment with this. Would you care to have me look for you?" He paused. "Your uncle suggested you might wish to retain me for *your* affairs, too."

Jane recalled Uncle Ben at Papa's funeral. Talking of how a widow lay beached, like a whale, wherever her husband had left her. "That's damned different," he'd said, "from a woman who's chosen to live alone." This was now, perhaps, his way of telling her, for the first time, that he admired her. She was someone who knew how to make it on her own.

Sid Arkoff, who'd joined the William Morris Agency, was talking to John Wilding about her doing another classic: Turgenev's *A Month in the Country*. Meanwhile, Jane roamed the East Side, matched her discoveries with Raney's. Elsewhere, people were responding to Russia's explosion of the A-bomb by building bomb shelters. Here, the days were cool and sunny, everywhere women hurried along in their new long dresses, young girls had let down their hems or added flounces to lengthen them. Refusing to permit herself to think of what had brought her this new affluence, Jane felt a sense of power, of a new life ahead. It was she who found the house on Sixty-first Street, between Second and Third avenues, a street lined with graceful plane trees.

Seven steps led to the grilled doorway. There were ornate cornices, a large three-windowed bay on the second floor, five arched windows at the top, a basement entry, and garden. This was the place she had to have as her own. Walter Raney had it inspected, swung the financing for fifty-three thousand plus closing. The els on Second and Third would be coming down, he'd discovered, in three to four years. At that point, the value could almost double. She should be in by Thanksgiving.

When she'd first left, Danny had taken on a weekly cleaning woman. Faith, a tall, comely Jamaican, had stayed on. Now, Jane asked if she'd care to live in, graduate to housekeeper. Someone else would be hired on a weekly basis to do the heavy cleaning. Assured of separate quarters on the top floor—Faith had a boyfriend—she agreed. It would be somewhat harrowing, moving into the house and opening in a play almost simultaneously, but also rather fabulous.

This Jane told Claire, who came to visit at the start of October, with her not surprising glance of scorn at the apartment.

"You mean you've lived here for years? Wow."

"I'm not exactly a welfare case," Jane told her. What could she add? That, dear girl, she dropped into the St. Regis with a fellow actor and Noël Coward leaned above her with a complimentary quip? That she came to a party at John Wilding's penthouse and Katherine Cornell informed her she was spellbinding? That John Gielgud stopped by her table at Le Pavillon? That three millionaires, in as many months, had offered to set her up in a dwelling of her choice? "You know, I *am* famous, damn it!"

"Okay. Don't get in a huff." Claire stepped about in her tiny elegant alligator shoes. "I don't need *you* biting my head off. My parents are doing it quite nicely, thank you."

"You haven't gone back to Miss Chapin's?"

Claire shook her head. "I'm at the Barbizon-Plaza. Lucky I have my own trust fund from Grandmommy Ham. Guess you could say I'm bidin' my tie-am. 'Cause that's the kind of girl I-am." She sent Jane that glance, the sly eyes over the half-opened mouth like a cat's. Jane hesitated.

"Were you planning to come back to New York anyway? Before last June?"

"You mean: before I met you?" Jane was silent. Claire waited, then shook her head. "No. I don't guess you could say I was."

Jane turned away to hide her pleasure, then invited Claire to the first rehearsal of *A Month in the Country*, two days from now. She'd be playing Vera, the ward, and Cynthia Blackwood, against all expectations, would act the lovesick wife, Natalya. Aurelia was doing the costumes. It was as though she wished to force Claire's attention toward her own achievement.

The following day Jane met Aurelia at the house. It was the first chance she'd had to show it and Aurelia had brought along Gregory Hatfield, the set designer, to suggest decorations. Gregory, who frequently enjoyed becoming swishy, enthused over the sunken living room with its small stagelike area below the long front windows. He'd take out, he said, the ugly black railing there, replace it with a graceful wooden banister, painted the same color as the mantelpiece and paneling.

"Williamsburg green, don't you think? The walls have to be done in some variety of cloth, red-and pale blue-striped damask, most likely."

"You might have two small brocade couches facing each other on either side of the fireplace," Aurelia offered. "The room's long enough."

"And the floor stained dark, very dark." Gregory held a hand to his forehead as he mused, then leaped forward. "A matching chair next to a small round table here, opposite the fire. Just a large area rug between the couches. Yes. . . ."

Whistling between his teeth, Gregory was on his way, pad in hand, making notes, sketching. Jane left them, wandered to the French windows in the dining room that opened onto the neglected garden. Their voices hinted of the future when she'd be settled in, giving parties, actually living here. There'd be a carelessly flung newspaper on a couch, a cup and saucer on a coffee table, a sweater thrown across the back of a chair. Dappled sunlight would slant through the windows late in the day. The sound of footsteps would be heard from the sidewalk, the wrench of gears as a delivery truck went on its way. She saw it all, like a stage set.

She didn't know which came first. Her knees buckling or the sound of Sal's voice. "In my opinion, you should invest this money and just hold it for her. To her now, in her present condition, it's blood money, see? . . ."

Her forehead was clammy with sweat, Sal's voice erased by a sudden ringing in her ears, the garden outside misted over. When she opened her eyes, Jane was on the floor, her head in Aurelia's lap, a wet hankie at her temples. She was aware of Gregory scurrying back and forth, snapping about the fact that one couldn't even find a tin cup in the blasted kitchen below. Aurelia's face, full of the old concern, hung above her.

"Aurelia!" Jane clasped her hand. "I'm not sure what I'm doing. I feel this strange compulsion. . . ." Then she was silent.

How could she ask if she had a right to contemplate life in this house with the money that had come from Peter's loss of it? How could she tell Aurelia of the dream that had come again only last night? The swing, and Claire's face, where Joanie's should have been. She sensed that Aurelia knew the first half. There was no way to tell her of the second.

The rehearsal next day was in a loft down in Chelsea, a light long room with many windows. By the time Jane and Claire had mounted the metal staircase, the propman had already placed tapes on the linoleum floor to represent where people should stand. John Wilding, bald head gleaming, looked even more as though an invisible string attached to his long nose pulled him toward his object of interest. Which was, at this moment, a choice between two boys to play the role of Kolya, Natalya's son. The improbability of Cynthia Blackwood as a mother had perhaps induced a hesitation unusual for Wilding.

138

One of the boys, well built and blond, with an appropriately Slavic cast to his features, came on first. In a moment, Cynthia had left the area John had blocked, and the boy followed her rather awkwardly. Audibly, the mother complained to John, who sent her to sit by the windows. He listened politely, thanked the boy, called the other.

Jane reflected she'd never seen quite such a beautiful ten-year-old child in her life. He was lean, tense, with very dark hair, thick eyebrows, startling gray eyes that seemed to catch whatever light there was. He was so excessively polite, she couldn't imagine him unbending enough to act. Possibly the equally tense and handsome little woman nearby was simply pushing him because of his looks. When he spoke the lines, however, he did indeed become the eager petted Russian child. To Jane, it seemed no contest. When John, his gnomic face bland, announced for the other boy—"Merely on the basis of resemblance to Miss Blackwood: they're both equally good"—Jane was taken aback.

This was, of course, a concession to Cynthia, a bribe to bring out her best. As the dark beautiful child—his name was Nicholas Spenser—turned away with tears hanging to his long lashes, Jane had an impulse to comfort him. Before he left, he came with exquisite manners to both John and Cynthia to thank them, gave each a small, graceful bow. Jane saw how the boy clung to his mother's hand as they walked to the stairs.

"Now," John said. "We're going to start right from the top." He seated himself at the bridge table, his script girl at the other side. "And, Cynthia, I'd appreciate it very much indeed if you'd write down the blocking as we go along." This in recognition of Cynthia's reputation as a "money" actress, someone who saved herself for the performance. Of course, they'd all forgive her anything—she knew—if her acting came off. No one could withstand the damning expression in the eyes of others onstage.

For two hours they went at it without a break. Claire, Jane decided, had conducted herself quite well during the long morning. Now, as they broke for sandwiches, she introduced Claire, saw how Aurelia, like a hunting dog, nose lifted to the scent, scanned the girl. Cynthia, rewinding the silk scarf about her neck, asked if Claire were studying drama.

"I went to finishing school," Claire rather loftily informed her.

"Darling, if you were any more finished, I'd sell you as a Hepplewhite chair," Cynthia responded.

Aurelia snickered.

Rehearsals were far rockier than they'd been for *The Wild Duck* and the weather turned wintry early. There was the hectic triumph of Truman beating down Dewey. Then, in freezing rain and blasts of polar winds, Jane ducked in and out of taxis between the rehearsal hall and shops Aurelia and Gregory favored, to furnish the house. There was little time for Claire. When she called to suggest Thanksgiving dinner together, the desk clerk informed her Miss Hamilton had left for the holidays.

Claire, to Jane's surprise, made it back for opening night, was on hand to join in reading the unanimously favorable reviews. One critic remarked how superbly fortunate Jane Belmont had always been: she'd had to weather few of the struggles of the usual aspiring thespian, was truly one of the blessed. While Claire read the review aloud, Jane met Aurelia's eyes. That link broke through the guarded nastiness Aurelia projected when Claire was present. For a moment, they shared together their past.

Then, it was time to move. Completed were the kitchen and pantries in the basement; the living, dining, and breakfast rooms on the first floor, Jane's bedroom— wth the three windows of the bay overlooking the street —and her study above the garden on the second, a guest room above the study on the third, Faith's bedroom on the fourth. The rest would have to wait.

Her first Sunday in the new house, Jane dressed to meet Aurelia for brunch. The doorbell rang and Aurelia stood before her, holding an enormous box, a large bag. Behind her, most of the cast of each play from the past, Claire, Walter Raney, even Uncle Ben.

"Housewarming party, darling!" Cynthia squeezed her way in quickly from the cold.

There wasn't enough furniture but people spilled outward and upward, squatting on the floor to drink champagne, consume the catered food. There were gifts, many expensive, some humorous. Jack Tanner, who'd discovered the outdoors, mewed piteously for it, then sat on the low breakfast window, mewing to return. Faith, eluding Natalie, smiled a lot and joined in the drinking. Over the downstairs rooms hung the sweet smell of marijuana.

Before the party broke, Aurelia took Jane aside in the bedroom. Her box had contained an heirloom patchwork quilt. (Claire had supplied enough satin sheets and pillow cases to seduce an army.) Now she held the large bag she'd first set aside.

"Sweet, in here are all the scrapbooks I've been keeping of you. I think it's your turn to work on them. I'm turning them over."

Into the festive mood of the day Jane sensed the approach of something she didn't want. She sank down on the bed, Aurelia beside her, and opened the books. There they all were, all the clippings. The first walk-on part in the play in the Village, the schoolgirl role she'd had when she'd first run into Danny again, the raves for *Here Be Monsters*. Interviews, pictures. The items from Walter Winchell, other gossip columnists. The one about her being replaced in *Monsters* "for personal reasons." (Her heart paused a moment, as though it would never resume.) *Zeal for Thy House*. The TV show. *The Wild Duck*. *A Month in the Country*. Jane glanced up at Aurelia.

"My darling," Aurelia said, "you're now almost the age I was when we met at High Hills. Do you know that?" She took a breath. "I can see you're headed for something very different and I think it's time I moved on. I'm taking up my latest Hollywood offer."

"Oh, no!" Jane seized Aurelia's hands.

"Oh, yes!" Aurelia retrieved them. "I can't stick around now," she told Jane softly. "Danny and Scott were one thing. This is another."

"I don't know what you mean," Jane countered. But Aurelia broke in.

"Maybe you don't," she said thoughtfully. "Maybe you really don't. But I do." She rose, bent, kissed Jane swiftly on the lips, was gone. To Jane, staying on alone in the room for some moments, it seemed there was no time she could recall beyond that when Aurelia had not been there for her.

She wondered, later, if Aurelia had sensed that Claire was poised to put her question. No sooner, shortly after New Year's, had Aurelia's train left for Chicago and the trip west, than she asked it. Could she now move in with Jane? All that space. . . . The Barbizon-Plaza was so stuffy. . . . It was only while Jane helped her to unpack in the guest room that she realized she'd been furnishing it for this moment. Everything in it was a statement, a compliment to Claire. Aurelia must have known.

Now, of course, what she herself came to know was more of what Claire was really like. The sophistication she'd first projected was superficial; the spoiled child, the narcissist: the bedrock. She slept late—never descending for breakfast without mascara on her almost white lashes—met friends from Miss Chapin's to go for clothes fittings at the best shops, entertained her friends in the living room—where Tommy Dorsey records, half-finished Cokes, and issues of *Vogue* and *Harper's Bazaar* lay scattered—condescended so insufferably to her friends that Jane was often obliged to conceal her own amusement.

Claire showed no inclination to know of Jane's inner life, her past. What she did want was to whirl in the bright life. It pleased her to see Jane open a charge account at Sardi's, to watch others defer to her. As they walked through Shubert Alley, Jane reflected that it wouldn't signify to Claire the pulse of theater life—the brightly lit passageway with its posters of plays and musicals, its street magicians, its crowd of commuters and actors. What Claire noted were the limousines with their special parking privileges, the eyes of the fans, all that was most superficial.

Even when Jane was awarded the Obie for Best Supporting Actress, it didn't mean as much to Claire, Jane knew, as another tentative offer from a movie agent. Or as Jane's appearance on another TV special. Truly a child of the age, Jane decided with something between a sigh and a shrug.

Claire was interested in good times. Opening night for *South Pacific* qualified. Evenings at the Copacabana or the Stork Club qualified. At parties, she was the last willing to leave. She didn't care to be "bossed," as she put it, but if Jane appeared to neglect her in any way—from her viewpoint—she sulked. Jane remembered Joanie sitting on her lap that last day, Joanie demanding to play school, and recognized an old capacity to efface herself. Claire's special demands were accompanied by that secret sly look, the lips half parted.

It was in April they had a visitor. Claire was out, not unusually, shopping, when Faith called up to Jane, who was reading scripts. A man named Steven Elder to see her. Could she please come down? Something to do with Miss Claire.

Jane descended the stairs. A very sober gentleman in a camel's hair coat and holding his hat in his hand. In his thirties, mahogany hair, matching accusatory eyes. He introduced himself as the Hamiltons' lawyer, his subject: Claire's defection from the ranks of well-reared young girls.

"After all," he said, his hat dangling between his legs as he sat forward on one of the blue brocade couches, "we know she lives here with you. A nineteen-year-old girl drops out of school and moves in with an actress? You can see how the family feels."

Jane stifled an impulse to laugh. First Danny's parents, now Claire's. She supposed she just wasn't what one would call eligible. "Claire's old enough to live on her own, surely? Would you prefer she had a job? Is it that she's being indolent? Or not moving in the proper circles? To make the proper marriage, I mean."

"There's no need to become unpleasant."

"Good. Then I won't," Jane cut in. "If Claire's family can only communicate with her—or with me, for that matter—through a lawyer, I'd say she's well enough as she is."

Jane informed Claire of the visit. In her room, Claire slammed packages about, fumed that her family would prefer her to be the zombie Bill was. That night, Jane lay in bed to continue reading the script she'd been studying earlier. Claire appeared, in her nightgown, walked with her dainty mincing steps across the rug, curled up at the foot of the bed as she often did.

"Mind?" That special little half-teasing glance. As though she knew something Jane didn't.

"Why should I mind?" Jane continued to read. But Claire hadn't brought anything to amuse herself and, in a short time, the silence became oppressive. Jane looked up. Claire still watched her. But her face had assumed a new tension, as though she listened for a mysterious signal. Jane laid aside the script.

"What is it?"

"I was wondering. What *am* I doing here, anyway? I mean, with you? Why aren't I living with some guy?" Jane was about to speak. Claire rushed on, as though she had prepared the words. "You—the big actress! The high-life gal! The wild one! I had more excitement in school! What are you waiting for?"

The words were taunting, the tone scornful. But the slim body moved toward her, the pale eyes narrowed to slits, the prim little mouth hung open. There was a quick flash of pink tongue, tiny white teeth, the swing of flaxen hair against Jane's cheek. Then the feel of Claire's arms, the skin silkier, more satiny than the sheets she'd given her, and between which they now lay entwined.

When Jane awoke in the morning, Claire lay asleep beside her, the fair hair spread like a fan on the pillow, the closed blue lids like a dim reflection of the pale eyes beneath, the pallor of her face seeming to indicate the outflow of energy the hours before. Momentarily, Jane buried her own face in the pillow.

Then she turned on her back. She must incorporate into her understanding of herself this new dimension. All right, she reflected. This, too, is me. So be it. She leaned over, kissed Claire's mouth, the milky cheek.

Claire opened her eyes, stared, slowly smiled. She raised her arms, twined them about Jane's neck.

3

If Faith were aware of the changed relationship, she gave no sign. Jane, faced with her own reflection, saw in it the flush of new life. She was, now, far more subservient to Claire's demands, her moods. But she didn't care. Claire, no matter how bored she might be at times, how detached, now stayed, now clove to her. When Claire decided they, too, should don men's clothes—shades of wicked Dietrich—as Cynthia and Natalie did, Jane went along. It was as though Claire wished to outdo the two older women at their own game. The four went out to dance together, two weeks before *A Month* ended its run, and Claire affected a long gold cigarette holder like Cynthia's, moved slowly in Jane's arms to the music of "I Married An Angel," wore that satisfied small smile.

It was on one of these evenings that a large loose-built Irishman cut in, sent Claire back to their table in a sulk. Owen Durant, an editor of *Theatre Arts.* Jane had met him briefly before. He had the pink and white prissy face with pouting lips of a Gainsborough portrait, but with a cocky leer to it. Plus the well-known verbal sting of an asp. Long wisps of brown hair floated like a halo askew around his head.

"Tell me." He swung Jane into a rumba. "You're so beautiful. You're basically such a smooth and elegant gal. You find it far-out—flirting with that world?"

"Tell me how to act. Not how to live," Jane retorted.

He ignored this. "You've heard of Narcissus. What you're up to is narcissistic adolescent crap." He saw her face. "Oops. Handkerchief on the field? But look: staying bisexually—homosexually—I don't give a damn about labels—absorbed in someone like yourself, your own sex? Instead of losing yourself in someone completely different?"

"Like?" Jane tried to control her anger.

"Like that great Edelman guy you cut off from. For lack of anything better: like me." He pulled her to him as the orchestra went into a fox-trot. Jane tried to pull away from him and he crushed her against his massive chest. "I've had my eye on you for some time. I don't intend to lose you to a slab of candy."

"You can't lose . . ." Jane began.

"I know. What I don't have. Balls. What's your next play? Another revival?"

"As a theater man, can't you call them classics?"

"Okay. Hang loose." His hand worked up and down her back. "At least dead authors don't puke on you opening night. Anything in mind?"

As a matter of fact, Jane had. She'd decided to take up Paul Talbott's project for *Man and Superman*. Omitting the section of *Don Juan in Hell* that contained Jack Tanner's speech: that would entail two evenings. Shaw, at last, after the aborted plans for *Pygmalion*. Contracts had to be signed in a flurry of preparation: for Jane's twenty-fourth birthday, Claire had determined to take her off, all expenses paid, to Europe. They sailed in June on the *Queen Mary*.

As they watched from the open deck the lights of Long Island disappear into darkness, Jane thought of Peter's last glimpse of America. This would be the sixth birthday without him. Her throat tightened. Then Claire slipped a small gloved hand under her arm, asked:

"Happy?"

Jane nodded.

Claire hadn't been to Europe in over ten years, she told Jane as she led her through the Tuileries. Here she and Bill used to watch with their governess the puppets, as they were doing now.

"What is it with you and Bill?" Jane asked. They were crossing a bridge over the quietly drifting Seine, back to the Place Vendôme and the Ritz. "Why are you so estranged?"

"He's hairy." Claire's small mouth stiffened. "He never even goes out with girls."

Jane turned on her. Mock horror. "No! You mean . . . ?"

Claire's eyelids dropped. She repressed a slight smile. "I mean: he never goes out with guys either. He's a yo-yo, that's all."

Jane could discover nothing more. Besides, there was far too much else to occupy them. Lunches and dinners at La Tour d'Argent, Maxim's, Fouquet's. Visits to Chanel, Balenciaga, Dior. Books at Shakespeare and Company in Rue de la Bucherie, tickets to the Comédie Française, wine at La Dôme or an even more fascinating small café at St. German des Pres. "Excuse me," breathed a young girl with white powder, blackly smudged eyes, "aren't you Jane Belmont?" "Check it," Claire drawled, in her best brat manner. Claire would have nothing to do with cathedrals, museums, permitted Jane to visit these on her own. Paris, bathed in blue light at dusk like a stage set, awaited another time when she could come really to learn it, Jane decided.

Now, they were off to England where, though rationing was still in force, the English displayed that indomitable spirit Peter had remarked. From the Dorchester they strolled through Hyde Park, Green Park, St. James's Park, had tea at Harrod's, saw two plays a day, gazed at night from Waterloo Bridge over the old city toward St. Paul's in its yellow glow, the Houses of Parliament, the spire of St. Martin-in-the-Fields. Later, renting a car, Claire drove them through the Cotswolds and up to Wales to show Jane the real thing in castles, in Scotland taught Jane to drive. There, it rained every day but, at evening, the sun came out in time to set over Loch Lomond. On the mossy bank beside the water, they made love.

Once, at sunset, they came into a small town square where six bagpipers played. From unfamiliar songs they swung suddenly into music that made Jane's knees buckle, as they had that day at the new house. "Amazing Grace." Played very slowly, very solemnly under the pearly sky. Jane saw Scott's face, smiling, then in a pool of blood. The tears formed. To Claire's frown, she didn't reply. Danny had labeled everyone a reconstitution of her family. He hadn't known who would become her sister, he hadn't foreseen Claire.

But Scott had been someone different, out of time. . . . Jane perceived, in the music, a statement of how fleeting life was, its despair and loss, a despair and loss that hovered over the past and that she saw coming dimly again in the future. Yet, there was an aching sense not only of the pity of life, but of its triumph. How strange . . . how sweet the sound. . . .

Then they were back in a sweltering New York, rehearsals, occasional escapes to the Hamptons where Mary Nodine and Ralph Gurney, the famous theater couple who'd taken Jane up, insisted they spend any time there was to spare. Ralph, long, narrow-shouldered, graceful in an almost offhand manner, with a pale face, strangely luminous hazel eyes. Mary, dark, theatrically statuesque, her face eloquent and taut, mouth as tense as Ralph's was almost flabby. Theirs was a large old house at Sag Harbor, constantly filled with guests, among whom Jane met one evening Owen Durant.

"Still lezzing it up?" he asked. Claire's fair head was visible across the room full of people. "Why not stop being a cube? Let me haul you off to a passion pit. I hear drive-in movies have arrived even this far out on the Island."

"I hear you sail. You can take me sailing," Jane said, and drifted off. Rehearsals had been strained. Sailing, even with Owen, would be one way to unwind. Claire always slept late.

Back in the city that Monday, Jane tried to understand what was happening to Paul. He was pale, haggard, on edge. Harold Channing, who'd played her lover in *Monsters*, was now to be Jack Tanner, took her aside.

"I think he's cracking up." At Jane's startle: "Never mind. I also think he's still one of the best in the business."

Jane hoped so. She had a horror, in her role as Ann, of slipping over into coyness, depended on Paul to let her know if she did. She reread Shaw's dedication to the play, the description of her character, as if it had been addressed personally to her:

"This is the true joy in life, the being used for a purpose recognized by yourself as a mighty one, the being thoroughly worn out before you are thrown on the scrap heap; the being a force of Nature instead of a feverish selfish little clod of ailments and grievances complaining that the world will not devote itself to making you happy."

Jane adored Shaw, gave herself up to the joy of his radiant prose. Anthony Brahm played the chauffeur and very creditably, too. They were to try out in New Haven, Boston, and Philadelphia before New York. Claire opted for Newport during the early part, met Jane at her room above the Public Gardens at Boston's Ritz-Carlton at the end of August. They strolled, hand in hand, along St. James Avenue from the Boston Common to Copley Square, through the cool church and into the Copley-Plaza. After drinks, they dined alone together at Kaysey's, returned to find Paul had been scouting for her everywhere, intent on making some change.

The tension returned, bringing with it, to Jane, a new spate of dreams about the swing. Claire turned toward her, stepped down, disappeared. The tension lingered, despite good notices, through the run in Philadelphia. It wasn't until they hit New York in October—her name in lights above the marquee, her face on posters at the doors—that the play appeared to expand, to grow into its own. The critics went overboard, outdoing one another in superlatives. Just before Christmas, the man who did the caricatures for Sardi's came to Jane's dressing room, took a dozen Polaroid shots. In the middle of a February blizzard Jane, Claire, Paul, Harold Channing, and the Gurneys went to midnight supper to sit beneath the completed drawing.

"My dear," Ralph said, holding her hand, "you've really arrived."

This statement was accentuated when, a few months later, Jane won the Tony for Best Actress. *Variety*, in its follow-up review only the week before, had singled out the delivery of her last line as worth the entire play. When she stood onstage to receive the award, after Ralph Gurney's laudatory introduction of her as truly a force of Nature in the theater, she declaimed it now:

" '. . . Go on talking.' "

The audience cheered.

With it, the award brought four dozen roses from Aurelia, pleas from other agents to forsake Sid Arkoff, five offers of marriage (two from unknowns), a message from Owen Durant that he now considered her fully ripe for him, another from Walter Raney about investments, a new TV special at Black Rock, CBS's elegant quarters.

But Claire was edgy, annoyed that Jane would continue through the summer in *Man and Superman*. She'd taken to going about with various vacuous young men while Jane was at the theater, found amusement in letting them know she wore no bra or underwear under her cocktail dresses. She wouldn't hear of a job, couldn't imagine rising early each day, being tied down. For Jane's birthday she gave her a Jackson Pollock painting Jane had admired, went off to Philadelphia shortly after, then Newport.

While she was gone, war broke out in Korea, and Uncle Ben died suddenly at High Hills. His will left half his assets to Mama, the other half to the hospital, various charities. Paul Talbott and Jane met for drinks, compared memories. He had that new settled look of strain, when questioned, wouldn't—couldn't?—say what was wrong.

Claire's absence stretched through the summer. It was Mary Nodine and Ralph Gurney who made the difference, insisting Jane come out whenever she could. Which happened most often, as it turned out, with Owen Durant. He took her out not only sailing but also deepsea fishing. With his help Jane caught, off Montauk, a small tuna.

"Wish someone would help me catch you." Owen mourned. "I'm still leching. There's only one cure."

Claire returned. She appeared mollified by her vacation, eager to pick up city life. Jane felt as though she were letting go a long-held breath. Sharing it with Bill, Claire celebrated her twenty-first birthday at the Bellevue-Stratford in Philadelphia, where Jane at last met the Hamiltons. The almost albino side came from him, the frostiness Claire knew so well to project from her. Bill's diffidence—he'd been given a fifty-five-foot yawl anchored at Chesapeake Bay, Claire, a "cottage" of her own at Newport—remained a mystery.

The Hamiltons' attitude toward *her* did not. Steven Elder took Jane aside at one point in the dancing.

"You're absolutely ruining an innocent young girl's life. You know that, don't you?" Tiny bits of caviar clung to his mustache.

"Claire's a free agent," Jane replied. She didn't add, as she watched Claire smile loftily in the arms of a tobacco scion, that she herself wasn't. Later, Claire smiled in the same fashion in Steven Elder's. To Jane's surprise, Bill asked for a dance. His hair, against her cheek, might have been Claire's.

4

In New York, Jane again urged Claire: why not a part-time job? Grudgingly, Claire went in as assistant at a haute couture shop, before Thanksgiving was bored and quit, caught up in the holiday mood that annually gripped New York. She was impatient that Jane had to perform Thanksgiving Day, turned up her nose at the cast dinner at Fraunce's Tavern on Pearl Street. Paul Talbott called brush-up rehearsals just before Christmas and Claire flew into a temper.

Suddenly, everyone was talking of Estes Kefauver, of his Senate Investigation into Organized Crime in Interstate Commerce. His show had played in many cities already, exploding in Las Vegas and L.A., was now returning in March for a major opening in New York. For the first time it would be televised. Stations on the eastern seaboard and throughout the Midwest were fighting for it.

Who, the papers asked, *were* all these crooks and influence peddlers? *Was* there a national crime organization? If so, what were its sources of power? Kefauver had centered his probe on gambling, which he considered the lifeblood of organized crime.

From earlier testimony, Americans had learned: *H* and *C* stood for heroin, cocaine. Now, at the Foley Square Federal Courthouse in New York, the spotlight was on crime on the waterfront, bookmaking, police who looked the other way. Tickets for matinees were turned back. Stores were sold out of TV sets. Schools closed, movie houses stood empty—except for those whose marquees announced they were showing *IT*.

For eight days, forty witnesses paraded before the court to reveal a crime syndicate that operated with police help. Joe Adonis, hair slicked back, appeared not to recall his bootlegging days, called himself a law-abiding citizen. The moll, Virginia Hill Hauser, created a sensation. Frank Costello, refusing to permit his face to be televised, put on a show for the cameras with his hands. Critics enthused: the type-casting for the production was perfection.

151

What the show revealed was a rub-out operation—
Murder, Inc.—its chief killer a stevedore named Albert
Anastasia. He owned a seventy-thousand-dollar house at
the Palisades on one hundred twenty-five a week. Other
star witnesses included a syndicate purchase, former
Mayor O'Dwyer, recalled from his ambassador's post in
Mexico to appear in court. And one Salvatore Celucci,
who followed the others' lead with his refusal to testify
because he might incriminate himself.

Halley shot his questions at Sal. Bootlegging from
the past. Black market during the war, in gasoline, cigarettes, liquor. Connections with bookmaking at Roosevelt Raceway. And what about H and C? Yes, he had a
home in Scarsdale, a modest place. He lived there quietly with some friends. Weren't they bodyguards? Why
were they needed? How had one of them, somebody
known as Dino, recently and mysteriously died? (Jane
hadn't known.) Had *Sal* ever given orders to Anastasia?

Like the others, Sal's belligerence crumbled. He
kept mumbling appeals to the Fifth Amendment. Jane
watched, smoking cigarettes she didn't know she held,
taking from Faith—they were in her room, upstairs—
glasses of bourbon she didn't know she drank. This was
the man who'd held her, walked her about the paths in
Scarsdale, next to whose bed she'd curled up on the
floor, in whose room she'd slept for months. At her evening performances, she fumbled her lines, glanced frantically toward the prompter, apologized to Harold and
the others. Sid Arkoff came to her, said:

"It was all my fault. I lined you up with that hood.
That's honestly all I thought he was. Jesus Christ!"

Then it was over. Kefauver and his men packed up,
returned to Washington. But there were charges of perjury, contempt, income tax evasion. It *wasn't* over. The
Rosenbergs were convicted of spying for Russia, condemned to death. Bill, Claire said, had been drafted for
Korea. *She* went out, had her hair cut in the new poodle
fashion, making her look a stranger. Jane went about
with a taste of ashes in her mouth. She had a sense of a
gathering storm. In Hollywood, Aurelia won the Academy Award for costumes but, in one month, there were
two funerals.

John Wilding, driving out to the house at Sag Harbor, was instantly killed when a car driven by a drunk teenager collided with his, head-on. Paul Talbott, immediately after signing a contract with MGM to direct three films, traveled to High Hills, and hung himself in the theater. He left no note. Jane moved from funeral to funeral. How many fathers she had lost. . . . *Man and Superman* announced its last two weeks. The closing party was depressing.

Claire, who during all this had taken to spending more time than ever in Philadelphia, decided to accompany a friend from Miss Chapin's to Reno, look in on Las Vegas.

Jane was studying her lines, rather desultorily, for a *Television Theatre* show one rainy afternoon at the end of May, when the mail arrived. She'd been thinking, once she did this script, she and Claire might go off together for a real vacation. An embossed envelope obtruded from the mass of bills and ads. She opened it, read:

"Mr. and Mrs. Thomas Hamilton request the pleasure of your company at the wedding of their daughter, Claire Ann Hamilton, to Steven Blair Elder at Christ Church, Saturday, June 15, 1951, at 4 P.M. Reception, dinner and dance at Hamilton Castle, New Cardiff. R.S.V.P."

The phone rang. It was Cynthia.

"You never let on. When did little Miss Moneybags decide to cash in her chips, darling?"

Jane's mouth constricted inanely. Her fingers around the phone were icy. "You received one, too? You're going?"

"Wouldn't miss it. Have to roll on to Washington right after. But Natalie can take us down in her car, bring you back. Unless you're included in the honeymoon?"

"No," Jane said. "I don't think I am."

The rain appeared to heave itself into new fury, lashing the fragile trees in the garden below. Jane replaced the phone, sat with the card in her hands. Then she went downstairs, paused in the living room, not knowing quite what for, descended again. In the kitchen, Faith looked up at her.

"What? What happened?"

"Nothing. Nothing's happened." Jane walked to the liquor cabinet, brought out a bottle of Scotch, turned back. "Have you a glass? Can you get me some ice?" Suddenly, she was shaking so she had to sit down. Faith came to her side, placed an arm around her. Unseeing, Jane stared into her face. "Claire's getting married. She's marrying somebody, two weeks from now."

"The hell you say!" Faith brought out the ice, two glasses. As they drank, Jane giggled.

"The little bitch! Right?" Faith raised her glass.

"The little bitch! Right!" Jane raised hers.

It was Faith who, unbidden, took charge of packing and sending on Claire's things. The day of the wedding was, of course, serenely beautiful. Cynthia had reserved a room at the Barclay for them to change in, kept sending Jane, in the back seat of Natalie's car, sharp inquisitorial glances. There'd been no word from Claire and Jane hadn't called. Her cold hand lay atop the wedding gifts on the seat beside her.

Limousines lined the streets for blocks. Christ Church, austerely beautiful as in Revolutionary days, was packed with people and flowers.

"At least she made sure we got good house seats," Cynthia observed as the usher led them forward. Jane saw Mrs. Hamilton turn from the front pew to watch her. The small frosty smile was much like Claire's. Bill, in uniform and up from Washington, also examined her. For that interval, his diffidence was gone. Jane was aware not so much of his resemblance to Claire but of the difference the deep blue of his eyes made between them. And that they were somehow both, she and he, Claire's victims. Bill turned away. The organ sounded the wedding march.

A retinue from Miss Chapin's marched resolutely down the aisle. Cousins. This was, after all, a tribal rite, reenfolding one of its own. Jane, lifting her chin, watched for Claire.

Ah, the pale face barely visible behind the pearl-encrusted veil. The flaxen hair, grown longer again, a silvery cloud about her face. As she stepped daintily, her small gloved hand on her father's arm, she stared straight ahead. But she didn't allow the moment to be lost. When she came abreast of Jane, her step perceptibly slowed. The pale flat eyes slid sideways, the little mouth came open in that catlike way. She passed on to the altar.

Outside the church—her throat ached almost too much to speak—Jane asked of the others: "I suppose you both have to see the castle? There's no way just to beg off?"

"Oh, no way!" Natalie swore. They were in the car again, past the river where the boys had sculled that day three years before, into the suburbs and the country, past the small shops of New Cardiff, down the road to the castle.

"This it?" Cynthia asked as Natalie followed the line of cars. "I'll be a son-of-a-bitch!"

The swans, in alarm, had sailed to the other side of the pond. Jane remembered dancing Claire about the ballroom. She didn't think they'd dance tonight, wondered if Claire would try, at any time, to speak to her alone. She drank but couldn't eat, watching Claire at the table on the dais. When the dancing began, Claire went into Steven's arms, then her father's.

Jane was in Bill's then, like the night of the birthday celebration at the Bellevue-Stratford. Claire's two rejects, she told herself, made no effort this time at small talk. She and the Hamilton family would seem to have had it.

Bill, however, had been drinking, too. That, or the uniform, or the wedding. Who knew what brought on the rush of words?

"Twin sister works in mysterious ways, doesn't she?" His voice was low, the intonation wooden, like his face. "She and her 'husband.' Guess they figure they'll get control of the money. What they don't know is: I don't give a shit. Pardon." Awkwardly he moved her about the floor another moment. "Think they'll take time off for a tumble in the hay? Or was I really the only guy Claire was ever hot for? . . . I suppose she told you." He caught her up as Jane briefly stumbled. She recalled that first night, the quick flash of pink tongue, tiny white teeth, swing of flaxen hair against her cheek. . . . "I suppose it's been good for a few laughs over the years, huh? How she made us celebrate our sixteenth birthday? What a reluctant virgin I was? And how I've never been able to get it up since? Huh? Did she laugh about it all to you?" The music ended. He bowed. "Thank you. For the dance. If they play that one about the poor little sheep, the ones who lost their way, I'll come looking for you again. . . ."

It must have been the flashbulbs that made Jane's head ache. Cynthia announced, quite suddenly, she was satisfied, had to make the train to Washington. Jane waited for Claire to leave the floor. Then she walked to her side. The noise, the smoke, the radiance of Claire in the shimmering white gown clouded her eyes, made it difficult to focus on the small translucent face of a fallen angel.

"Claire Elder! We have to be off." At least her voice was steady. "I suppose this is the time. For me to say I hope you'll be very happy."

People were watching, listening. Claire glanced down a moment. "I meant to tell you." Then her eyes slid toward the others. "Thanks for coming."

"Thanks for having. Keep in touch."

In the car, Natalie glanced back, saw—in the headlights from the car in back—Jane's face. "Here," she said, and fumbled in her bag. "Take a couple of these." She passed her some pills. Jane swallowed them.

Back at the Barclay, they changed again, dropped a fidgety Cynthia off at Thirtieth Street Station. Natalie began to mumble about hitting the Schuylkill Expressway, the Pennsylvania Turnpike. "Guess I'd better not indulge, eh, hon?" and she passed a bottle to Jane, who'd moved up front. Jane closed her eyes to the roar of the traffic, drank what was left, felt herself sleeping as with a fever, heard *The Third Man* theme music come on the car radio, saw Claire's face, dozed, woke suddenly as the car stopped.

"Is this New York already?"

"I'm dead, darling," Natalie announced casually. "This is a motel and we're staying over."

Of course. Whatever Natalie said. Jane followed her into the office, leaned against the wall as Natalie spoke to the desk clerk, had to be nudged to sign the register, followed numbly back to the car and watched without curiosity as they pulled up before a row of rooms away from the highway.

"Here, you look too pooped to take care of yourself," Natalie said after she'd locked the door. She stood a moment, stared at Jane. "Want another couple of pills?"

Jane nodded.

Then it all went hazy. The room swung out of focus. She was aware of Natalie undressing her, cursing under her breath, tucking her into one of the two double beds. She turned on her stomach to escape the dizzy lurching of the room. Now, Natalie's arms were around her, strong, demanding. Jane remembered the swans on the pond and it was as though she were Leda, as though strong wings were beating her down, a beak pressed against her throat so she couldn't cry out, even if she'd cared to.

But she didn't care. She was coming in and out of brightness that alternated with dark, the room turned a full three hundred and sixty degrees, she clutched air, saw a body not her own doing things she didn't recognize. A strange rumbling noise. . . . That must be the highway, not the heavens falling down.

If only they would . . .

5

In the morning, the sky was gray, swollen. Jane stared at a stranger's face in the mirror. This same stranger accompanied her, during the sullen oppressive heat of the weeks that followed, through ineffectual rehearsals of James Hooper's new play. There was a disastrous opening in the fall, perhaps the kindest review suggesting that the drama was still "in the workshop phase." Her first theatrical fiasco, it closed after four performances. James Hooper fled to Europe.

In the same issue of the *Times*, Jane noted that Salvatore Celucci had been convicted of income tax evasion and narcotics smuggling, would begin a seven-year sentence almost immediately. The phone kept ringing. Condolences about the play. She didn't respond. Faith brought her a wire from Owen.

"Coward! Answer phone. Have best remedy for what ails you. Let's be polymorphous perverse." And another one: "So you finally didn't have a hit. Tough *t* and it ends in *y*."

She walked. Never on Fifty-fifth Street. But through Central Park where she'd played games with Scott. Around the reservoir where a bitter early wintry wind brought tears to her eyes. Down to the Village where she and Aurelia had shopped and strolled for so many years. It was while she struggled against the gusts up toward Harlem that she understood where she must go.

The Scarsdale station was thronged with police. The taxi driver, when she gave the address, eyed her like a curiosity seeker. At the estate, Sal had a different contingent of guards. It was finally decided to admit her. Mr. Celucci would leave tomorrow. Under escort.

Jane asked if she might first take a quick turn around the grounds. She walked past the empty pool where they'd danced on her twenty-first birthday, straight to Bonzo's cage. His disappearance was somehow more revelatory than the presence of police, rather than Frank or Dino. She held to the bars of the cage a moment, as she'd done so long ago, remembering the leathery paw on her fingers. The past appeared to rush in on her with a roar. Why had there seemed to be an innocence to those days? Even—or especially so—with Sal Celucci? Was the primal garden always free of sin? Somewhere, because new loss always returned the memory of that early one, it was as though Joanie lingered unseen, unheard, in the leafless tress beyond.

In the familiar hallway, dust had gathered. Jane was led to the Chinese room. The heavy figure sat alone in the shadows, struggled—unsuccessfully—to come to his feet when the massive head had turned, had seen who it was.

Jane stood in the doorway. Her voice was like a child's. "I had to come. To say goodbye, Sal."

158

Sal leaned forward in the chair. His head drooped, and she saw, from the workings of his face, that he was shamed. Still, he rallied. "So. . . . In my opinion, you never really believed all that stuff against me." He groped for the words. "You never would really turn against your old pal, Sal Celucci." But the timing was off. The deep voice trembled. Jane stepped forward.

"I believed it, Sal. Maybe now I believe it even more. But I had to come."

He looked up at her, his eyes suddenly moist. "I'm sorry, kid. Honest."

She hadn't known she'd do this. But she was on the floor at his feet, her arms around his knees, her face pressed against them, and weeping. Sal's heavy hand came down on her hair. He made sounds of comfort, nothing she could comprehend. Then another hand was on her, the policeman bringing her to her feet, telling her she must leave. Not looking back, Jane held out her left hand toward Sal, felt him grasp it, allowed herself to be led away.

Two days later there was a picture in the *Times* of Sal stepping out of the car at the prison gate. Two days after that an envelope, again postmarked Maryland. The photographs dropped out, as they'd done before. The group of colored people standing around the grave. A close-up of Scott's tombstone. . . . How had Clyde Simpson known of her visit? What revenge did he plan?

The winter dragged on. Letters from Aurelia told about HUAC trying to destroy Hollywood. In one phone call, she mentioned how stars who were already at the mercy of the studios now lived in terror of being investigated.

"Did you hear Mort Sahl?" Aurelia asked. " 'Every time the Russians throw an American in jail, the Committee throws an American in jail to get even.' " When Jane didn't laugh: "Why don't you come out for a visit? Get away from New York."

Jane declined. She told herself it was because she'd lost weight, looked too awful to have Aurelia see her. Her hair, that she'd never had to do more than wash and brush, now refused to fall as it should. She wasn't sleeping. There was no good part in the offing. It occurred to her that she had everything still to learn about acting, and a limited lifetime to do particular roles. The pressure of time was on her. She'd not yet done Shakespeare, Chekhov, O'Neill.

One dreary Sunday in February she took a bus to Atlantic City, walked along the deserted boardwalk, sand blowing along it, stopped to lean against the railing. The ocean appeared sullen, insistent, the gray waves wrenching themselves in uneven spurts against the dirty beach. She remembered the green waves hissing in the wake of the *Queen Mary*, the ocean at Wellfleet with Danny where the foam had resembled the white manes of spirited horses. The wind, wet with rain, beat against her face. Gulls swooped low with piercing, mournful cries.

For some reason, the scene at "21" presented itself as though on a screen. Danny lifted his glass. "Now our fortunes swing up. May they never swing back."

Then, it was as though Peter himself stood silent behind some drape of burlap, hovering near but out of reach. She heard herself cry out into the wind, "Come back, come back!"

But to which figure she cried, she couldn't have said.

As spring tried feebly to assert itself, Walter Raney appeared. Embarrassed, fumbling like a stock actor for his lines.

"You'll think me presumptuous. I know our lives don't have much in common. But from the first day I met you . . ." He took courage. "I don't suppose you'd consider marrying me? You know, you'd never have to worry about money ever again. You could go on with your career. Do what you want. . . . I don't see why your uncle didn't leave you anything."

Jane reached for his hand. "He did. You. The best bequest of all." Walter flushed. "I doubt I'll ever marry, Walter. But you'll stay my dear friend?"

He raised her hand to his lips. "Always."

It was at Sag Harbor that Jane gave in, at last, to Owen. Curious that something that meant, ultimately, so little to her, evoked such romantic fervor in him. She was satin and silk, he told her. He'd thought bedding her would rid him of his rut for her. It had worked the wrong way, damn her!

Through the dog days of August it became natural to spend the night frequently at Owen's apartment at the Chelsea Hotel. Dylan Thomas, the Welsh poet, sometimes joined them for drinks. Together, Jane and Owen watched the returns come in Election night. Owen muttered darkly that Eisenhower had better take care of himself. Imagine that greaseball on the ticket with him ever moving into the White House?

After Christmas, when Jack Tanner suddenly died, Jane wept for days, as she hadn't been able to do for John Wilding, Paul Talbott, though these tears were, at last, for them, too. She no longer attended the gym, lessons in voice or dance. Too expensive. Perhaps she'd never act—seriously—again. Aside from two television roles, there were only the evenings with Owen. Ballet. Opera. Plays. In the spring, at *Picnic*, Jane recognized one of the townspeople as that beautiful child who'd tried out for *A Month in the Country*. He was a high school boy now, taller but slight. Something about him reminded her of Peter in his modeling days. . . . Suzy Parker was the top model. People talked about Zen. A new song, "Sh-Boom," was popular.

In the autumn, shortly after a brief trip to Europe with Owen, Jane opened the door to Bill Hamilton, now in civilian clothes. As he moved about the living room, his dark blue eyes vacant, Jane dwelled on the familiar pale face, the flat cheeks, the almost white hair, all so like Claire's. She realized she no longer felt pain, even wondered that she could have allowed herself so long to be under that strange dominion. Bill accepted a drink, mislaid it.

"How's Claire?" Jane, on the brocade couch, held her own drink in both hands and watched him. At that, Bill sank on the couch opposite. His thin white hands drooped between his knees.

"In Bermuda now. The rest of the time leading Philadelphia society." Yes, she'd seen pictures of Claire and Steven at Newport and the Caribbean, Claire's small round chin flaunting a new truculence. "Hoping I'll drown in that yawl. Or slit my wrists. Guess she doesn't care how it happens. So long as I disappear."

"Aren't you ascribing a little more bestiality to Claire than her due?"

161

He glanced at her. "Am I?"

Jane shifted in her place. "Is this—is it all related to what you told me? On her wedding day?"

To her dismay, Bill struggled to control his quivering lips. "You don't know what it was like. In the army. Living in the barracks. Other guys knowing I can't do it. You don't know. . . ."

"I don't." Kindly: "Why have you come here?"

"She wronged us both, didn't she? . . . I want you to tell me why I shouldn't go ahead and gratify her. My parents, too. Why *don't* I kill myself? I *have* a gun."

"Because one doesn't, that's all," Jane said flatly. More slowly, she went on: "I can't say why, Bill. It only seems to me everyone must contemplate it at times. Some more seriously than others. For longer times." She saw Paul Talbott's ashy, distraught face. "Maybe the reason some people finally go ahead with it is that they can't take the indecision anymore. Maybe the only barrier against that is to *make* the decision, once and for all —now—that one *isn't* going to, no matter what . . ." A demon inside her yearned to say, instead: Let's do it. Now. Together. "And to know there's always someone there one can turn to. No matter what." She looked at him. "Does that make sense?"

It became a ritual during that fall and winter for Bill Hamilton suddenly to reappear, demand to know, again, why he should not do away with himself, allow her to cajole him, take him for walks. As with Claire, Jane found herself asking him to *do* something with his life. She discussed him with Owen, who agreed that an occupation, a calling was the only true protection against the drearies, as Owen termed them.

What else was, Jane wondered? Sid Arkoff placed her in a short run as the young wife in *Desire Under the Elms* but the off-Broadway theater was small, the salary commensurate. She was, too often now, when not with Owen or Bill or the Gurneys—busy most of the time in their latest play—in bed with some stranger she didn't care about. On impulse, she made an appointment with a psychiatrist.

"I have no family. I'm an orphan. I'm alone. I hate myself. I feel useless, unreal," she stammered.

"Oh." He smiled. "If you talk like that, I'll have to turn you over my knee."

Jane fled.

She was drifting again. The monthly visit to Mama became too much for her; weeks went by. *Confidential Magazine* (All Fact—No Fiction) came out with a picture of her with one of those actors she'd slept with, a leering blurb about how she spent her nights. Jane flushed with humiliation. As though in answer to her question about purpose, and to rebut her shame, Ralph Gurney showed up alone, businesslike, one squally February day.

"We can't believe how long it's been since you've been onstage."

"Neither can I."

"I want to direct for a change. You've never done Shakespeare. Think you can handle Cleopatra?"

Jane began to speak, instead was laughing. Then crying. Ralph waited for the emotions to dissipate. He wanted Harold Channing for Antony. The two of them acted well together. What did she think?

Shakespeare! And under Gurney's direction! Ralph gathered them at Sag Harbor for a read-through. He was not a Method disciple, never suggested that Jane rely on the sorrows of the past when she came, for example, to the words:

> "Noblest of men, woo't die?
> Hast thou no care of me? Shall I abide
> In this dull world, which in thy absence is
> No better than a sty?"

But Jane saw herself, unbidden, seize up the emotions of loss, take from them what she needed, go on from there. One had to distill that personal experience of bereavement that was shared by everyone, had to find a way to express it that transcended the merely personal. Or encapsulated it forever? She wondered still which it was. Primarily, she sensed that art, of any kind, must not allow so much an escape from the present as an immersion in it that would be impossible without art to lead the way. Now, she told herself that everything till this

163

time had been an apprenticeship. She was on the verge, at last, of becoming what she'd traveled toward all these years.

Owen said it: what she sensed as she saw her reflection. "You've never been so beautiful. You've emerged."

It was as though she were a long-disused instrument being played at last by a genius. Jane trembled as she spoke the lines:

> "Give me my robe, put on my crown; I have
> Immortal longings in me. . . ."

Chapter V

1

Long before formal rehearsals, a flurry of publicity surrounded the mounting of *Antony and Cleopatra*. In May, at a lavish party at the Pierre to celebrate the end of the Army-McCarthy hearings, both Jane and Ralph were feted. She moved through the festivities with a dazed awareness of joy. For everyone here connected to theater, she held a special overpowering reverence: for their talent, their courage in laying themselves on the line. As she'd soon, at last, be able to again.

She was busy, once more, all the time. Back to the gym. Lessons in voice, dance. Books about Rome, Egypt. At the Metropolitan, she gazed on the busts of Roman senators, traced in the lineaments what had drawn Cleopatra first to Caesar, then Antony. From the museum shop, she bought a reproduction of an Egyptian necklace, wore it as a talisman. She slept now, ignoring Owen's complaints, always alone. It was as though she held herself inviolate for what was coming.

Briefly, in June, she acceded to Bill's plea to accompany him on the yawl. When the play opened, he argued, if it were a hit—if!—there'd never be another chance. On deck, the crew discreetly in the background as they sailed the inland waterways, Bill blurted:

"You know, don't laugh. . . . But I'd been hoping you'd marry me. So I'd have something to live for. Now, you never will." The fair hair, so like the hair she used to twine about her fingers, blew about his face in the wind. Jane leaned forward to pat Bill's knee.

"I never will, period. Anyone. I don't intend to marry." Then: "You *have* everything to live for, Bill. Part of life is to find it."

Bill shook his head. "I can't. Not without you. I can't help it. And I still think of dying. All the time."

Jane gazed out at the sunlight glinting on the almost purple water. The wind hummed in the sails as the ship leaned into it. "You have to dedicate yourself, Bill. To something."

"I could. To you. . . . Do you remember the day we met? I was on my horse. You took a scarf off your head and your hair came down around your shoulders." He regarded her, as though the common memory might pull her into his orbit. It was her turn to shake her head.

"People are too frail to deserve dedication. It has to be something outside you. Something concrete. What Eliot called the 'objective correlative,' I suppose." Jane saw that she'd lost him. "Maybe I'm one of the lucky ones, Bill. I found what that was early. Something to which I can give my full self. . . ."

Bill stood, walked to the rail. "I can't find anything. I don't want busy work. I need a *person*." In the dark blue eyes, Jane read reproach. "I need *you*. Maybe with you I could even—get well."

"Sorry, Bill. Not for sale." Already, her mind was on rehearsals.

Was there any sound, Jane wondered, like the hollow sound of voices on an empty stage in an otherwise empty theater? The border lights blazed on and it was like entering a magical cavern to move into their illumination. The familiar stir of some unknown breeze rustled the muslin flat Ralph had had erected to serve as background for rehearsal. Meanwhile he discussed with the stage manager the exact height at which the grand drape should hang as top frame for the stage. There was the sound of hammering as carpenters constructed the Elizabethan inner stage, the small area enclosed by curtains and in which certain actions took place before moving forward to the outer stage, once the scene was in progress. Already, the skydrop to be used in the battle scenes hung above the flies, and a trap was readied from which soldiers would emerge. In all this activity, it was as though unseen drums marched them forward.

To greatness, Ralph Gurney assured her.

On opening night Jane saw from her taxi the lights come on all over the city and, with them, her name soaring above the theater marquee. There had been such a rush of scalping for tickets that that story itself had made the top news of the theater section. But Jane was suddenly sick, as she'd never been, with nerves. At her dressing table, a burlesque image danced before her dazzled eyes. The audience would rise, en masse, throw vegetables as they had in Shakespeare's day. She wondered if she might rush out again from the stage door, out to Broadway. She might catch a bus that would take her to the Midwest. There she could lose herself, sell lingerie in a department store. In the mirror, she stared at her reflection: the dark wig cut in bangs and sprayed to hang stiffly down, the slant of her eyes heavily accentuated, the amulet hanging in the center of her high damp forehead.

The stage manager knocked, called, "Time!"

Harold Channing, handsome in his costume, met her, offered his arm. The small string orchestra, seated in a box, was already playing, a tune by Henry the Eighth. Jane's mind went blank. She stared at Harold as though at a stranger. He pressed her arm, murmured, "Steady!"

The houselights had gone down. The music ended. The curtain rose. Demetrius and Philo met, center stage, to express their disgust with Antony. There sounded "the flourish within." As Philo spoke his next four lines, Harold led Jane forward onstage. The lights blinded her. There was a tremendous noise that prevented her from speaking her opening line.

Applause.

As it died away, Jane gazed up at Antony. " 'If it be love, indeed, tell me how much.' "

The acclaim, when it was over, resembled an assault. It was as though the audience hungered to come over the footlights, sweep them up in its arms. At Sardi's, the atmosphere bordered on hysteria. By the time the reviews came out, it was as though they'd always known what these would be.

"Ralph Gurney's direction, at once subtle and passionate. . . ." "Harold Channing belies his years, recalls the Antony who spoke for Caesar and summons for us the noble and tragic passion of his ending. . . ." "It is Jane Belmont who, from her first entrance, transfigures the stage, who compels us equally to condemn, admire and mourn her. A performance for the ages. . . ." "Miss Belmont has given us the definitive interpretation of Cleopatra. Miss this at your peril. . . ." Perhaps the *Times* summed it up best: "It should run forever."

Aurelia flew in to see the show, wept openly when she came backstage. She stayed over at the house on Sixty-first Street, they walked arm in arm in the October sunshine along Fifth Avenue, the shadows of the tall buildings dappling the street. There was a roar of traffic going by, the bustle of shoppers darting in and out of stores with packages, passersby smiled at one another and the wind whipped coat flaps open. At the Plaza's Palm Court, where they stopped for lunch, Aurelia told Jane she wasn't worried about her any longer.

"You made my heart stop a while there," she said.

"I know," Jane answered.

Afterward, Aurelia worked on the long-planned exhibit of her stage and screen designs. Before she left New York, nearly one thousand people crowded the Grand Ballroom of the Plaza to view one hundred garments in less than half an hour. *Now our fortunes*, Jane recalled, *swing up. . . .*

In December, Tiffany was selling a special Cleopatra necklace and bracelet, designed for the Christmas trade, paid Jane handsomely to model it. McCarthy was censured by the Senate and Jane's picture, a close-up in costume, appeared on the cover of *Life*.

From simple exhaustion, Jane declined invitations to all the glittering parties, reduced her evenings after theater to quiet ones with Owen, occasional afternoons with Bill. The house came in for a much needed repainting, and often, to conserve herself, she simply watched TV with Faith, whom she'd caught, several times, bristling with delivery men: this new success had quite gone to her head. Jane was moving on two planes all the time now: the elevation on which she existed as Cleopatra, the dim sense below that despair and loss could again not be far behind. This June she'd turn thirty. Somewhere, somehow, despite everything, there was still something she desperately needed, didn't have.

This sense was briefly dispelled when she won, in the spring, the Tony for Best Actress and the Drama

Desk award. Children were walking about the sunny streets in Davy Crockett hats when she dropped into Bergdorf's for an evening bag. From cars stopped at traffic lights, radios blared "Rock Around the Clock." Walter Raney and Bill Hamilton again proposed marriage. Faith made her work, for relaxation, in the much neglected garden. Together, they trained wisteria to grow up the front of the house. The demand for tickets to *Antony and Cleopatra* continued.

It was July then, the end of the performance on a Thursday night. As she creamed the makeup off her face, the stage manager brought Jane a note. A replica of the one thirteen years before.

"May I see you? Danny Edelman."

Jane's hands turned cold, trembled. The impulse to refuse arose, she realized as she stared into the mirror, from a terror that Danny would see this face, wide-eyed, frozen, that he'd no longer love it.

But everyone was saying she'd never been so beautiful. More important: why should Danny love her? Hadn't she sent him on his way—how long was it now? Seven years? Seven years of drought, said a voice within. Surely a gesture of friendship could be resurrected from their past?

The stage manager waited. Yes, she told him. Of course she'd see the gentleman.

The stage door was open to the summer night. Its soft air touched her cheeks as Jane stood a moment, preparing herself as for an entrance onstage. Then she walked forward to a flurry of fans, programs held open for autographs. Danny, a few paces from the door, turned, watched her.

She hadn't remembered—this was Jane's first impression, as the others left—that Danny was so big. Of course, he'd always been tall. Of course, now, he'd filled out, become broad-chested. Perhaps it was the mass of curly hair, the curly beard he'd grown. He was handsomer than ever and her vision clouded as he came to her, appeared to envelop her.

But he only took her quickly in his arms, stared down, kissed her lightly. Yet, even when he held her off, grasping her hands in his, Jane found it difficult to see him clearly. She searched, as though blindly, in that familiar face, found at last what made her own eyes clear: *his* eyes, his golden eyes, brilliant and expressive. What she felt made her fearful.

Danny smiled, broke the silence between them. "You were magnificent! Thank the Lord Sid Arkoff could scrounge me a ticket. But you: an Egyptian! How could you do this to a nice Jewish boy?"

Jane felt shy. "The Romans and Egyptians had their problems, too. That didn't stop Antony and Cleo..." No, that was the wrong thing to say. "When did you arrive? How long will you be here?"

They began to walk, his hand over hers as he held it on his arm. "Two days ago. My father had a stroke. I leave tomorrow night." Jane reassured herself: Good! "There's trouble brewing in Israel. . . . When isn't there? But this time it looks even more serious. I have to get back."

"What do you do there? I have no idea what you do."

"Teach stagecraft. Theater in general. Teach flying. . . . We're all in the army, you know. When war comes, I'll fly."

" 'When?' It's that certain?"

"Oh, yes." As though he owed this to her: "Besides, I'm getting married. To a sabra."

He must have felt her arm stiffen in his. "What's a sabra?"

Danny laughed. "So much for your political IQ. Somebody born in Israel. She lives on a kibbutz. You do know what that is?'"

Jane lifted her chin. She had developed a stitch in her side from Danny's stride. "I think so. . . . So you'll live on one, too? Aren't they dangerous? Right near the borders, I mean?"

"Israel's all borders. But I'm hoping to get Rachel to forsake the field life, move to Tel Aviv." So. Her name was Rachel. Jane had a vision of a vigorous figure in coveralls, dark hair flying in the desert wind, healthy teeth bared in a smile. How loathsome. Her own legs felt weak. "We haven't worked that out yet. . . . Where can we eat? I haven't been back for so long, everything's strange to me. Does the Stage still have pastrami sandwiches?"

"They do."

Suddenly, they were silent, walking through the thinning crowds. Did Danny remember, too, all the nights they'd walked, arms around one another's waists, up Broadway after *Zeal?* To the Stage, to the apartment on Fifty-fifth? The ease of those first moments, the ease Danny had labored so diligently to inject fell away. Jane sensed he must feel it, too. There was too much between them to act like comrades. As they stood on line for the crowded tables, as people turned to point her out to one another, she saw—almost with satisfaction—that a slight film of damp had gathered beneath the curly hair on Danny's brow. The golden eyes avoided her, betrayed a certain tense desperation as he gazed above the crowd. When they met hers, she murmured:

"Let's not stay. We can have something at my place."

Sharply, he inhaled, nodded. At Fifty-fifth Street, he began to lead her to the corner. She pulled away.

"No. We don't have to cross here. We can walk up to the park and over."

Danny glanced down at her. "We don't *have* to. . . . You'd rather not?"

She nodded. They walked on. Past Carnegie Hall and to Fifty-ninth Street, down past the horses and carriages, past the Plaza where they'd stopped together so often. There wasn't a step of the way they took that wasn't full of memories. They should, Jane thought, have taken a cab.

Danny asked about Aurelia. She told him about Paul Talbott. Sal Celucci. It was better when they approached Madison, walked on up to Sixty-first Street and east. The only memories here were hers, not shared ones.

"That's it," she said, as they reached the corner of Third Avenue. "The one with the wisteria growing up it." Across the side street, near the unsightly yellow brick church, a man was walking his dog. Tomorrow night, it occurred to Jane with startling pain, when he's out there again with his dog, Danny will be on his way back to Israel. He'll be gone again. Forever.

The house offered a passage to impersonality. Here, within its walls, it spoke of her new life, of the years they'd passed apart from one another. Jane realized she was chattering, explaining, while Danny had become both constrained and polite in praise as he followed her through the downstairs rooms. He admired the Jackson Pollock. Jane excused herself to go to the basement to prepare sandwiches, left him to fix drinks in the living room. Downstairs, she dropped the bread, almost shattered the jar of Dijon mustard.

"I'm impressed, very impressed," Danny announced, as they sat beside one another on one of the brocade couches.

"I suppose you'd be living in the city. Maybe like this. If you'd stayed on in theater," Jane observed.

Danny stood. He began to pace the room. "You've heard, I suppose? In Israel we've made the desert bloom."

"Do you always speak in iambic pentameter when you talk of Israel?" Jane knew she sounded jealous.

"It's difficult to describe what you feel when you live and work there. You know, the musicians we have: some of the greatest in the world. And you remember, always, the ones who might have played like that. The ones who died at Auschwitz, Treblinka. . . . Maybe I saw their corpses. . . . We have such scientists! And you think of *those*. Who never lived to grow up. What they might have contributed to the world. . . . We've snatched one remnant from the fire, made it glow and burn. . . ."

As he strode about the room, Jane realized that Danny saw not this room but that land over there. He'd found his purpose. Better that his dedication was now to Israel than to her.

And their lost love.

Yet, as she watched him, Jane barely heard his words. The lines she spoke onstage hung silent on her lips:

> His face was as the heavens; and therein stuck
> A sun and moon, which kept their course, and lighted
> The little O, the earth. . . .

She knew that she was gazing up at him, that her heart appeared to have spread through her chest, risen to her throat, that her vision had clouded again. Her own voice onstage seemed to reverberate above them:

> His legs bestrid the ocean; his rear'd arm
> Crested the world. . . .
> Think you there was or might be such a man
> As this I dream'd of?

Danny, she saw, had stopped his pacing, stood above her. The ruddy cheeks visible above the curly beard had paled. The golden eyes glowed down at her. Then he had lifted her from the couch, was holding her against him, pressing her to his chest.

"Oh, God," he groaned. "Why can't I stop loving you?"

She was limp in his arms. Everything else had been a wandering. This was home. They were on the stairs then, speaking nothing but the other's name. In her room, Jane swiftly threw back the bedspread, the covers. Their fingers raced to undress one another, they were clasped in bed in one another's arms, kissing away the other's tears, fumbling to come close everywhere.

When he came into her at last, Jane was reminded of how she'd studied what might have been Cleopatra's last night with Antony, had seized on a passage from *Madame Bovary,* thought now that this was what she herself must resemble: "There was something wild, something strange and tragic in this forehead covered with cold sweat, those stammering lips and wildly staring eyes, in the embrace of those arms. . . ."

Then she was floating far out into darkness. Gravity was Danny's body, his arms. What she'd never been able to give before, now—when it was too late—she gave entirely, clinging to him. There was only him.

For just a few moments during that day they left the room. To descend to the kitchen—it was Faith's day off —where Jane made eggs, toast, coffee. Danny stood behind her and held her as she moved. Upstairs again, she bathed, combed her hair, saw her eyes, pupils enlarged, stare into this day that would have to last her her life. She'd been, without Danny, sexually and spiritually alone, and hadn't known. She opened the drapes, forgot to close them as she came to him again on the bed where he waited for her.

Then it was time for him to bathe and dress. They'd brought up a bottle of Scotch, ice bucket, glasses. Now they sat by the round table at the window, knees touching, and talked as they drank. The room darkened gradually, like a stage set, to denote the passage of time. Time was what they had so little of.

For there was no way they could close the chasm between them. Danny couldn't forsake Israel. Jane knew that. She'd already wronged the woman waiting for him. Her own life held her here. At the last, they could only hold hands, gaze at one another in the darkened room.

Then he was gone into the New York streets, headed for Idlewild. She, in a room that seemed to shriek with silence, dressed slowly for the theater. In these brief hours, Danny had taken with him, she felt, the world.

She stared into the dark streets. Perhaps in a small apartment nearby that same man with the dog sat reading a newspaper. Later, when she'd be on her way back home, he'd rise, call his dog, again pause near the yellow brick church as he had the evening before when she'd foreseen this pain. Every evening it would be the same, the same figures on these sidewalks. Only she would be aware that, years ago, when Joanie still existed in her life, Danny had entered there. Only she would remember that, for one night only, Danny had walked here, too.

Yes. He'd taken the world.

2

It wasn't until late August—Danny's wedding announcement already received—that Jane allowed herself to believe what she'd been dreading might be true: she was pregnant.

"Don't tell me whose it is." Owen's tone was cold

174

when, needing somebody, she told him over lunch before the Wednesday matinee. "You wouldn't think of blitzing your career when it's at the point it's at now. . . . I suppose you can find somebody to fix things? If not, I will."

"How soon?" She was miserable.

"I'll let you know. How far gone is it?"

"Almost two months."

His rather pouty lips twitching, he eyed her. "I'll 'bring you liberty' . . . and not in the form of an asp. Though that may be what you deserve."

He called next day. The doctor would await her on Sunday at his office. Then he'd check her into a hospital as a miscarriage case. She wouldn't miss a performance.

Her acting that evening was mechanical, even execrable. Before the condemnation in the eyes of others onstage, Jane cringed. She awoke, Friday, to a depression such as she'd never known. It was as though a stone statue rested on her chest, on her abdomen. She drank coffee, brushed aside Faith's queries, dressed, decided —despite a heavy rain—that she must walk.

As she stepped through and around puddles, she tried to decipher what this was that gripped her. She had no moral qualms about abortion. It wasn't that. Then why, as she turned up Lexington Avenue, stepped for a moment into the entrance of Bloomingdale's to dry off, was she trembling?

Not for her physical safety: Owen had chosen the doctor carefully. She stared at the people hurrying in and out, at those standing about to wait for friends, as though they could offer an answer. Outside, buses lumbered by, women stood under umbrellas with hands raised to call for taxis. In the store, behind her, customers moved restlessly from aisle to aisle. Two women, recognition in their eyes, stepped toward her. Jane pulled her rain hat further over her forehead, ducked outside again into the downpour.

She was on Fifty-fifth Street then, was slowly approaching the seated lions that guarded the doorway to the house where she and Danny had lived. It was the first time she'd permitted herself to walk here. She had been cut off, all through those years, from life, from love.

175

Her capacity for love had ended, she'd thought, when Peter had died. She hadn't been able to give, from that emptiness, what Danny had needed. What difference did it make now that she had found that source again? It was too late. This child inside her was only an ironic footnote to her own tardiness. What affirmation was she seeking? She had chosen her way, hadn't she? It was only onstage that she had decided to live to the full. It was sentimentality that brought her to a standstill here, before the lions, with tears streaming down her face in the rain.

Like a child, not the new one inside her, but her own self, she cried out in silence: I want! I want! . . .

But what? She couldn't bring herself to believe it: that the depression that had settled within her, like some beast taking up its rightful abode, appeared to lift slightly when she permitted herself even to think the answer to that demand. Did she want this baby? Wasn't it only a whim? Did one casually bring into being an entity so unplanned? The child she was herself kept crying out. Each time it did, the beast shifted within, slightly, as though to contemplate departure to the jungle from which it had come.

That night, onstage, Jane recouped. Her heart was still painful, she still had come to no clear decision. But some lightness had returned to her step. It was as though she had set back time and thought, had decided that somehow, during these moments, perhaps the answer might reveal itself.

It came sooner than she had hoped. In Scene Three of the first act, she gazed at Antony with her full anger at his marriage to another woman. But as she spoke her lines, she realized that they expressed, too, her bond to Danny, to the growing life inside her.

> Eternity was in our lips and eyes,
> Bliss in our brows' bent; none our parts so poor
> But was a race of heaven. . . .

It was as though a voice within asked: "I may? It's completely up to me, then?" Another answered, with reassurance: "The choice is yours."

She knew then what it must be. A commitment to that affirmation of life she'd been seeking. The last of the depression lifted. Perhaps she'd found it, in part. Amazing grace. . . . Then Danny hadn't, after all, taken the world. He was gone but had left her another.

The one aspect that saddened *was* Danny. Danny could never know.

It was simple to cancel the doctor's appointment. Not so simple to answer Owen's phone call Sunday night.

"Have you flipped? I called the hospital to see how you were. What happened? You lost your cool?"

"I couldn't tell you before. I've decided to go ahead. To have it. . . ."

Silence. Then: "Does it have anything to do with who the father is?" Quickly: "No. Don't tell me. . . . You're really going to enjoy pushing a pram through the park, matinee days? How long will you do Cleopatra with a belly?"

"I'm hoping to go on till December. I may need different costumes."

"What you need . . ." Owen didn't finish. Instead: "I'd find it a little difficult to escort you about the city in these coming months. You *will* understand?"

"And after? You don't want to play godfather?" What was so unsettling? His rejection of her—or of the baby?

"I hate kids." He hung up.

In September, the Gurneys returned from Europe. Jane broke the news. Ralph whistled. "I imagine we'll have to wrap up the show when you go." At her guilty face: "Better to leave at the top of demand than let it peter out. Don't worry. . . . Plenty of actresses, despite Owen's horror, have children. You'll be back."

Mary's dark, eloquent eyes widened. "But without a father? What will people say? And, Jane, what will you do?"

"Yes, there is that," Ralph agreed.

"What Scarlett O'Hara always did," Jane responded nervously. "I'll think of that tomorrow."

In October, Bill Hamilton was at her again, demanding she give him a Sunday. *The Threepenny Opera* had opened a month ago; Jane suggested they take in a performance, have dinner. By the time Bill had brought her back to Sixty-first Street, he was importuning her again. If she married him, it would turn his life around.

"Bill." Jane sat him down on one couch, walked over to the other. "I have to tell you something. I can't marry you. Even if I loved you. Which I don't. I can't ever again let you mention marriage. I'm more than three months pregnant."

The white, strained face lit up. "You're pregnant?" And dimmed. "Who is it? Who *are* you marrying?"

"The man's already married. Though he wasn't when it happened. So that doesn't signify. He doesn't even know. . . ."

Bill was at her feet, her hands in his. He looked so vulnerable, so young. "Jane! Then marry *me!* You don't want to bring up a child without a father. I'd take care of it as though it were my own, I swear! It would be yours and mine. No one would ever have to know differently." His face was radiant, beseeching.

Jane shook her head. "Bill, it's not possible. I can't ask . . ."

"*I'm* asking! I'm begging, don't you see? I said I needed you to turn my life around. I thought just you. But a *family!* Jane, I'd love it like my own." Bill stood, began to stride about the room as he waved his arms. "My God, what a life we'd give him! None of the mistakes my parents made. But we won't spoil him. But at Easter he'll have the biggest damn chocolate rabbit the factory can turn out. He . . ." Bill stopped. Jane was laughing.

"First things first?" she managed.

Bill hesitated, laughed, too. "I can't help it. I can't think straight." He was at her feet again. "No, I *am* thinking straight. It's not as though I didn't want to marry you before. This only makes it better. Come on, Jane. Say yes. For the baby's sake."

She stroked his cheek, pushed back the silky hair. "Bill, you *are* a dear. But there are obstacles. Besides the obvious ones. . . ."

"That I can't? . . ." The face clouded.

"Not that, not that at all. . . . I wouldn't want to stay on at the castle once the baby was six months or so. I'd want to return to the stage." The blue eyes darkened.

"And then, there's you, Bill. You're excited and elated now. But what about the suicide threats? Do you think I'd want to bring up a child with all that?"

He spoke very slowly. "I won't make those threats, Jane. I promise. And we'll see how you feel about the stage when the time comes. You know I'd never stand in the way of your happiness. . . ."

Incredibly, Jane felt herself weakening. "It would be such a strange marriage, Bill. . . ."

"Not more than many."

"If we went ahead: there are things we'd have to promise one another."

"What things?"

Jane reflected. "I suppose we'd have to repose absolute trust in one another. More than in the ordinary marriage. That we'd never lie to one another. About anything." As he began to nod his head, she shook her own. "No, don't say yes, yes. You have to consider this. Very seriously. Remember: if we're going to present this child to the world as yours, we'll never say anything different. Even to the child."

"Don't you think that's more important to me than it could ever be to you?"

She laid her hand to his cheek. "Is it, Bill? Really?"

He held her hand to his lips. "I love you. I'll never lie to you, Jane. I'll keep the promises I make."

3

They decided to keep the ceremony secret. The Gurneys stood up with them, provided simple gold rings. After, from the Rainbow Room, Jane called Aurelia, asked if she'd care to become a godmother.

"Are you serious? Who's the guy?"

"Bill Hamilton."

A moment's silence. "Claire's brother? . . . You're not still hung up on *her?*"

"This is your last offer." Jane's tone turned cool.

"I accept, I accept. When does my office begin?"

"Keep open the end of April."

She returned to the glittering terraced room where Bill and the Gurneys waited, passed her own dazzled reflection many times in the long mirrored columns. To her dress was affixed Bill's gift: a gold peacock, its claws clutching a large pearl, its feathers encrusted with diamonds, emeralds, rubies. The floor-to-ceiling windows framed the sparkling city below and, as she sat, she took Bill's hand.

Bringing her home later, he stood shyly at the door.

"Bill, you'll spend the night?" As he hesitated: "I don't expect anything. Beyond that we hold one another."

Faith, always discreet, had left a bucket of ice in the living room, champagne, glasses. They toasted their marriage, the child. Evading the memory of Danny on these stairs—or Claire—Jane asked Bill to follow her up.

His body, when he undressed, was smooth as a child's. Like a child, he allowed her to tuck him in, watched as she crossed in her nightgown around the bed, crawled in beside him. Jane was aware of his tension, turned toward him, laid her hand on his forehead, her head on his shoulder. In the dark, his profile was Claire's, the hair the same silken texture. She raised her lips to his cheek, moved her hand slowly along his chest and down his hip. She didn't know if his hand arrested hers, or memory. Danny's strong flank came back to her, his special smell, the touch of his lips. Bill said, his voice choked:

"Don't." As she regarded him in the dark: "It won't matter? You said it wouldn't matter."

Jane turned on her back, took his hand. "There's nothing I really need less. Ever. Bill, feel. You can feel the baby kick."

He allowed her to move his hand to her belly. She saw his slow smile. As she stroked his hair, she forced herself not to think of Danny.

In the next weeks, Jane had to reprimand Bill for the influx of gifts—flowers, animals of porcelain, a jeweled watch, a gilded anthology of Shakespeare, *objets d'art*, a sable coat. The ads for the last weeks of *Antony and Cleopatra* brought a groundswell of new demands for tickets. At the big onstage closing party, Ralph made the announcement that she and Bill Hamilton had been married for some time, would await their baby at New Cardiff. Obviously, the Gurneys had sent alerts: gifts cascaded across the tomb setting. Although, as Harold Channing remarked:

"What do you buy for a Hamilton?"

Jane, gazing across the stage, sensed a premonitory pang. What if she never stood onstage again? To Ralph, she put a question: what would he think of directing her, eventually, as Lavinia in *Mourning Becomes Electra?* Ralph thought he'd like very seriously to consider it.

"So you do forgive me for cutting out?"

"Dear, I'd forgive you anything."

Bill had prepared a suite of rooms on the second floor of the castle. (Claire had said that day: "But can you imagine *living* here?") Connecting bedrooms and sitting room with kitchenette. He was having the playroom redone. Afternoon sunlight slanted across the floor of her room as Jane stepped into it. At some signal from Bill, Don Giovanni's invitation to the castle—her favorite aria—sounded from hidden speakers.

Armed with a cautious courtesy, on a seesaw between suspicion and relief, Bill's parents arrived from South Washington Square for dinner their first Sunday. Jane made no mistake that Mrs. Hamilton was fond of her, but the wait-and-see attitude she could tolerate. To Jane, free to revel in maternity clothes, Thomas Hamilton observed:

"So. You're making this boy of mine a family man, are you? I must say: we never expected it." His scrutiny was surprisingly friendly.

"He'll be Big Daddy himself," Jane said.

"Well." He watched her over his cigar. "Claire seems in no hurry to make grandparents of us. All she and Steve seem to care about is getting control of the business. Think you can persuade Bill he's got a responsibility to hang on at the factory?"

Jane met his regard. "Where the baby's concerned, you'll find Bill very greedy."

"Good!" Thomas Hamilton puffed at the cigar and

grinned. "Good." During the week he had sent over, as a wedding gift, a gold dinner service for twenty-four. From Claire, in Bermuda, there arrived a Hallmark congratulatory card, one handwritten line:

"I never realized, Jane, that money meant this much to you."

Those next months appeared to Jane the most idyllic of her life. Evolution had caught up with her at last, and she was glad of it. When Bill was not at work in Media, they walked hand in hand through the frozen fields and woods, told one another everything of their pasts. To her memories Bill listened, rapt, as Claire never had. Around them animals leaped, startled, from their hiding places—rabbits, deer, grouse, pheasant. Their presence was symbolic, a sharing in life, the life that grew inside her. She and Bill would return to the small upstairs dining room near the long windows that looked out on the castle entrance. Caldwell, the chief butler, served them with heavy silverware, pretty pink Spode she'd selected from the pantry stores, Waterford crystal, always fresh flowers. Plus, at her place, a glass of milk which he possessively watched her drink. When it was gone, they exchanged smiles. As the weather warmed early she swam—to the alarm of the swans—nude in the pond. There was only one visit to New York: for *My Fair Lady*. Jane remembered the plans for *Pygmalion*. So long ago . . .

She had to scold Bill for buying presents, this time for the child. When Jane came across his .22 caliber gun, she admonished him: the best gift to the child would be to cast the weapon out. Bill insisted he kept it against intruders. Besides, didn't alcoholics retain one bottle as proof of their new will? Jane shook her head, told him to feel the baby turn somersaults.

It was during labor, the last day of April, at the hospital in Abington, that Jane had to struggle against longing for Danny. Instead, it helped to curse him, silently, for putting her through this. It was most unusual, the doctors insisted, that Bill be allowed entrance to the labor room to rub her back. Husbands—but possibly not Hamiltons—were supposed to wait in the lounge. Later —the baby was a boy—the nurses made jokes about Bill.

"Here he comes," they told Jane at visiting hour. "The mad father. Twitching all over with excitement." They'd been scandalized by her decision to nurse, ascribed this bizarre determination to her being an actress, were resigned now when Bill arrived with a movie camera, Caldwell bearing lights. Later, after the baby had nursed, Jane handed him to Bill, who gazed down in awe at the sleeping face.

"He looks like he's making up poetry." Then: "How about a tremendous favor? It would mean so much to him. Can we name him after my father?"

"Yes. If I get to choose the middle name."

Bill's elated face clouded. "Not Daniel?"

"How about Thomas Scott Hamilton?" It was a simple memorial.

"Thomas Scott Hamilton!" Bill peeped into the baby's peaceful face. "Can you handle that? Huh? What say, Tommy ole boy?" His lips brushed against the soft fair hair.

What Jane found difficult to handle, alone with her son, was her sense of the birth that had accompanied his. A rage of love of which she hadn't known herself capable—as though held, since Peter's death, in some frozen waste—was now renewed, heated back to life. Like an avalanche it tumbled forth, sweeping strength to itself as it poured, inundating and surrounding her, while she held this small, fragile, still almost insensate being in her arms. By his third day, as a thin spring rain dripped beyond the windows, Jane—who seldom cried—allowed tears to drop on the thin blanket encasing the baby's warm body as, fatigued by nursing, he slept with his satin cheek against her breast.

This apotheosis of their love—hers and Danny's—would never know the feel of Danny's strong arms, would never be carried on his shoulders, not kneel to play in the sand with him, nor throw a ball, never lean against his side. The nurse, come to retrieve the baby for the nursery, patted Jane's shoulder.

"It's natural, you know. Post-partum blues. All new mothers get them. You'll be over them once you have your baby home. . . . Oh, what a handsome boy!" She lifted the sleeping infant from Jane's arms.

How much the choice of name meant to Bill's father was soon apparent. Aside from the five-million-dollar trust fund set up in the baby's name, a Mercedes-Benz arrived, registered to Jane. It was a good thing, Jane scolded at one of Mr. Hamilton's constant visits, that Bill *was* taking such hold of the business. Otherwise, it might really slide downhill, with the top boss here so often.

"Never mind, never mind." Mr. Hamilton held the baby in his arms. "Claire's nose is out of joint but she had her chance. Mm? Isn't that right, fellar? Isn't it?"

The baby gave a smile, from gas.

"Yes, I like your Mama, too," Mr. Hamilton added to Tommy. He hesitated, laid his hand on Jane's hair. "You're quite a girl, Jane."

"Hardly a girl anymore." Jane blushed, still uneasy about how to address him. She squeezed his hand.

Claire, with a set of silver infant dishes and cutlery, sent a stiff little note in her perfect handwriting. "For your child," she wrote, rather pointedly addressing it to Jane. With Steven Elder she came, at last, to the christening. Her one comment: "Amazing how little he resembles either of you."

Jane was only relieved by the absence of feeling at sight of the cool little face. Their past together might have been another life. What mattered now was the bundle she held in her arms. Faith, who'd also arrived, didn't—naturally—want to leave, once she'd seen the child. Jane was constantly taken aback, herself, by the platitudes that poured out of her while she nursed:

"*Are* you a handsome boy? *Yes,* you're a handsome smart boy!" And so on.

Now, while the minister intoned the blessing, she whispered, as though her only message to Danny, "You little *goniff!*" At which the baby awarded her another lopsided gas-inspired smile. Followed by an angry protest as the water splashed on his light hair, already beginning to curl.

It was only a few weeks later that Jane, on impulse, led Bill away from the crib to which the baby had graduated, brought him to her bed. Neither of them questioned why, this time, it worked. Being a father? Accepted at last by his own? For all its satisfaction, Jane saw two consequences that troubled. The new relationship deepened Bill's love for her. It also fanned the suspicious jealousy of other men that always smouldered below his quiet surface.

When Bill found her reading plays while she fed the baby, he frowned. "How long do you mean to nurse him?"

"Six months. That should give him his immunities. By then, he'll probably start to bite."

"And then?"

"Bill, you know I don't want to give up acting."

"But we've been so happy. Tommy needs you. I need you. . . ."

"We *could* all move back to New York, to my place. Maybe you could commute, a few days a week."

"Tommy should grow up here in the country. And I can't see commuting." Bill's face turned sulky. "I also can't see you living with him in New York without me. What is it? You want other men?"

"I don't need other men. Get away from me. You'll upset me and that will upset the baby."

It was their first fight. Later it occurred to Jane they'd never been so happy as when she was pregnant. This she didn't divulge to Aurelia who made it east in June, was properly staggered by the castle. She took one look at Tommy, whose eyes had already turned from neonate blue to gold, and remarked:

"My God! When did you have it on with Danny?"

"Danny? He's in Israel. You know that as well as I do."

Aurelia cocked her head. "So. Fifth Amendment. Okay." Then: "He doesn't even know?"

Jane refilled Aurelia's glass. "We didn't send a birth announcement. No."

"Playing your cards close to the chest, eh?"

"Look. Tommy's laughing at his godmother."

Aurelia, slated to begin work on another movie wardrobe, left in a few days. Not before listening to Tommy, nude in his carriage under a tree, gurgling: "Mum-mum-mum!" and "Da-da-da!" at the leaves.

"Hm," Aurelia observed. "Smart! Just like his daddy."

It was the following week the newspaper item caught

Jane's eye. Salvatore Celucci, sentenced to seven years in prison, had been released to die in a hospital. Bone cancer. That night Tommy was awake with colic. Bill, walking the floor with him, asked what had upset her.

"I have to go to New York," she said, and told him why. As she'd anticipated, Bill first objected, then said he'd drive her in.

They left Tommy, with a bottle, in Faith's arms, drove down to see Mama—who appeared better than she had in years—then slowly through the Village. Girls hurried along the street in tube dresses, men flaunted their new pink shirts, graceless Bermuda shorts. At street corners, young boys mimicking hoods stood about in black leather jackets, tight jeans with real or painted-on tattoos. Walking down Eighth Street from the parking lot toward the Brevoort, they heard rock and roll blaring on radios overhead, the new young singer, Elvis Presley. They'd decided to spend the night, see *Tiger at the Gates* that evening. At last, over their demitasses, Jane told Bill she was ready. It was a relief to concentrate on the ache in her heavy breasts, bulging with milk, rather than on what still lay ahead.

One of the policemen guarding the private room at Flower Hospital on Fifth Avenue expressed chagrin that Jane was to be admitted without being frisked. Bill grew so belligerent that Jane warned him not to get arrested. Alone, she was ushered into the shadowed room.

The figure on the bed was shrunken, the hair white. Had they brought her to the wrong man? Then the familiar face turned toward her. Jane moved to the bed while the dark, clouded eyes watched. Sal's lips began to quiver. He lifted his hand and she caught it.

"I came to see you, Sal. I had to come."

The voice was a hoarse whisper. "My little girl . . ."

Still holding the wasted hand, Jane sank down on the chair by the bed. "Oh, Sal, I'm so sorry." Quickly, lest he think she was asking forgiveness: "To see you like this. Is the pain bad?"

The massive head tried to roll in its old way on the pillow, lay still. "They give me stuff. You know. . . . How you been, kid?"

"I'm married. I have a child. A little boy."

The dark eyes lit up. "No joke? How old? Whaddya call him?"

"Two and a half months. His name is Tommy."

"It sure woulden be Sal, would it?" A smile trembled on the cracked, dry lips. "Your husband? He good to you?" The questions, as much as his appearance, indicated how much he'd slipped out of life: that he didn't know.

"The best, Sal."

There was the sound of rasping breath, an obvious effort to recollect. At last, a frown. "But you didden marry—you know—what's-his-name?"

"Danny Edelman?"

"Thassa guy. . . . What happened?"

"Nothing, Sal. He's been in Israel many years now."

"Ah. A Maccabee. . . ." The eyes closed. He appeared to sleep. Suddenly, the rasp deepened as Sal gathered himself for another comment. "So. See. You're happy now. In my opinion, somebody had to bring you to your senses. . . ." Jane's fingers stiffened in his. With surprising strength, his hand refused to let hers go. "You wuz mad. You wuz so mad at me, huh? But I coulden let you go runnin' around like that with that spade, could I? Who else was goin' to watch out for you?"

Had this been her ulterior motive? That Sal should tell her at last that she'd been wrong, had wronged him? She saw that, with something like the old shrewdness, he was watching her.

"Sure, you wuz right," he whispered. "But it was Dino done it, you know. Not me. . . . What did you have to go runnin' with spades for?"

Jane glanced down at her hand in his. Her hand, as in a movie montage, lay in Scott's, moved through the soft, bushy curls on Scott's head, over his shoulders and chest. She saw again the bright eyes, the smile. Out the window lay the further extension of the park where they'd played. . . .

"Oh, Sal!" Jane freed her hand, covered her face. In that silence, a nurse entered.

"I'm afraid you'll have to leave, Mrs. Hamilton." Jane saw the professional pity of her glance. The nurse thought she was grieving for Sal's sickness, for his death. She rose.

Sal's fingers groped along the coverlet, the ravaged face lifted. "Hey, kid! You gonna remember me, huh? You're not gonna forget your ole pal, Sal Celucci?"

Jane allowed him to find her hand. She closed her eyes so as not to see that beseeching scrutiny. "Of course, Sal. I'll always remember you." She stood a moment, irresolute. It came to her how long and how final death was. *Vengeance is mine, saith the Lord.* She bent, laid her cheek to his.

But at the theater that evening, she left her seat during the first act, paced—under the suspicious regard of the aged attendant—the lounge downstairs. She had been, after all, an accomplice. What a price Scott had paid for their brief interlude! What could she ever do to set things right? All those whose loss lay at her door. . . . Beginning, as always, with Joanie. . . .

At the castle, two days later, there was another envelope from Maryland. The same photos. What, she wondered again, could she do? Tell Clyde Simpson he'd been right? What was it he'd said the night they'd met? Repeated at Scott's death? "I'd get back there, hell or high water, and gun down every damn bastard killed anyone belonged to me. . . ."

Jane looked down at Tommy, and shivered.

4

In July, the trouble Danny had foreseen a year ago appeared to reach a climax. Nasser nationalized the Suez Canal. In Jordan, parliamentary elections reflected his influence. Throughout August, increasingly violent threats of Arab invasion. Mobilization in Israel.

Bill, understanding Jane's concern, insisted they go off on the yawl with Tommy for a couple of weeks. As they scudded before the wind, he climbed a few feet up the rigging with Tommy in his arms. Above the shimmering water, the baby laughed, his light brown curls blowing about his face.

"We'll make a sailor of this kid!" Bill promised, exultant.

When they returned, Thomas Hamilton had plans. They must permit him to give them a party. At the castle. For Bill's birthday, for their anniversary. There'd been a sudden flurry in Washington in September of antimonopoly activity, but in October they could celebrate. He'd take care of everything. Hire an orchestra. See to the menu, invitations. Would Jane give him her guest list? He wanted to show her off. Of course, sometime during the evening, Tommy would be awake? Could be brought down to the guests?

To everything, Jane answered yes. The festivity would punctuate the end of her nursing, might endow Bill with enough sense of himself to allow her to do what she must: return at last to New York, to the stage. Remember, she'd been admonishing him lately: we trust each other. It wasn't that she needed to leave the castle, leave him, but that she must go *toward* something, toward—despite her passion for the child—the still-existent center of her life. That center could be neither Bill nor Tommy. It couldn't be a person. . . .

"Just a little longer, Jane. Don't think of leaving yet. Let me work it out. We'll manage. . . ."

Jane bowed her head, returned to the guest list. The Gurneys were off on tour. She supposed she should ask Owen. Sid Arkoff. For a moment, she considered. Her agent was the only one—aside from Aurelia?—who knew of Danny's visit. All the acting friends available on a Saturday night. If they were performing, they could drive out afterward. She was having a fitting of a Dior gown when the news arrived.

The Hamiltons' private plane—both of them aboard —on its way back from Washington, had gone down in Chesapeake Bay. There were no survivors.

Her own pain surprised Jane. Another father lost— before she'd been able to reciprocate fully the affection he'd shown her. Tommy robbed of grandparents. Each morning, as she awoke, tears filled her eyes.

"We must cancel the party," Jane told Bill as they prepared for the funeral. "It's still almost a month away."

"No. I don't think my father would have wanted that. I think he'd have said it was his last memorial." A small muscle twitched in Bill's cheek. She saw how he kept swallowing.

"I know what this means to you, Bill. You had really just begun becoming his son."

Bill turned to her, wide-eyed. Then he was holding her, his face against her shoulder. "Do you think he felt that? Do you really think he felt that?"

If nothing else, the terms of the will appeared to indicate it. Not for herself but for Bill, Jane felt her own lips tighten in something like triumph as the castle and controlling stock in the company were handed over to him. The houses at South Washington Square and West Palm Beach, with the remaining stock, went to the Elders. Under the black veil thrown back from the chic little hat, Claire's pale face turned whiter. Jane saw the knuckles tighten in Steve Elder's fist. The partings were barely civil.

A day later a note arrived to decline the invitation to the party. "We hardly see a gala as being in good taste," Steve Elder wrote.

Two days before the party, Jane took Tommy in for his smallpox vaccination. He had a strong reaction, was still awake most of the night, feverish the day of the festivity itself. On which Israel made a lightning attack on Egypt. Jane saw the dark shadows under her eyes, tried to nap, instead held Tommy, tried to get him to drink water or to nurse, but he only fussed. Bill chided her for her timing on the vaccination, apologized as he took the baby, watched almost mournfully as she stepped into the black Dior gown.

"All your old friends will be telling you how beautiful you are. And asking when you're coming back."

"One hopes." She tried to smile. Her heart was still heavy with those deaths. The hairdresser had come earlier. Now, Jane slipped a diamond pin into the shining coils of hair, pulled on the above-elbow black kid gloves. "*You're* very dashing in your tails, sir."

190

In everything, Thomas Hamilton's hand was visible. He'd hired more than two dozen extra staff. In the ballroom, an elegant cold table had been set up, decorated with ice carvings of swans surrounding a baby. Platters were piled high with shrimp, salmon, hams, two garnished pigs, turkey, lobster. As the orchestra tuned up, the kitchen help were laying out on a hot table chicken, veal, potatoes, a standing rib of beef. In the living room-chapel would be trays of hors d'oeuvres: artichoke hearts, smoked oysters, snow crab claws, cherry tomatoes, cheeses, caviar. Out in the kitchen, platters for dessert waited: ice creams, ices, pies, pastries, petits fours. Two bars were ready, in the chapel and the ballroom.

The guests who'd attended that twenty-first birthday party at the Bellevue-Stratford arrived first. In just a few weeks, Jane supposed, they'd all be voting again for Eisenhower, she and her friends for Stevenson. Jane was dancing with one of the men when she spotted Owen with Sid, excused herself.

"Well." Owen, apparently dispensing pardon, eyed her with obvious relish. "You've kept your figure and your impressive carriage, I see. Had enough of Kirk, Küchen and Kinde?"

Jane was startled by her rush of elation at seeing them, took one on each arm. "Come say hello to Bill."

Bill barely nodded before he turned to her. "Have you checked on Tommy?"

"Anything wrong?" Owen was watching closely.

"Not really. He's been fussy." To Bill: "The nurse knows she can call me, any time."

As though she were an errant wife, Bill formed a small sour smile. Cynthia Blackwood, a long cigarette holder in one hand, sidled up.

"Heard about Natalie Young's new plaything? Gives blow jobs at one hundred dollars per. I suppose the hours are short enough to leave her time for Natalie." Cynthia sent a long stream of smoke toward Bill.

He stared, turned away, strode across the room. Owen suggested to Jane: "Let's dance."

In his arms, Jane was aware of Bill brooding. It would probably be best to keep her contact with Owen to a minimum. What she felt for and owed Bill would forfeit a hundred Owens. Still, he was so amusing in his old way about everyone they knew, it was so good to hear the old bitchy gossip, that she soon forgot, was laughing as they circled the floor, only remembered when Sid Arkoff cut in.

"Something tells me you were asked to do this," she commented.

"You doubt my gallantry?"

But Jane sensed she'd guessed correctly. At the end of the dance, she excused herself, hurried up to Tommy's room, found him sleeping well, his light brown curls in damp ringlets from the subsiding fever. She saw, when she returned, that others of her own crowd had arrived—Harold Channing, the cast of *Antony and Cleopatra*. Also that Bill had been drinking heavily. After embraces, talk, Jane asked Bill to dance, suggested he go easy on the liquor.

"Afraid I'll embarrass you? Is that why I'm getting some attention? . . . When you were dancing with Durant, you were laughing. With him, you really enjoy yourself, don't you?"

"Are you trying to ruin the evening?" His drinking, his mood were new to her. They should have canceled the party.

"Are *you*?"

He left her, as soon as the music ended. Several others had noticed his temper, were exchanging glances. Jane fetched herself another drink, laid it aside to dance with somebody else, found herself again in Owen's arms.

"So? When are you leaving Levittown and the uxorious millionaire?" He swirled her around, began to sing in her ear to the music: ". . . um . . . um . . . nights of love —but not for me . . ."

Jane pushed him off a bit, remembered as he crushed her closer the night they'd met: he'd behaved the same way. The music ended but he didn't relinquish her, stood waiting for it to resume. Startlingly, instead of dance strains, the orchestra began to play, very slowly, in hymn cadence, the music of "Amazing Grace."

Puzzled, everyone faced toward it. Jane felt a chill.

"What's this?" Owen asked. "A revival meeting?"

"Excuse me." Jane left his side, walked across the floor, stood below the dais until the leader had finished. He bent toward her.

"Was that satisfactory, Mrs. Hamilton?"

"What in the world made you choose that?"

"You didn't request it? Somebody said you'd requested it."

Jane smiled lightly. "Yes? Who?"

"Some guy from the kitchen. Negro? Really high yellow, I guess you'd say."

Jane turned away. She forced herself, smiling as she went and exchanging small talk, to move across the room, till she came to the kitchen. Here there was such activity that, for a moment, she went unnoticed. One of the chefs glanced up.

"Anything wrong, Mrs. Hamilton?"

"No, nothing." She gazed out over the room, walked through the outer pantries and back. Found the head of the newly hired staff. "Do you know everyone you've employed?"

He stiffened. "Each of them has bond posted. Is anything missing? Any complaint?"

She refused to be stared down. "Is there someone by the name of Clyde Simpson, by any chance? A sort of mulatto? Heavyset? Glasses?"

"The name's not familiar, ma'am."

Jane nodded absently, returned to the ballroom. Bill was still drinking. Her head had begun to ache. Bill saw her.

"Ah, there's the little missus," he called out. "I thought you'd run out on me already! Tonight of all nights!" He turned to those around him. "Supposed to be our anniversary, you know. Married only a year and already she wants to leave me."

"Bill." She spoke close to him. "You know that isn't true. Don't make a fool of yourself. Please."

"*I'm* not making a fool of myself! *You're* doing it. You . . ."

Owen had pushed his way through. "Can't you cool it, man?"

"Oh, the big theater swell! One of the sharks waiting around the raft. Think you're getting her back from me, don't you?" Bill waved his glass about, drink spilling out of it. His eyes were bloodshot, wild. "Well, you're not, see? I'm not about to let her go. She's *my* wife, not yours. See?"

To Jane's dismay, Owen murmured: "We all know how much you own, Willie boy. You don't have to set off the burglar alarm.... Maybe your problem is you haven't earned entrée to Jane's world. I mean: no tickee, no washee."

Several people tittered.

"Christ, you're so smart, you theater people!" Bill noticed Jane's face. "I'm disgracing you, huh? But what do *you* plan to do when you go back to New York without me? I'm not supposed to care when you're fuckin' away with everyone in sight?"

"Shut up, Bill." Her voice was cold, low.

"You'll be sorry." Bill heaved a deep breath. "You'll be sorry when your kid has to grow up without a father. I'm not sticking around to watch. I'll kill myself first, you hear? I'll get my gun and kill myself."

"Have one handy?" Owen smiled around toward the large audience.

"You, too, Owen," Jane said. She walked off.

Tommy was still asleep. She laid her aching forehead to the side of the crib. As she crossed to the window and gazed out toward the gardens and fields, she faintly heard the orchestra: "Some Enchanted Evening." The door opened behind her. It was Bill. He glanced at her, crossed the room, continued into his. Jane hesitated, then followed.

Bill was holding the gun.

"You swore you'd never use that threat again," Jane said. Somewhere on the other side, beyond Bill's dressing room, another door softly opened and closed. She supposed it was the nurse, going the long way around for some reason, to check on Tommy.

"You hate me now." Bill's eyes filled with tears. "What do I have to live for now?"

"You were keeping that gun the way an alcoholic keeps a bottle. Remember? And you were never going to use that threat again."

"You do hate me, don't you? For humiliating you in front of everyone?"

"How can I hate you?" she asked. "You're Tommy's father."

Bill stared at her. With a quick movement, he tossed the gun on the bed, came to her, cast himself on his knees, grasped hers. "Sorry, Jane. Sorry, sorry. Please forgive me?"

Jane stroked the fair hair, damp with sweat. She sighed. "Of course I forgive you, Bill. Do you think I care what everyone down there thinks? What's important to me is what *you* think. You're my husband, Bill."

Bill rose, caught her hand to his heart, held it there. "Okay. I *do* swear, Jane. I swear on Tommy's life." She moved in protest. "You know I love him. Almost as much as I love you. I'll never make that threat again. I won't kill myself. And I won't say I'm going to. Ever again. You believe me?"

"I believe you, Bill." She touched a tear from his cheek. Tommy let out a cry. "Stay here, darling. I'll be right back."

It must not have been the nurse. Jane was leaning over the crib to pull the quilt over Tommy when she heard Bill emit a strange cry. A shot rang out. For a moment, Jane stood, swaying. Then she whirled, ran back to the room she'd left.

Bill lay on the carpet, the gun near his right hand. Blood streamed from his right temple. His face looked puzzled but already his eyes had glazed as Jane leaned above him, cradling his head in her lap.

"*I* didn't . . . ." he stammered. "I didn't lie. . . ."

A film crossed the dark blue eyes as Bill gazed up at her. His life receded as she watched. He lay, immobile, his head in her lap, his blood staining her gown, when people began to crowd in. Strangely, Jane could still hear the orchestra: "Luck, Be A Lady Tonight."

It was Owen who tried to move her. But she remained fixed, only gradually aware that the figures about her held off in a wide arc. . . . The orchestra had finally been silenced. Police had arrived. Then it was possible to distinguish the words that showered down about her, these minutes. These hours.

"He *said* he was going to kill himself. . . ."

"He *said* he had a gun. . . ."

"But did you see how they were fighting? Did you see the way she looked at him?"

"Maybe she did it in self-defense. Maybe she didn't mean to do it."

Jane stared up at the police. Her whole countenance, she was certain, had become only eyes. Before them hung a vision of Michelangelo's Pietà. She could see the policemen's lips moving, the impassive faces. The room appeared to tilt. They were questioning her.

Questioning her again about Joanie? Was Peter in another room? Were they again questioning Peter separately? They'd forced her to her feet. The black gown was wet, wrinkled and stiff with blood. No wonder Bill's pale face was whiter than usual. His blood was on her gown. On her hands. . . .

Of course, Peter wasn't in the other room. The men she became involved with died. Scott was dead. Bill. And Peter . . .

"I'm afraid, Mrs. Hamilton," an officer said, "we'll have to take you in. We're booking you on a murder charge."

"At least let the woman change." It was Owen. His eyes glittered, his pouty lips twitched uncontrollably.

"We don't have all night. It's a long ride to Norristown."

Jane was aware, as they led her down, of faces turning past her, like a kaleidoscope. Harold Channing stood by the wide entranceway, his hands clasped before him, a praying statue. In bewildered surrender, Sid Arkoff held his arms wide. The hubbub of voices cleared to silence as they passed through. Someone had hung the sable coat over her shoulders by the time they emerged into the chilly night.

Before she stepped into one police car (others strewn about the grounds like toy cars left by a child while their overhead lights twirled), Jane gazed back at the castle, bathed in floodlights and by the moon. It seemed to breathe and sigh a message of doom.

Chapter VI

1

Norristown, the county seat, resembled a setting for a small town American tragedy. The shabby main street wound up and down hills. Halloween decorations hung in the dime-store windows. A drunk stumbled as he turned to watch them pass. The town clock sounded three. In her ears, Bill's stammered words: "I didn't lie . . ." His strange cry. Somewhere, beyond his room, while they'd talked, a door had opened and closed. . . . It hadn't been the nurse. . . .

Owen, Harold, Sid, and Cynthia had followed. During the slow hours of the preliminary arraignment, Walter Raney appeared, his face contorted with grief. It was he who repeated to her the words of the charge: murder. He who arranged to post her bond. If she had to stand trial, he told her, she wouldn't be in jail.

Jane nodded, managed a dim smile.

Cool light had spread across the city sky by the time they emerged from the courthouse. Owen wondered darkly if one could find breakfast in this godforsaken town. Walter procured directions to a diner, placed Jane delicately in his own car as though she were a fragile vessel that might shatter.

In the diner a few men, hunched over their Sunday sports sections, turned to stare at them in their evening clothes, exchanged comments. Walter listened to the story the others told, the same they'd repeated several times to the police. Harold, hand over his eyes, sat silent. Mechanically, Jane sipped her coffee, watched the eggs they'd ordered for her congeal on the plate.

"Of course, it was suicide," Walter said. "I'll have a lawyer at New Cardiff this afternoon. George Kersnick. Works for the firm that always handled matters for High

Hills. The grand jury meets tomorrow—you may not need a trial lawyer. But just in case . . ."

Jane would have liked to lay her hand on the grief-stricken face. But her movements had become constricted. What was the animal that rolled itself into a ball in self-defense?

Then they were back at the castle. All but Walter murmuring goodbyes. In the windy sunshine, vans were hauling off the residue of that long-ago feast the night before. Tommy, when he saw her, stretched out his arms, gave a demanding cry. As well she'd begun to wean him. Her milk, overnight, had dried up.

In what seemed a very short time, George Kersnick arrived. Small, round-headed, slightly protruding teeth, bulging gray eyes, a watch and chain across his vest. He'd already made inquiries, he announced, watching her. The district attorney for Montgomery County—Robert Moyer—might be said to be in the pocket of her brother-in-law, Steven Elder. Relations between her and her in-laws were not the best?

In the sitting room between their two bedrooms, Kersnick sipped the coffee furnished by Caldwell. He, eyes rolling, had already managed to take her aside, stammer out his sorrow. For a moment, she'd held his hand. Jane saw that, like her, Walter let his coffee grow cold.

"Yes, suicide, of course," Kersnick intoned. "No doubt of it. Powder burns on the temple from holding the gun close. No other fingerprints. . . ."

Walter sighed. "They'll say she was wearing gloves."

"No." Jane's voice, each time she spoke, had to be dragged up from some stone quarry within. She'd turned, she thought, to stone.

"Not suicide?" Kersnick's fussy eyebrows rose.

"Jane!" Walter protested.

"Oh, I didn't murder him. . . . But he was murdered."

Kersnick sat back. "You have a list of suspects?"

Jane spread her hands. She heard again the unexpected hymn last night. The sound of that door closing beyond Bill's dressing room. His cry. Like footprints in sand, swept by receding waves, the answer sank from her mind.

"I have no suspects. But Bill told me. He swore, just

before I left the room, that he'd never kill himself. And when I came back after the shot—he told me. Before he died. He said he hadn't lied."

Kersnick studied her, made a clicking noise with his tongue. "You'd risk a murder rap rather than some misplaced guilt about driving your husband to suicide? Is this some form of useless loyalty?" She started to speak. He held up his hand. "If you're indicted, you'll plead innocent. You *will* do that?"

"Yes. Technically, I'm innocent. But Bill kept his word."

By noon the following day, the grand jury had met. Odd, Jane agreed as Walter paced the room, that the district attorney should be allowed to share in their proceedings, not her own counsel. The indictment came in. Murder. Kersnick presented himself.

"I imagine Moyer will expect me to ask for a continuance. More time to prepare for the trial." He was wound up, she saw, like a tight spring. "I'm going to surprise him. A speedy trial date might work in this case to *our* advantage."

"How so?" Walter relit his small cigar, bit down on it.

"Publicity surrounding a case like this. All the detritus he may be able to dig up. Given time."

It was Walter who saw to the funeral arrangements. At the small private affair it was possible for Claire, again in her chic black hat and veil, to approach Jane once, to state:

"You won't get away with it, you know. There's no way you'll get away with it."

Steven Elder, at the reading of the will, gripped his hands so that the knuckles audibly cracked. Eight million dollars in cash and securities to his beloved wife, Jane. Five million dollars to his only son and heir, Thomas Scott. And, to his wife, the castle. All his holdings in the Hamilton firm. . . .

"Mrs. Hamilton does not inherit, I believe? If found guilty?" Steven interposed.

"As an attorney, you must be aware of that," the other responded.

Walter, staying on at the castle, suggested Jane read

no newspapers. Kersnick, also ensconced, suggested this was pointless. Just as well to know what was being said. What prospective jurors were reading.

The Sunday papers featured the story. Among other items: that Bill had been five years her junior. His parents had not been dead a month before Jane had thrown the lavish party. An explosive argument between them. Powder burns on the scion's temple suggested suicide. But a trusted and vindictive killer could have held the weapon close enough to the drink-befuddled victim's head. . . . Photos of Bill. The castle. The yawl. How busy they'd been! Jane stared at the picture from the cover of *Life*, another of her onstage at High Hills. The shining hair, the dazzled face, her hands on her heart: she might have been praying. . . .

She was discovering, if she never had, that they—the Fates?—didn't fool around in their harshness. But why was she so stunned? And why had Bill had to pay?

"I've asked," Kersnick announced, "for application of Rule Three-Oh-Five." At her questioning glance: "Pretrial Discovery and Inspection. Involving mandatory disclosure by the prosecutor of any results or reports of scientific tests or expert opinions about the defendant to defendant's counsel."

Her new role. Defendant. "Only about me? Not Bill?"

"I can't ask what they're going to root out about your husband."

Jane met his insinuating glance. She wondered what he knew, about Bill. The dead weight on her heart that held her loyal to Bill kept her silent.

She continued to read the papers. The Israelis, in five days, had captured Gaza, Rafah, El Arish. Taken thousands of prisoners. Occupied most of the peninsula east of the Suez. Jane, moving in confused dreams about playing Cleopatra, woke drenched with sweat. She'd heard Harold Channing's voice. But bending above the body onstage, she saw that it was Danny who lay there, his bleeding head in her lap. It was Danny's voice that said, close to her ear: " 'I am dying, Eygpt, dying.' "

Jane rose from the bed, hurried to Tommy's crib. Moonlight lay across his peaceful face. One knee was thrust up, a chubby brown hand lay enmeshed in the curly hair. Wouldn't he, too, have dreamed? Wouldn't he, too, have awakened?

Telegrams, full of concern, arrived almost daily from the Gurneys, Aurelia. It was surprising, wasn't it, Kersnick asked, as he sat in the upstairs study, papers spread before him. With the news about Israel, the election, everything else—including an item about the death of Salvatore Celucci—there could still be so much coverage of her case? Elvis Presley had appeared on the Ed Sullivan show. Critics had castigated his obscene body movements.

"This is what I mean about a trial involving showbiz," Kersnick noted. "The less time the prosecutor has to develop any details that link you in any unsavory way with showbiz, the better off we are."

Jane finally understood why Danny had not come to her side, had sent no message. The war was suspended after six days. The cable was signed Rachel Edelman.

"Daniel severely wounded. Am praying for both of you."

She should have foreseen this, Jane thought. *Zeal for Thy house has consumed me. . . .*

Aurelia arrived. In her arms, at last, Jane wept. The same day Kersnick revealed that Moyer had indeed asked Jane's doctor for her blood type.

"On the strength of that, I put in a call to your husband's doctor. And your pediatrician. Yes, they've been queried, too. Fortunately, your husband and son have the same blood type. You can't prove a man *is* a child's father. But you *can* prove he *wasn't*." Kersnick turned away. Before Aurelia's knowing stare, Jane lowered her eyes.

Norristown, under dismal wintry skies, was decorated for Christmas when they arrived for the start of the trial. The main street had garlands strung across it. A sidewalk Santa Claus, with a bell in his hand, shivered as he worked the crowds. Christmas music from a dingy department store assaulted the air. The lines fighting to gain access to the courtroom resembled, Jane reflected dispassionately, those that had wrangled for tickets at the box office of *Antony and Cleopatra*. The same good-humored impatience, the pushing, apologies. Just like in the movies. . . .

There was a surge as, accompanied by Kersnick, she emerged from the car. Flashbulbs. Shouting. A few cries of: "Good luck, Janie, old girl!" Several of: "Murderer! Why aren't you in jail?"

The courtroom was handsome, a fine stage set with its gleaming mahogany paneling, shining fixtures. The judge, a large man with long white hair that curled around his ears, appeared both weary and excited. He would call, he announced, on Rule 326. "Special Orders Governing Proclaimed or Sensational Cases," Kersnick whispered.

"The court will make certain that the seating and conduct of spectators and the news media lead to no interference in this investigation," the judge intoned. "The court will also put into effect Rule Three-Twenty-Eight. There will be no photographs in the courtroom or its environs, no television or radio during the proceedings, whether the court is in session or not. These prohibitions will apply to the area immediately surrounding the entrances and exits to this courtroom as well."

Moyer, Jane decided with an almost impersonal dread, resembled General Douglas MacArthur. The *Voir Dire* proceeded against a rather embarrassing series of peremptory challenges of prospective jurors from Kersnick. He'd already explained to her:

"I have to make certain nobody gets through who has it in for anyone that's a showbiz personality. . . . Of course, most of them would kill to get in on this panel. Christmas shopping or not. . . ."

Aurelia had bristled. "Jane is something more than a showbiz personality. And I do wish you'd stop saying showbiz!"

"Not to them, she's not," Kersnick, unruffled, had shot back.

The jury, the judge announced several days later when the final selection had been made, would be sequestered for the remainder of the trial. He was not about to have these proceedings turned into a three-ring circus, nor would he allow them to be influenced by the media or the crowds in any way that he could help. The indictment was for murder. It would be up to them, on the basis of the evidence and arguments they'd hear, to ascertain the degree.

Or decide for acquittal.

Jane studied the faces on the jury as the jury studied her. They were, after all, each individual, "acquainted with grief." But would that intimacy turn them toward generosity or retribution?

More than with any audience, she was in their hands.

2

Moyer's opening statements made clear what he'd demand. First degree. And how, according to Kersnick, he aimed to obtain it.

"He's relying on character assassination, in lieu of concrete evidence."

Among Moyer's points, delivered in mellifluous tones: The defendant had married a man far younger than herself to gain control of his fortune. Defendant's background was questionable. She'd relied on common knowledge of the victim's suicidal tendencies to goad him to despair. The victim had, at this point, everything for which to live. He'd taken over the reins of the Hamilton business. Had a son, so far as he gave out, he adored. Defendant had deliberately set up a situation in which premeditated murder would pass for suicide.

Kersnick's statement was short. The deceased had often threatened suicide, had kept a gun, had perhaps been more upset than he'd realized by the recent deaths of his parents, had been drinking heavily that evening, had quite possibly felt threatened by the presence of many of his wife's old theater friends, had done on impulse what he'd so often threatened.

"Starting low-key—he'll wind up ruthless," Kersnick murmured as Moyer called his first witnesses. Party guests. The story repeated several times. Bill's drinking. The public quarrel. It rather resembled the *Rashomon* story: the differing viewpoints. Claire was called.

"Mrs. Elder. You did not attend this party. Were you invited?"

"We received invitations." The pale blue eyes flicked once toward Jane, returned to Moyer's face. "We thought it extremely poor taste to hold a big celebration immediately after my parents' death."

It was Kersnick's turn. "Mrs. Elder, were you aware of the person who planned the party?"

"I was told it was my father. He handled the details. Possibly because he considered my sister-in-law incapable."

Jane could have sent some object flying toward the fair little head. Kersnick lowered his own. "I wasn't aware my client's intelligence was held in such low esteem. . . . Wasn't your father enthusiastic to have this party? As a belated celebration both of his son's marriage and his grandson's birth?"

"The original wedding ceremony was kept a secret from my parents. Naturally. They considered Jane Belmont odious. They accepted the birth of my sister-in-law's child as their grandson out of the goodness of their hearts. What could they do? They didn't want to hurt poor Bill."

Jane saw Kersnick bite his lip. Claire's little mouth hung open in catlike triumph.

"Mrs. Elder." Kersnick almost spat out the words. "You've been married five years? How many children do you have?"

The pale face remained impassive. "None."

"Your father was extremely fond of his grandson, was he not? Wasn't that very hard to take for a sister who'd always disparaged and despised her brother?"

"Objection!"

"Overruled."

Claire stared above Kersnick's head. "I didn't like to see my father made a fool of."

To Steven Elder, Moyer discreetly lowered his voice. "From what your wife states, are we to understand that there was a doubt in your minds about the parentage of the child born to this marriage?"

"More than a doubt. Everyone knew William Hamilton was impotent. He talked about it himself, all the time."

The judge gaveled for quiet.

"In your opinion, then, did he know the child wasn't his?"

"Objection!" Kersnick was on his feet. "We're not here to take an opinion poll."

"Sustained. Rephrase the question, if you will."

Moyer stared toward the jury. "From your knowledge of your brother-in-law's sexual problems, from what he himself gave out about them, is the child, Thomas Scott Hamilton, the son of William Hamilton?"

"He is not his natural son."

"Objection. This is rumor and innuendo."

"Overruled."

"Thomas was the name of the victim's father. Have you any idea, Mr. Elder, where the name Scott comes from? Is that a family name?"

"Scott was the first name of a colored lover the defendant had when she was young."

Again, the judge gaveled for order.

"Mr. Elder, under what circumstances did you first meet the defendant?"

There followed the tale of his visit to New York to entreat Jane to release Claire from "psychological bondage," a description of Jane's reaction as cold, defiant, insulting, how he'd managed at last to rescue and marry Claire. "Little did we suspect that the woman would get her hooks into her twin brother. . . . I've often wondered if it wasn't simple revenge."

To Jane it didn't much matter about the hints of perjury. Kersnick was still wavering about putting her on the stand. When and if he did, it was doubtful she could escape committing perjury herself. Bill hadn't lied to her. She'd keep their vow about Tommy. That was all she could give him now.

Kersnick had one question for Steven Elder. "If the defendant is found guilty, an enormous fortune left her by her husband reverts to your wife and you, does it not?"

Steven sucked in his cheeks. "That's a likelihood."

"No further questions."

Owen was called. "Mr. Durant," Moyer said briskly. "Were you intimate with the defendant before her marriage?"

Owen's eyes glittered. "There's no way I have to answer that."

The judge leaned forward. "The witness will answer."

Moyer smiled. "I admire the witness's chivalry. Let me put it this way. Would you have been willing to have your child regard the murdered man as his father?"

"Objection! It has not been established that murder . . ."

"Sustained."

"Sorry. . . . Your child look on the *deceased* as his father?"

"No. I don't care for whimperers that are always threatening suicide. And finally do so, injuring everyone around in the process."

"But, Mr. Durant. If you were indeed the father, and were unwilling to marry the woman yourself?"

"Objection! This is all speculative, Your Honor."

"Sustained."

Moyer had, Caldwell had already austerely informed Jane, tried his hand on the servants. But he had no interest in hearing the two had been like lovebirds, always hand in hand. Jane was touched by Caldwell's words, was now mystified at the presence of the next witness, could not place the man until he replied to Moyer's question: he managed a motel between Philadelphia and New York, off the Pennsylvania Turnpike. She saw Kersnick stare at her, and looked away. Outside, it had begun to rain.

Yes, the man told Moyer. Although it was five years now, he could positively identify the defendant as one of the two women who'd stopped for the night at his motel.

Kersnick was on his feet. "Objection! What is the prosecutor's goal with this witness and this line of questioning?"

The judge pulled at his lower lip, signaled Moyer to approach the side bar. There was a hurried conference. Moyer returned to the witness.

Was there any behavior on the part of the defendant, he wanted to know, that would make it obvious why the victim objected to his wife's return to the theater world —thereby angering the defendant?

Oh, the defendant had appeared drunk, right out of it, maybe worse—maybe like she'd been taking drugs or something. Next morning, the maid reported only one of the two double beds had been used. Even as a motel manager, he'd been shocked, he didn't mind telling that right now.

"I will not hesitate to clear this courtroom if I cannot have order," the judge declared, banging his gavel.

Kersnick strutted forward more jauntily than he could have felt. Asked how the witness was certain the defendant had slept in the room at all? The other woman had had to drive the car around to reach it? If Miss Belmont had been so under the weather, perhaps she'd simply stayed in the car? The witness was annoyed, strongly doubted that.

As they left the courtroom, Owen took Jane's arm. "Try not to walk so damn gracefully. Those jurors may resent it."

Kersnick had rallied. "Moyer has no one else to call. He's waiting for his thrust and we'll give it to him. I'm putting you on the stand," he announced to Jane. "If I don't, the jurors may resent not getting their chance with a celebrity. And wonder what we have to hide."

Faith had arrived during the day, helped Jane to wash her hair. Elated, that evening, Tommy crawled from one to the other, crowed with delight. He pulled himself, for the first time, to a standing position at Faith's armchair, emitted a scream when he couldn't figure out how to get down. Faith lifted him to her lap, commented:

"My! Just look at the color of those eyes! I swear . . ."

Smiling, Tommy interrupted. He waved and said his first words: "Nigh-nigh!" Aurelia, at the doorway, observed:

"If only his father could hear that!"

Jane, momentarily enraptured, turned to her. Aurelia met her glance and looked away.

Jane dreamed that night again of Danny. But now he was suddenly transformed to Peter. They were sixteen again, she and Peter, together in the pine grove at High Hills, a bee humming on a shaft of sunlight. Peter, in a blaze of radiance, spoke, but she couldn't hear his voice.

He rose, beckoned, disappeared through the trees

before she could tell him her deep trouble. He was there again but now far off, strange, elegant, in evening clothes and opera cloak as he'd appeared in an ad in *The New York Times,* yet turned away from her. Jane floated toward him and Peter turned again, lifted the cape wide. She understood what he was offering her at last and she closed her eyes in gratitude, came in close, while he wrapped the black cape silently around and around them both.

3

At breakfast, Caldwell placed the morning paper by her cup but could not meet her eye. He—the others, too, of course—had read it all. The testimony was there. The day was windy, a thin sleet falling. Before Thanksgiving, Walter Raney had left for New York. Now he'd returned, determined and bellicose, with Sid Arkoff who gazed at Jane and shook his head, as though in argument with private demons. Several umbrellas blew inside out and many of the crowd outside the courthouse had turned belligerent when they were rejected. Word had got out: Jane was to take the stand. Someone called from the throng:

"Yoo-hoo, Janie! How're your girl friends today?" There was a wave of laughter and catcalls.

Inside, Ralph Gurney waited, tall, imperial. "My dear. I had to come."

Dazed, Jane clung to him a moment, then entered the courtroom. She walked, head high, to the clerk who swore her in. The jury watched with something akin to hunger. Kersnick approached softly.

"Mrs. Hamilton, you have an infant son. How old is he?"

"He'll be eight months at the end of the year."

"You love him?"

"Very much."

"Did your husband love him?"

Jane swallowed. She saw Bill, his cheek pressed to Tommy's. "Very much."

"Was he a good father?"

"The best."

"Would your son be better off if your husband were alive?"

"Of course." The words tumbled out. "The baby said his first words last night. And Bill wasn't there to hear." She saw Moyer's face, knew he'd make her pay for the reaction this called forth from some of the jurors. But he'd make her pay, anyway. . . .

Kersnick let the moment sink in. "Do you wish your husband were alive?"

"Yes. Yes, I do. Very, very much." Her voice trembled.

"Would you ever knowingly or unknowingly have harmed your husband?"

"No."

"Did you kill your husband?"

"No, I did not."

"Your witness." Kersnick walked away, more poised than he could possibly feel.

Moyer moved in, almost visibly savoring what would follow. "Mrs. Hamilton, I'm sure we're all very moved by this little exchange we've just heard. Motherhood and apple pie. Very American. Of course, violence is as American as motherhood and apple pie . . ."

Kersnick hadn't yet sat down, was shouting, "Objection!"

"The prosecutor will confine his expository remarks to his closing statement," the judge intoned. Moyer bowed his head.

"Mrs. Hamilton, you were celebrating a one-year anniversary in October when your child was six months old? I must congratulate you on your efficient use of time."

Kersnick called out during the laughter. The judge ordered Moyer to proceed with his questioning or sit down.

"Mrs. Hamilton, would you describe to the court your first encounter with the police?"

"They came very soon after the shot, I believe. . . ."

"I'm referring, as you must know, to your first encounter. At the age of ten, I understand. With the New York City police."

Jane sent him a glance, mingled admiration and contempt. As she stated, briefly, what had occurred that March day with Joanie, the judge had to gavel for quiet.

"Your sister was never found?"

Jane glanced toward Claire. The swing revolved, empty. "No. She was never found."

"Would you say you'd taken good care of your little sister?"

"Objection! This is irrelevant!"

"Your Honor, if it please the court, I should like to show another reason why the dead victim was so set against the defendant returning to New York with the infant son to whom he'd given his name. . . ."

"Objection! Objection!"

"Because if she could be so careless with a child of five, what might she neglect to do with an infant?"

"Objection sustained. The jury will ignore the remarks of the prosecutor."

Moyer tried, in vain, to hide his small smile. "Mrs. Hamilton, will you tell the court where your mother resides?"

"In a hospital. In New York City."

Moyer turned his back, gazed toward the jury. "For treatment of what?"

"Mental illness." Jane was shamed by her own flush.

"No diagnosis, Mrs. Hamilton?"

"They've varied. Manic-depressive illness has been the predominant one."

"Manic-depressive *psychosis* is the medical term for this form of insanity, is it not? In the manic stage, did your mother give vent to uncontrollable rages?"

"What do you mean: uncontrollable? If you mean . . ."

Moyer interrupted, his reptilian lower lip thrust out. "Have you ever worried that your mother's illness—and rages—might be hereditary?"

"Objection!"

"Sustained."

"Mrs. Hamilton, did *you* ever visit a psychiatrist?"

Jane frowned, the memory was so faint. "Yes. Once."

"You never returned?"

"No."

"Why, may I ask?"

"What he said was ridiculous and irrelevant."

"Did it ever occur to you you might have needed his help? And were resistant to recognizing that need?"

"I thought *he* needed help."

Laughter. The judge gaveled.

"Mrs. Hamilton, in this courtroom you are attended by a friend of many years' standing. Aurelia Anderson is now, if I'm correct, a costume designer out in Baghdad-by-the-sea." Moyer smiled conspiratorially toward the jury. "Sorry. Hollywood. How old were you when you first became acquainted with this woman?"

"Sixteen."

"Did you, some months after you first met, move in with her at an address in Greenwich Village?"

Jane saw Aurelia's tan face pale, grow strangely puffy. "Yes."

"How many beds did her apartment have?"

"Objection!"

"Overruled."

"One."

"You shared that bed with your friend?"

"Yes."

"And when you moved to a larger apartment on Sheridan Square, and you were both making rather good money, as I understand, you didn't lay out any of it for another bed?"

"No."

The judge gaveled for order. Jane noticed Ralph Gurney, his nose lifted in distaste as he watched Moyer.

"Mrs. Hamilton, in those next years, you kept the gossip columnists fairly busy with your comings and goings. . . . You and Claire Hamilton took a trip to Europe in the summer of 1950. Who footed the expenses of that trip?"

"Claire insisted on that."

"Indeed! You *were* under her thumb, weren't you!" Laughter. The judge frowned. "And you had a very good idea of the extent of the Hamilton fortune. *And* the existence of an eligible heir?" Before she could respond: "Mrs. Hamilton, does the name Salvatore Celucci mean anything to you?"

Her heart slowed. "Yes."

"Mr. Celucci very recently died?"

"Yes."

"You visited him at the hospital before he died. . . . Would you tell the court where he last resided before that?"

"He was released from prison to die in the hospital."

"Why was he in prison?"

"He was convicted of income tax evasion. . . ."

"And racketeering? I believe Estes Kefauver uncovered his dealings with the crime syndicate? Was it not revealed that he also dealt in smuggling? Do you know what he smuggled?"

"Your Honor, Counsel is not permitting the defendant to answer."

"You will confine your questions to one at a time."

"I beg pardon. Do you know what items Salvatore Celucci smuggled?"

"I realize . . ." Again, her voice trembled. "I found out he dealt in gasoline, cigarettes. Other things."

"What other things?"

"Drugs . . . cocaine."

"How old were you when you first sniffed cocaine with this Salvatore Celucci?"

"I think . . . eighteen."

The judge demanded order.

"How many times would you say you took cocaine?"

"I didn't count."

"Too many times to count?"

"I don't know."

"Would you say you had a close relationship with this racketeer?"

"Yes. We were close."

"I understand you actually lived in the Scarsdale home of this gangster for close to a year?"

"I was very young. And my brother . . ."

"You moved into this gangster's house," Moyer thundered, "and you slept in the same room! Isn't that true?"

The judge gaveled.

"Is that true, Mrs. Hamilton? Did you sleep in the same room with this gangster?"

212

"Yes. But not in the same bed . . ."

"Did you sleep in the same room with your dead husband, Mrs. Hamilton?"

"No . . ." When would he bring up Scott? What would come up about Scott?

"Then you got this gangster to back a play by a young man you were living with—without benefit of matrimony—before the age of twenty-one? The chance of success with this play was enough to lure you from your lady friend and your gangster friend, right?" Before she could reply: "But it seems you just couldn't remain loyal. Who, exactly, was Scott Williams?"

Outside, the sleet had turned to rain. Jane watched it a moment.

"The witness will answer the question," the judge pronounced.

"Scott Williams was a very dear friend. A very talented folksinger."

"Friend? Your definition of friendship is so unique, Mrs. Hamilton. Wouldn't you also characterize him as another lover? One so important to your life you gave his first name to your son for his middle name?"

"Yes."

"And what race was Scott Williams?"

"Objection. The court has already heard . . ."

"Overruled."

"Scott Williams was a Negro." Somebody let out a low hiss.

"Would you say you got a certain kick from having sexual relations with a Negro?"

"Objection!"

"Sustained."

"This Negro was your lover. Yet, when he was shot to death on the streets of New York, you didn't even go to his funeral? . . . Mrs. Hamilton, were you pregnant at the time of your wedding?"

Jane realized she was rubbing her hands together to warm them. "Yes."

"Was your deceased husband, William Hamilton, known to have a problem with impotence?"

"That was said about him."

"Mrs. Hamilton, wasn't he your scam? Do you know the meaning of that term? You find a mark and make your score?"

"Objection! Objection!"

"Overruled."

"Bill," Jane said in a low voice, "had wanted to marry me for some time. I hadn't actually ever planned to marry. When he was so happy about the baby ... it seemed like a good idea."

"Why, I wonder, was he so worried about your returning to the stage? Was he worried about your predilection for—'friendships'?"

"He may have been somewhat jealous. Though he had no need to be."

"Are you sure? Wasn't your husband, in fact, impotent? Hadn't he always been impotent? Wasn't, in fact, the child he gave his name and fortune to, not his? Did you ever, in fact, have a sexual relationship with the victim?"

"Objection!" Kersnick was on his feet and waving his arms.

"I have warned Counsel. He must allow the witness to answer questions one at a time."

"Did you ever have sexual intercourse, Mrs. Hamilton, with your husband?"

"Yes." Jane almost smiled toward Claire. "I did."

Taken aback, Moyer hesitated, took a deep breath. "Very well. I'll ask this. Was Thomas Scott Hamilton your husband's child?"

This was it. She'd promised Bill long before she'd taken this oath. "Yes," Jane said. "He was." Claire, eyes narrowed, shook her head.

"Then, would you," Moyer demanded, "ask this court to believe your husband, driven to despair, committed *suicide*?"

Jane gripped the rail before her. For a moment, the courtroom receded. Photographs spilled from an envelope. Scott's tombstone. *Had* it been Clyde Simpson? Was he now satisfied? Was Fate? *In my end is my beginning.* ... But why had Bill had to pay? Music appeared to swell inside her head. Scott's voice. The bagpipes in Scotland. The orchestra the night of the party ... *how sweet the sound ...*

"No." Jane saw Kersnick, as though he could compel her to his will, lean forward.

"No—what? He *did* commit suicide, but not because driven to it?"

"No. He did not commit suicide."

Moyer, in triumphant flight toward the jury, stopped short. Kersnick, head lowered, sat back. "Mrs. Hamilton! You *are* admitting then that your husband did not take his own life? Please think carefully. If you intend to change your plea to guilty, you must consult with your attorney."

"Objection." Kersnick's voice was feeble.

"Sustained."

"I'll rephrase my questions. Did your husband commit suicide?"

"No."

"How, then, do you say he died?"

"He was murdered," Jane said. "But not by me."

"I will have order in this court," the judge bellowed. Faces flowed past her vision. Claire, a tiny satisfied smile as she shook her head, this time in triumph. Aurelia, fingers to her lips like an old woman. Kersnick, mouth awry in despair. Moyer smiled.

"Our task is simple then. All we have to do is pinpoint among the two-hundred-odd present that evening who it was that had a stronger motive for murder than you, Mrs. Hamilton. I wonder how we'd do that." He paused. "That's all."

On the way back to the castle, as they had every evening, they passed houses decorated for Christmas. Some floodlit, a few with mangers in the front yard, lights strung on trees. Electric candles glowed in many windows. Wreaths on doors. Upstairs, in many of these houses, children were secretly wrapping presents. In the kitchens, women baked Christmas cookies. People were speaking on telephones, watching TV. Would one ever wish to exchange lives with another? Theirs had reached no heights, perhaps, as had hers. Nor sunk to such depths. . . . Tommy's first Christmas. A year ago, Bill's last.

There were urgent messages from several newspapers and magazines. They wanted first rights to a serialization of her life. Would she return the calls? The evening paper's headline blared: ACTRESS SHARED ROOM WITH GANGSTER, SNIFFED COCAINE.

". . . They are not moral: only conventional. They are not virtuous: they are only cowardly. They are not even vicious: they are only 'frail.' . . ." But when had she begun to use those lines, not as a guide for her own life, but as a condemnation of others?

Most of that night, Jane sat up by Tommy's crib. It appeared to her necessary to identify to herself who she was. Before tomorrow. Before her life was cut, perhaps, in two.

There was a day she'd held Joanie on her lap at the round maple table and listened, with Peter, to her parents quarrel. The swing had revolved, empty. Men drew in colored chalk on the sidewalks and she and Peter had walked, carrying groceries with Papa, toward West End Avenue, crossed paths with Danny Edelman who'd hesitated, guilty to be alive in the midst of their own death. There had been nights with Peter while he spoke of a girl in a Fifth Avenue penthouse. High Hills. Aurelia. *Here Be Monsters.* Hours in Orlando, clinging to someone she must already have recognized as a ghost leaving her behind. Somewhere—everywhere, there—Danny. A day in June she couldn't even now face. The long months in Scarsdale. Sal Celucci. Danny again and *Zeal for Thy House.* In the background of that time with Danny, why had no piano sounded the music of *Sleepers, Awake*? . . . Scott. Claire. The others who'd swept in and out of her life. Triumph and sorrow. Bill and, at last, Tommy. Now this. . . . At dawn, Jane was no nearer to knowing. She tried, unsuccessfully, to put through a call to Israel. If she could only hear Danny's voice. . . . This, her life, might now be falling through her fingers. Like the sands of the desert where Danny, himself, had fallen.

On the way to Norristown, she faced Kersnick. "What do you think?"

He shook his head. "I don't know. I can't see any evidence to convict. But I just don't know. . . ."

To the attentive jury, Kersnick explained that, unwilling to accept her husband's death as suicide, the defendant supposed some stranger had somehow got to him, committed murder. All evidence other than suicide was, however, circumstantial. She'd had no motive to kill. Whatever the prosecutor had brought up had nothing to do with the case. Character assassination was not evidence.

Moyer instructed the jury to look closely at the sort of person with whom they'd been asked to deal. Associations with gangsters. A mentally ill mother. Unnatural sexual liaisons. A compelling drive to return, unhampered by a naive, doting husband, to the stage.

"Remember," he told them. "Whatever it is you've heard the defendant say: she *is* an actress. . . . And, if you acquit, it will always be said of you that you were blinded and humbled by glamour."

They sat, then, in a private room and waited for the jury to deliberate. Aurelia, Owen, Walter Raney, Sid Arkoff, Ralph Gurney, Faith, Kersnick. The papers had made the most of every detail. There were stories of wagers being made on the outcome. Jane laid the papers aside, turned the pages of a book Aurelia had brought along. Coffee was brought in. Sid laid out cards for solitaire.

"How much longer?" Aurelia asked at one point. Her leathery skin, even her eyes, appeared to have paled.

"I just have no idea," Kersnick said.

Deeply, Sid sighed. Owen left to take a walk. Ralph noticed Walter staring at Jane, as though she were lost forever, took his arm, led him from the room. Jane looked down. She tried to concentrate on the page before her. After all, if she ever emerged from all this, there was Chekhov to do, and Strindberg. . . . She was reading a definition of *Katharsis.*

". . . a state of mind produced by the spectacle of tragedy, the stillness of the heart in which compassion and fear have been dissolved, the purification of the soul which springs from having grasped a deeper meaning in things; which creates a grave and new preparedness for acts of duty and the acceptance of fate; which breaks the hubris as it was seen to be broken in the tragedy; which liberates from the violent passions of life and leads the soul to peace. . . ."

She was cold, very cold. It was as though her soul struggled against the message. She'd been surrounded by others so long now. At the very center she was, at last, alone. She relived her deaths onstage. Yes, that definition was what she'd commanded in herself. That had been the meaning of those moments. But each time the curtain—the magic living curtain woven into her being —had descended, she'd reemerged into life. She didn't know if she was now ready . . . "a grave and new preparedness. . . ."

Surprisingly, the jury had returned. "They must want to do their Christmas shopping," Aurelia cracked, her face drawn. They filed back into the courtroom. Jane gazed toward the jury, tried—with something like shy embarrassment—to read the impassive faces. The foreman was called, rose.

"Have you reached a verdict?"

"We have, Your Honor."

"The defendant will please step forward."

Jane obeyed.

"How find you? Guilty or not guilty?"

"Not guilty, Your Honor."

Pandemonium. Aurelia let out a shriek, then a sob. Jane stared at the foreman, at the other faces of the jury. In vain, she waited for that moment to descend, that epiphany.

In a very short time they were out in the corridor again, Aurelia clasping her, Walter Raney and Owen shaking hands with Kersnick, Ralph Gurney clapping Faith's cheeks while Faith lifted her fists in triumph.

"Thank God, thank God, you're acquitted." Sid Arkoff pressed both Jane's hands in his. "I never doubted for a minute you would be."

Beyond the glass doors to the street, photographers waited, cameras held on high. The muffled roar of the crowd grew louder.

"Hallelujah!" Owen sang out, in the tones of a Gregorian chant.

"There's something else I don't doubt for a minute, either," Sid continued, after a moment.

"What's that?" Jane lifted her eyes to his. Perhaps now it would come. That moment. *A grave and new preparedness . . . the acceptance of fate. . . .* She waited.

Again, his hands pressed hers. "I know. I know. They—the world—they'll never ever let you act again."

Part Two

Chapter VII

1

WAS JUSTICE DONE?

Scraps of paper, gold-embossed: From the Desk of Jane Hamilton. She didn't remember scrawling those words so many times. The tabloid, its headline that had prompted her, lay rumpled on the floor. From its page stared the image of her brooding face.

No. The stern voice behind the tabloid exposé, the audience still apparently avid to listen: they didn't consider justice had been done. The death sentence, life in prison. . . . Had the defendant not been so rich, so famous, so glamorous, the jury would have dealt with her —drug fiend, sex pervert, gangster's moll—as she'd deserved. . . . Was justice done? . . .

Obviously, from that repeated scrawl, she questioned, too. From, of course, the opposing view, the night hours' stance of self-pity. Her angular printing, on another scrap, admonished: "Think of THEM!" There tumbled names in illogical sequence: Gershwin, Mozart, Schubert, Keats, Van Gogh. . . . A litany of early loss, the untimely end of promise and of hope. Injustice, all.

Beside those names, how did she and her misfortune signify? That was, quite simply, the lesson she'd set herself the night before, the hours she always spent awake now before the dawn. She could see her face as though on a screen: large dark eyes glistening, moist, staring into the somber garden below, pen held to her lips, pen cast across the desk, a glass lifted to her lips instead. . . .

In the morning light, Jane again perused the list. Justice? Beyond that enigma, underlying all thought, persisted the guilt, the grief for Bill. As though this latest sorrow had released again the pain of an earlier one, the personal affront she'd never really accepted: Peter, dead to *all* possibility before nineteen.... Did it matter, then? Into what interstice of fate, of justice did the loss of her vocation fit?

But she rebelled, could not accept. There had existed, always, after Peter, an essential emptiness at the center of her life, from which she'd watched others and herself as on a stage. Only on a theater stage had life ever since been real. Nothing could repay her the forfeit of this center of her life, after the early loss of her heart's center. She understood, as perhaps never before, how much of her, with Peter, had died.

It appeared to her now—why now, when it was too late?—that all her acting life had passed at the edges of, in the shallow waters of, a vastly deep pool whose depths she'd glimpsed, peered into, but whose mysterious chill she believed—despite all accolades—she'd never really risked. Now that she sensed in herself the courage, the will, the need to dive headlong into those frigid awakening depths, she was placed behind an impenetrable barrier, denied—perhaps forever—access.

It appeared to her at times that, if she herself could never fall deep to those marvels, it might almost be enough to urge another to them, to watch the flash of limbs descending down and down to discoveries now closed to her, but to await the rising up from those depths of such an unknown figure, clasping in its hands the secrets of those hidden glories....

Then she checked herself. The memorable danger of desiring another to emerge "with vine leaves in his hair...."

... Poor little rich girl. In daylight, as she crumpled these scraps of paper, Jane's lips tightened. Was it only a year since she'd said goodbye to Sal Celucci, had learned irrevocably the truth about Scott's death? The death that had triggered all that followed? Who would imagine the widow Hamilton spent time in this manner, filling the wastebasket with scraps of futile desperation? She was rich, beyond calculation. Mirrors, store windows reflected back to her the proud creature presented for public consumption. Fine thick hair tumbling about her shoulders over the dark fur coat, or now—in June—

the linen frock. Graceful carriage, long, elegant legs, fingers flashing rings. In an aura of perfume she floated, head held high. . . .

Who, glancing in her closets, would find it incumbent on them to pity the widow Hamilton? A spending spree after the precipitous return to New York had filled those closets with rows of Ferragamo pumps, with gowns and furs from Givenchy, Chanel, Dior, on padded hangers. A neat array of Jax slacks, of cashmere sweaters, of Gucci handbags. Linen handkerchiefs embroidered with her initials, handsewn underwear stocked the dresser drawers. She slept between Porthault sheets. Across Tommy's carriage, in winter, had lain a cover made of lynx. One day, she'd had all the doorknobs replaced with eighteenth-century French bronze handles.

As though these could ever open again the doors to her life.

The Gurneys, after the trial, had finished their tour, were traveling now in Europe. Aurelia had returned to Beverly Hills. Like an animal running to its lair, seeking sanctuary, she'd come to the townhouse in New York.

It was Owen who'd urged her. If Sid Arkoff could find no one willing to take a chance on her—would Westchester now pay to applaud her?—why not act in a play she backed herself? How better spend her cursed loot?

He hadn't foreseen. The hungriest boys and girls, scrounging for meals, napping in the fourth-floor lounge at Equity, the theater management itself, hadn't the fortitude to buck the bomb threats that venture had brought on.

What next? Escape on the yawl from the reporters, curiosity-seekers still besieging the house. . . .

No, the trip had been Faith's idea, a direct result of the climactic afternoon following the demise of the play. Why had Faith allowed the woman in? Jane had sung her usual songs to Tommy before his nap, had been descending the stairs. There the woman had stood, across from her, at the railing above the living room. Tousled blonde hair beneath a knitted cap, large blue eyes. She'd hesitated, the woman had thrown wide her arms, cried out:

"Jane! It's Joan! Your sister! I've come back!"

In Faith's stunned face near the door Jane, immobile on the bottom step, had glimpsed a collage of what should have been her own reaction. Doubt, joy, incredulity, horror? Initially, there'd been nothing. The woman had taken courage, stumbled quickly into the room, hurried the length of it—a low fire gleamed in the hearth, it was March—while Jane had hung there, staring. It was Faith who'd interposed herself between them.

"Here. Sister is as sister does. Where's your proof? Can't have every female with a free afternoon falling in here to stake a claim . . ."

"No," Jane had said. "Let her speak."

The girl—shabby nubbly coat, red hands fumbling knit gloves, worn galoshes, the poor thing needed money—perhaps hadn't imagined she'd get this far. She'd begun to cry. She was so sorry she'd got down from the swing. Nobody had been paying any attention to her and she'd just got down for the fun of it, to hide a little. This man had come along, had put his hand over her mouth—she realized later it was chloroform in his handkerchief—and he'd carted her off. Living with this nice old couple in California, she hadn't known how to get away, hadn't wanted to hurt their feelings, you know. And—and—but now . . .

"So. You're Joanie." Jane had walked close to the young woman, who ducked her head and sniffled. Jane's hand had shot out, knocked the knit cap to the floor, seized the blonde curls, forced the girl's face up under her own.

"Joanie, where did you sleep in those days before you disappeared?" She'd given the girl's head a small shake. "What was your favorite game—the one you used to make me play with you?" Another small shake. "What was your favorite dessert? Tell me!" The girl had emitted futile squeaks.

"Should I call the police, Miss Jane?" Faith had asked.

"No." Jane had stared down into the round flushed face. "Joanie's going to disappear again. Isn't she?" She'd picked up the cap, handed it over, given the girl a slight push.

It was only after the door had closed that Jane had allowed herself to sink in a heap on the floor. Unable to speak, to take the brandy Faith brought. Simply aware of staring into space as though, eyes wide, she'd died there. . . .

It was the following morning Faith had suggested the cruise on the yawl.

Those first days out toward Key West had been restorative. Privacy, fresh air, the glinting water with the wind whipping off it, clouds butting each other like lazy porpoises, the sails humming. . . . Of course, beyond Tommy's curly head, the constant presence of the crew, the measured knowing glances a couple of them kept sending her. Not far off the coast of Florida, they'd come with the proposal.

How would she like, the two had asked, to use the yawl for a little smuggling? Cocaine and marijuana. Surely it would be a familiar game to her. Grinning and squinting against the sun, they'd told her: "It's a real rich run off these waters."

She'd gone below to Faith, bathing Tommy. Jane had felt her lips pale, her hands shake as she lit a cigarette. "We're turning back," she'd said. "It's no good." And told Faith why.

She'd sold the yawl. In that next month, everything was reorganized. Faith married her longtime beau, Ted Wilcox, and sent for her younger sister, Joy, from Jamaica. The top floor was redone for them. Faith took over cooking, marketing, laundry, Joy, the housework, while Ted performed as chauffeur, heavy housecleaner, gardener, general repairman, bodyguard. Laura Crowell, a small determined Englishwoman in her forties, came on board as Tommy's nurse, shared with him the second floor and—with Jane—unmitigated delight in his sunny disposition.

Some time in the midst of all this had come another reassuring bulletin about Danny. Recovering nicely from unspecified wounds. . . .

Other business: Jane met with Walter Raney. He'd already given up all other work to take over her affairs. Under sharp observation, Steven Elder was kept on at the Hamilton factory. The castle would be converted to a home for orphans, Walter as overseer. He'd already accomplished the first task she'd set him on her return to New York. To find Clyde Simpson.

There'd be no more envelopes from Maryland, photographs of Scott's grave. Clyde Simpson had died in a car crash the week of her trial. Life, and death, appeared at times too pat.

Then, what of Mama?

The hospital had had Mama on lithium for a while now, was nudging Jane to bring her home. Jane had picked her up several times, escorted her to Elizabeth Arden's where she'd had the faded hair restored to pale shining gold, the shyly eager face freshly made up, the nails shaped and varnished. (She looks like Joanie again, Jane had thought, and pressed the cold hand. Mama's eyes had lit up.) On his first birthday, Mama had fussed nervously over Tommy, who'd held her face between cake-sticky fingers, had christened her "Lil Mum." This additional source of love for her own orphaned child somewhat diminished for Jane her sense of the loss Tommy had suffered. She kissed his warm cheeks as she dressed him for bed in his favorite yellow pajamas with the red sailboats crisscrossing them.

But the city frightened Mama. Could Walter, Jane asked, find a nice secluded place in Connecticut where Mama might live with a companion? Walter's gratitude at being of such large use was, as always, disconcerting. His call came quickly. Jane must bring her mother to see the house. Greenwich, on Long Island Sound, was only thirty-five minutes by car. He'd even located the companion: Helen Eustace, in her twenties, had already put in time as a nurse at High Hills, was imperturbable, liked the country. He'd hire other staff.

On the ride up in the Mercedes—they'd made a day of it—Walter had chatted about Greenwich. A wealthy community with all the appearance of a small town: maple-lined streets, single-shopping thoroughfare. Mama would like it very much. Papa would have, too, Jane reflected, shielding Tommy's eyes from the sunlight that shot through the trees on Merritt Parkway as he snuggled in her lap. No Jews. . . . Gratifyingly, Tommy would mar that ambiance.

They'd moved along North Street, past smaller

houses, and out toward intersections with signposts set in neatly clipped hedges. Behind these, Walter explained, lay vast hidden estates. Among them, with a view of the water, hers. . . .

A stone-pillared entry framed the private road that led to a circular parking court with a fountain. Six acres of landscaped grounds. Heated swimming pool. The house was Georgian, replete with sitting rooms, bedrooms, sundecks, terraces, stone fireplaces, servants' quarters, three-car garage. While the others explored, Jane wandered—Tommy strutting flatfooted beside her until she gathered him in her arms—over a masonry bridge. This spanned a narrow stream to a converted grist mill with living room, sleeping loft, kitchen, bath.

"Maybe you'll live here, darling, when you're big," she told Tommy. "When you want freedom from your stuffy ole Ma."

Tommy looked soberly about, stuck a thumb in his mouth, stroked her cheek with his other hand. The thumb came away as he decided: "Tommy big boy."

While settlement went forward, Jane escorted Mama to showrooms and auctions. Mama proved to have retained her good taste, an insatiable appetite for spending. Much of Uncle Ben's money remained, but Mama was secretive about that, preferred to use Jane's. Truckloads of furniture set out for Greenwich twice weekly. "Is that all right, Jane?" Mama would ask, her eyes alight with concern and greed.

"Of course, Mama. We want it all to be nice." For every dollar spent on Greenwich, Jane sent two to the colored minister down South fighting for civil rights.

So now Mama was settled in the country, and urging Jane to come out for the summer with Tommy—June, and so hot already. After her call yesterday—Mama hadn't remembered it was her birthday, that she'd turned thirty-two—Jane had walked for a long, long time. She'd stopped in at the Russian Tea Room, consumed a round of bullshots that had sent her out to the street dazed, searching for a cab. She'd rejected Faith's offer of a light supper—"I made your favorite mustard sauce for the artichoke, and there's heavenly large shrimp, Miss Jane"—had hurried like a dog with its bone to her study, to peruse in secret the tabloid she'd picked up at the kiosk near Bloomingdale's.

It was that night, that early morning, she'd sat at her desk, overlooking the dark garden, and scrawled on all those slips of paper, while she'd filled and refilled her glass of Scotch, setting it down on the picture of the brooding face.

Yes, she had more money than she could ever spend, had Tommy, some reassurance about Danny, had done her part for Mama. But she was cut off from her source, from her talent. Was justice done?

The phone rang, startling her into familiar guilt over the prevailing self-pity. It was Ralph Gurney. They'd arrived only yesterday on the S.S. *United States*. Would she meet them for lunch?

"Yearning to see you, dear." Mary's languorous voice on the extension. "Isn't it lovely McCarthy died? Has it been this hot for long?"

Over salmon aspic and white wine at the Colony, they exchanged news. London theater better than ever. The French, if possible, ruder. The house in Greenwich. The castle with its new sign: Scott Williams Home for Children. Ralph reached out, held Jane's chin a moment.

"You look different, my dear. So—aloof and mysterious." Before his kindly eyes, Jane lowered her own. "You never looked this way. . . ."

"Well, 'that was in another country. And, alas, the wench is dead.'" Jane forced a smile.

"It seems impossible," Mary began. Jane broke in. "Don't pity me. I do enough of that, myself."

"That's not it." Mary sipped at her wine. "We've been so full of our travels, we haven't got to the gist of things, was what I meant."

Jane glanced from one to the other.

"James Hooper sent us his latest play," Ralph explained. "Best thing he's done. Marvelous parts for us both." He read her hopeless, unreasoning query. "And for a young man. But we need someone truly special." Ralph signaled the waiter for coffee.

Jane admonished herself for that unreasoning hope, lit a cigarette. "What's the title? What's it about?"

"He's called it *A Dead Language*. . . . Recognize the source?"

Jane reflected. *"Pictures at an Exhibition?"* Her Julia Richman Latin reassembled itself. *"Con mortuis in lingua mortua*. . . . With the dead in a dead language."

Ralph nodded. "Lovely."

"It's about family," Mary put in. "Parents who've never truly communicated with their son, allowed him to gain an identity. James has obviously discovered psychology. Something about placing a child in what he calls a 'double bind.' "

"By the time the play begins," Ralph added, "the boy is already beyond reach, schizophrenic. The action concerns their recognition of this, his breakdown. . . . Fantastic opportunity for a young actor."

"Does James have anyone in mind? Do you?" Jane asked. (Not: Isn't there a maid's part I can do? A walk-on? Anything?)

"There *is* someone," Ralph ventured slowly. "He already has the script. We're looking in on him tonight. Does readings at a coffeehouse in the Village. . . ." At Jane's raised eyebrows, Ralph hastened to add: "But he's had experience onstage. Nineteen years old. Summer stock. Crowd scenes at the Met and on Broadway. A couple of leads recently off-Broadway. Splendid reviews. He's no neophyte."

Mary gave her slow, languorous smile, her long eyelids drooping. "One drawback. He's too good-looking to be accepted as our son."

"We have boring amounts of business to attend to this afternoon," Ralph said. "But you'll join us tonight, will you?" He pressed Jane's hand.

"Of course." She wondered, when he told her the boy's name—Nicholas Spenser—why it should sound familiar. To find in it what Ralph had mentioned, she regarded her reflection that evening as she prepared to go out. Yes, what she knew to be the wound to her being might appear to anyone else as an aloofness, a diffidence that would hold the other at bay.

At her very center lay a death.

2

At the Village Pump, James Hooper chatted at a front table with the manager. Conversation stopped while the usual bearded youth in faded dungarees and sandals came out to sing protest songs to a thumping guitar accompaniment. During the brief pause for orders—this was not the usual coffeehouse, liquor was served—the manager raised his eyebrows toward Ralph as they all settled in.

"Hear you're interested in young Spenser for Mr. Hooper's play. I was just explaining to Mr. Hooper. You prepared for a package deal?"

James Hooper smiled nervously. "Seems we've landed a whopper of a stage mother."

The manager leaned forward. "Listen. The kid had the lead in that off-Broadway production of *Ghosts?* This mama-lita used to have him delivered to the theater in a limo when it rained." Ralph shrugged. "Nice kid. But he probably lets her change his diapers."

"He *can* act," James Hooper mumbled worriedly.

"Oh, yeah!" the manager conceded. "And good-looking!" He whistled. "Hates to model but he sure must rake in dough on that. You should see the invitations he gets here every night." A smirk. "Everything from debs to Wall Street bankers. Well ..." He stubbed out his cigar, rose from the table, walked to the center of the small stage area, held up his hands. "Ladies and gentlemen, the featured attraction a lot of you've been waiting for. A nice hand, please, for Nicholas Spenser."

To the sound of applause, a couple of piercing whistles, the burlap drape beyond was pushed aside. As soon as he stepped out, Jane recognized him: the beautiful child who'd tried out unsuccessfully for *A Month in the Country.*

Lean, if anything more startlingly beautiful now. Dressed impeccably in sharply creased slacks, polished shoes, a gray cashmere sweater that accentuated the wide gray eyes—those had impressed her even then as wells of light. As he almost diffidently slouched toward the stool set out for him, Jane thought quickly: that posture can hurt his voice in years to come, someone should warn him of that. . . .

Nicholas Spenser settled himself on the stool, adjusted the microphone, gazed around with a large, strange, unblinking stare, as though to memorize each face. It was an exceptional poise that commanded an impressive silence. Jane was aware of that scrutiny resting briefly on them at their table, like a private summing up of who they were, what they signified, to be filed away for his own inspection. As though he were considering them, not the reverse. The lean face with its long bony forehead and high cheekbones, its perfect, slightly aquiline nose, sensual mouth would have been too delicate, exposed, vulnerable, she thought, were it not for the thick flags of his eyebrows that dominated it, strangely shielded it. He sent toward the audience a shy, awkward smile—the result, Jane recognized, of conscious practice.

"Folks." His voice was a little high, a little reedy. He gazed around with that wide stare. "I give you Jack Kerouac." Scattered applause, some whistles. He waited for the perfect silence to return, his left hand—Jane noticed before he thrust it into his pocket—trembling slightly.

" 'The only people for me,' " Nicholas Spenser told them slowly—it was not a reading, he had it memorized —and it was as though he spoke in somebody's living room, assembled his thoughts as he gave his private meditations to one close and private friend, " 'are the mad ones, the ones who are mad to live, mad to talk, mad to be saved. . . . the ones who never yawn or say a commonplace thing, but burn,' " the wide gray eyes sought them each out, made certain each understood, invited them each, " 'burn, burn like fabulous yellow roman candles, exploding like spiders across the stars. . . .' "

For some moments, he continued with Kerouac. Applause. The lights changed, pinpointed his face as he softly announced: "Poe speaks. *William Wilson.*" He raised his right hand. As he delivered his edited version of the tale of the double, of conscience and of ruin, the face grew haggard, haunted, damned.

" 'Men,' " he informed them slowly, " 'usually grow base by degrees. From me, in an instant, all virtue dropped bodily as a mantle. . . . Death approaches; and the shadow which foreruns him has thrown a softening influence over my spirit. I long, in passing through the dim valley, for the sympathy—I had nearly said for the pity—of my fellowmen. I would fain have them believe that I have been, in some measure, the slave of circumstances beyond human control. . . .' "

Somebody coughed. Aside from that, there was only the hush as smoke drifted and curled in the light toward his face. "The boy's a spellbinder," Ralph murmured.

Barely moving his thin frame, Spenser recounted the attack on his masked double. He paused, gazed around, and his voice took on a deepened note of wonder.

" 'It was Wilson; but he spoke no longer in a whisper, and I could have fancied that I myself was speaking while he said:

" '*You have conquered, and I yield. Yet, henceforward art thou also dead—dead to the World, to Heaven, and to Hope! In me didst thou exist—and, in my death, see by this image, which is thine own, how utterly thou hast murdered thyself.*' "

There was a chill on her limbs as Jane joined in the applause. The wide gray eyes momentarily closed, shutting them all out. The lights changed again to a soft blue and the aged face grew young again, fierce, as Spenser launched into a stunning presentation of the son's denunciation of the mother from *Ghosts*. (A coterie cheered as he began it.) He ended, staring into the lights with that disturbing, unblinking command of his eyes, the blank unseeing stare of a statue: " 'Mother, give me the sun.' "

"I'll give him anything, if he'll do the play." James Hooper's voice trembled.

Ralph nodded: yes, yes, yes. Mary's long eyelids drooped, as though to hide a private suffering. They lifted as Nicholas presented himself at their table. The men rose.

"Good evening." With that precise Little-Lord-Fauntleroy manner Jane remembered, he shook hands. Over hers, he paused, the clear contemplation holding her. "Jane Belmont!" There was a rush of color to the thin cheeks. "I've seen you in everything."

It was as though he peered into her brain to dissect her talent. It was unclear how much the shyness was real, what portion feigned. They were all sitting again. While Hooper and Gurney talked, Jane was highly aware of the glances Nicholas Spenser sent her from under those heavy dark brows, and she looked away.

That mantle of aloofness, of indifference Ralph had mentioned, enveloped her like a protective sheath. The boy had been mesmerizing, she'd felt she could listen, watch interminably. Yet here he sat, a very young man, a boy really—she could see the dark roots of his beard in the smooth tan cheeks, his breathing vitality and fragility at once—who was he, after all?—his long nervous fingers clasped as though in self-restraint. . . . Again, she looked away. She disliked in herself the taste of bitterness at listening to their talk of theater, talk that excluded her. A waiter stood at the boy's side, set before him a plate of raw steak, a glass of milk.

Conversation halted. Nicholas glanced at each face with a slow, serious smile.

"I was in Mexico last summer. Picked up amoebic dysentery."

Ralph eyed the dish with controlled concern. "You plan to consume that?"

"See." That slight hesitation. "They had me in a clinic in New Orleans. For two weeks. On all kinds of drugs. A special diet. My intestines were shot. Actually, I still get this acute colitis. Comes and goes." That serious individual scrutiny. "Don't worry. So long as I stick to raw meat and milk, I can control the cramps." He reached quickly in his pocket, popped two pills into his mouth, swallowed milk. "And these. That helps with the diarrhea and bleeding," he explained with something akin to pride.

Jane exchanged with Mary small smiles that deprecated the gaucherie of these details. Nicholas sliced the meat, with his fingers selected a morsel, glanced up, quickly transferred it to the fork, and chewed. Ralph cleared his throat, resumed talk about the play.

He'd direct, he'd already explained. Might they set

up an audition for tomorrow morning? He reached for Jane's hand. "Jane, dear, why don't you drop in, too? We can use your wise counsel."

Nicholas set down knife and fork, placed his hands in his lap and contemplated her. She'd been about to refuse. Why, under that waiting, watchful stare, did she assent? The drinks she'd had—both before coming and here—garbled her thoughts. *What's he to Hecuba?* flashed through them.

Outside, Ralph again pressed her hand, commented: "My dear, you must show yourself tomorrow. You've made a conquest."

"Cradle-robber!" Mary murmured, before ducking into the Mercedes where Ted awaited them.

There was a blaring of horns, a slight mist hung under the streetlights. Despite the warmth of the summer night, Jane shivered for a moment. When she woke, as usual, at three, for the first time it wasn't to that sense of bereavement. Had she imagined it? The way the hair grew on the back of Nicholas Spenser's head. . . . Was it possible she could still recall, so clearly, Peter's?

In the morning, Jane dressed carefully. A dark plaid Mainbocher dress, wide-brimmed hat, slim-heeled linen pumps. The boy was onstage at the Broadhurst when she arrived. Clean and slick as a child on his first day at school. Long-sleeved silk shirt, tan cashmere vest, Brooks Brothers' slacks, polished shoes. Not at all the rumpled effect Method actors went after.

Jane saw how Nicholas invented bits of business, defining the character each moment. She intuited that his strange staccato delivery—breaking up the lines with small pauses—helped the rather high, reedy voice to carry, besides adding an awkward sincerity. He was highly professional. On the seat between herself and Hooper—damp with his usual anxiety—lay a *Vogue* magazine, open to a Cecil Beaton portrait of Nicholas. This stopped the viewer's throat with its stillness, catching all at once the sensuality, intelligence, distinction, and—what was it, too?—a sense of torment in the face that leaned toward the camera.

A voice inside Jane seemed to capitulate. *He's breathtaking*, it admitted.

Later, while Nicholas stood onstage in a muted colloquy with Mary and the stage manager—only some current of electricity in him signaled his triumph—Ralph sat down beside her.

"Our young man was after me. Questions about you. Your air of mystery intrigues him." He bit down lightly on the side of his lower lip. "Why you aren't acting. . . . We're taking him on, of course. Would you believe this? Naturally, we wanted to take him to lunch. But he's running home. To celebrate with Mother. Hey, diddle-dee-dee . . ."

They were walking up the aisle, all of them, out into the sunny street where the heat wave had given way to a day like spring. A slight breeze ruffled the shining dark hair as Nicholas stood suddenly shy, very young, very eager to please, shaking hands and thanking the Gurneys, Hooper, the stage manager. Herself, for coming. Jane saw how he kept watching her. Ralph took her arm.

"You'll come with us, of course?"

"No." There was no forethought. "It's such a lovely day. I think I'll walk. . . . I have some shopping to do." A lie.

Mary sent her a conspiratorial smile. As though in denial, Jane gave a cursory nod to Nicholas, strode into the mingled sun and shadow of Forty-fourth Street, headed toward Broadway. A cab braked nearby, somebody shouted, a blast of horns. A sound of footsteps close behind her. Nicholas fell in beside her.

"Do you mind? I'm going this way. Tell me if you mind."

"Heavens, why should I?" What was this light-headed confusion his presence aroused? She was almost old enough to be his mother. Of that he apparently had already more than enough. They walked on, the air gentle on her forehead as she discarded her wide-brimmed hat, shook her hair loose.

"Why can't *they* put you on in something—the Gurneys?" His voice was abrupt. "They have their own production company. Why can't they?"

Jane sustained a light tone. "Even good friends don't court a boycott. Believe me, good friends they've been. There *are* limits to friendship."

"Are there?" That sober encompassing scrutiny.

"Aren't there?"

They'd turned onto Broadway. Sunlight sparkled in the sidewalk like diamonds. Jane fumbled in her hand-bag, slipped on dark glasses. Tourists were taking pictures of the sign that blew smoke rings. A line had formed outside a movie house showing Brigitte Bardot in *And Man Created Woman*. It was a novel experience: to notice that attention was paid not to her, as they swung along together, but to him. People turned to watch him as they passed.

"You're not a Method actor." Her tone implied approval.

"Nah. I don't go for finding my way to a role through my own personality.... I've seen the way Strasberg works. It's depressing."

She was illogically pleased. "What type of acting *do* you go for, then?"

He was silent so long Jane turned, saw him contemplating her. "I think it's Belmont." He blushed. "And like Olivier, maybe. You know: craft. I think an actor has to study his part, he has to know his character perfectly, I think he has to have it all completely in his hands without wallowing in any depths...."

"Create his own manner? Deliver on cue?"

"Yeah!" He took her up eagerly. "That's it, exactly it!" Again, that hesitation. "Am I wrong? Isn't that what *you* do?"

"You're not wrong." Easily, she changed the tense. "That's what I always *did*."

He stopped so that Jane, too, was brought up short. People pressed around them. From a record shop, music blared: the album from *The Music Man*. "Always did." He shook his head. "That's hell. Miss Belmont, that's hell."

Jane shrugged. The sunlight bothered her eyes. She replaced the hat, hiding her face under its broad brim. "Look. I have to go over to Fifth. I'm terribly pleased with your triumph today. And I wish you the best of luck."

"Miss Belmont!" His hand shot out, dug into the soft flesh of her upper arm. "Would you think me brash if I

236

invited you to lunch? I live just over on Fifty-third, between Fifth and Sixth." He scuffed a shining shoe on the sidewalk. "Naturally, you don't have to . . ."

It was curiosity, of course. To meet, observe the stage mother recalled vaguely from that morning long ago. How old had he been that day? Ten? Eleven? Still, Jane was mildly astonished to find herself turning down the side street with him. As they passed a row of honky-tonk hotels east of Broadway, a man with a toothpick in his mouth, crew-cut hair, brushed against Nicholas, whistled softly between his teeth. She saw Nicholas duck his head, flush, frown.

In the elevator of the small, elegant apartment building, Jane wondered if she weren't intruding on the mother's rightful joy. This compunction was underlined when the door was flung wide, the handsome little woman—her dark hair now slightly streaked with gray —stood before them, arms outstretched, gray eyes shining.

"Well?" she cried out. The glow faded as her gaze found Jane.

"Mom, I got the part."

He stood before her, arms slack, laying at her feet, like a sacrificial victim, his triumph. Quickly, he turned, again laid a hand on Jane's arm. "Mom, brace yourself for a great honor. This is Jane Belmont."

Something in the mother's eyes clicked over, barely disguising a combination of awe, anger, anxiety. Jane was ushered into the apartment where a small round table had been tastefully set up near the sunny window. It would be no trouble, none at all, Mrs. Spenser fussed, to lay another place.

"This is such an honor," she repeated several times, the fury, the apprehension preventing her from glancing directly at Jane. "You must call me Daisy. Nicky, my darling, bring a chair. Look what I've had ready, just in case!" In a silver bucket, a bottle of champagne stood ensconced in ice. "Oh, dear, Nicky sweet, you'll have to find another glass. And then, do the honors, darling, will you?" To Jane: "My son's had lots of practice opening champagne. He's given me a lot of pleasure already." The gray eyes, physically, were his. But their glance darted, like a bird's. "*Young* as he is," she added, her measured stare at last meeting Jane's.

Like a rejected daughter-in-law, Jane bowed her head. She might have been amused but for her solicitude for Nicholas. In his whole manner now she perceived the languorous supercilious calm that overlays an anger—and a grief?—too deep to express. It was a revelation that stirred in her a desire to protect, to gather up and guard him. Above her rancor, as their three glasses met in midair, Daisy smiled and smiled. They drank to Nick.

Almost immediately, Daisy lifted the glass from his hand. Nick's face turned sullen. "Remember, sweetheart. You mustn't drink too much." To Jane, the lips arched in feigned warmth: "He suffers terribly from diarrhea."

"I've heard." Jane took the seat Nick pulled back for her.

Lunch was rice and beef fondue, with milk and two pills for Nick. While Daisy and she cooked their morsels of meat in the hot oil set out in a chafing dish, Nick popped his pieces raw into his mouth.

"Later," Daisy fussed, "you'll have to tell me all about the audition, sweetheart. I'm dying to hear. But I'm sure Miss Belmont is such an old hand at all that, she'd be bored."

Jane hid a smile. "On the contrary. I'd like very much to hear the conqueror's version."

Nick leaned toward her. "I intend to be the greatest actor on the American stage."

"It may be possible," Jane said. A half-remembered vision of white limbs flashing, deep down into waters she's never plumbed. . . . "with vine leaves in his hair. . . ." "Perhaps I can help you in some way."

Daisy cut in. "All Nicky needs is to continue to develop his talent as he always has. As I've seen to it. He's taken lessons in everything, believe me, Miss Belmont. Nothing's been too good for him."

Nick slammed down his glass so that milk shot out onto the damask cloth. "Okay, Mom. Tell our guest all about the sacrifices you made for me. . . ."

Daisy trembled and smiled. "I never saw it that way. You know that."

Nick leaned toward Jane. The large gray eyes widened. He spoke as though this were a litany. "We didn't always live like this, Miss Belmont. When we first came to New York, we lived in a walk-up on West Ninth. We left my father in a little town in California, to go on with his gambling. . . ."

"Nicholas!" Was Daisy trying to stop him or compel him to continue?

". . . but we slept, Miss Belmont, between silk sheets even then. And Mom made sure I began all sorts of lessons right away, when I was eight." His breathing was perfect, the way he brought the phrases out. "See, Mom was once a bit starlet in Hollywood. Till she had the misfortune to go on location. Where she met and married my father. But then she saw me in the school play, Miss Belmont, and God spoke to her in her dreams. She knew we couldn't go on living there. . . ."

Daisy poured herself more champagne. It was as though she no longer cared about Jane's presence, as though this were a lover's quarrel. "The children made fun of you because of your looks. And your natural grace. They used to imitate the way you walked and talked. Calling you Miss Spenser. . . ."

"Oh, don't get me wrong." The heavy dark brows shot up. "I didn't mind seeing myself as superior. I took everything Mom had to give."

"You surely did. Oh, you surely did." Daisy sipped and sighed.

"Finally, my father did right by us. Died and left a whopping insurance policy. We moved here, right, Ma? And *I* began bringing in the shekels, too. There's always a modeling job for a good-looking little snot. . . ." The gray eyes glittered. A long swallow of milk left a slight mustache on his upper lip.

"Good-looking?" Daisy bristled. "You were always more than good-looking! Anyway, I expect you not to throw it all away, now."

Nick emitted a high barking laugh. "How am I throwing it away, Mom? I just got a lead in a play. With Ralph Gurney and Mary Nodine."

Daisy's lips tightened. She sent Jane a half-placating look. "It's not that I don't want Nicky going out with girls. You understand. After all, you're closer to my age

239

than to Nicky's, aren't you! It's just that I have to make sure he conserves his energy. . . ." She ignored another bark of laughter. "And remains on the high moral plane I reared him on." Without warning, the eyes flashed, the voice grew sibilant. "No vulgarity. And no scandal, Miss Belmont! Nicky is a young innocent boy."

It was certainly, by now, time to speak. "Do you think I'd harm him, Mrs. Spenser?"

Daisy caught her breath. Her hand went to her throat. "I didn't say that. I didn't mean . . ."

Jane rose and smiled. "I really must be on my way. It was good of you to include me. Thank you so much, Mrs. Spenser." She looked down into the gray eyes alight with victory and concern. "Believe me, I admire your son. And everything you've done for him." An incoherent sound from Nick. "As well as what he's done for himself. I can only wish you both the best of everything."

Nick was on his feet. "I'm walking you home."

"Really, there's no need."

"For me, there is."

They were on the street again, walking in silence. She didn't know quite what to say. At last: "You know, when you were just a little boy, you came to audition for *A Month in the Country*. The other boy got it. But I was on your side."

"You remember that?" His smile was tender, as though she'd awarded him a gift. "Believe it or not, eventually I did the tutor in summer stock." They walked on. "That's the problem. She *has* done so much for me."

Again Jane tried to keep her tone light. "I suppose nobody's mother is ever entirely right for them." Abruptly: "Don't you have a girl?"

"Oh, sure."

In a flash of intuition, Jane knew he was lying. Probably a virgin, too. They were on Fifth Avenue, walking toward the park. He was obviously deep in thought. "She never listened," he burst out. "Whatever she told her husband, that became truth. So when the son *tried* to communicate, she never really listened!"

A moment of confusion. "I thought you said your father . . ."

The high barking laugh. Two women, approaching, the breeze whipping their dresses about their thighs, smiled in sympathy. "I'm talking about the play. The way Erin O'Neill keeps moving back behind a veil—a shroud, really—where it's the only place he can be himself. Because neither of them, but especially the mother, ever listened."

He began to speak about the part. It was evident the thought hadn't been far from his mind all these hours. He'd had the script a week now, already knew almost every line. All the way to Third Avenue and Sixty-first, they discussed his role. As they approached the house, Nick hit his forehead with the heel of his hand.

"You wanted to do some shopping!"

"Not really." Jane smiled. "Come in and meet my son."

He was shy, eager, pleased. Upstairs, Laura Crowell was slipping Tommy into fresh overalls as they entered the big room full of sunlight, paintings, toys. Tommy emitted a shriek of joy at sight of Jane, wrested free of Laura's grasp, hurried in his flatfooted gait to be lifted in the air, hugged, kissed. Over her shoulder he spotted Nick, gave a shy smile, grasped a lock of her hair in one hand, a lock of his own in the other.

Over introductions, Jane saw how Nick's slow dazzling smile brought to Laura's small, squashed Pekingese face a blush with something akin to lust, how Nick derived from this an obvious pleasure, the gray eyes shining like a lover's. Back on the floor, Tommy regarded him soberly.

"Hey, hey!" Nick crouched to Tommy's level. "What have we here? Can I have a feel of those curls?"

With a gentle smile Tommy grasped Nick's hand, guided it to his hair. Nick ran his fingers lightly through the brown ringlets. Then he was on all fours.

"How about a pony ride? Know how to ride bareback?" he asked.

Tommy giggled, hoisted himself up, grunting with effort, onto Nick's back. Nick began to run about like a large spider, narrating the difficulty of avoiding the blocks, wooden puzzles, furniture, while Tommy grasped his neck and shouted with laughter. Nick tossed him lightly to the floor, sprawled beside him, brought his face close.

"Wanna see something, fella?" In a moment he was on his hands, walking across the floor. Tommy doubled up with laughter that turned to awe. At the fish tank, Nick halted, imitated the gaping mouth movements, padded on, ending with a somersault. Tommy immediately tried to follow suit, landing on his side.

"Fan-TAS-tic!" Nick cried, and gave his high barking laugh. He lifted Tommy into the air, then crushed him against his chest in a hug. Tommy snuggled against him. Laura had watched the pyrotechnics with her hand to her throat. Jane let out a breath.

"You've made a conquest."

"So has he," Nick said. Suddenly, he appeared stricken. "Hey! What time is it? I have to get home and shower. I'm on at the Pump in a couple of hours!"

Jane, at the door, thanked him for walking her home, wished he had time for a drink, that he'd had a better way to celebrate the day.

"This wasn't celebrating? Spending the day with Jane Belmont?" He appeared very young, very vulnerable, as he slouched there.

"Kerouac's lines last night," Jane said, on impulse. "Did *you* mean what they said? Or was that acting?"

"Oh, no. . . . 'The only people for me *are* the mad ones, the ones who are mad to live . . . who burn, burn. . . .' "

Then he had grasped her hand, crushed it painfully in his, was gone. Jane leaned against the door, her fingers where his had been. Danny's warning about reconstituting the family returned to her. And more: the image of a moth dancing around a flame. . . .

3

A line throbbed in her head. *How wayward is this foolish love.* . . . It obsessed her as she ordered Laura to pack

Tommy's things, had Ted Wilcox bear the three of them off to Greenwich. She was in flight again, could not confess to herself that this time it was from a demon she carried within. After only two days, she was in a large outside cabin on the S.S. *France*. The line beat on with the rhythm of the glittering waves beyond it: *how wayward, how wayward. . . .*

At Cannes, Jane lay on the golden beach and watched, through narrowed eyes, behind sunglasses and under a wide straw hat, the young girls in their bikinis, their smooth skin shining with oil. She glanced down the length of her own legs, still firm and supple. These days she'd begun to lavish moisturizer on her face, body oil on her limbs as never before. Everywhere, as she drove back and forth in her rented car on the Corniche —the pervasive fragrance of carnations and lemon trees, the blazing colors, the radiance of the sea—at St. Tropez, at Cannes, at the Hotel de Paris at Monte Carlo, there were lovely young girls. Or beautiful young men in pairs. Especially she noted the old women with haughty young men in tow.

She wondered. Was this what she'd brought herself to witness? She stopped in at the museums of Antibes and Vence, couldn't concentrate. At a sidewalk at Cannes where she sat alone sipping Pernod, she allowed herself to be picked up by a film producer from Paris, boarded his yacht, sniffed cocaine. It made the sex so much easier.

Alone again on the way to Paris, she stepped off the train at night at a rural station. Stars glistened in the black sky, there was the high cry of another train whooshing south, a smell of cinders in the air. Like the thrust of the train, like the rush of cocaine came a swift access of joy, as though everything were, after all, possible. But what she meant by everything, as she stepped back into her *couchette,* she couldn't say. For a long time Jane sat encapsulated in the rushing dark, her forehead against the window.

In Paris, it rained. Days of gray, lowering skies, gray buildings, gray streets, gray river—as though the city's promise were veiled in shrouds, to be revealed at last at night when lights glittered in the river and streets turned black and shining. She was taken up by Albert Poster, still living on the publishing and film royalties from the war novel he'd written years ago at twenty-six, *The Mighty and the Damned*. He was short, good-looking, pugnacious, fed her Scotch and marijuana in his room at the George V, read her great swatches of his new manuscript. When he got her into bed, it turned out he had a thing—she'd heard that—against birth control.

"Thanks," she said. "But no, thanks."

She was no longer in flight, she decided, sailed home, hurried directly to Greenwich. What she most needed—an actual physical need—was to sink her lips into Tommy's soft round cheeks. She gathered him, brown and sturdy, into her arms, only reluctantly let him down so he could show her how he'd learned, already, to swim in the pool. "Mommy, mommy, look!" His stamina was heroic as he showed off for her, drops of water hanging from his lashes, sunlight glinting off his wet arms.

Jane now sent Laura off on holiday. It was the only way to have her child to herself. In the early mornings they romped barefoot in the wet grass sparkling with dew, later swam, built castles in his sandbox, picked wild raspberries. When Tommy napped, Mama engaged her in demoniacally competitive games of croquet, only occasionally allowed her to lie about and read. She was, Jane felt at last, restored. An awful, undefined danger had passed. By the end of September she was eager for the sunny windswept streets of New York in the fall.

At least, so she told herself.

Not that she'd returned in time for the opening of *A Dead Language*. She had flowers sent, with a warm message, to the Gurneys. To Nicholas, too. Over the phone she hesitated over what the note to him should read, at last simply instructed the florist to sign it with her name.

In a new Balenciaga gown she moved on Owen's arm —"You're particularly glowing this evening," he observed—through the crowded lobby of the Broadhurst. The excitement reminded her of *Antony and Cleopatra*. Harold Clurman, Brooks Atkinson, Walter Kerr seemed to pass to their seats on the waves of it. Inside the *Play-*

bill, facing each other, were photographs of the Gurneys, the Cecil Beaton portrait of Nick. Owen gazed at her curiously as her fingers tightened on the page. Behind her, a man was reading aloud to his companion about Nick in the Who's Who section. Avidly, she listened as she gazed toward the dark red curtain, rustling with that mysterious life.

Gradually, the houselights dimmed, the footlights came on like small waves washing toward the curtain. There was that intensity of silence and the curtain rose with that swiftness that always cut the world in two.

Applause, as Mary Nodine was discovered drinking coffee and writing at a secretary, stage left. Elegant living room with garden at stage right, stairs descending to stage center. Mary rose, walked to the foot of the stairs, gazed intently upward, turned as Ralph entered from the garden. More applause. Mary spoke. A discussion of their son. A brief argument. Mary returned to the desk. Ralph stood at the small table to fix drinks. Jane tensed.

As Nicholas came down the steps to scattered applause, there was the same rush of joy through her abdomen that she'd known that night at the station on her way to Paris, the rush that had reminded her of cocaine. To Jane, he appeared larger than life, crossing gracefully, despite the slouch, to stage front. Obviously, it was his line. Jane's fingers curled into tight fists. What was he waiting for? How could he take such a chance, so prolong the silence? He turned, gazed out over the audience, turned back. At last, he spoke. The entire audience appeared to release its breath as she did. Daring, bordering on the reckless . . . !

At intermission, Jane knew she had not imagined it, the phrase was on others' lips, too. Tonight's was a historic performance. Women's eyes had brightened, their cheeks had flushed beneath the rouge. She was aware how she kept her face averted from Owen: he mustn't read there what would be so obvious. The houselights gave their warnings and she hurried toward the darkness where she could be alone, as it were, with Nick.

The second act, taut with tension, moved swiftly. She was not fantasizing: the same surge of protective tenderness she'd known at Nick's apartment went forth from the audience as the young actress attracted to Erin O'Neill reached out to touch him, and he cringed. The embarrassed strangled phrase was whispered, yet audible, throughout the theater.

"Careful!" He smiled apologetically, the overhead lights illuminating those eyes. "I'm made of glass."

Later, when Ralph smashed a goblet and Nick emitted an anguished animal cry, arms limp at his sides, gaze darting wildly at the floor around him as though to find himself shattered, a shudder ran through the audience.

The applause was accompanied by shouts of "Bravo!" The Gurneys led Nick forward for a separate bow on a stage massed with flowers. Later, there was a tremendous crush in the struggle to reach backstage. James Hooper loomed, eyes glassy, face damp. People were wringing his hands. Jane was pushed forward, wrapped in his embrace, congratulating him. The surge carried her and Owen to Ralph's dressing room. Over someone's head she caught sight of Daisy, just entering another door.

The babble of voices, the aroma of perfume, the press of bodies were overwhelming. There was one moment when she was in Ralph's arms, then she was swept on, into Mary's dressing room. Champagne spilled over her hand and gown as she accepted a drink. Owen towered above the others, was speaking to Hooper, brought in on the surge of the crowd. Jane pushed her way out. Between her and the door where she'd seen Daisy stood the stage manager.

"Sorry, Miss Belmont. Mrs. Spenser's order. Nobody's to be let through just yet."

Jane didn't know if it were resentment or a sense of reprieve she felt. The door opened and Daisy, flushed with victory, skipped out, as though for a moment. Nick's head emerged. He saw Jane. In one movement he had grabbed her arm, locked the door so that they were alone together. He stood waiting, the gray eyes full of light. Jane hesitated.

She was this individual who'd been in flight with her pride, her vulnerability. But he was this other who stood before her, who onstage had somehow at once both illustrated and destroyed the barrier between what it was to be male and female, between immediacy and eternity, who had brought together the particular and the universal so that, for a short time, chaos was eradicated, everything understood. She lifted her gown slightly and bent in a deep curtsy to the floor.

"I abase myself to your talent," she told him.

Then they were in each other's arms and Jane felt his heart racing, his wiry body wet with sweat, trembling. There was a clamor at the door. They broke apart. For one more moment he sent her that long, unblinking stare, at last opened the door to Daisy, to the crowd beyond.

There was no time at Sardi's when Jane could get close enough to speak to him again. This enabled her to watch as others did—openly, with a smile on her lips, in reverence. He was sweet, deferential, his dark brows lowered in concern as he listened to the analyses of his performance. She was very aware of the pervasive sensuality he projected, it was as though they were all in love with Nick, with his every expression and gesture. The general adulation made it the more disconcerting when Owen gripped her hand under the table, whispered:

"Don't look at him like that, my love. He's never going to be for you. For me, maybe, yes. But not for you."

Jane rose, ascended to the powder room, passing as she did so her picture on the wall. Upstairs she gazed into the mirror and remembered her own young triumphant face the opening night of *Here Be Monsters*. By the time she returned to the table, the papers had arrived.

They came through, all of them, of course, paying homage to Hooper, to the Gurneys, to Ralph's direction. As though at last released, to the performance by Nicholas Spenser. An actor of tragic dimensions who combined both strength and delicacy. They spoke of his sensuality and sensitivity, his intelligence and sincerity, his naturalness and spontaneity, his combination of self-ridicule and self-respect, his distinction and overwhelming talent. Several mentioned the uncanny fashion in which he'd aped Ralph's mannerisms, his way of speaking, biting his lower lip, so that he truly appeared to be Ralph's son. One advised: "Mark September 1957 down. Tonight history was made."

Jane spent almost the entire night—what was left of it—awake, pacing from bedroom to study and back, at last going out into the garden to walk there. She wondered if, after all, Nick's principal appeal lay in his age, the fact that he had this life still to shape—the same age as Peter when he'd lost his. Before dawn, she took a sleeping pill, awoke in a couple of hours. The morning light brought a harsh answer. Nick was on his way. She could merely be one of those who stood on the sidelines to cheer him on. What else?

He did call her, twice, when she wasn't in. Self-protective again, Jane didn't return the calls. There were many parties that fall, she was amply busy with details about the children at the castle, with Tommy, there were visits from Mama who insisted on total attention. Still, Jane knew she was keeping tabs on Nick's progress. Articles kept appearing in the weeklies, interviews, pictures. He was busy enough, himself, with his lessons in voice and dance. He worked out regularly at a gym. One photo showed him, barechested and surprisingly hairy, hanging upside down from hand loops.

Toward the end of October Jane's usual insomnia mounted as she relived the party at the castle only a year ago. Guilt and sorrow for Bill tormented her. Now, in November, a year ago, she'd awaited the trial that had cut her life in half. Refusing an invitation from Cynthia Blackwood for lunch and a fashion show, Jane went instead one Monday afternoon that first week of November for a walk on Third Avenue. The els were long gone, new tall buildings were going up. There was the incessant sound of drilling at one corner, then sirens, then comparative quiet. On impulse, she stepped into a rundown bar, putting off—till this sense of despondency, of being at loose ends, should mitigate somewhat—coming home to Tommy. He was often sensitive to her moods.

She ducked into a dark corner, gave her order, sat and watched a sullen man in his early forties—cabdriver? unemployed?—bent over the bar. . . . How differently Americans drank from Europeans: like animals hiding in the dark with their prey. A slash of light fell across the bar as the outer door opened, the gloom enveloped it again as a young man in jeans and dirty jacket hunched in. He leaned against the bar, raised a hand to the bartender, said something. A young hoodlum. When he turned to the sullen man beside him, Jane saw—with a catch at her throat—that it was Nick.

For perhaps ten minutes she sat motionless, a voyeur, watching Nick with garrulous good humor gradually unwind the stranger from his mood. By the time she held her gold lighter to a cigarette, the man had wrapped his arm about Nick's slim shoulders, was hitting the bar with his fist. The flame of the lighter attracted the bartender's attention. He jerked his chin at her.

"You okay, lady? Ready for a refill?"

Nick turned, the slack grin on his thin face changed to startled recognition. He cast the man's arm from his shoulders, gave him a swift absent jab in the upper arm, grabbed his drink and moved with something like uncertainty to her corner.

"Jane? What are *you* doing here?" As he leaned above her, the tension she'd carried within her this month was released in a flood of joy.

"I might say the same. Aren't you under age to be drinking here in a bar? Sit down." He pulled out the wooden chair opposite her, crouched into it and searched her face with that demanding unblinking stare. "Who's your friend?"

Nick shrugged. A small deprecatory smile pulled at the fine lips. "Crazy hobby. I like to drop into bars, light into some honcho, string him on." He gave a quick look around where the man—watching in surly disappointment—turned back to the bar. Nick's voice dropped, his voice slurred. "Give a dame an inch—I'm tellin' you! one fuckin' inch is all you gotta do—and they got you by the goddam fuckin' balls. My fahdda tole me dat alla time I wuz growin' up—you tink I evah lissened?" The mimicry was perfect, even the eyes had dulled to an animal stupidity. They cleared and he grinned. "You probably think I'm rotten. Or crazy."

That night at the Village when he'd joined their table, she'd had the same thought. He was, after all, only a boy, a person like any other, not larger than life as he'd momentarily seemed. Today, the growth of two days' beard covered the tan cheeks. There was a flash of thin bare ankle as he crossed his sandal-clad foot over one knee. He was only a person like any other. She remembered the feel of his warm, sweating body as they'd clasped one another in the dressing room, and smiled. The smile released a fraction of her hidden joy.

"Of course I don't think you're rotten or crazy. I do wonder. About your being under age. At a bar like this."

The heavy dark brows drew together. His lips twisted. "I'm twenty today. This is celebrating my birthday." Suddenly, his Adam's apple worked up and down. "My mother wanted me to go out alone with her, of course. But we had a fight. I had to get away. I had to be alone." Quickly: "I mean, alone away from her." There was a quick shine of childish tears as he averted his face.

Again that rush of protective tenderness. Jane reached for his hand. "Nick, what is it? You're doing so well. Aren't you happy?"

The face he turned back to her was barren, stark. His voice had a hollow tone. "A horror. . . . There's a horror growing inside me," he blurted. " 'Men,' " he intoned, his eyes wide and blank as he stared at her, " 'usually grow base by degrees. From me, in an instant, all virtue dropped bodily as a mantle. . . .' " The clasp of their hands changed. His now gripped hers, painfully. He grimaced. Then, that staccato bark of laughter. "I'm kidding. I'm only kidding. . . . Why haven't I seen you? Why didn't you call? I thought you liked me!"

"I do." It came from her in a rush. "I like you very much. Your life, from my distance, looked very busy. I didn't think . . ."

"I figured to you I was small potatoes. I mean, I thought about you a lot. . . ." That slow enunciation, as though he read his words from her face. "You seem so independent, so mysterious. . . ." Again, that bark of laughter. "Don't worry that Daisy isn't happy you're not around. Hey, know what she said?" Jane wasn't certain she'd like to hear. "You're the Hamilton candy fortune. If I see you, I'll start eating sweets. Sweets have always been a no-no!" The heavy eyebrows shot up with wonderment and anger as he stared at her.

Suddenly, they were both laughing. The sullen man at the bar sent over a threatening glance, threw money on the bar, walked out. The bartender, wiping the surface, watched suspiciously.

"Come on," Jane said. "*I'm* taking over your birthday."

Chapter VIII

1

Later, she supposed that was when it really began. Nick beside her as she steered the Mercedes across the George Washington Bridge and into the country, where the setting sun touched the last of the autumn foliage ablaze. Dinner at a country inn in the Poconos, overlooking the tranquil Delaware. On the water a lone fisherman's boat bobbed up and down.

They took separate rooms for the night. At dawn, Nick insisted they must seek out—slipping along the leaf-clogged paths—the owl he'd heard calling through the night. They never found it but, perched on a high rock, recited lines from plays. If the other couldn't guess the source, the next turn was forfeited. An argument about *Cymbeline* turned into a scramble in which they tossed armfuls of leaves at one another. With a sudden access of tenderness, Nick combed them from Jane's hair with his fingers, his still unshaven cheek against hers, his breath warm.

"This," he said, "was the best birthday I ever had."

After that, there was no question. If they couldn't get together, Nick phoned. Even if they did, he called later. Between his lessons and the gym, before performances, they argued about his next role. Offers from Hollywood kept arriving.

"I saw you and that gorgeous Nicky Spenser arm in arm on Madison Avenue yesterday," Cynthia informed her. "You certainly looked all wrapped up in one another. What gives?"

Jane's reply was evasive. She was growing accustomed, she confided, to the way people—even those who didn't recognize him—turned to stare at Nick's beauty. When they did, they squealed, screamed, followed him. Nick smiled, turned pale, clasped Jane's hand, ducked with her into hiding. He was aware of his beauty, aware, both proud and self-conscious about it. A top model agency selected him, despite his age, Most Eligible Bachelor of the Year.

Owen, whom she rarely saw these days, scoffed. "Eligible bachelor! Since when's a pansy an eligible bachelor? No sour grapes, my love. Nothing could go on between you that threatens *my* balls."

That there *were* only embraces, only kisses, held Jane silent. Yet the situation felt right somehow, familiar. She'd dreamed again of swimming alongside Peter in the lake at High Hills. In the dream, again, she lost him. But this time he returned, moving below the surface beside her. When they crawled up on that mossy bank where Alec had taken her, she turned in her dream to find that it was Nick. . . .

Jane took Nick down to the Lower East Side, past the open-air stalls of clothes. When she decided to fit him with a new jacket for spring, the expansive salesman nodded and smiled. "Oy," he congratulated her, wagging his head. "Some *shaneh mensch!* Boyfriend?"

Jane smiled noncommittally.

"Nice voik," the salesman said. "So? Vat's a few years?"

"An even dozen." Nick grinned, raised his dark eyebrows in surprise as Jane winced.

Aurelia called from the Coast. "Hear you're shacking up with the *wunderkind* of New York."

"You hear wrong."

"The shacking up? Or that he's a wunderkind?"

"Oh, not the latter. That's not wrong."

"Hm. . . ." Aurelia arrived, flying in for a weekend visit, saw the play. "Yes. I see what they mean. Broadway won't keep him long. Let me know when he tumbles for Tinsel Town." She peeped into Jane's face. "And then what, my darling?"

Nick kept meticulous scrapbooks of his career. One evening, in her bedroom, he asked to see hers. As he sprawled across her bed, the item about her leaving the cast of *Here Be Monsters* caught his attention. Why, he asked, had she left at the height of her triumph? Jane, propped against the headboard, looked at him a long moment. His face faded into Peter's. . . .

She let it happen: again, she was drinking coffee in the kitchen at Sheridan Square, Jack Tanner purring on her lap. The ring of the phone. The blow to her belly. The blind stagger into the other room, the swing crashing into her back as she stumbled and screamed. . . .

Nick's face swam back into focus. Slowly, then in a tense rush, she told him of Peter. "That kind of pain never disappears completely. But something I never thought could happen. . . . Someone *can* come along to fill that empty space. To live in your heart in the same way." Wide-eyed, Nick watched her. "With you, my life swings up again. As though I've been returned a life to make up for Peter. You're my acting life now too, Nick. When you come onstage, I'm there, too. Do you know that?"

He moved close. Solemnly, they exchanged a long, chaste kiss.

Intermittently, those "horrors" Nick had mentioned on his birthday inexplicably returned. He dealt with them with an assortment of pills, most with some element of opiate. Boasting: "I've a whole private pharmacy. I really know about pills."

One day Jane awaited him at the Museum of Modern Art. She hoped they could get through it without too much furor. Nick had an aversion to autograph hunters. "What Einstein called the last vestige of cannibalism," he grumbled. Jane understood that he, like she, felt a curious ambivalence toward such fans.

Seated in the lobby as she read a brochure, Jane became aware of a group behind her—what Owen liked to call "flaming faggots," the sort who flagrantly advertised.

"Ooh, look at her, is she something?"

Another responded: "You can have her, I'll take the one coming out of the elevator."

The *shes* and *hers,* of course, were men. Several women nearby expressed shock and annoyance to one another. As Jane lit a cigarette, one leaned toward her: "They shouldn't be let out of their cages."

Jane sent her a cold stare. At that moment, there was commotion in the group.

"Help, I'm going to faint, she's slaughtering me!"

Intuitively, Jane knew. Nick, just inside the entrance, saw her, saw them—one of them advancing. He wheeled about, fled into the street. When she caught up with him, he was clutching his belly, pouring pills into his mouth. To no one, he mumbled something that sounded like "the horrors." . . . Jane tugged at his arm.

"Nick! What's got into you?"

"I hate mental illness." His face was haggard. "I . . ."

"Those boys? They're *not* mentally ill, Nick!" They passed onto Fifth Avenue and he pulled away from her.

"They *are!* With their bleached hair and their makeup and their simpering. . . . They're sick, they're diseased." His steps slowed. "And if not, they're evil! *Evil!*" His twitching lips were stained green by the capsules he'd swallowed. "Still, at least they're honest. I hate deceit! I hate pretense! I *hate* it!"

Suddenly, he was running from her, head lowered, as he knocked blindly into people. At the next corner he just as suddenly stopped, stood looking up at the tall buildings. When she reached his side, he was humming and grinning.

"How about afternoon tea at the Plaza?" he asked.

Daisy, when Jane infrequently dropped in to pick Nick up, displayed a fine control over her rage. She'd selected a clever ploy: to treat Jane as a colleague in maternity, someone to watch with her over a child they both loved. Wouldn't Jane try, she begged, to stop Nicky from looking a bum in those jeans, the frayed leather jacket he often now wore? Would Jane see to it that he ate properly, took his medicine, watched his language?

"I brought Nicky up to be a gentleman," Daisy announced.

"You know what, Mom?" Nick shot back. "Fuck being a gentleman!"

Daisy's thin, handsome face paled. "I know you only use such language to rile me, Nicky darling." To Jane: "He never used to speak to me that way before."

2

Toward the end of spring, Daisy's anger slipped out of control. Nick's cramps had begun to double him over with pain and Daisy confronted Jane. "It's you that's doing this to him. You take him out drinking and heaven only knows what! You've got a two-year-old son! Why don't you spend time with *him*, instead of corrupting young boys?"

Jane knew Nick's cramps were largely a result of his constant stage fright. Also, she couldn't have explained that the flow of emotion released for Nick made her love Tommy, if possible, even more. She brought Tommy out that week to stay with Mama in Greenwich, swam alongside him in the pool as his sturdy brown arms and legs thrashed. Later, as they lay on the grass to dry, Tommy discovered a long fat worm for whom he concentratedly built a bower with leaves and twigs. By the end of half an hour, Tommy's ministrations were proving almost beyond the worm's capability to cope.

Jane intervened, pointed out to him the various types of sailing boats that skimmed the Sound. He was quick to learn their names and, that evening, as Jane read to him *Millions of Cats*—Tommy's curls damp from his bath, his warm presence redolent of soap and zwieback —she had an idea, took him with her next day to the Cape.

There she rented for the summer a sprawling house tucked into an inlet that overlooked the Wellfleet bay. Even if they weren't there continually, it would be good to have available—also like some link between Tommy and Danny. Surely it was no disloyalty to Bill to bring Tommy to that little bookstore restaurant on the waterfront where she and Danny had eaten that first evening in Wellfleet? From his highchair, Tommy excitedly identified the boats coming in with their running lights, just as they had that evening long ago. Jane found a strange delight in walking the wide beach near sunset with Tommy, climbing the dunes with him, watching him slide down them. From the dunes, where they snuggled together against the wind, it was almost as though she could look down on herself and Danny on those sands years ago, send him some silent message about his son.

It was from the papers Jane first learned that Nick had had to bow out of *A Dead Language*. He was in New Orleans again, at that clinic. The understudy had taken over. Perhaps, the paper said, for the run of the play.

Yes, he told her when she called. If he were sprung from here, if they ever stopped using him as a guinea pig with their needles and pills—he was learning some new ones, incidentally—he'd join them on the Cape. When he did, he was pale, thinner than ever. A highly emotional reunion took place between him and Tommy, Nick trotting Tommy up and down the cove beach on his shoulders. Nick returned, panting, his hair fallen across his forehead, and laughing.

"In all the excitement, Tommy let out a you-know-what," he explained privately. "When I yelled, 'Hey, what's that noise?' he said, 'There's a duck in my diaper.'" Nick emitted his loud staccato bark.

Owen had arrived briefly in Truro, invited her to a beach party. Nick didn't care to go, stayed behind with Tommy. Albert Poster, recently arrested in Provincetown for disturbing the peace, arrived with a new lady friend. At sight of Jane he scowled, remembering Paris. When he tried to monopolize her, to insinuate some sort of relationship between them, Jane awarded him a cool regard.

"I know," he snapped. "You don't wanna make babies. You only wanna fuck 'em. . . ."

There was a small bonfire on the cove beach when Jane returned. Beside it, Tommy lay asleep with his head in Nick's lap and covered by Nick's jacket. A young couple, drinking beer and smoking, sat with him. They rose to their feet as Jane descended through the beach grass. In the shallow water a Rhodes-19 bobbed, its rope tied to a cement block in the sand.

"Jane, this is Steve and Kathy Hearn." Nick's voice was low, not to waken Tommy. "They gave us a sail this afternoon. Hearns, meet the great Jane Belmont."

An attractive couple, they might have been brother

and sister. Both with reddish-gold hair, that fair, freckled skin that often went with it. Light brows and lashes, blue eyes, snub noses. Kathy's long hair blew in the wind that came over the water and she had an easy, confident manner, a ready smile on her clean-scrubbed face. Steve was tall, muscular, with the same down-to-earth quality.

It turned out he'd known Nick at the High School of Performing Arts. He and Kathy had just worked a couple of music tents on the Cape, were on holiday—"by request of the management," Steve explained. They'd only recently acquired the sailboat, secondhand.

"We always wanted one," Kathy said. She reached out a freckled hand and smoothed Tommy's curls, ruffled by the breeze.

"Yeah, we don't all become stars overnight like Nick here," Steve added, without rancor. He handed Jane a beer from the ice chest, brought ashore from the boat.

"Did I miss anything?" Nick asked.

Jane described the party, mentioned Albert Poster.

A moment of silence. "You met him in Paris?" At Nick's tone of jealous curiosity, the Hearns exchanged glances. Jane smiled.

"I escaped without physical damage."

"Mm. . . . Everyone knows what a womanizer he is." Nick's voice had turned flat, hollow, with that reedy quality.

"We were talking about a new script everybody's in a dither about in New York," Kathy broke in tactfully. "Nick hadn't heard."

"Yeah!" Nick moved so violently that Tommy came awake, looked about at the firelit faces with sleepy golden eyes. "Sid Arkoff"—Jane had persuaded him during the year to go with Sid—"didn't even let me know. A play about David and Jonathan. Sounds like it's *made* for me!"

Jane leaned over Tommy, gathered him into her arms. "Call him." The Hearns rose to their feet, brushed the sand from their cut-off jeans. They had no running lights, had to get back to their mooring. They were renting a small house near town. Nick took Tommy from Jane, carried him up the hill. While she prepared Tommy for bed with his favorite lullabye, Jane heard Nick on the phone.

"Sid, what kind of agent are you, anyway. I have to hear about a part that's tailor-made for me by accident?" Pause. "Of all the *chutzpah!* What a *momzer!* Listen, I couldn't care less *what* you think!" Jane, bending to kiss Tommy, cringed. "I don't *give* a fuck. You send me a copy of that play by the next mail, you hear? I don't want to be beaten out of that part!"

In a moment he was lounging, a grin on his face, in the doorway of Tommy's room. "*You* know I like Jews. I want to play the king of the Jews." Then he was revolving through the room, his body bending and swaying, arms raised above his head. "David dancing naked before the Ark as he enters Jerusalem."

Tommy giggled, ready to come awake for the night. Jane pushed Nick out.

But Nick was in high spirits. Sid Arkoff had told him of several new Hollywood offers. Jane sank down on the couch in the glass-enclosed porch that overlooked the water. Across the way the lights of Wellfleet glittered. Faintly, the chimes of the church—the ones that sounded ship's bells—rang. Nick strode across the room, stood with his back to her, flamboyantly damned Hollywood. He turned and gave his barking laugh.

"That's how they talk on TV and in the movies. With their backs to one another, to express emotion. Hollywood!" The scornful face turned grave. "I know someday I'll go. It's in the cards. But not yet. Not yet. . . ."

3

The Hearns came by often to take them sailing. Tommy, almost lost in the orange life vest, couldn't get enough of it. (*We'll make a sailor of this kid!* Bill had exulted, holding Tommy to him.) Privately, Jane ordered a thirty-six-foot cabin sailboat to be trailered down from Hyannis after the Hearns left.

Steve and Kathy joined them at the ocean, too. Both,

with their fair skin, had to shield themselves from the sun, while Jane and Nick quickly grew brown. Remembering Cannes, Jane observed Kathy in her bikini, saw that—despite the girl's age—her own body remained superior.

On the wide ocean beach, children twirled with hula hoops, young people threw Frisbees back and forth. Kites blew against the cloudless sky and the smell of suntan oil evaporated into the wind. Nick and the Hearns built mermaids and whales out of sand for Tommy, rode him on the waves, chased one another. When Nick's identity—and Jane's—were discovered, they wandered further toward the empty expanses of beach that still remained.

One day the Hearns arrived with a hula hoop. Neither had much skill with it, handed it to Jane. She rose from the blanket, held her wrist to her forehead, palm outward, gyrated like a stripper while Nick, clapping in rhythm, called out admiringly, "Hey, hey!"

At his turn, he swiveled his slim hips while the pelvic muscles rippled. Then he became aware: she and the Hearns caught up in the sight of him against the flashing sea, all abandoned to awe of his beauty. He stopped and laughed, the hoop dropping to the sand.

Meanwhile, Sid had sent the play, Nick had been right, the part *was* made for him. They flew down to New York for two days, she and he, where he auditioned, was signed immediately. Before and since, Jane had been helping, coaching him, dissecting motivation. Rehearsals wouldn't begin until October. Above all, Nick wanted to know: what was the quality of love between David and Jonathan?

"I mean, they can't come on like two fags." He repeated what he'd said about liking Jews. He wanted, he said, to show in one person the glory they represented, what they'd given to the world. "Look at David, alone," he pointed out. "The Psalms. . . . And his son: Ecclesiastes. The Song of Songs. . . . 'Thou art all fair, my love; there is no spot in thee. . . .'"

Jane laughed. On Nick's lap, where perched a marvelous example, Tommy was searching for the spot Nick had mentioned.

When the Hearns left, there were promises to keep in touch in New York. They lived in a third-floor walk-up in a condemned building on Tenth Avenue and Fifty-first. But Nick was deflated, lounged at loose ends in the house while it rained. When it did clear temporarily, he announced he was ready to investigate Provincetown. He'd been avoiding it because of its "reputation."

"Everybody knows about Provincetown," he'd declared.

Nick admired the beauty of the town as they drove the shore route—the small wooden houses, the roses straggling over fences, the hollyhocks, the shining bay dotted with boats. But as soon as they walked the crowded streets, still damp from the storms, a small group of men emerged from a shop on a side street, began to follow them. One made kissing noises directed toward Nick.

"Let's go," he jerked out, his face dark.

"Don't be paranoid," Jane argued. "Come on, we can stop here for a drink."

It was a sidewalk café, fringed umbrellas, hanging plants. But the group followed them, sat at the next table. Nick, wooden as a puppet, stared ahead while one of them leaned across.

"Hi," he purred. "Let me introduce myself. My name's Polly Ester." He let out a low shriek of laughter. "What's yours? And why don't you join us?"

Nick bolted from the table. Without warning, it had begun to rain again. He ran, knocking into people as he'd done that day on Fifth Avenue, toward the parking lot. When Jane arrived at the Mercedes, he was lying in the puddle beside it, curled in a fetal position.

"Nick! For God's sake!"

"Unlock the car!" he snarled between clenched teeth. "Unlock the goddam car!"

They drove home in silence, only really made up later that night when they met, unable to sleep, exchanged a measure of pills with shamefaced smiles. For the remainder of that week, while it continued to rain, they investigated the effects of various doses.

Before Labor Day, the weather cleared, the new sailboat arrived. They had several good days on the water, though Nick liked to go out when the bay was too choppy for Jane's taste, especially with Tommy. She carted Nick off to New Bedford for a beginner's license, taught him—to Ted's dismay over the Mercedes, if not her safety—to drive. Then Mama was clamoring for Tommy's presence. Ted flew down to New York, returned with the Hamilton Rolls.

Tommy was inconsolable at not being allowed to show "Lil Mum" all the horseshoe crabs he and Nick had collected, the stiffened carcass of the sand shark nailed to the shed door. He wept bitterly until Nick took him aside, told him the story of *The Three Bears* transformed into cats, acting all the parts as he meowed, purred, hunched his body, tapped Tommy's face with delicate paws. Laura led Tommy in dazed enchantment into the Rolls. She'd stay on at Greenwich with him while Faith, Ted, and Joy readied the house in New York for Jane's return.

They spent most of their time now—Jane coaching him—on the play, *The Sceptre and the Harp.* "Why does the title list Jonathan first?" Nick grumbled.

"Don't you see? David is the one who eventually becomes both."

Nick regarded her, his eyes alight. "Ah so."

They lived very simply, the two of them, hardly ever venturing to the ocean beach with the crush of the Labor Day weekend coming on. But Jane acceded to an invitation from a painter and his wife in Provincetown. She must come to a costume party at a dilapidated saloon on Commercial Street. An occasion like this Nick could not forego. They acquired black leotards and tights, smudged their faces with charcoal, arrayed one another in seaweed, set forth in the Mercedes.

When they arrived, they had to push their way in. It took some doing to find the couple who'd invited them. Rock music blared, the waiters—also in costume—were perspiring and harassed. By the time drinks were brought to the round wooden table that the couple had managed to sequester, a tall, leggy girl in a skimpy bikini bottom, bare-breasted under her necklace of seaweed, with face and long blonde hair tinted green under more seaweed, had surrounded Nick.

"Hey, you're my soulmate!" Obviously unaware of his identity, she insisted he dance with her.

Nick, who loved costumes, was in an antic mood. Jane gave up trying to talk to the painter and his wife above the music, drank, watched Nick. Making up dance steps, he was taken over by one girl after another. He beckoned to Jane and, for a time, they danced. She saw, through the dim light and smoke, the glittering eyes of men watching Nick—wasn't one of them Polly Ester?— had a sudden sense of animals gathered in hiding, observing their prey. It occurred to her that perhaps they should soon leave.

But Nick, holding a drink above his head, swirled away from her, tipped the glass to his lips without losing the rhythm of the music, was embraced by three girls at once. The couple at the table had risen to wave goodbye. Jane fought her way back to speak to them. When she glanced again at the mobbed dance area, the three girls surrounding Nick had been joined by several men. Nick was in the center, they were all clapping to his movements.

Through the tangled seaweed, in the darkened face streaked with sweat, the light eyes blazed, trancelike. It was some mixture of boogie and ballet he did to the blast of rock and roll music, a dark sea god rising through churning waves. *The only ones for me are the mad ones, the ones who are mad to live. . . .* More than before, Jane was aware of that sense of animals watching. They'd moved out from cover now, were creeping toward him, drawn by that beauty, by that wild androgynous force, accentuated tonight by the makeup, the costume, the way he moved. Someone tapped Jane's arm.

"Hello, again."

It was Albert Poster, costumed not too originally in a red devil's outfit. "Come on out for a smoke. It's too hot in here even for Lucifer." At her hesitation, he gave his cocky smile. "Scared?"

"You're not armed? Aside from the pitchfork?"

"Harmless as the driven snow."

They pushed their way out to the rear deck where the wind from the dark bay was soothing. Poster informed her he'd bought a house in Provincetown, invited her to see it. At her scathing glance, he shrugged his stocky shoulders. "I remember. 'Thanks, but no, thanks.'" They finished their cigarettes, Jane began to shiver, they went back inside.

Nick had disappeared.

For a time Jane watched the door to the men's room, then wandered out to Commercial Street where groups of people from the party staggered about and shouted. She returned to the noise and smoke within. Nick had not shown up. She drank alone, refusing entreaties to dance. She saw that the bare-breasted girl had disappeared, too, was aware of a constriction in her throat that made it difficult to swallow.

But it occurred to her that perhaps Nick had tired of the party, was searching for her. Jane squeezed her way out again, walked the few blocks to the parking lot. Nick wasn't there. She wandered along the pier where several groups had taken their share of the party. The glow from the lighthouse at Race Point shot spasmodically across the dark water. No Nick. Back to the saloon, now rapidly emptying. One of the girls who'd clapped to Nick's dancing was finishing the dregs of several glasses. Jane asked if she knew where Nick had gone.

"If I knew, you think I'd be here?" the girl jibed.

For an hour Jane sat, smoking cigarettes and seething, in the car. Several times she started up the engine, decided to give Nick ten more minutes, turned it off, lit another cigarette. When the pack was empty, she revved up the engine again. The lot was almost empty by now. Slowly she drove along Commercial Street to its end, swung past Race Point, back along Bradford Street, and down around again into town.

The streets were empty now. Again to Race Point. This time, from Bradford Street, Jane gunned the engine and swerved left to Route 6.

Damn him! she muttered under her breath. Only a faint sense of worry underlay her anger. The anger was easier to bear than the sick jealousy that curled like a wounded cat in her belly. The dim hope that he'd hitch-hiked for some reason, awaited her at home died away as she swung up to the dark house.

Jane rid herself of the costume, showered, sat with a

bottle, glass and cigarettes in the glass-enclosed porch overlooking the bay, watched the sun come up. If you love him, she told herself, you should be glad he's finally ridding himself of his inhibitions. How long could one expect a Nicholas Spenser to remain virginal? She thought of the story of *The Lady and the Tiger*. Which door would one open for a loved one?

Ah, she told herself scornfully. Perhaps she didn't love him that much.

She must have dozed. The front door had slammed. Jane sat erect, brushing the hair from her eyes. Against the anger and hurt, her heart lifted as she heard the footsteps draw nearer. She turned.

Nick stood slumped in the doorway. Someone had given him clothes—a work shirt and jeans. He was barefoot. His face, still slightly smudged with charcoal, was red, raw, swollen, especially the lips. He stared at her. His teeth were chattering.

"What happened?" Jane asked.

Nick started to speak. Instead, his whole body shivered uncontrollably. Jane rose, aware of sunlight warming her shoulders, her tongue furry from the long night of drinking and no sleep. It was as though a vast distance separated them, as though she were trying to reach him in slow motion.

"What happened?" Her voice sounded faint.

"I—I . . ." The ravaged face lifted. His throat worked spasmodically. Sobs broke from it. "Ah—ah—ah . . ."

Jane covered that distance between them, tried to take hold of him. He wrenched away from her, sank to the floor, began to crawl, moving his body from side to side and baying like an animal. She dropped to her knees beside him, gripped him, and he fell over on his back, covering his face with his arms in an awkward, crippled gesture.

"Nick, stop it! Stop! Tell me right now what happened!"

The arms dropped away. He lay back and stared at her, his eyes bloodshot, the swollen lips moving without sound. A hoarse whisper. Jane leaned close, aware of a fetid smell emanating from him. It was the smell of vomit, of liquor, of sex.

"I'm one of them," he whispered. "I'm one of them. ... I always thought I was. Always. I was always afraid I was. Now I know...."

Jane sat back on her heels. An image of those men like stalking animals, their eyes glittering in the dark. Which one, gathered around to clap while Nick danced. ... And had it been only one?

"Nick! Nick, darling, it's not the end of the world," she began, trying to take him in her arms. He twisted away.

"It is! For me, it is!" The sobs were more human now, almost childlike. "I'm sick, like *them*. Like all of *them!* I don't deserve to live. It's the horror, the horror . . ." His body convulsed with sobs.

"Nick, please." Jane felt helpless. "Don't you think plenty of people have done what you've done? Peter and I both . . ."

He stopped, quite suddenly, peered into her face with calm solemnity. "You and Peter went for the same sex to escape each other," he snapped. "That's not what's wrong with me. . . . 'From comparatively trivial wickedness I passed. . . .' " Quietly now, he began to weep. This time, he allowed her to hold him.

"There's nothing *wrong* with you, Nick," she crooned. "It's not sick and it's not wrong. Because some of society says so, doesn't make it true. It's only—different."

His head, against her breast, shook violently in denial. "It's wrong. Or it's sick. Or both." He pulled back from her, searched her face with frantic reddened eyes. "Jane, I don't want anyone to know. I guess *I* always knew. But honestly, I tried like hell to fight it. Jane, you've got to help me keep anyone else from knowing. Ever! Swear! Do you swear?" His hand tightened on her wrist.

"If this *is* true about you, can't you accept it? Besides, eventually people would know. . . ."

He sprang to his feet and let out a cry. "No! No! I don't want them talking about me the way they talk about that. I can't take it! I won't!" He stared about him wildly. Jane, still on the floor, looked up at him.

It wouldn't change anything. It might even be a risk. But worth it.

"Nick," she said quietly. "Come here."

He frowned at her, slowly bent till his face was level with hers. Jane laid a hand on his wet swollen cheek, rough with his heavy morning beard. His stench was almost overpowering. Of course, she must always have known, too. But life was not that limited. She leaned forward, softly kissed the puffy lips, was aware of the grieving eyes that watched her.

"Come," she said gently. "Come on."

At first, he didn't understand. She laid him gently back upon the floor, slowly unbuttoned the shirt, placed her cold hands on the hairy heaving chest. Then she slipped the blouse above her head, began to undo her skirt. The grey eyes widened.

"Come, my sweet," she told him. "I'll show you. . . . 'Thou art all fair, my love; there is no spot in thee. . . .' "

Chapter IX

1

There was a problem in the David-Jonathan play no one
could have foreseen.

Though encased in pink sheets and blanket at Elizabeth Arden's, hot water bottle in pink towel at her feet,
Jane lay tense. It was surely this issue that held her
muscles rigid under the calming hands of the masseuse,
surely not the lunchtime meeting ahead. In the elevator,
two women had restated the problem, before stepping
off at the hair salon.

"That's what happened when *I* saw it." The speaker
folded a raincap into her alligator bag. "Everyone iden-
tifies so with Jonathan's sister—waiting for Nicholas
Spenser to come to her in that tent. . . ."

". . . and wishing they could take her place!" The
other woman giggled furtively, slid a glance toward
Jane, who quickly averted her eyes.

"Mm, those legs?" The first woman lowered her
voice. "Wrapped in those leather thongs? I mean, all he
does is reach out a hand to her hair and all around you
hear this—this *grunt*. . . . Everyone's groaning with
lust. . . . And this absolute ripple of laughter. . . ."

"It's a goddam mutual orgasm," Joseph Kahn, the
director, had fretted. The wave of embarrassed amusement that relieved the audience of its tension also broke
the rhythm of the play. "This I never had to deal with
before."

It was Kahn's one complaint. Since the try-outs at the
Colonial Theatre in Boston (Elliot Norton, in the *Her-
ald-American*, predicting Nick's triumph, had noted audience reaction to his projection of erotic innocence),
there'd been only critical acclaim, the S.R.O. sign out for
every performance, the demand for tickets phenomenal.

The demand for Nick—Jane's right leg was unwrapped, the soothing hands applied oil—no less so. Across the sky of her life she'd watched the trajectory of his star shoot, had known fear: that he'd fly so far he must be lost to her. She was thirty-three and he just twenty-one. At present—today? tomorrow?—the fear seemed irrelevant. It was understood that for this present, Nick was hers. No matter that all desire was on her side. To flaunt their affair, to make no secret of it helped Nick to hide that other, with which he could not come to terms. Occasionally—Sundays, Mondays—he disappeared.

"Who," a gossip columnist asked in one column, "was the shabby loafer Nick Spenser was seen with down in Union Square the other night?"

That alarmed Nick. He'd concentrated, when he wasn't with her, on his relationship with the Hearns. "What," another columnist had demanded, "goes in the fourth-floor walk-up on Tenth Avenue where Nick Spenser hides out so often? Do we have a ménage à trois?"

This last comment, that only amused Nick, aroused in Jane a flare-up of unreasonable jealousy. She was irritated by women who bragged of their lust and sexual prowess. All the "desirable" heroines of best sellers, of drawing-room comedies—they had names like Kay and Maggie, they liked to drink, were always available for bed, instantly orgasmic, good sports, experienced only an amusing sexual jealousy—were totally unreal. What she knew now was real. Nothing she was proud of, but it was real.

Jane turned on her belly, the hands were at work on her shoulders. Yes, she'd yielded herself up, her life, she was possessed. Eyes closed, still trying to deal with the problem in the play—and to avoid what lay ahead—she let her thoughts drift instead to the wide bed where they lay together, she and Nick, between the satin sheets. Outside, the first damp snow of the season drifted slowly upward.

"I like your slanty eyes. It's as though you pulled your hair way back on your head to make them slant." His fingers traced her eyelids. "But your nose is too long." The slow smile.

"So's yours."

"Mine's perfect. You know that."

"*This* is." Her mouth lifted to his, brushed it lightly. The luminous gray eyes closed as, bodies turning, her lips surrounded his, moved to his throat, his shoulders, the hairy chest. His arms strengthened around her but she sensed him watching her as they came together, as she floated outward on that dark encompassing wave. Only once she'd asked, not wanting to, unable to stop herself:

"You don't feel I'm using you? You're not just trying to please me?"

He'd pulled back from her. "Is that what you think?"

"You have so many permutations and combinations. Why do people do things, for what reasons? Is this one of them?"

"This," he said, in the slow, hesitant voice that intrigued audiences, "is the right thing for the right reason. . . . That other: it seems right and natural at the time. But after. . . . No matter what you say, I know it's wrong. But I can't control it." His face was hidden against her neck. "Jesus. It's going to destroy me. I know."

"Only one thing can destroy you. More than the world knowing. That's self-hatred." His head moved vehemently in denial. She'd sighed. "I suppose I'll have to love you enough for both of us."

The massage was finished. Jane moved to the long narrow tiled room for the Scotch hose hydrotherapy. Under the jets of hot water, as the blood sped through her body, she realized she hadn't yet come up with a solution to the play's problem. But now she must concentrate on what was coming.

At the Four Seasons, she and Nick would be meeting for lunch. There, Danny would join them.

He had called the evening before, displacing, all in a moment, the life she'd fashioned for herself since he'd taken with him—as she'd imagined, that evening—the world. He was in New York for his father's funeral, in the morning would place his mother on the train for Florida where she now lived. When Jane had suggested they meet at the restaurant, there was disappointment in his voice.

"I hoped I could see your child. Isn't he almost three already?"

She could still act. An agony of regret was masked by her words. "Oh, Tommy's in Connecticut, with Mama." For this truth, she should, she knew, be grateful. She couldn't remove all the photographs of Tommy from the townhouse. There was no way she could risk Danny seeing them—though a part of her needed him desperately to do so. Only in these last months, watching Tommy, had she become aware of a movement of the eyes, of the eyelids, that she'd never identified with Peter, but that she now saw had been his.

Otherwise, he was all Danny—the curly hair, the golden eyes, the tender curve of the lips. Danny would see it at once. Even Nick, who knew about the past they'd shared, didn't know the truth about Tommy. That truth might bring Danny back—or shatter the life *he'd* built. Her very soul—like iron filings to a magnet—had felt a leap toward him at the sound of his voice. It was, then, as though some warder had placed a monitoring hand upon her, pushed down against that thrust. . . .

Nick was waiting when she arrived at the restaurant. The new suit from his English tailor, a cashmere sweater beneath the jacket, Gucci loafers, dark hair shining, gray eyes alight when he saw her. Jane's chin lifted as they followed the maître d' to their table while heads turned, smiles of reverence for Nick's beauty appeared, as always. The waiter pulled back her chair and she raised her eyes to Nick's face. She always enjoyed that consciousness of the impression he made, that combination of embarrassment and pride. In secret acknowledgment, their eyes met. The maître d' lingered.

"Want to wait for drinks till he comes?" Nick was elated at this prospect of sharing her past. Before she could answer, she saw his eyes widen, heard the sharp intake of breath. "Oh! That's him, isn't it?"

Jane turned.

Yes: Danny. The large figure, the curly beard, the wide-set golden eyes searching toward them. For a moment the old pang of love turned to an unbearable pain. For a moment it was as though this that now enmeshed her was what was ephemeral, Danny again who filled her whole horizon. Her gaze cleared. She saw, simultaneous with that spasm of pain, the crutch on which he leaned. He smiled toward her as he made his way slowly to the table.

"Hey. . . . He has a wooden leg?" Quick tenderness roughened Nick's voice as he stood.

"Please. . . . I didn't know." Jane rose and reached out her arms.

Amazing, the special grace still evident as he came to her, held her to him. So this had been the unspecified wound. Danny handed the crutch to the maître d', was pulling the artificial limb under the table as Jane made introductions, explained that Nick would leave early for the matinee, that she had house seats so Danny could see the performance. Good, good, he was saying. Jane held his hand in both her own.

"Oh, Danny! How did this happen?"

His plane had been shot down. The leg, too mutilated to be saved, had been amputated while he was in coma. Vaguely, Jane was aware of another sharp intake of breath as Nick listened, studied Danny with his wide, curious gaze.

"Do you think," Danny asked, his hand tightening over hers, "anything else could have kept me away during *your* ordeal?"

"My poor darling!" She raised his fingers to her lips, saw that Nick had now sat back to stare at her.

The knowledge of her secret lay open on his face. Over drinks, Danny grew sensible to the curious element in Nick's unabashed scrutiny, his sullen refusal to scan the menu. Nervously, Jane ordered for all three. Pike and salmon pâté. Asparagus maltaise. Danny brushed aside her questions. He had his own. He glanced toward her purse.

"At least you have pictures of your boy?"

"Somehow I never carry them." A spasm of grief, of mute apology accompanied the thought that a director would have told her not to reply so quickly. Nick's hollow, reedy voice was dangerously loud, accusatory.

"You never carry pictures of Tommy? Since when?"

"Since. . . . No, I don't." Nick's lips tightened and she looked away toward Danny. "How about you? Do you and Rachel have a family?"

The wide-set eyes lowered as Danny turned the stem of his glass. She recalled the feel of those eyelids under her lips. "We don't seem able to have any." With swift loyalty: "Must be me. Rachel did have a miscarriage once, before we met. So we know *she* can have them." Momentarily, the full lips twisted in the curly beard. Nick leaned forward, his dark brows drawn together. As he cleared his throat, Jane savagely gripped his knee under the table.

Did he think it was all so simple? Did he expect her to burst out with it: Oh, it isn't *you* that's not able, Danny. Our child exists, yours and mine—the child of our lost love. . . . Nick, responding to the drama of the moment, not knowing her vow to Bill, wouldn't see how that confession might tear apart Danny's life, his marriage. Her fingers tightened on Nick's knee.

Still bent toward Danny, Nick said in a rush: "You should have seen the kid at Hallowe'en. Jane made him an elephant costume with wrapping paper. She went along the street in front of him carrying this big wrapping paper trunk for him." Danny smiled. To her, Nick sent only a sullen regard, sat back in tense silence.

As they ate—each only picking at the food—Danny enumerated Israel's problems, its achievements. Still, he shot puzzled glances toward Nick's denunciatory scrutiny. As though to deflect this, he questioned Nick about theater. That broke the tension.

"I've read *Zeal for Thy House*," Nick said in his deliberate way. "I was a kid in California when it was on. But I've read it. It's a great play. How come you don't write anymore?"

"Guess I lost my inspiration." Danny smiled. "I've heard: you're a powerful David."

Now Jane tried to control her pride while Nick spoke, with increasing passion, about his role. How Jane had helped. His ideas of the stage. As she sat back over coffee, lit a cigarette, she knew her face must reveal what she felt. When Nick had left, Danny turned back from watching him. His hand touched hers, then her cheek.

"So, my lovely bright-eyed darling." His expression said they were alone now, encased in their common past. "You have it bad, don't you! Is that it? You found the one love you needed?"

His smile said, too, that *his* feeling for her hadn't changed. Again, Jane sensed that pain. Grief over his mutilation. Relief that he had lived. Guilt for the secret she held from him. . . . Briefly, there flared the desire to confess, to argue that they both fling away what tied them to others, that they come together from that past they'd shared. Between his face and hers came that other—the heavy dark brows, the wide gray eyes, the texture of his skin. She bowed her head.

"To my probable ruin, yes. . . . He's *become* my life."

Danny sat back, his gaze guarded. "Well. You had a lot of unused care left in you to lavish on someone. Not the sort *I* needed. At least the search is over. The one that always came between *us*. You've found that reincarnation." It was, in its way, more a farewell than the one they'd said that day in June when the light had gradually dwindled from the room like a stage set.

She wasn't prepared, after Danny left, for the sweep of Nick's rage. Perhaps she should have been: in the dressing room after the performance, the icy courtesy he accorded her measured out against the deference paid to Danny and his praise. When he discovered that Danny was leaving for an airport motel, wasn't staying with Jane, Nick's face flushed ominously. His plane left at dawn, Danny explained, careful to conceal any hurt at the lack of hospitality. He was grateful to have seen Jane, met Nick, caught the play. Before Nick could say more, Danny was offering a solution to the play's problem.

Nick mustn't touch the girl at all, not at least till they'd been together several moments. Simply their reunion in the tent would ease the tension beyond the footlights. Only then should Nick reach for her.

"Ah!" Nick breathed out slowly, the gray eyes glittering. "I'll try that. Tonight. I have to warn Stella. . . ." The shy, winning smile. "Do you have a favorite moment in the play?"

"When Jonathan warns you Saul is out to kill you. And you say goodbye to each other." Nick nodded. "And you climb that promontory and look out over the lights

274

of the tents in the distance, with that terrible sense of loneliness. . . ."

"You get that?" Nick put in quickly.

"And then, the way you begin to recite . . . no, *speak* what you're feeling. . . ."

" 'The *Lord* is my shepherd,' " Nick murmured, watching Danny. " '*I* shall not want. He maketh me to lie down—in green pastures. . . .' " It was the mode of delivering the Psalm they'd hammered out together, she and he.

Jane had dinner alone with Danny. As though there were nothing more to say to one another, they attended a showing of *The World of Apu*. Ted waited to drive them to the airport. Only once did Danny refer to Nick, who'd obviously not said goodbye to Jane.

"Moody chap, isn't he? Is that the theater in his blood? Or youth? Or him?"

"Oh, youth. The idealistic impulsiveness of youth." She didn't explain. For a moment, as Danny caught her roughly to him—she felt the wooden leg against her own, remembered those strong flanks against hers—she was tempted to. "How can I tell you . . ."

"We owe nothing to the past," he broke in.

She gazed at the glittering lights of Manhattan behind them. "It's not possible, is it, to love more than one person at a time?"

"In our way? No."

Then, since the temptation to confess everything arose as much from the desire to exonerate herself as to give any ease to him, Jane held silent, converting their last moments to an unfamiliar banality. On the ride back across the bridge, remembering his eyes, tears stood suddenly in her own.

Nick was pacing the living room when she returned. The room was ablaze—like her life, these days—with flowers: orange lilies, birds of paradise, deep red carnations. He whipped around as she stood at the railing above the steps.

"How could you do that to him?" The wide eyes were glassy, staring, pupils dilated. He was trembling. It occurred to Jane that he'd taken Seconal to sleep, had changed his mind, come here instead, was wildly over-

stimulated. She started to speak but he picked up a pillow from a sofa, smashed it down, sent a light coffee
table over on its side.

"You loved him! He was the one guy you loved, before me. . . . And he's Tommy's father, right? You never
even told *me!* How did it happen? Did your husband
know? How could you send him away—Danny—without knowing? And thinking he can't even *have* kids?
How *could* you?"

Upstairs, Faith and Ted moved about. Jane gripped
the railing. "You don't understand . . ." she began. He
picked up another cushion, hurled it at her.

"No!" he barked. "I don't understand! The great Jane
Belmont! So wonderful! So misunderstood! Is that all
your love means? You going to give me the shiv someday
too, huh?" He advanced on her. "This isn't just some
guy you use like a rag and throw away. He's a Jewish
hero, he's . . ."

"Oh, come. . . . You're not David now." Jane hated
herself as she moved down the steps. He stared at her,
then grasped her shoulders.

"You're a monster. Daisy was right. Maybe all those
news stories about you were right, too." It was more
than Seconal, she decided, trying not to feel. "I'm getting out of here."

"Do. And leave the key, while you're at it!" Was this
shrill, anguished cry her own? Nick turned, sent her a
long, scornful stare, dug into his pocket and held up the
key. For a moment he wagged it back and forth before
her dazed face, emitted a strange, nasty snicker.

"The key to your house. The key to your heart. If you
had one!" He flung the key underhand, carefully, toward
the center of the rug. It was the way she used to throw a
key into hopscotch boxes. " 'Parting is such sweet sorrow. . . .' " he whispered, and was gone.

2

Jane spent several dull days in Connecticut where
Mama engaged Tommy in tourneys with wooden puzzles, at which she always won. In frustration, Tommy
punished two of Mama's goldfish, laid them under a
table for biting one another. They were rescued, Jane
admonished him, "in the nick of time." Seated on a
wooden potty chair Jane had painted to resemble a
throne, Tommy grumbled: Where *was* Nick?

Back in New York, Jane read the gossip columnists.
Nicholas Spenser was seen in company with various
debs or actresses each night. Sid Arkoff was quoted: film
offers inundated his office, they were pleading for Nick
at least to fly out to the Coast for a screen test. Daisy was
interviewed. Daisy had hoped Nick's frequent careless
dress was only the result of a passing influence, now
over and done with. Well, her son was young, you know.
Despite his brilliance, he was only a boy. . . .

With Owen, Jane attended the opening of the Gug-
genheim Museum. She visited the castle with Walter
Raney, joined the board of the Museum of Modern Art,
took Tommy to performances of children's theater. With
the Gurneys, she wept at *Hiroshima, Mon Amour,* was
ashamed to use the film as a release for her own pain.
Albert Poster accompanied them, informed her he'd
even marry her to field her in bed.

Then it was spring, the delicate air soft and vibrant
as it could only seem in New York. Down South, Martin
Luther King—to whom she still sent money—pressed
harder for civil rights. There was a song they had: "We
Shall Overcome." By now, in 1959, off-Broadway was
booming. Tommy went about singing "Mack the Knife,"
like Bobby Darin. One afternoon as Jane returned from
a meaningless foray to Bloomingdale's, as she walked
drearily along the sunlit street toward the house, she
saw a dark head emerge from an upstairs window two
buildings before it. Her steps slowed. She raised a hand
to shield her eyes from the sun, her face from his. It was
Nick.

"Hi!" The breeze ruffled the thick hair as he leaned out. "Why don't you come upstairs and see me sometime? Like now?"

Jane walked to the sidewalk below him. The boyish smile disappeared. "What are you doing up there?" She could barely speak. "What are you *doing*?"

"I've rented the place. With an option to buy." His voice was so low, it barely carried. "I have to be near you."

It was as though a casing of ice around her heart cracked. Jane held up her arm toward him, he reached down as though their hands might touch. Then she was running up the few steps toward the door, he'd flung it open, they were in one another's arms, rocking, holding one another, laughing, half sobbing. The hallway smelled of fresh paint. There were cartons of books in the room beyond, a fencing foil leaned against the wall, a broom lay on its side on the floor.

"Don't ever let me go away again," Nick was saying. "I've been dying without you."

"*You've* been!" she breathed. "This was barely in time...."

With his move, Jane overtly handed to Nick her investment in the future. There was not only decorating the house, helping him to entertain, making out reading lists, working on his constant stage fright. After he won the Tony Award, they had to plan his next move in theater. Her role, Jane believed, was to deflect him from the pull of Hollywood.

"On Broadway, in London, you don't have to worry," she argued. "Look at all the theater people that are known homosexuals. Out there, they'll tear you apart. They're Victorians. Immoral hypocritical prudes. They do anything and condemn everything."

"Oh, but it's coming. It's coming," he insisted. "I know there's no way not to give in. Eventually." Throughout the summer, the following year, they argued about it.

By the next spring, the papers were full of stories about the widow Todd, who'd gone off with her best friend's husband, and with news of the young senator from Massachusetts who was seeking the Democratic

278

nomination. A Catholic, people said, would never get it. When *The Sceptre and the Harp* finally closed, Jane and Nick had passage—her first long separation from Tommy—on the S.S. *United States.* As it moved slowly out from its berth, paper streamers floated past its enormous red and black hulk and Nick paced the deck in excitement. They sailed past Ambrose Light, were barely aware by then, so deep in argument about his next role. By the time they'd reached Le Havre, then Southampton, Nick had acceded to Jane's insistence that he do Romeo. There hadn't been a Broadway production for more than twenty years, not since the ill-fated Olivier-Leigh staging. The public, Jane insisted, deserved to see Nick as the archetypal lover.

At the Dorchester, Nick spread notes across the taffeta bedspread while Jane, as she did each day, called Tommy at Greenwich. She shopped for the new Mary Quant skirts that ended above the knee, and Nick, deep in thought beside her, wondered aloud how best to emphasize the pervasive imagery of light and dark in the play. At the Guinea, in Bruton Place, where someone had mentioned they served the best steak, Nick—eating his raw—declared he was afraid, not ready to tackle Shakespeare. This wasn't, after all, Orlando, in summer stock. They walked arm in arm through Hyde Park, near Sloan Square bought more toys for Tommy, later sat at a sidewalk café, imitated the veil of boredom of those around them, broke up in laughter. Yes, Nick said: he wanted to do it, after all.

"Only because of you. You lift me up, you make me believe in myself. . . . No matter what *they've* done to you, there's such a core of artistry in you, such a sense of self-worth. . . . Hey! We'll get Steve Hearn for Mercutio."

But that night he disappeared from the hotel, didn't return till late afternoon. The days left to them in London, a young Italian followed them. Nick pretended not to know why. Their last evening he disappeared again, this time from a party given by a star of The National Theater, barely made it to the boat train where, face wet with tears, the young Italian stood by.

Jane, desperately missing her child, was silent in

fury. There was still constraint between them when they sailed for home. Nick, aggressively pleasant, chattered at the table they shared with a drama critic and his wife, forced questions on Jane that she answered toward the others. He played like a porpoise in the pool, entered the Ping-Pong tournament, danced with graceful abandon the latest craze called the Twist. Jane, still sullen, watched as young girls pressed forward to be his partner. As though to question her role, they slid furtive glances toward her. The third day out, Nick cornered Jane as she walked the corridor on A Deck toward their suite.

"Hey. You not going to speak to me ever again?"

"You wouldn't want to hear what I'd have to say."

"So, look. I may as well jump off the ship."

"Be my guest."

"Oh. Yeah?" Nick turned the key in the door, walked in, left it ajar. Jane slowly followed. Nick had already opened the porthole, was climbing out as she entered. In a moment, only his fingers were visible as he hung the equivalent of ten or twelve stories above the water.

Jane heard her own fluttering cry, ran to hold his hands while Nick, hair flying in the wind, laughed and shouted for forgiveness. When he pulled himself back in, his lean body and face damp with spray, Jane struck him, twice, then burst into tears.

They made up in bed.

But at home, Jane swept Tommy up, bore him to Wellfleet for what remained of the summer. In the spring-fed pond between the town and ocean, he displayed a fine fearlessness, disdained her arms ready to catch him, jumped from the wooden float into the water. Parents of bigger children, hanging back, harangued them: "Look at *that* little fellow!" When Nick flew up to join them, she couldn't show Tommy off to him: Nick's growing fame made any appearance at the crowded pond unthinkable.

In the fall, Jane enrolled Tommy in nursery school, as leaves drifted slowly to the sidewalk taught him to roller-skate. Before *Romeo and Juliet* opened, Kennedy was elected president. Nick now had top billing, top salary. The critics lauded his "brooding sensitivity . . . controlled spontaneity. . . ." His, they said, was the essence of male sexuality, as he shifted in mood from intro-spection to a sudden electrifying smile. MGM, Warner Brothers, Paramount renewed their bids, each offer more generous. Aurelia, winning the Academy Award for Costume Design, reported by phone to Jane that Nick's name came up at almost every party she attended.

By summer, Sid Arkoff—traitorously, Jane believed—had convinced Nick to fly out for a screen test. *Romeo and Juliet*, despite all acclaim—there was a limited au-dience for Shakespeare—was closing. Jane spent some time at Greenwich with Mama, then back to the house at Wellfleet with Tommy. Almost every day she took him sailing, holding his hand on the tiller to give the feel of its hum. Almost every night, from Hollywood, Nick called.

She wouldn't believe, he told her, the way Holly-wood treated talent. "Like odds and ends for sale at Bloomingdale's." The swimming pools, tennis courts, private viewing rooms in movie moguls' homes—Aure-lia was taking him around—these were impressive. "But the studios treat actors like morons. And the actors let them. They cringe to their business managers and pub-licity people. And their agents. Oy! I guess the agents are the dregs."

Still, the arrowhead, Jane saw when Nick returned, had left its poison. As of old, Nick escorted Tommy—now enrolled in kindergarten—to the Museum of Mod-ern Art, announced with glee that, as they'd inspected an abstract sculpture, Tommy had boomed out, "What the hell is *that?*" After an evening with Jane at the The-atre of the Absurd at Cherry Lane, he scolded Sid Arkoff for not placing him in roles like *The American Dream*. He signed, at last, a mortgage to buy the house near Jane.

But he kept refusing parts, didn't want to be tied down in a role that might not further his career. It was as though he awaited a call he didn't wish her to hear. As the winter progressed, as the city lay weary under dirty crusts of snow, strangers showed up at his parties. They'd met Nick, they revealed to Jane's cool query, at dingy bars, poolhalls, street corners—clues to his fre-quent disappearances. Derelicts most of them, Nick hugged them to him, plied them with drinks, caviar, gifts of his clothing.

"Don't be such a snob," he told Jane. "Your nose is going pug from turning it up at my friends."

She supposed it had to come. Tommy often dropped by, after kindergarten, to visit Nick, whom he regarded in part as his private property. One afternoon, he returned quickly.

"I sure don't like that guy Nick has staying with him," he complained over milk and graham crackers. "How long is he going to be there?"

"What guy? And don't say guy."

"I don't know. Maybe he's sick. I went up and first I thought it was Nick. 'Cause I saw somebody in bed, asleep. But I heard the shower going, so I got kinda scared. And this guy turned over and said, 'Hi,' and he was wearing Nick's pajamas. You know: with the initials on them. Why does Nick let a sick guy sleep in his bed? He could catch something."

"That's so. But maybe the man was only tired. Maybe he isn't sick. And don't say guy. . . . Did Nick know you were there?"

Tommy rubbed a hand through his curls, spreading a fine powder of crumbs. He appeared shamefaced. "He poked his head out of the bathroom. 'Cause this guy yelled to him he had a friend. The guy was laughing. . . . And Nick told me to go home." The lower lip trembled.

"You had no right to go upstairs without being invited, darling. You had no right to go into the house. . ."

"I rang first."

". . . without Nick opening the door to you and asking you in. No matter how friendly you are with someone, you must always wait to be invited in."

"But when I'm with you, we go in lots of times. Just with that key in the box."

"Yes. We won't do that anymore."

He was hardly more than a boy, Nick's friend. Almost defiantly, that evening, Nick invited her over to meet him. Buddy Del Ray was the stage name he'd chosen. He had the impossibly slim hips, the muscular calves— these bulged through the tight pants—common to the

282

gypsies that populated Broadway chorus lines. He sat very erect on Nick's couch, held his drink very tightly in both hands, was very aware of being on trial. Nick, passing by to refill his drink, ran a hand quickly over the dyed blond hair.

"Relax, Buddy. Jane's not going to eat you."

But behind the boy's back, he sent Jane a long, wide-eyed stare. Sleepless later in bed, Jane reassured herself: Nick wasn't rash enough to allow Buddy to live there. But what was it Nick was telling her? Pleading for her sanction? Or showing her what must happen if he continued, rudderless, in New York? Was he insisting he needed the straitjacket of Hollywood to hold him on course?

She should, perhaps, be glad Nick had found the courage to be true to his own nature, she contended with herself as the weeks passed. Was it only sour grapes to feel that the tenor of his life had changed, sickened? Was she only struggling to hold to him now by the teeth, like a terrier? Ambivalence: she had never as truly defined it as now, wanting Nick for herself, wishing him—for his own sake—to do what he was compelled to do, loathe to see any other assume a role of importance in his life.

3

Jane had planned a dinner party in Connecticut, only old theater friends. Nick, staying at the grist mill, had sent for Buddy—and who knew how many of these others? Her dining room resembled the cast of a Fellini film. Ralph Gurney—he and Mary had frequently told interviewers in the past that they viewed Nick as the son they'd never had—looked toward him and murmured to Jane: "What is the dear boy up to, do you know?" Like the other invited guests, they left early. Mama—"I don't think I like your new friends," she confided to Jane— went up to bed. Nick and his cohort stayed on.

At the head of the table Jane sat, her food untouched.
The air was heavy with marijuana, small dishes of cocaine were being passed around, not by her order. It was
as though they were waiting for her, too, to leave. When
the cocaine arrived at her place, Jane held the tiny spoon
to her nose, closed one nostril, inhaled deeply.

She felt as lost as when she'd first sat in Sal's red
Oriental room and, a refugee from another earlier world,
taken it from his hands. From that world she'd brought
with her even now only this singular need, this hunger
that no one but Nick had ever assuaged.

Ah, she thought, as a blue glow appeared to encase
the room, and changed to red. It was all a matter of rela-
tivity, her life rushing forward, this was the famous Dop-
pler effect, the blue signifying Nick's coming toward
her, the red his passing by, leaving her behind. . . .

Some weeks later, when the next offer came from
Hollywood—a firm one, a Western, with Jim Wyatt, the
popular older star famous for his cowboy roles—Walter
Raney, acting as Nick's business manager, confided to
Jane that Nick was in financial trouble. Jane told Nick
he ought to go.

"Go and be damned, you mean." That slow, hesitant
drawl that still enchanted her, the searching stare.

"Do you need my permission?"

"Come with me. I'll need you." His apprehension
gladdened her.

"We'll be in Wellfleet, Tommy and I. . . . Good
luck."

Before she reached there, Mama—quite suddenly, in
the middle of the night—had a massive heart attack. It
was Jane's thirty-seventh birthday when, at the funeral
parlor, she leaned above the face now closed to her forever. It was as though those silent lips asked only now
the question they hadn't in life. *Is she still alive—Joanie
—somewhere?*

The child *she'd* been that day long ago cried now for
the comfort that had always been withheld. Again and
irrevocably, Mama had eluded her. Mama's life must
have passed like a dream.

Friends came to stay in Wellfleet. Walter Raney, in
his hopeless way, again proposed marriage. Hugh Kirk-

land, a producer with three hits on Broadway, and the first man she'd taken to bed since Nick, was increasingly emphatic that she needed a husband, that he'd be a good father to Tommy—strangely quiet these days in his first encounter with death. *He* was willing, Hugh insisted, to take any risk to get her back onstage. Small, wiry, athletic, he strutted back and forth across the glass-enclosed porch while sails scudded along the shining bay beyond.

"If you haven't the courage for that, at least get back into *some*thing. Start a drama school. You'd be a spectacular coach. Everyone knows what you did for Nicholas Spenser. People would flock to you."

Jane turned the goblet in her hand. She'd thought of that, she confided. Down at a mooring, a dog barked wildly on deck while his master straightened the sheets of his day sailer. Tommy, running in and out of the incoming tide with small friends, stopped to watch.

"Ah, I see." Hugh Kirkland studied her face. "Nicholas Spenser was different. You're waiting. To see if *he* still needs you. Right?" He bit at his small gray mustache as she looked at him. "That one—out there in Hollywood. You're just marking time with me. . . ."

"I don't think," Aurelia confided by phone, "Nick's awfully happy." To please Jane, she flew out to the Tucson location. He didn't fit in, Aurelia said. Others viewed him as too damned polite, too controlled. Between takes, he went off by himself to his trailer. Jim Wyatt had been heard to say he was just waiting for that fight they had to stage. He'd told the cameraman to be sure to catch the moment he broke that conceited little prick's jaw.

To Jane, Nick revealed ambivalence. The technology of film-making was awesome; it made you understand what a different and still nascent art film was. He especially admired the stunt men, the second unit director, the special effects men, all stunningly professional. But the arc lights and reflectors used on these exterior locations were awfully hard on his eyes. And Wyatt, the director, the others on location: "Every night," Nick reported, "they pitch into these big he-man dice games. Always acting the studs! It's enough to make me sport the green carnation." This last, rather tremulous.

Still, the night he'd finished the big fight with Wyatt, Nick called again, elated. Wyatt was, after all, the symbol of the Western hero, of brawling manhood. He *was* bruised all over, Nick admitted, but he'd hung in, surprised Wyatt, surprised them all. "You're a tough little prick, after all," Wyatt had decided, insisted on standing him to drinks. "Can't say I know what the hell you're up to in your acting. But you're one tough little prick."

Jane returned to New York to enter Tommy in Dalton's first grade. Suddenly, everyone was talking about the Cuban missile crisis. For some days, it appeared that the unthinkable was at hand. Wind and grit whipped between buildings on Election Day and Nick, back in California for interior shots, called to crow about Nixon's defeat for governor. "Jane, *The High Mountains* will be wrapped in a few days. I'm going to be a star."

Aurelia corroborated this. She'd seen the rough cuts, admitted that Nick brought some personal blend of tough innocence and idealism to the role she was certain had not been written into it. "His life will be permanently changed when that film comes out. I think he knows it and he's a little scared."

It was his back Jane saw first when she met him at the airport and her breath caught in her throat. That was the way, she decided, he should first be seen in his next film. (His next? But what of Broadway?) As though to serve up his beauty only by degrees, she thought, as he turned and saw her. He was too singular to be savored all at once. As his arms went around her, she recognized that she'd lost the battle she imagined she was waging for his sake. If he had to go on in films, if he needed her, she'd by by his side. Her own need was too great.

Still, since there was something he wanted from her, she'd be adamant. Before joining her at her house with the new script he carried, Nick could have his reunion with Buddy. But that reunion must be an ending. When Nick appeared, after midnight, she averted her eyes from the ravages of that meeting that marked his face. If *she* could never possess him totally again, she'd not share him with anyone that threatened even partial permanence.

The Rescue, Nick had explained coming in from the

airport, would be shot in India. He'd play an American artist, seriously ill at the start of the film, with dysentery. Sandra Bellamy, at last willing to accept the role of an older woman with fading beauty—she'd been fading for more than a decade, Jane mused—had agreed to play the European wife of a Hindu doctor. "She saves me and takes me into her home so I'll fall in love with her daughter and take the girl away from India. She doesn't realize it herself: *she's* in love with me, too."

At the hill station to which the family retreats for a holiday, Nick concluded, the mother discovers he has no intention of marrying her daughter. Tumult, hysteria. The parents have the American expelled from India. The film would end with him gazing out over the Himalayas as his plane flies across them, and wonders what it is he's lost.

Now, his eyes glowing with excitement, Nick laid the choice before her. "I'm only waiting for you to say you'll come along. This is the film that will make me. But I need you. You want to be there with me, don't you? In the most fulfilling dramatic experience of my life?"

4

All spring, after Nick signed the contract, they read about India. Submitted to the necessary shots. Nick bought an easel, began to paint to feel out his role as an artist. Tommy, who would spend his first summer at camp, assuaged Jane's reluctance to leave him by his own excitement. "I *am* seven years old!" he boasted.

Still, she'd be unable to visit him and, when Jane heard there would be an enormous march on Washington in August for civil rights, she wondered if she shouldn't, after all, send Nick on alone. Nick, on hearing this, threw down the paint brush, threatened not to go himself.

"All right, all right," Jane conceded. Nick left for costume fittings on the Coast. At Gristede's, Jane ran into Cynthia Blackwood, told her of the projected journey.

"Will the director appreciate your help?" Cynthia, holding an avocado, appeared doubtful. The hair was as brilliant as ever but the familiar scarf was now more than decoration, only partially hiding the flabby, worn throat.

"Oh, I plan to stay very much in the background." Jane averted her gaze to Tommy, where the clerk allowed him to weigh out grapes. How tall Tommy was growing! The clear innocence of his eyes, the smooth, downy cheeks, the shoulder blades behind the thin shirt smote her with remorse that her own need should separate them so long. Cynthia was speaking.

"Really? Will Nicky allow that?" Jane was about to retort that Nick's contract permitted him to leave the picture any time in the first five weeks if he were at all dissatisfied. But Cynthia smiled. "I guess you *will* be able to give him a lot of help. On that relationship with the older woman. . . . Ta, darling. Don't let the cobras bite."

By the time they arrived in New Delhi, she and Nick, Grant Hastings, the director, had been in India a month to scout locations. An air-conditioned car—it was one hundred twenty degrees at the airport—waited to drive them to Almora, eighty miles away, five thousand feet high. They'd shoot the hill station portion of the film first, go down to Baroda in the northwest for the beginning scenes in the monsoon, the ending as the weather cleared.

Two hundred miles of Himalayan peaks stretched before the rose-covered bungalow Hastings had arranged for them. He was gentle, smiling, attired in Indian *khadi*, white hair neat, mild brown eyes alight with anticipation. He'd already filmed, he told them over dinner, shots for the opening scenes. Indian crowds, festivals, classical dancing, water buffalo in the scant waters of village tanks, desolate cows in search of food, bats hanging black and numerous as leaves from trees—all to be montage scenes passing before Nick's eyes while he lay sick and the sound track recorded his labored breathing.

"Unfortunately, Sandra's under the weather. We'll

shoot around that climactic diary scene, if we're to keep to schedule—two to four pages a day. . . ."

By morning, gasoline generators were pumping electricity for the exterior shots—Almora was lit by kerosene —and Anne Franklin, a new, exotic young actress who played the daughter, appeared, shy and nervous, for the scene where she and Nick walked hand in hand through the woods. Carefully, Jane watched as the clapsticks were held aloft. Grant ordered a take. There were several, and, with the final cry of cut, Nick glanced toward Jane.

She shook her head. Nick turned to Grant, asked for a retake, came to her side for a whispered consultation. Lines that had appeared adequate in script Jane now felt didn't express his character. Nick walked back to Grant who'd finished his tea, was reascending the ladder to peer again through the camera. As Nick offered the suggested revision, Jane saw the reproach Grant sent in her direction, and turned away. It was she who knew Nick's special quality, how it must be evoked.

That evening, in the bungalow, she went over the next day's lines with him, rewriting the script as they rehearsed. Like a dancer, Nick asked where she thought he should turn, how he should move. By the third day, when Sandra Bellamy at last felt herself well enough to join them, Grant Hastings had turned rather cool. An element of the good humor with which they'd begun had been dissipated.

Sandra saw to the remainder. The circles under her eyes troubled her. Did the set have to be so well lit? Grant reassured her: a somewhat haggard look—"despite your beauty, my dear"—would underline her stress, her unacknowledged passion for Nick.

But Nick, Sandra insisted before the first day of shooting had ended, had added bits to his close-up performance that simply weren't there in the script, or even in the medium shots they'd done together. "What is he up to?" she fumed. "He's reacting to all sorts of things I'm not doing at all. He's absolutely invalidating *my* close-ups!"

Grant ordered their scene together repeated in medium shot. As was customary, when the lines were redone for close-ups, Sandra's were taken first. Nick repeated his own lines as he'd first done. But when it was his turn for close-ups, there was an indefinable something. . . . Jane smiled toward him in secret triumph, such a small nod that surely only he would see it. What, for shame, she would never have done for herself, she promoted without compunction for Nick. It was a flicker of the eyes, a slow gaze toward the camera. . . . Sandra stalked off the set.

And when they viewed the rushes that evening, she had hysterics, demanded to know what that Belmont woman was doing here anyway. It was *her* doing, she who'd set Nick up to this bitchery. Jane, uncaring, sat dazzled. Nick's face, this first time she'd glimpsed it even on this blotchy screen, had mesmerized the camera, compelled it to commune with those features, those eyes. She was now ultimately seduced by what he could do in film.

By the time they descended to the monsoon in Baroda, Grant had taken Nick aside, insisted he'd have to order Jane off the set. Nick, one day short of his five weeks' option, refused to go on without her. At the guest house where most of them stayed, Sandra hid, afraid to go out among the rabid squirrels, the hidden cobras, the huge monkeys with dark faces and white Elizabethan ruffs. She didn't know why she'd let herself in for this torture, the heat, the constant rains. The *Hollywood Reporter*, Aurelia let Jane know in a laconic note, had aired Sandra's complaint that Nick was a bum, India's weather foul, the food inedible, and a goat had eaten her straw bag while she haggled at a bazaar over copper vases.

Then the weather broke, the pristine blue skies of the warm Indian winter began, scene after scene fell into place. Grant had submitted to Jane's presence but there was no socializing after work. When the film was wrapped, the producer cabled Nick: he was damned lucky not to be sued for the trouble he'd caused. Did Nick realize Sandra Bellamy—she'd defiantly eaten salad at the farewell dinner, despite all warnings—was now in a London hospital, because of him and that Belmont woman?

Angry, Nick laughed, handed the cable to Jane to preserve for his scrapbook, announced he'd stay on, tour the whole damned subcontinent. Jane, wanting by now only to see Tommy—he'd won, at camp, Tommy had written in his square uphill printing, the junior trophy for sailing—prevailed on Nick to come away.

Besides, while they'd been gone, *The High Mountains* had opened in the States.

If even the studio had been unprepared for audience reaction to Nick's film debut—the role, after all, had been secondary to Jim Wyatt, number one this year at the box office—surely she, Jane assured herself, had the right to feel as though shock waves were assaulting her. The first signal sounded as they landed at the airport where police restrained the screaming fans. Her own fingers were cold as she held Nick's hand on the drive into the city. His house was in a state of siege. Nick's smile was icy, his face pallid as they fought their way inside. "I told you, didn't I?" he exulted, his shaking hand reaching for a drink. In less than a week, his pleasure had turned to panic.

"I can't even walk to Gristede's for a loaf of raisin pumpernickel anymore," he mourned to Jane, the day he applied for an unlisted phone. Nick was, Sid Arkoff marveled, as he popped a Valium, washed it down with milk, "the hottest property in town." Movie offers, demands from Broadway producers had inundated his office. Scripts arrived both there and at Nick's house, from around the country, gradually from around the world.

This was a different sort of fame from any Jane had ever known. At the parties on penthouse terraces above the East River or across from Central Park, around tables at Regine's, at the Gurneys' in Sag Harbor, Nick was the center, the solar energy around which all others orbited. How soon, everyone asked, would the Indian film, his first starring role, be out? Grant Hastings was cutting it now and the producer, apparently rendered amnesiac about past anger, had reported there were hardly any outtakes; these few should be preserved forever as lessons in acting. To Nick and Jane each he sent a case of Chateau-Lafite Rothschild 1961: "a simple memento of my appreciation." He was running scared, Sid chuckled: Nick might sign on elsewhere for his next film.

In November, the country came to a halt: the energy, the vigor of the handsome and charming prince who'd stood at its head wiped out. As they watched the mourning crowds on television, Jane reflected that this universal grief was not for Kennedy alone, but that catharsis of tragedy that embodied all human sorrow. Nick brooded about the wheel of fortune:

"We must remember these days of our lives now, when everything's running lucky. We can't expect it's going to last."

Remembering Danny's image of the swing, Jane nodded. Perhaps, she told Nick, the greatest favor Providence had given mortals was not to know the future.

It was strange that in just this period Tommy should discover Scott's record of "Amazing Grace." "Who *is* this guy? The castle's named for him, right? And that's my middle name!"

Jane told him only that Scott had been a dear friend, like Kennedy also gunned down—in this case by hoodlums, because he wasn't white. With sudden pride, she added: "To him, *I* was Amazing Grace."

Death was, after Kennedy, in Tommy's thoughts. The golden eyes gazed into the distance a moment. "When I die, play that at my funeral."

Jane shuddered. Once, Nick had told her that. A sense of foreboding numbed her. It was as though she saw herself in some future, bereft of all she loved.

5

It wasn't until spring that their spirits really picked up. To deal with the influx of mail, scripts, fan letters, Jane prevailed on Nick to hire Helen Eustace as his secretary. Nick had always liked her—slim, pale, short hair in a pageboy, the face of an ascetic choirboy—and she'd been at loose ends since Mama's death. *The Rescue* was released simultaneously in New York and California. Immediately, several magazines announced achievement awards for Nick's performance. He was, they said, "the most promising star on the horizon . . . the star of tomorrow."

In dimly lit bars, Jane and Nick discussed with the Hearns his next move. Kathy was appearing in off-Broadway modern dance. "From bare feet to bare breasts," Nick warned.

"Are you sure," Steve asked, "you don't want to get back to Broadway? Isn't that your real home? You really want to subject yourself to Hollywood and everything that goes with it?"

Nick hunched over the table, the clear eyes hidden by dark glasses. "If Jane comes with me, I'll be all right."

The day he signed with Paramount at the MCA office where Sid was now affiliated, Jane went along. Three films at three hundred and fifty thousand dollars each. The right to pass on any script or director. No publicity duties beyond simple ones to publicize each production. On his side, the agreement could be scrapped at any time.

"This is an incredible contract on the basis of only two films," Sid crowed. "I've never handled one like it."

Would Paramount give Steve Hearn a screen test while they were about it? Nick wanted to know. Of course, Paramount answered. Nick smiled. "Anything Lola wants, Lola gets."

Alone, Nick went off to Europe. He needed to tour France in preparation for the first film—Stendhal's *The Red and the Black*. "Funny," Sid rather tactlessly pointed out. "*The Rescue* and this one: Nick's loved by an older woman."

At the pier, Jane saw Nick smile as he talked to a young crew member on deck. Before the tugs had pushed the *Queen Mary* out to its position on the river, while the tremendous blasts sounded from its smokestacks, he'd moved off, his hand on the boy's arm. A familiar jealousy flared in her as Jane turned away from the streamer-littered pier, her hand on Tommy's shoulder. Something in her child's regard of her halted her steps. Strange how patient he'd always been with her obsessive love.

At Wellfleet, Jane bought a Lightning for Tommy so he could enter the children's sailing events, watched the sunlight pour through the brilliant colors of the spinnakers, wrote a letter of protest against the Gulf of Tonkin resolution, LBJ's bombing assaults on Vietnam. *The New York Times,* she noted, had found that eighty-five percent of Americans approved these. But it was as though she couldn't begin to live again fully till autumn with Nick's return.

She greeted him with the *Life* magazine that had his picture on the cover. There was time to see *Fiddler on the Roof,* several other plays, before Nick was due in Hollywood for makeup tests, hairstyling, wardrobe. Aurelia was already sketching that. Paramount had lined up the best in every field: screenwriter, director, cinematographer, cast. A famous composer had agreed to do the score.

Together, Jane and Nick went through the hundred-forty-page script. In the margins he'd already listed the qualities describing Julien Sorel in the novel: reflective, fiery spirit, pale, gentle beauty, passionate nature, girlishly shy. . . .

Over lunch at "21," Jane recalled the idea that had come to her that day at the airport. "Here, in the first scene, the camera picks you up looking shy and scared when you come to meet Madame de Rênal. And she realizes she doesn't have to be afraid of this tutor her husband's hired for her kids." Jane's pen hovered above the script. "That first view of you—her view—should come from the rear, in your shabby seminarian's frock. She—and the camera—have to catch that sudden flood of emotion when your face is first seen."

" 'They call me Julien Sorel, Ma'am,' " Nick recited slowly, his wide eyes watching her face as he recited the lines from memory. " 'I am trembling as I enter a strange house for the first time in my life; I have need of your protection, and shall require you to forgive me many things at first. I have never been to College, I was too poor. . . .' " The hesitancy, the vulnerable pause by which he gained control. " 'My brothers have always beaten me, do not listen to them if they speak evil of me to you; pardon my faults, Ma'am, I shall never have any evil intention.' "

"They're going to say you were born to do this part." The force of her love frightened Jane. "In general, the script's an excellent job."

"But there are nuances you'll have to help me get across." As they stood, Nick turned to the waiter who hovered beside them. " 'Sir, I am uncomfortable in these new clothes: I, a humble peasant, have never worn any but short jackets; with your permission, I shall retire to my bedroom.' "

Bewildered, the waiter spread his hands, smiled, wished them a good afternoon. At the next table, several diners who'd recognized Nick beamed and applauded.

Before Jane flew out to the Coast to join Nick—with Tommy and Laura Crowell, who would tutor him—the New York Film Critics named Nick Best Actor of the Year for *The Rescue*. About her own role in Hollywood, Jane was apprehensive, strolled down Fifth Avenue as though in a ceremony of farewell to a significant portion of her life. Why, she wondered before her own reflection at Blanchard's, was she so anxious? In the wide mirrors as she had her hair done that last day before leaving, she watched several screen stars posing before the fireplace and rotating to view themselves. Jane studied her own image. She was almost forty. Was her face really as curiously unlined as her dark hair remained free of gray? She knew, objectively, she was still what was known as a striking beauty. Who were those unseen rivals she feared?

Aurelia had rented a bungalow for them in Brentwood. Tommy, his hair long like the Beatles—"Are you a boy or a girl?" a little old lady, her own tresses blue, reprimanded him. "Yes," Tommy, all innocence, replied —was excited at the sight of the fifty-foot-high letters that spelled out Hollywood on Mount Lee, at the famous arched gate of Paramount Studios off Melrose Avenue, where tourists peeped through. The house was surrounded by orange and olive trees, the air fragrant with acacias and azaleas, ablaze with hot pink and flaming red bougainvillea. Lovely as the bare gray mountains and the turbulent sea appeared, Jane felt strangely out of place. To Tommy, she explained: "I can't get used to facing the ocean with the sun in my face in the evening." She took him to Disneyland, introduced him to Mexican food. At his relish: "You're quite the gourmet for an eight-year-old, chum."

But it all seemed to her here too new, too foreign, it was as though she were constantly aware—always riding in cars, never walking as one did in New York—that this continual sunlight, these palm trees, this surfeit of luxury lay above a geologic and emotional fault that would send them all tumbling into that sea. At the parties they attended together—she, Nick, and Aurelia, her bosom grown top-heavy, her manner increasingly laconic—Jane had a vision of all these egos as so many underwater tendrils waving about to reach above one another for the light that filtered downward from the source of the moguls' power.

Nick delighted in taking her—he'd bought a cheap convertible—along Rodeo Drive to point out the shops crammed with imported luxuries, the stars' limousines parked outside. He dressed more sloppily than ever as he escorted her to Oblath's, outside the Paramount gate. They watched, over sandwiches and drinks, the stars and their agents argue. It was as though, Jane reflected, Nick were always watching *her,* asking that she render this life real to *him.*

It was only when rehearsals began that it became so.

The entire sound stage had been transformed into a nineteenth-century French village. The cinematographer, who'd already won three Academy Awards, had perused paintings of the period, announced he'd be reaching for some combination of color and light from both Constable and Turner. ("Ah!" Jane breathed. Turner was her favorite painter.) Nick had suggested to Martin Rasmussen, the director, that notion about the opening shot of him. Rasmussen, tall, with a rigid bearing and shaved head, had turned grave, murmured he'd consider it, then cold when Nick explained the idea had come from Jane.

Soon, he began to mimic the way Nick turned to Jane

after each take. Jane didn't care, didn't mind the constant waiting always involved in any film, the coolness of the script girl when she and Nick brought revisions in the morning. Whatever they were doing, she and Nick, would prove worth it. Her own popularity meant nothing to her.

There was a weekend during which Jane transported Tommy to San Francisco, introduced him to the sight of the gleaming bay, Chinatown, Fishermen's Wharf. Across the water in Berkeley stood the tower of the University of California. She allowed herself to imagine Tommy attending classes there, his hand in that of a young girl's, instead of, as now, her own. Tommy's question brought her back to the present. He indicated several slim youths at Union Square.

"How come they look like that—so different, Mom?"

She wasn't certain how to answer, how their outer difference was unique from that which Nick bore within. Tommy's attention had wandered, by then, to the cable cars.

It was the continuous influence of the dailies, soon after their return, that softened Rasmussen's harshness toward her. It was as though even he hadn't foreseen how the screen would come alive with Nick's grace, his beauty. The first slow smile, a momentary emotional setback, each effect they'd planned together the night before, consulted about on the set between takes, made the viewer captive to his appeal. His hair, his skin, his eyes, illumined by the sound-stage lights, would mount an erotic appeal to any woman. Nick was truly a man now, Jane reflected, watching his image on the screen—no longer the boy she'd first loved. . . .

But he was a rebel, the *Hollywood Reporter, Variety* cautioned. The papers were crammed, these days, with ads paid for by the studios and by the stars, bucking for Academy Awards. About Nick's nomination, the producer of *The Rescue* remained ominously silent. That, Dando—Nick's West Coast agent—fumed, was because Nick had signed with Paramount.

The night of the awards the studio sent a twenty-thousand-dollar rented limousine to deliver him to the Civic Auditorium in Santa Monica. The klieg lights burned through the fog drifting in from the ocean as they passed the stands erected for the hysterical fans. Just like in the movies, Jane thought. . . . The ABC-TV announcer thrust his microphone toward Nick's face as they stepped onto the red carpet lining the sidewalk from curb to entrance, and Jane, pushed aside, saw Nick turn pale as women screamed, tried to break through the police lines.

"No, I have nothing to say," he mumbled to the announcer and the watching audience at home. He flashed his slow puzzled smile toward the shrieking women. The camera caught a young girl letting out a squeal as she fainted into a policeman's arms.

Nick didn't win. It was Lee Marvin, for his role in *Cat Ballou*, who stood upon the stage, made his acceptance speech as he clutched the statuette. Nick's face remained impassive, only once his nose wrinkling. Bohdan Galitsky, the Rumanian director with the kinky reputation, had alerted him beforehand that he was having a party for losers. Now, as the ceremony broke up, a note arrived.

"So. I'll be expecting you. Bring your lady."

"Let's not go," Jane said. She didn't like the look on Nick's face.

"You ready to sleep yet?" he asked roughly. *"I'm sure as hell not."*

Outside the night was cold and she saw Nick shiver. The wide eyes stared at the orange and olive trees, the fuchsias and camellias as the limousine wound up the roads of Holmby Hills toward Galitsky's house. "There's always something blooming out here, isn't there?" Nick mumbled. "Just not me. . . ."

Each person entering the Tudor mansion was handed a medieval costume. "We're all rebels and freaks here," Galitsky called out, his lean face damp. At the rear an enormous ballroom was equipped with stereophonic sound and "Carmina Burana" played, over and over. "Defrocked monks and nuns singing, darlings!" Galitsky cried. "They got tired, too, of sucking on the tit of Mother Church." He'd had the windows covered with paper-stained glass, told them all to drink their champagne, hurl off the goblets at the windows, each bearing the name of a major studio. "Oh, mother!" he giggled, pulling back to fling his own glass.

The music was deafening. Jane, in a mock nun's outfit, saw Nick in a friar's burlap gown slit from neck to floor. He drank, wound up as though to throw, shrugged, turned away. By the time the paper hung in shreds from the windows, a long string of tables had been set up. A medieval feast of sorts had been prepared, the music still blared, only a few people were actually eating, a dish of small sugar cubes was being passed around. Jane, at first hesitant, sighed, swallowed one.

Soon the table began to tilt, Nick had disappeared, voices closer than those of the people about her were shouting in her ears, faces streamed up dangerously near as they emerged from the food before her. Then she was on some track that must be carrying her swifter than the speed of sound—prisms, triangles, spirals of color shot past her as she dived into them, flowers exploded in her face and turned to weeping eyes, she was in a tunnel with something loud and fierce pursuing her, a wind caught her up, rescued her, she was lying on the floor with cold fingers at her temples, she struggled to rise and a wooden swing hurtled from one end of the room to the other, Joanie was snuggled in her lap, Peter took her in his arms at the hotel room in Orlando, turned into Nick, " 'I have immortal longings in me,' " she heard herself whisper through cracked dry lips. . . .

She was still hallucinating, of course. This wasn't happening. Or was it? A monstrous tray and the music playing again the song of the roasted cygnet. Nick, naked on the platter, his limbs contorted like that of a trussed fowl, and the tray being passed down the table while hands reached. . . . With the tenor on the record, who sang in Latin, someone else in falsetto shrilled the words in English:

"Once I dwelt in the lakes,
once I was
a beautiful swan.
O miserable me!
Now I am
roasted black!

The cook turns me on the spit,
the fire roasts me through,
and I am prepared for the feast. . . ."

Jane, the silent scream of nightmare rising in her throat, reached to rescue Nick, but she floated upward, beyond, hovering above him as the hands picked at his dead white face. . . .

6

It helped that the Cannes Film Festival, in May, chose Nick as Best Actor. One film critic assessed why—aside from the lack of promotion—Nick hadn't won out in Hollywood. His technique, so natural, simply didn't come across as acting. Rasmussen let it be known that, while he admired Nick as an actor, he didn't care if he ever directed him again. Nick was an eccentric little bastard. *The Red and the Black* would reveal him as the hottest sex symbol of the day, but thank God the film was wrapped.

Two days later, as though in reentry from outer space, they were back in New York. Jane went on to Wellfleet with Tommy, received a call from the Hearns.

"A friend saw Nick at some joint in the West Village. Nick was sitting at a table and stroking the hair of some young boy. . . . People don't understand how affectionate Nicky is. He shouldn't behave like that in public."

The Red and the Black, on a reserved seats basis, opened in December in New York. Police on horseback moved across dirty snowbanks to hold back the crowds as celebrities arrived. Everything they'd labored on, she and Nick, worked. At the end, in the prison cell where he awaited execution, Madame de Rênal arrived to tell him she still loved him. Nick caught her to him, wept, kissed her hands. He kneeled before her, his face in tight close-up, and cut across her words, his voice slow, on one even pitch throughout, in the way only he could control.

" 'Know that I have always loved you, that I have never loved anyone but you.' " In answer to her question about the girl he'd married, Nick's face filled the screen, wide eyes staring. " 'It is only true in appearance,' " he pronounced. " 'She is my wife, but she is not my mistress.' "

The competition this year for the Academy Awards would be stiff, the critics noted. But surely this time Hollywood would recognize what they had in Nicholas Spenser. After the reviews were out, he appeared, late, at Jane's house. "It's all you," he insisted. "I could never have done it without you."

"If I make you believe that about yourself, I'll never work with you again," Jane protested. But the camera had rekindled all the dormant physical love repressed for so long. Like any shopgirl, her fingers ached for the feel of his hair, her body against his. Suddenly, as in the film, Nick was on his knees before her and kissing her hands.

" 'Know,' " he repeated, " 'that I have always loved you, that I have never loved anyone but you.' "

"Oh, God," she heard herself breathe, "I don't want to use you."

"Use me, use me!" He kissed her hands. "Everything else I am," he said, paraphrasing the lines of the film, "is true only in appearance. It's only you that can make me real."

But though, upstairs, he allowed her to undress him, the sweet remembered rituals of love between them, so long disused, failed. He lay asleep beside her and Jane traced the heavy eyebrows with her fingertips, the fine cheekbones, the strong shoulders, the hairy chest. There were new fine wrinkles around his eyes. . . . It didn't matter. All that really mattered was that he lay beside her.

The new film Paramount had lined up, they learned with incredulity, was now titled *Young Love*. Something, Jane affirmed, would have to be done about *that*. Paramount, Dando informed Nick, had signed Gloria Randolf, the beautiful seventeen-year-old who'd recently emerged from childhood roles. "You'll be the knockout couple of the year," he wired. "Assume you've seen the cover of *Time*."

Who hadn't? The blazing red hair cascading over the white gleaming shoulders, the eyes iridescent like green crystals fringed by heavy lashes, the full lips glistening, slightly parted. "Grown up now, Gloria exudes sensuality," the article had gushed.

Again, Nick flew out to the Coast for the requisite makeup tests, costume fittings, publicity shots. Jane, Tommy, and Laura Crowell—he'd attend school this time but Laura could still baby-sit—would have a house high above Coldwater Canyon on Eden Drive, Nick's place next door.

While the Vuitton bags were brought out of storage, Jane turned on the television. LBJ expressed his rage at the "nervous Nellies" who objected to the twentyfold increase in one year of American forces in Vietnam. Marines were setting fire to villages with cigarette lighters. Napalm and defoliation were commonplace. From Tommy's room, where two friends visited in farewell, over and over came the recorded sound of Arlo Guthrie's high voice in crescendo: "I wanna kill . . . kill . . . kill. . . ." On the phone, Jane spoke to Sybil Fox to whom she'd turned over the house in Greenwich to convalesce from a different sort of war: only she knew of Sybil's suicide attempt. As soon as she hung up, the phone rang again.

Aurelia thought Jane should know she'd succeeded in squashing a rumor about Nick. He'd driven up the Coast highway to Santa Barbara, had been recognized on a street corner with a couple of gays. "Guess he needs you here to play nanny."

The risks Nick dared—considering his public—always took Jane aback. She recalled Tommy's puzzled reaction to the boys at Union Square. It occurred to her there was something cabalistic about her thinking. Let her own child understand, accept—and the world, itself, could be transformed. One worked, after all, only through one's own life. But that life was not, should not be how one took the measure of the world. There must be some balance between personal principle and openness to the negation of others. Meanwhile, what it was she made of her son—his capacity not merely to tolerate but to embrace diversity—this itself could presage that "brave new world," that had such people in it: those never ready to cast the first stone. If she shaped her child to nothing but this, she might consider her motherhood successful.

Nick, when they arrived, had filled her house with flowers. Paramount was really pushing his nomination for the Academy Award. In town lingo, he was the "hottest property in Hollywood." On this basis, Jane arranged that they meet with Dando and the publicity chief from Paramount at the Polo Lounge, offer her new title for the film: *A Rose at Christmas.* The two faces across from them looked blank.

"This is a young couple essentially out to exploit one another." As Jane explained, she saw herself through their eyes: the New York outsider. "The crux of the movie is that they each discover an unexpected depth they're not prepared to handle. The epiphany of the story lies in their learning really how to love."

"The epiphany?" Puzzled, the publicity chief allowed his cigar to dangle from his lips.

"From Shakespeare. But we could keep that secret," Nick said.

"At Christmas I no more desire a rose
Than wish a snow in May's new-fangled mirth;
But like of each thing that in season grows."

There was, apparently, a price for Nick getting what he wanted. The studio agreed on the title. But the morning of the award ceremonies, the publicity chief called. Jane, on her way back from bringing Tommy to school, sat on Nick's bed with a cup of coffee. Nick was to pick up Gloria Randolf—whom he'd not yet met—was to arrive, for publicity purposes, with her in the limousine Paramount provided.

"Nyet!" Nick barked into the phone. Since arising, he'd been doubled up with cramps, was alternating shots of Scotch with glasses of milk. "I'm going with Jane Belmont."

Argument at the other end. At last, a concession. Jane could "go along." Gloria was not to be kept waiting. As far as the studio was concerned, this was the beginning of the movie, this night when Nick and Gloria would first appear together.

Gloria lived with a mother known for a certain tough good sense and strictness in a house in Hidden Valley. The street turned off Coldwater Canyon on Mulholland Drive toward the summit with large homes, impressive gardens. The limousine had almost reached its destination when Nick leaned forward, told the chauffeur to slow up.

"Goddam it, I don't care if the little twit has to wait all night!" To Jane, as he pressed the fist into his abdomen: "I should get some raw meat into me. I'll throw up in the little twit's lap if I don't."

Jane was silent. She was aware that she was elegant, exotically lovely in her apricot-hued Oscar de la Renta gown, her hair smooth and pulled into a French twist. Nick had helped her to clasp the emerald, diamond, and sapphire necklace, bracelet and earrings. But the evening was spoiled for her, having to share it. As the car moved on to the summit, Nick kept clearing his throat, pulling at his tie.

"I'm not going to win anyway," he muttered. "It's got to be Burton for *Virginia Woolf*. . . . He deserves it."

"*You* deserve it," Jane snapped. Through the open windows drifted the fragrance of camellias. The orange and avocado trees were heavy with fruit. The chauffeur kept making tsk-tsk sounds and shaking his head as he glanced at the dashboard clock, swept the car into the curving driveway. The open door framed Gloria in a green sequin and chiffon gown, cut low to reveal her voluptuous gleaming breasts. The pictures didn't do her justice.

"Hi, kids," she called out. The studio publicity chief appeared behind her.

"Where in hell you been?" he growled as he handed Gloria into the car.

Nick mumbled something, barely glanced at Gloria who leaned across him to shake hands with Jane. He hadn't offered his own.

"What'd you say, chum?" Her voice was curiously little-girlish, at odds with the shattering sensuality. She spread the green gown across his knees.

"I said I hope you're going to get rid of that gum before we get there," Nick muttered. He held himself stiffly away from her.

"Oh, sure." Gloria took his hand. "Don't lose your cool. You're going to win. I know it."

Nick gave his short bark, tried to withdraw his hand. Gloria held it more firmly. "How *jew* know? Play ouija with your dolls or somepin'?" As though to underline his contempt, Nick slurred his words.

Gloria, the masses of red hair falling about her shoulders, threw back her head and laughed. The glow of the street lamps revealed her arched white neck. "Hey, you're a surly little shit, you know that?" She squeezed his hand, wrinkled her nose at the publicity man, who glowered on the jump seat across from them. "Cheer up, buster," she told him. "You look like your fucking hemorrhoids hurt."

Nick turned to look at her for the first time, emitted his first real laugh of the day. Pleased, Gloria again squeezed his hand.

"He's just worried we won't come on like we're laying each other. To get ready for our parts in the movie." Her voice, if not the vocabulary, mimicked Hedda Hopper. "Look, chum," she explained, as though much older than Nick, "I've been in this racket since I was ten. They're all assholes. Don't let them bug you." She settled back against the upholstery, one hand on Nick's, the other playing with the heavy radiant hair. As the arc lights cut across the sky and the screams of the crowd became audible, she cracked her gum loudly, spit it into her palm, and handed it to the publicity chief. "Here, buster. You can chew it now."

The chief maneuvered the gum into the ashtray. They were now a block from the Civic Auditorium. He leaned toward Jane. "This is where you and I get off."

"What?" Nick snarled.

"Studio orders." The man's smile was tense. Gloria leaned forward to flash beautiful even teeth at Jane.

"Shitty, isn't it? You should say, 'Hell no, I won't go!' " She giggled. "But we'll sit together inside. They give me any trouble on that, I'll pee on the seats."

Because the line of limousines moved at such a crawl, it was possible for Jane—the publicity chief grasping her elbow—to reach the area of the long red carpet just as Nick and Gloria arrived. Nick turned to hand Gloria out of the car and a tremendous shout went up from the fans. The ABC-TV announcer thrust himself toward them and swept them to the microphone.

"The audience out here and all of you out there," he cried hoarsely, "at last have a chance to see Hollywood's most romantic—I guess you could say most beautiful—young couple together. Together at last for their new film, *A Rose at Christmas*. The way they're together every minute off the set. Would you care to say a few words, Miss Randolf? Who's going to win for Best Actor, in your opinion?" He held the microphone to her full, smiling lips.

Giving the camera a good view of her high white breasts, Gloria leaned toward it. Again, Jane was struck by the contrast between the opulent splendor of her appearance and the strangely little-girl voice.

"If they had the Oscars right out here," she said, "I could save us all a lot of trouble by handing one to Nicky right away."

The fans cheered, screamed, applauded. Gloria turned away, with a proprietary air straightened Nick's tie. Briefly, Nick smiled, shook his head as the announcer thrust the mike before his face. Gloria pushed her arm through Nick's, swept on toward the entrance with the train of her chiffon gown lifted in one hand.

"Come on," the publicity chief growled to Jane. His sparse hair shone with spray. "I don't know why in hell he couldn't say something. The fans like to hear the stars talk in real life."

Real life. . . . Of course, it was real life that their seats were *not*, after all, together. The TV monitors showed the heavy red hair fall across Nick's shoulder as Gloria talked to him, buoyed him up during the long ceremony. It was also, Jane supposed, real life that *The Red and the Black* won for Best Film, Best Screenplay, Best Musical

Score, Best Costume (Aurelia, heavy, dignified, on-stage), while Paul Scofield, with *A Man for All Seasons*, won for Best Actor and Fred Zinnemann for Best Director. That led, Jane imagined, from the self-congratulatory pleasure audiences—bored as they might have been by the film—derived from identifying with the martyred Thomas More. They, who supported the war in Vietnam, congratulated themselves that they, too, would have behaved with such high morality. A man nearby said to his companion:

"It's just what that critic said. Nicholas Spenser comes on as so damned natural, it doesn't seem like he's acting."

"Oh, well, he's young yet. Anyway, I think Burton should have won," his companion answered.

Should have.... She should have been at Nick's side, Jane thought, to comfort him. But it wouldn't be long now. There would be no losers' party tonight. They'd go home together, leave this crush of strangers behind. The publicity chief was lost in the crowd as she pushed her way outside, waited in the cool air, damp from the ocean, and shivered. It was taking a long time for the limousines to drive up. The red carpet was littered with flower petals fallen from corsages, the air heavy with perfume as the throngs streamed out and Jane was jostled to one side. A hand grasped her elbow and she turned in relief. It was the publicity chief.

"Come on," he muttered, not looking at her. "I'll get you home."

"Where's Nick?" she protested. "I want to wait for Nick."

"Use your eyes." His own flicked with impatience.

Nick was surrounded by a small group of well-known stars. A few were reaching for him, others had already squeezed into the limousine that waited with all its doors open. That was Jim Wyatt with his arm across Nick's shoulders. Wyatt was shaking his head at a reporter and shouting. Nick's face was pale, stunned, a fixed smile, and Gloria laid her hand on his cheek, leaned forward to kiss him. Jane pressed closer.

"I'm saying," Wyatt cried out, "what does the kid need a lousy award for? Here's the greatest bundle of beauty in Hollywood in love with him! You wanna learn about love, bumchick? You watch these two!"

They were gone then, all of them, into the limousine. For one moment only, Nick had appeared to hesitate, to search the dark sky still crisscrossed by the arc lights playing toward it. As the car moved off, the lights went out. There was still the press of the crowds about her, noise, the smell of expensive perfume, of flowers. Somebody stepped on Jane's gown, there was the sound of a rip, the person turned quickly to see who she was, shrugged, pushed on. The fog had turned to drizzle. The publicity chief's fingers were hard on her arm.

"Hey," he said, looking into her face. "This it? This what you meant by epiphany?" He chuckled. "Come on. I gotta get that limo turned back in."

Chapter X

1

A shuttlecock, Jane brooded: that's what she'd become, slammed between rage and fear. The rage was mortifying, for the first time brought with it a dread of viewing the dailies. For their many two-shots, the long arm of the Chapman crane reached across to Nick and Gloria under the special lighting the cinematographer had devised. A soft high light in front of their faces with a hard back light, it stressed the romantic tension between them. In the evening, those close-ups filled the screen, illumined it with their beauty, the tenderness they evoked in one another. Nick's wide-eyed stares, his hesitations, his vulnerability summoned in Gloria a trembling luminous Madonna-like quality. Jane still coached him and Nick was teaching Gloria. The success of this team effort brought, in the dark of the screening room, bile to Jane's throat.

The fear was different. When Nick vacated the house nearby to move into a bungalow at the Beverly Hills Hotel, she imagined it was to elude her for possible meetings with Gloria. The day Gloria escorted them to the Farmers' Market, Bohdan Galitsky showed up at the stall where they were buying black bread. From the look exchanged between him and Nick, he'd known Nick would be there. That night, Jane lay wakeful, staring through the bedroom skylight at the giant palms overhead. She imagined Nick drawn on that drive up to Holmby Hills where, like some giant spider, Bohdan waited. This was a first, so far as she knew: Nick going to an older man. . . . There were times now when the dailies traced signs of stress on Nick's face. Scenes had to be reshot. This was the apprehension that wove itself through the jealous anger Gloria's presence in Nick's life had ignited.

One Sunday morning at four Nick showed up at Jane's house. He was very drunk.

"Know what? Hey, you know what?" Face pale, sweating, Nick lurched against a coffee table. "I'm in bed, see? Like a good boy. And comes this knock at the door. What the hell—I figure the asshole'll check out if I just lie low. But no. So finally I get up. You know what's there? Some naked dame. An open kimona, and naked." Trembling, Nick fumbled for the pills he always carried. Jane dashed them from his hand.

"Are you crazy? On top of all that booze?"

"You know what it is, don't you?" He stumbled over his own feet, sank to the floor. "The studio put her up to it. A publicity gimmick. Supposed to make me come off their big he-man star!" On his knees, he groped for the pills in the heavy shag rug. "Damn it! How'm I going to sleep now? I should've gone to Bohdan. I don't need a nursemaid."

"Then get out! Go!" But as Nick struggled to stand, Jane sank to his side, her hands on his shoulders while the gray eyes stared wildly. "You *can't* go! You can't drive in this condition. . . ."

He lifted a quivering hand to her hair, smoothed it back. Then his face was against her shoulder. "You don't know what it's like, Janie. Christ, you don't know!"

"What? What, my darling?" She held the lean body close.

"You know, in my own way," he mumbled against her neck, "I do love her. Glory, I mean." Jane's muscles tensed. "I mean, how can you help loving her? Here's this fantastic creature wants me to go to bed with her. And I can't. I just can't. She supposed to keep thinking I turn her down for her own sake? Because she's too young?" A feeble bark of laughter. "A coupla times I imagined myself actually marrying her—like she wants me to. You think I wouldn't like that? I wouldn't like to have kids? Huh? But then I always know . . . know how impossible . . ."

From the patio beyond came the pleasant sound of the fountain. It had probably accompanied many small woeful dramas enacted here. Nick said: "I know what you think—me and Bohdan. But how else can I punish myself? How else do I drive it home to myself once and for all? That I'm the dregs of the earth?"

Tommy, golden eyes stricken, appeared in the doorway. Shamefaced, Nick turned away as Jane urged Tommy back to bed, said she'd be with him shortly. She fed Nick milk, steamed a pot of rice, laid him to sleep as the sun crept through the early morning smog. In his bed, Tommy lay rigid, watching her.

"It's the pressures of Hollywood, darling," Jane began, as she sat on his bed.

Tommy nodded. "I know. People are different out here, aren't they?"

Jane smiled. "How do you mean?"

He shrugged, his brown fingers playing with the rumpled sheet. "I don't know. Like at school. All these film stars' kids. I like them all okay. But it's like I always feel they're different—or maybe I am." A frown between the dark brows as Tommy puzzled it out. "Maybe it's like they're Coca-Cola. And I'm milk and orange juice. . . ."

Jane leaned over, hugged him to her. "How would a nine-year-old milk-and-orange-juice boy like going back to sleep with his favorite lullaby?"

Tommy laughed. He snuggled back into the pillows as she sang:

"Hushabye, don't you cry,
Go to sleep, my little baby;
When you wake, you shall have
All the pretty little horsies,
Blacks and bays, dapples and greys,
All the pretty little horsies."

Gloria appeared the day after the film was wrapped. There'd been an elegant party at Le Bistro the night before, camera flashes reflected in the mirrored walls of the rococo restaurant. Jane had watched Nick leave with Gloria, his arm around her gleaming shoulders in the low-cut taffeta gown. Today, as the green crystal eyes filled with tears, Jane learned that Nick had only seen her home.

"It's a good thing," Gloria whimpered in her little-girl voice, "the picture's done. Now I can let myself cry. I've really tried to be brave. And I didn't want to hold up shooting, with bloodshot eyes. But what am I going to do now, now that we're finished?" she wailed. "I love him so!"

Surely, Jane thought, she was herself too young to play the maiden aunt? Then she remembered Nick's torment. "Nick's more than ten years older," she offered lamely. "Isn't this really too soon to think of love? Or marriage?"

"Oh, shit!" Gloria moaned. "You sound like my goddam mother." The green eyes widened, teardrops clinging to the long curly lashes. "Listen! What *is* it with Nick and that kinky director, anyway? They don't *really* fuck each other, do they?" Lips innocently apart, a child asking about Santa Claus. Jane assayed a light smile.

"You shouldn't listen to rumors. You know Hollywood by now."

"Um. Well. That's not the only rumor, you know." Gloria pulled a strand of heavy red hair across her face as though to conceal behind it the sudden sly expression. "How about *you*? Are you in my way, too?" Jane was silent in the familiar protection she gave to Nick. Gloria smiled. "Okay. I already asked Nick. He says he doesn't kiss and tell. But look. If I'm too young for him, aren't you too old?" The clear direct gaze of a child in the woman's face. That gaze changed at something, an intuition of the distress in Jane's. Suddenly, she was at Jane's knees and hugging her, the smooth satiny arms clinging to Jane's waist, the red hair—so beautifully lit by the late sun flooding through the open blinds—tumbling across her lap.

"You do love him, too. You're mad for him, just like me! Oh, damn, damn, damn! How do you stand it? Tell me! If you can't have him, how do you stand it?"

Perhaps, Jane thought as she stroked the heavy hair, this was a foretaste of her future role. Still, it was the first time anyone had identified with her own pain. Gloria grew quiet, looked up at her.

"I'll always love him," she announced matter-of-factly. "I know he won't marry me. At least not now. But I'll always be his friend. That," she declared, with an element of satisfaction in the drama, "I solemnly swear. No matter what I'm doing or where I am, if he ever needs me, I'll always be there for him." Another flash of that intuition. "That's the way it is with you, isn't it?" Yes, Jane reflected: reduced to this marginal creature, this half life. "But I guess the thing is: he has to let us. I mean, he's just going to have to let us *into* his life." Turning at the door as she left, Gloria gave Jane a direct adult stare. "His life. I guess it's such a kind of hell. Isn't it?"

Was it, Jane wondered alone, the tyranny of the weak that was essentially Nick's hold on her? Or that she so revered the genius that expressed itself through his acting? And why, after all this time, was it only through *his* acting that her reverence for theater emerged? A pallor appeared to dim the scene before her. Was it only Danny's old construction of her life? That night, for the first time in years, she dreamed of Danny. He tried to tell her something, something he'd said many years before. In her dream, she called out, "But I can't hear!" There was suddenly an exquisite stillness and his voice was plain in her ears. "Don't you know work *is* everything? . . . But only together with love."

Summer was over when they returned east. Nick, restless, left to join the Hearns, touring Europe. Jane hadn't fully understood how restful it would be with him away. Weekends at Sag Harbor with Tommy and the Gurneys, evenings out with Hugh Kirkland, meetings at the Museum of Modern Art. There were long walks, tennis and ice-skating with Tommy. It occurred to Jane more than once: there was no one with whom she enjoyed herself more. Stopping with him to glance in a shop window on Madison Avenue to look at imported baby clothes, she had a sudden image of Tommy grown, married, and in her arms his infant girl, fragrant and babbling in a tiny smocked dress like these. This was, she conceded, rather rushing things: he *was* only ten years old.

The night Nick was back at the townhouse he invited her to join him and the Hearns. Sprawled on the floor to cut up his raw steak, he suddenly—though she'd seen him drink nothing—began to crawl upstairs on his hands and knees. Before she and Helen Eustace could reach him, he'd blacked out.

Yes, Kathy said, that had happened before, on little or no liquor. In Europe, he'd consumed pills as though there were no tomorrow. Especially since he'd heard of Gloria's marriage to a young tobacco heir. Kathy, pregnant, was clearly out of patience with Nick, relieved to see him and Steve leave almost immediately for Hollywood with an original script they'd been working on. It was turned down everywhere. What appeared to bother Steve more, on their return, was the rumor that had followed them. That he and Nick were lovers.

"Where in hell do they get *that* kind of shit?" Steve fumed. Incredibly, the Hearns still didn't know about Nick.

Meanwhile, there was a long delay in the release of *A Rose at Christmas.* The director had been ill and Dando confided that holding off till later in the year would help its chances for Academy Award nominations. Twice a week, Nick showed up at Sid's office to argue about scripts.

"He's being offered the cream of the crop," Sid complained to Jane. "But he calls them all crap."

To Jane, Nick countered: "Listen. I have to have some principles. No?"

"Oh, you should." In his living room, Jane looked toward the stairs. Halfway down, in a black satin robe, Gregorio Petruzzi, seeing her, stood hesitant. Supposedly, Nick had picked him up when Gregorio had waited on him at an Italian restaurant in the Village.

"You mean you met him in Rome and gave him the passage money over," she'd challenged, only half believing it. Nick's dark brows lifted in surprise. He gave her a slow, admiring smile.

"You *are* a witch, aren't you?"

Weary of righteousness, Jane tried to convince herself this was preferable to the cruising that had preceded Gregorio's move into Nick's house. She sometimes wondered if he might have taken a lover worthy of him if she were not available to provide that equality of temperament. And how could she censure Nick for his various addictions when she had no control over her own—for him? This was 1966. Almost a decade he'd towered over her life, erasing from it the importance of so much else. To Tommy, she suddenly announced:

"You've never been to Europe. I think it's time we rectified that. Could you tumble to the Grand Tour?"

2

June fifth, the day they sailed, Israel answered Egypt's blocking of the Gulf of Aqaba to Israeli shipping. Syria and Jordan joined Egypt in Israel's third war. Quickly, Tommy became attuned to the agitation with which Jane awaited the daily ship bulletins. More than ever, she had to resist the old desire to tell him about Danny. Instead, as they paced the decks in the early morning, she spoke to him for the first time of her early life—of her twin, of Joanie. They paused to lean against the rail above the cabin class deck and Tommy was silent as his arm went around her, the wide-set golden eyes clouded with concern. Jane clasped his hand, smiled, pointed to the distant clouds that resembled land above the sparkling swelling sea. She spoke of her triumphs in the theater. Tommy, enraptured, accepted without question that she'd gladly given up all that for marriage, motherhood.

By the time they docked at Southampton, the Mideast war was over. In six days, Israel had won a stunning victory—as Danny said when she called. They'd bought, he told her, a little more time before the next conflict.

"Let's go there!" Tommy said, alert to Jane's relief. She offered a lame excuse about hotel reservations throughout the continent.

While they traveled, they read of race riots in the States, especially in Newark and Detroit. At something called a Summer of Love gathering, the so-called caviar of psychedelics—STP—was consumed. The *Paris Tribune* described smoke-ins held by hundreds of East Village hippies on sunny Sundays in Tompkins Square Park. "Wonder if I'll grow up to be a hippie?" Tommy mused. And Vietnam. Always Vietnam. . . .

Tommy sent a dejected card to Nick: the Beatles, since the *Sergeant Pepper's* album, with its new method of sound tracks, were no longer performing in concert. Jane's only communication to the States was a gift—a complete wardrobe of handsewn dresses—to the Hearns' baby girl. She told herself she was convalescing from a long illness. On the beach at St. Tropez, Tommy was pleasantly embarrassed by the women in topless suits. At Cannes, he took her sailing, gave her a bad few moments when, with a sudden gust, he let the sail jibe.

"Don't worry," he reassured her. "There always has to be a first time."

"Be sure it's the last." Under his tan, his own face had paled.

But Tommy's favorite jaunt turned out to be the Tivoli Gardens. "This is *really* where it's at, man!" He appeared especially satisfied to learn she'd never traveled there with Nick. "Of course," he put in quickly, amazing her with the strange comprehension in his eyes, "you can't drop Nick. You know that, don't you?"

She didn't want to think of Nick. It annoyed her, when they returned, that Helen Eustace called immediately with the information that Nick and Gregorio were at Cherry Grove on Fire Island. Jane didn't want to know. With something like distant pity she listened to Helen: she knew that Helen's passion for Nick was by now such that, simply to be allowed to talk of him, eased a part of her frustration.

In October, thirty-five thousand war critics marched on Washington, so-called flower children spiked the militia's rifles with blossoms. Two hundred demonstrations took place at colleges and young people chanted: "Hey, hey, LBJ, how many kids did you kill today?" Jane, watching body counts on TV, permitted herself some hope that the war would wind down. With the Gurneys, she attended the opening of *Hair* at the New York Shakespeare Festival's Public Theatre. In the lobby, during intermission, they ran into Nick.

He was alone, dirty, unshaven. The hollows in his

cheeks were startling, in the thin face his nose stood out like a blade. The Gurneys were clearly appalled. Nick grasped Jane's arm.

"Please. Come outside with me. I've got to see you." As she hesitated and the Gurneys moved off: "Now!" He was wildly overexcited, his pupils dilated. Walking out with him, Jane assumed an armor, resolved not to let him reach her.

"I had to break up with him—the little shit!" Nick shuffled beside her, his shoulders hunched. They passed stores with water pipes and roach holders in the windows. "He was always cheating on me." Nick shook pills out of his pocket, picked through them like a jeweler weighing out carats. Jane halted.

"I'm going back if you take anything."

He stared, spread his palm flat so the varicolored capsules rolled around on it, pitched them to the curb, and waited, as though for her praise. The armor held Jane silent, but she walked on.

"Don't you think I want to get off them?" he said. "You know what insomnia is. . . . We were fighting all the time. Greg kept taking LSD. Someone gave him chlorpromazine as an antidote. He went into convulsions. Almost died. He swore he'd be faithful and we'd start a new life. Two nights later I come back from the city and he has some leather-pants rat with him. I threw him out. . . ."

A flask had appeared in Nick's hand. Again, Jane stood motionless. Irate, he glanced over at her, took a few steps, leaned against a storefront. A cold gust blew across his forehead. It was as though an invisible bridge separated them. But already, the gray eyes staring toward her asserted their old power. As though he knew it, felt he owed her some freedom of choice, Nick looked away, peered off into the distance where streetlights illumined the slow drizzle that had begun to fall. A man walked by, glanced at her curiously, then at Nick, paused, walked on. The street lamp was, she saw, much like a spotlight on Nick's face while he continued to stare away from her.

"Nick. What's happened to you?" She heard the note of pleading in her voice.

He turned his head. The pale, staring eyes reminded her of that night in the Village when he'd recited the line from *Ghosts*. He spread his hands, let them drop to his sides. *His* voice was slow, husky.

"It was Gloria. She showed me what I'm losing out on in life. Being what I am." He seemed to draw himself inward, as though to disappear through the glass against which he leaned. A young couple approached, looked at them, whispered something as they passed, and laughed, glancing back.

Was it that old sense of having been remiss toward others? Or was it her own need that made her see him as handing her his lifeline, appealing to her to tow him in or leave him to drown?

"You know," Jane said, "you wanted to be the greatest actor in the world. Will you come back to the theater? Will you accept—grace under pressure—what you are, what you need? That's all that's necessary."

"That's all?" The voice was hollow now.

"Give up on Hollywood. The theater can embrace your talent. And you—as you are. Without camouflage—or debauching and destroying yourself."

A muscle flickered in his cheek. "You make it sound so easy."

"Life's not easy. If you take some responsibility for yourself, I'll help."

Sid Arkoff didn't want to.

"Are you saying you won't find Nick a play because the same money won't be in it for you?" she argued. His protest was too weak. She went to Hugh Kirkland.

"You're the top producer. You can have the top talent. If you find the vehicle for him."

"All producers, dear heart, are gamblers. But hasn't your protégé been working out for the basket-case lately? Drinking's bad enough. Booze and dope together?" Hugh leaned back in his leather chair, shook his head.

"He's straightening out. I'll vouch for him."

"Oh, *you*. No limb's too weak for *you* to go out on for him." At something in her face, he sighed. "All right. Let me think about it. I *do* have something by an interesting new fellow in Texas. Won a prize for it in a production out there. . . ."

So it was that when, at the end of November, with Gloria still on her honeymoon in Paris, *A Rose at Christmas* opened in New York, Jane was at Nick's side. For two weeks he hadn't had a drink, appeared pale, purged, yet radiant as their limousine pulled up to the theater. Colored lights twirled atop patrol cars and the police joined hands to hold back the crowds. But as their car stopped, the shout went up.

"He's here! It's him! He's in that car!"

Nick hesitated, stepped out, turned to give Jane his hand. Several policemen were thrown against him as the mob surged through. Jane saw the hands tearing at him, the buttons ripped from his tuxedo. As she reached futilely to help him—"Hey, who's *she?*"—other hands came at her. She lifted her arms to guard her face, felt a hank of her hair pulled, the cold steel of scissors at her neck as a strand of hair was clipped.

The police regrouped, amid the shrieks and wails came the thwack of billy clubs, she and Nick were hurled almost bodily into the theater. They peered at one another, both shaking, simultaneously yielded to weak laughter. As they were handed protectively toward their seats, Jane leaned toward Nick, still pale and disheveled.

"Can you give all that up? A few years on the stage and you'll never get *that* again."

"They're crazy," he said in his slow, wondering voice. "What do they want?"

"Darling, all of you. . . . That's one of the reasons you're bowing out."

The reviews, hailing Gloria and Nick as "the most beautiful couple in film history" could only be viewed as a setback to her plans. Critics pointed out how the camera underlined the almost mystical bond between them. It was said that Nick had opened forever a new path in acting for the screen, one no serious performer could ignore. "Even," said one, "that almost androgynous movement when he walks."

Nick should, Steve argued, if he were to begin again in theater, start seeing a psychiatrist. It was the only answer. Didn't Jane agree?

Jane had never been enamored of therapy. Still, Hugh Kirkland had come forward with the play. Steve

319

knew of a Dr. Samuel Winkler who'd treated other theater people. Kathy added that he tried to get his patients
to use their aggressions effectively. Perhaps that was
what Nick needed.

To Jane's surprise, after his first visit, Nick was
elated, announced he'd be going every day from now on.
A weight had dropped from her, been handed to someone else. They met at Elaine's where Hugh awaited
them. Nick, moving his glass of milk around on the red-
checkered tablecloth and contributing his new purified
smile, listened to a summary of the play. Hugh relaxed,
told Jane that Sybil Fox would have a strong part as
Nick's mother. It was as though Nick had passed some
test.

By the end of January, there was a change in national
affairs. With the astounding cost of the Tet offensive,
Walter Cronkite announced that, in Vietnam, the United
States was threatened with "cosmic disaster." Robert
Kennedy told the papers that Tet "shatters the mask of
official illusion." In the entertainment section, there was
news of Gloria's quickie divorce from her tobacco heir.
Nick, completely engrossed in a father-figure projection
on Dr. Winkler—"He never had a real father relationship," Steve Hearn explained worriedly—laughed with
delight, wired Gloria that now she'd starred in her own
UFF—Unfinished Fuck Picture, he told Jane.

Whatever Dr. Winkler did for him it wasn't, Jane decided, a change of his need for pills or liquor. It was,
Nick argued, his insomnia that made him carry in his
jacket pocket the old array of pills, together with vita-
mins. While he waited for rehearsals to begin, he fre-
quented a dingy bar on Third Avenue, from a dark
wooden booth and studied the customers.

"The pimps and winos come and go," he said, "talking of Joe DiMaggio."

It was here that Gloria, radiant and heavily made up,
joined him when she was "free—free at last." Her one
goal for 1968, she said, was to become Mrs. Nicholas
Spenser. After much laughter, many tears. Rebuffed, she
left for Hollywood. In March, Nick was nominated again
for the Academy Award and play rehearsals, to Jane's
relief, began. Gloria sailed for England without seeing

Nick. There was a rumor about a British screen actor that made Jane nervous for Nick. Rehearsals, she heard from Sybil Fox—Dr. Winkler had instructed Nick he should stand on his own feet in this venture, not add another mother to his life with Jane—were not going auspiciously.

The play was scheduled to open on tour at the end of April. Before that, Johnson announced he was deescalating the war, wouldn't run again. In Memphis, Martin Luther King was shot. What kind of country was this? people were asking. Violence abroad, violence at home. Although *A Rose at Christmas* picked up a number of prizes at the awards ceremony, Nick lost out. He promptly disappeared from sight—"You stay out of it," Dr. Winkler instructed frostily when Jane called his office—and, after four days, Sybil phoned.

"I thought you should hear it from me first. Nick's been dropped from the play."

3

The other news Jane read about: Sybil Fox and Hugh Kirkland planned to marry. Also, Albert Poster's latest novel—*Legend of Their Youth*—had won the National Book Award and been sold to Paramount. Nick—as one of a trio of men attempting the first climb of a treacherous mountain—would star, drawing down a million dollars for the role. Dando had negotiated a multiple picture, nonexclusive contract for him that appeared to give Nick every privilege. It was on this basis—resurfacing without explanation or apology—that Nick called, invited Jane to come with him to the Cannes Film Festival. He'd been nominated again for Best Actor.

"Think I should go?" In her question to Tommy, Jane heard a sulkiness that asked only to be wheedled. "It's like two straight weeks of Academy Award nights."

"Sure, Mom! Maybe I could get out of school and come along."

"Nice try. Get back to your homework or I'll send you to military school." Over crackers loaded with peanut butter, they agreed she wouldn't mention to Nick his aborted role in the play.

Cannes, Jane decided, was like a mob trance. Dozens of pictures alternated at theaters, hotel suites, and nightclubs while hysterical throngs on the Croisette pushed to identify the stars. Warren Lantz, producer of *Legend*, was already peddling foreign rights to it from his suite at the Carlton. Rushing out at intervals to the terrace to ogle the panoply of flesh on the beach below, he admonished his daughter, Susan, to behave herself. She was sixteen, blonde, blue-eyed, with exquisite skin, a tiny, high rib cage, a constant delighted giggle—especially when Warren Lantz handed her over for safe keeping into Nick's hands. The night of the awards, when Nick won, Susan sat between him and Jane.

At the party, later, Jane, sated with pleasure, saw Nick—very elegant in his evening clothes—hold forth to a group of younger actors. When she looked again, he and Susan were gone. At dawn, still sleepless in her wide bed, she heard him stumble across her room, watched as he searched out some Nembutals, washed them down with Scotch. He tumbled into bed beside her.

"Hey, Gawge," he said, like Lenny in *Of Mice and Men*, while he caressed her body under the sheet. "I done a bad thing, Gawge. Warren Lantz finds out what I gone and done to his little rabbit, I gonna be in damn big trouble, Gawge." His hand on her belly, he fell asleep.

Of course Warren Lantz found out. In New York, Nick showed Jane a cable from Gloria in England: "Marrying Kenneth Campbell unless you come for me in twenty-four hours." He flew off to Barbados with Susan, who wrote to her father: "If I died now, I'd die happier than any girl has ever been."

"Die?" Lantz raged to Jane. "She talks about dying? He's the one gonna die, believe me! He meets cute with my kid and right away it's a tits-and-ass production? I'll kill the monster! Who does he think he is, doing this to my child?"

322

Jane wondered. Since Nick had begun making love to *her* again, at Cannes, there was a lazy sense of joy throughout her limbs that almost, though not quite, obscured the taste of ashes in her mouth at the thought of Susan's young body in his arms. It was, apparently, Nick's taking up with a young scuba diver on the beach that drove Susan back to her father's shelter. As he lounged in Jane's living room, Nick grinned sheepishly.

"Guess I better keep out of Lantz's way. Huh?"

For the New York premiere of Gloria's latest film, she arrived with her new husband, the tall, bony veteran of several respectable English films and plays. His initial reserve with Nick fell away under Nick's considerable effort to charm. Jane saw how Gloria watched the two, as though to measure what she'd lost against the possible gain. To Jane, while Kenneth and Nick accompanied each other to walk off the effects of liquor, she confided: "It would still have been Nick. If he'd've had me."

It was too bad *Legend* was taking so long logistically to prepare. Gloria and Kenneth left, but Nick went on with his drinking, as though to make it a new career. "What does Dr. Winkler say about all the booze?" Jane asked.

"It's my *dharma*. . . . Ask him yourself!" Nick shot back.

When she did, Dr. Winkler's remote voice held its familiar frost. "Why don't you stop your menopausal nagging? What drinking?"

They were watching with disbelief the violence at the Democratic Convention in Chicago when a newsbreak told about the Gurneys. En route from Mexico City to Cuernavaca, they'd been killed when their car was smashed by a bus. At the widely attended funeral, Nick was tense with grief, with the guilt that, in their last days, he'd been estranged from them.

Throughout the summer with them at Wellfleet, even after, he behaved with a new morose gravity. Perhaps it was remorse about the Gurneys, perhaps it was the break with the Hearns. Steve had returned from tour about the time Gloria announced from England that she was pregnant. Nick, staggering drunk, had almost dropped Nicole, the Hearn baby and his godchild, after her bath. Steve had forbidden him further access to her.

In the fall Tommy—faced with the choice of another trip to the Coast or a stint at boarding school—left with his trunk and electric guitar for the latter.

It was when he was home for Christmas that Jane wondered if this were not the time to tell him—before she left for the Coast with Nick. Before others did. Tommy must know that once his mother had stood trial for murder. But Tommy, who disliked boarding school regimentation, was full of exultant tales of the rock group he'd organized. His friends visited before New Year's and, rear end slightly thrust out in Beatles manner, Tommy twanged his electric guitar and led the group as he sang. The fact that his voice broke in adolescent disharmony a couple of times was tactfully ignored, the applause of Jane and the household staff graciously accepted.

Her own explanation to Tommy, Jane, with acknowledged cowardice, put off.

4

A hundred-sixty-page shooting script had been developed from Poster's eight-hundred-page novel and Eli Jacobi, who'd directed *A Rose*, had set what seemed at first an impossible goal: two months for the entire filming. At least, Jane reflected, she'd be back soon to visit Tommy.

Filming began in Mendocino County on the Northern California coast. Early morning sunlight poured in shafts between the giant redwoods, glinted on the waves crashing against enormous boulders in the sea when they ran through the first technical rehearsals under work lights. This was the period of promise, of excitement, and hope. The electricians rolled out cables, propmen carried about boxes, camera assistants pushed equipment into position, the sound mixer conferred with the unit director. Nick, intensely sober, pointed out to Jane that Joe Conti was trembling, already—this early in the day—half drunk.

"He's *your* albatross," Jane observed. Nick awarded her one of his looks.

A thin, washed-up popular singer, Conti had spent years in peril from his screaming fans. Now he reached the nadir of his career. His vocal cords had hemorrhaged, his third marriage had fallen apart, MCA had dropped him. Jane wondered: had Nick fought for Conti to secure this—his first dramatic role—because in Conti, only a few years older than he, he'd seen the paradigm of his own possible future? When Nick, with Conti trailing him, came to her for a whispered consultation over lines, she suggested Nick relay her ideas about Joe's part—as well as his drinking.

By the time shooting began, Jane sensed the extent of Nick's coaching in the way Joe began to come across. The mess tent doubled for rushes at night and Conti's hangdog surliness changed to manifest adoration of Nick as he watched his own performance grow. The only rub: must Conti display his gratitude by encouraging Nick to drink with him at night, drag-race on the coastal highway? As Conti's confidence grew, only the quality, not the quantity of his drinking changed. To Jane's relief, before they could wrap the car around a redwood, Nick and Joe were arrested one evening, released to Jacobi's recognizance. Nick, still paying for his hour with Dr. Winkler, told Jane when she confronted him that his psychiatrist wanted him to stand up to her—or drop her from his life.

Jane returned to the Bel Air Hotel on Stone Canyon Road. She decided to call Winkler herself.

"Still nagging?" he challenged. "Nick doesn't drink. And there isn't any dangerous driving. Let him live, will you?"

By the time the crew moved back to the sound stage at Paramount, Nick was contrite. "Conti thinks everything's in my grasp. He doesn't realize how every minute I'm sure the talent—whatever I had—is going to ooze away."

"You do see," Jane argued, "that even the way Joe swills it, he somehow knows how far he can go? You don't."

"Yeah. . . . The last rushes. I saw how the Nembutal makes my eyes come off bloodshot. Come on. Let's go shopping."

What Nick had in mind—after picking up an array of jeans at Fred Segal's on Melrose, a few Italian designer shirts at Maxfield's in Santa Monica—was to deliver into her hands at Juel Park's the trouseaulike assortment of lingerie he'd had made to order for her. Nightgowns, camisoles, slips. As the salesgirl's long painted fingernails trailed lovingly over the embroidered monograms, Jane flushed. Never had she felt herself so much the older woman. The girl's thick artificial lashes fluttered. She sent Jane a sudden smile.

"Listen. What we usually see is the other way around."

"Gigolos?" Nick grinned.

"You're so right." The tissue paper whipped smartly under her hands. She gave Jane a frankly admiring glance. They passed out onto Rodeo Drive in a warm flush of triumph.

As the stress of the film intensified, Nick did confine the drinking bouts to Saturday nights, Sundays. Then Poster arrived. Poster was delighted with the rushes, embraced Conti like an alter ego, openly prodded Nick toward macho excess. Their arms about one another, singing dirty limericks, the trio swaggered through the hotel lobby, made their way to Poster's room and hurled toilet paper from the windows. The studio had to send flowers and champagne to the manager.

"Whassa matter? Am I pollutin' your baby?" Poster lounged mockingly over her as Jane studied the script for the next day by the pool.

"It's your book." She shrugged. "You want to see it ruined? I don't care."

But she did care. So, of course, did he. It became clearer each day how good the original source had been —its melancholy theme of irreplaceable loss from the waste of early potential. Nick had by now coached Conti through a powerfully controlled death scene and, de-

326

spite the tension, pressure of time, drinking, volatile moods, Nick was giving the greatest performance of his life. More than ever, Jane was reminded of that image, the figure plunging deep into the mysterious pool, the figure "with vine leaves in his hair." Nick's natural generosity, his constant help to others in the film was partly a spillover he couldn't control, one dimension of this profound dramatic energy. The crew often stood hushed when he did his takes, often broke into applause that only then brought him from the trance of his role.

Like a marathon swimmer plunging for the final mile, Nick was building steadily toward the last scene. In this, he returned to the mountain whose summit he'd renounced on the earlier climb while Bill Clark—the other lead—and Joe Conti had made it to the top. With this set, the Special Effects Department had done a masterful job, creating a storm sequence on the sound stage for Nick, fatally injured, to battle as he made his way back.

The night before shooting, as they went over the scene together, Nick studied Jane's face. "You know, don't you, that *Legend* is *my* story? I could have climbed that summit once—the stage. It's too late for me now." He awoke after even less sleep than usual. "Come on, I'm eager to die. 'The readiness is all. . . .' "

Fans whipped wind toward him as Nick lay back on the crag under the high-powered illumination of the arc light. A few feet away, the cameras and studio lights crowded in on him, the boom hanging just out of sight. Nick's face was tense, thin, paper-white. Slowly, he wiped his mouth with the back of his hand, wonderingly blinked toward the summit, a fleeting smile as he shook his head. A vein below his left eye began to throb. As though he understood something that had eluded him before, an ineffable smile touched Nick's face. Almost at once—that vein still throbbing—another comprehension slowly filled the wide staring eyes: they peered through an opening door no one else could see. The vein stopped throbbing as the eyes gradually grew vacant. Jacobi pointed, the clapsticks came together, on the hushed set the fans whirred to a halt.

"Oh, shit, Jesus Christ!" somebody said. In an as-

327

tounding concert of emotion, almost everyone involved broke down in tears.

"Know how a balloon vibrates and zooms to the ground when the air's let out?" Nick asked Jane after wrap day. "And stop searching my eyes to figure what pills I'm on this time."

She stopped. Warren Lantz, who'd shown remarkable self-control during the filming, had stuck his head in the door of the sound stage the afternoon before, while Nick did a retake on a reaction shot with Bill Clark. He'd caught Nick fondling the blond hair of a propboy. Someone had seen to it that the underground paper that imitated *Variety* had been left at Nick's door this morning with its headline: "Nick Prick Not Thick," its blurb: "There's no great mystery that Nick Spenser (remember England's *Faerie Queene?*) hangs out with a dame who's pretty long in the tooth. The lads the matinee idol favors know a camouflage when they see it."

Joe Conti challenged Nick at the party Poster gave that weekend for the cast and crew. Poster had taken over a private mansion in Bel-Air for the occasion. "Hey, man, you gonna let these turds get away with that crap? How about we hustle over and break up their office? How about it, Al? You game?"

Poster, his hand on the inside thigh of a blonde starlet, grinned, waved his hand. "Gimme five to finish what I'm doing." He pinched the girl's flesh and she giggled.

Nick had been consuming a full bottle of Scotch daily since the day of the news item. He was shaking so badly that when he tried to shrug, he almost tumbled off the sofa. Joe Conti pulled him back.

Sounds of merrymaking drifted from the pool in back. Nick looked unseeingly toward Joe, pulled himself up, shouldered his way through the crowd, disappeared. Poster watched Jane watching.

"Tell me, shweetheart," he said, imitating Bogart. "Ish it true about him? I mean, I'd'a fucked him myshelf, but he never ashked."

Conti scowled. "Not funny, man." He rose, tripped over the starlet's long legs, made for the bar. Jane held back. A Paramount executive's wife engaged her in worried conversation about her butcher. Bill Clark, always

328

relaxed and easygoing, was showing pictures of his children. One of the cameramen had a group shrieking with laughter as he did imitations of various celebrities jousting for the most important parking places on the studio lot.

Eventually, Jane wandered out to the front terrace that dropped to lower levels, bordered with ferns. It was overhung with banana, apricot, and peach trees like irrelevant sentinels under the strung lights. Here a group argued about exactly when the night-blooming cereus flowered. At last she permitted herself to make her way, past hibiscus and oleander, toward the ubiquitous kidney-shaped pool at the rear.

Water splashed on the Spanish tiles surrounding it as naked bodies thrashed about, others went off the diving board with scant concern for those beneath. Jane told herself to remove this fixed meaningless smile from her lips. Music blared from speakers affixed to the patio wall and, to the sounds of a tango—as the crowd parted, Jane saw him—Nick ("bare-assed as the Lord made him, God love him," someone murmured) danced in slow concentration under the colored lights with the blond propboy, also nude.

"*La Dolce Vita*," somebody else observed, began to clap in rhythm to the music. Others took it up. Nick's eyes had been closed but now they opened, met Jane's, remained fixed on hers as he moved to the music. She felt herself suddenly shoved aside, would have fallen if the person closest hadn't caught her. A stranger—she'd glimpsed him briefly inside—advanced through the parting crowd.

"Jesus H. Christ! So it's true! You goddam fucking fag!"

Like a football tackle, the man hurled himself through the air, pulled Nick from the startled boy, and swung. The first blow knocked Nick sideways, the second into the pool. The man was coming after him into the water when other arms shot out to restrain him.

Jane saw how Nick wriggled his way to the bottom. With something like hysterical laughter inside her came the image, the body flashing into that deep pool, the vine leaves in his hair. She saw how he seemed to rest there a moment, then moved slowly along it—his lungs must be bursting—at last rose gradually to the surface, eyes closed, water spurting from his mouth. A pink trickle of blood oozed from the side of it.

"Someone should get him out," Jane heard. "He's too drunk."

"Someone should get *him* out," came another voice, indicating Nick's attacker, who struggled to free himself. There was a brief scuffle, the man swinging wildly as he offered to ruin Nick's pretty pansy mug for him, then he was dragged inside.

In the pool, Nick moved back and forth, eyes closed, face turned toward the colored lights, water spurting slowly from his lips, the spray intermittently pink with blood.

5

When, after two days, Nick hadn't returned to the bungalow at the hotel, Jane assumed he was off somewhere with the propboy. Why stay on? Aurelia might have helped, but was traveling abroad. Why not fly east to Tommy?

Still Jane delayed. She drove the Pacific Coast Highway, was aware of gas stations, fast-food joints, motels, all the usual gaudy clutter that somehow she and Nick never really saw. The prime reality had once been the rustling red velvet curtain, was now the huge electric eye that gave life, the camera lens that refined it. She stared out toward the water as she drove. Long-limbed tan girls with flowing hair frolicked with boys whose hair curled—like Tommy's these days—down about their bare brown shoulders. The sea glittered, yet Jane was newly sensible to the fault on which the whole area rested. It was as though they must escape before the earthquake hit.

She recognized this as a displacement of her anxiety.

How ironic it was that Nick's greatest need in life, what he did best, was to act . . . for which he needed, of course, an audience . . . of whose disapproval he lived in a state of constant apprehension . . . which prevented him from finding a lover who could be his equal, with whom he might really share his life. For his sake, she'd now be willing to accept that. Meanwhile he ran his treadmill of self-loathing, self-destruction. With full new force the essential loneliness of his life—without her—hit: that he could not live openly with a man he might really love, appear with him everywhere, share with him the triumphs and setbacks of his life. If he could, there'd probably be fewer setbacks. American homophobia. . . .

She was set to leave when he returned. Dirty, unshaven, he only grinned at her silence. "What a patient Griselda you are! Don't you ever get tired of it?"

"Frankly, yes. Can we pack up and go?" Jane was lying on a chaise at poolside in the early evening where the ocean breeze cooled the air. Nick kept snapping his fingers. His eyes were bloodshot. "And go clean up, will you?"

"Yes, Mommy." Falsetto.

Jane watched him slouch toward the bungalow, picked up the letter she'd been reading—a corporate plan for a Broadway theater to be named for the Gurneys—lay back to let the relief flood through her at Nick's return. An attendant appeared with the telephone. She ordinarily called Tommy several times a week, was quickly alarmed to hear his voice.

"Hi," he said. "Don't panic. Just wanted to tell you: someone came to visit me. What a great guy! Why didn't you tell me we had a Jewish cousin? Though I still can't figure the connection."

"What are you talking about?" Tiny beads of sweat formed between her nose and the sunglasses.

"This guy. Dan Edelman. From Israel. He said he stopped by the house in New York. You weren't there. But he saw my pictures. And he always wanted to meet me. So he found out from Laura where I was and came on up. Took me out to lunch in town. Gee! You know he's got a wooden leg and he doesn't even use crutches? . . . He wants me to visit him in Israel this summer. Can

I? . . . Hey! Is that the guy you called in that six-day war? I didn't know we were related."

Jane's stiff lips framed what must have been an appropriate reply. She should expect, Tommy added, to hear from Dan herself. She dropped the phone into its cradle, saw several faces from nearby chaises turned toward her with curiosity, gathered up her things, made her way to the bungalow. Nick wasn't there. She sat staring out the window, heard how she cleared her throat, took deep breaths, as though to prepare herself. When the phone rang, she wasn't ready.

Not for that cold, accusing voice.

"I met him. When I came to the house and saw those pictures, I knew I had to. At least once. . . . How could you rob me of all these years?" Danny said.

"Danny! I know how you must feel . . ."

"Do you?"

"What can I say? You were married by the time I knew."

"What has that to do with it? Not to let me see my own child? Not even to know he existed? *Our* child?" His voice caught a moment.

"Bill—he and I—we agreed it had to be that way. We promised no one would know Tommy wasn't his." How feeble this sounded.

"You never did understand where your debts lie. That's your way. To give more to the dead than to the living."

Against the enmity of this voice, Jane's ears felt muffled. Foolishly, she asked: "He *is* lovely, isn't he? Now that you've seen him?"

"Oh, yes. What I always imagined a child of ours might be. . . . When I saw him, I felt I couldn't ever let go again. Thirteen! Thirteen years of his life! I could make him his Bar Mitzvah!" A short bitter laugh. "I wanted him to come to Israel. I wasn't thinking, then, of Rachel: what that would do to her. *She* doesn't deserve it. *She's* not a monster. She loves me."

"Danny! Don't turn against me!"

"Turn against you? Why not? Maybe this was what I needed to wash you out of my system, once and for all." Somewhere, Jane's thoughts raced, there must be the

332

right words. It occurred to her, in that rush, that Danny had been her anchor, always. His anguished voice went on: "I keep seeing him, damn it. That beautiful kid. The living symbol of our old love. . . . Listen. If I go on, I'll say more things I shouldn't. The old Jane-protecting mechanism takes over—one last time. . . . Well, Belmont, take care of that boy." A muffled sound. Then a click.

She sat, holding the phone to her ear and staring out past the bougainvillea at the smog that drifted constantly lower across the hills. Her mind appeared to have emptied. It was the noise of her own rasping breath that caught her attention. It was as though she couldn't hold on, the sense of the bottom falling out of all things that made her lurch, dizzy, when she tried to stand. The mirror reflected her, a woman almost forty-five who still appeared strangely girlish, but whose olive-toned cheeks had paled. The dark eyes glowed back at her as though feverish. She lit a cigarette, lifted the phone. The high voice in which she asked the desk to page Nick startled her.

Pacing back and forth, nursing the ache in her gut, Jane told herself that saving worked both ways. Of course, Nick might not be anywhere in the hotel. That rasping sound again. . . . She sat down to wait.

The outer door wasn't locked and Nick soon appeared. He'd bathed, shaved, changed, again her *parfait gentilhomme*. This is a test, a voice declared inside her. He frowned, came toward her.

"What's up? What's the matter?"

In a flat voice, she told him. At his look: "And don't say you told me so!" She kept staring, as though to find in his face some answer to her pain. She saw how the wild inner-directed torment gradually left it, as palpably as a cloud that moved across the sun. He lifted her to her feet, put his arms around her, held her.

"You lean on me," he said. "You just lean on me."

She talked. He sat, holding her, while she rambled. All those years with Danny—back to the forbidden childhood baseball games with Peter, the time in the war when he'd been reported missing, the walks home after the evening performances of *Zeal*, the first trip together to Wellfleet, his reappearance at *Antony and Cleopatra*. As she talked and Nick continued to hold her, she trembled with nervous tension.

Sometime later he ordered dinner sent in, dismissed the waiter, stood with a napkin over his arm to serve, insisted—until he made her laugh—on spoon-feeding her. Then he was doing imitations: actors, directors, producers. For Dando, he assumed the stance of a chimp, waddled across the rug with his arms dangling, rolled over on his back while she laughed.

"Thanks," Jane said. "I needed that."

Nick lay there and watched her as she smiled down on him. In the silence she saw the profound tenderness on his face as he stared at her. Somewhere was a vague memory of wondering why she put up with it all—his life—but she couldn't recall the details that had troubled her. It was as though, without words, they communed with one another, as though he were telling her that—as much as he could ever love—he loved her.

He came to his feet then, reached for her hand, drew her to him. He pulled her arms around his neck, placed his about hers, his forehead against her forehead, began to move with her in a slow dance, singing and smiling, a sardonic smile for what he sang, but holding her close.

> "See the tree, how big it's grown,
> But, friend, it hasn't been too long,
> It wasn't big. . . ."

He hummed, unsure of the next words, his forehead against hers, then:

> "And, Honey, I miss you,
> And I'm being good,
> And I'd love to be with you,
> If only I could. . . ."

Despite the chill that lay on her heart, Jane was laughing again, at first. Why did a small whisper tell her: *I'll remember this one day?* Then she nestled in against him, his breath warm on her face.

"I came home unexpectedly,
And caught her crying needlessly
In the middle of the day,
And it was in the early spring,
When flowers bloom and robins sing,
She went away. . . .
And, Honey, I miss you,
And I'm being good,
And I'd love to be with you,
If only I could. . . ."

Afterward, it was as though wherever Nick led her, she'd follow without objection. She'd thought this before but never, despite the urgency of her desire to get back to Tommy, so strongly as now. The heat of the races at Santa Anita, a quick jaunt to Las Vegas, the sneak preview of *Legend*, in the first fine cut at San Diego—"This flick's going to be a blockbuster," Dando promised, his small, exquisite ears pale with fervor—and at parties. Nick approved of Jane's air of floating acquiescence.

"No more Mama-san, huh?"

It was after a particularly riotous evening that she woke one morning to find Nick packing. Stumbling back and forth from one Vuitton bag to another, throwing in their things together. From her bed—she didn't know how she'd got there—Jane called lazily: "We leaving, *mon vieux?*"

Apparently they were. Aurelia had returned, arranged their flight, was seeing them off. At the airport she appeared more massive than ever—a Macy's Thanksgiving day balloon, Jane told herself with a repressed giggle—and very stern.

"You don't *have* to go down the drain with him, you know," Aurelia said. Nick was being sick in the men's room.

"Yes, Mummy," Jane said, imitating Nick. Her own hostility, compounded of guilt, shame, confusion, was suddenly so great she was compelled to fawn, glancing sideways into Aurelia's face with an evasive smile.

6

They were very sober, both of them, by the time they
reached New York. Tommy, after all, was waiting. In
these months he'd grown incredibly, was almost as tall
as Jane. There was something else, a new rebellious-
ness. Decidedly, after a year at boarding school, no camp
this summer. Either Wellfleet, he announced, or Israel.
In August there would be some sort of rock festival at
Woodstock. Tommy wanted to go.

"You're too young," Jane said. "It's out of the question."

"Hey, Mom! Don't treat me like a kid. I'm thirteen!"

"You *are* a kid, darling." They were on their way to
the Cape, were leaving Nick behind at Greenwich
where, Jane knew, he'd begun his heavy drinking again,
and the pills. In that company of male models and gypsies that he allowed to pursue him when he wasn't working. At a farewell weekend, she'd watched him crawl
about on all fours on the grass, come up to people to hug
and kiss them, sometimes to bite. The Hearns, with
whom Nick was attempting a reconciliation, took one
look at the scene and fled.

"Man, the Cape's sure getting crowded," Tommy observed, as she maneuvered the car into another lane.
Traffic had come almost to a crawl. "Maybe we should
give up on the Cape."

It wasn't until they passed Hyannis—the cars from
the lower Cape now also streaming toward it—and
pulled in for gas that they found out about Chappaquid-
dick.

"Ghouls," Jane murmured. "They're all ghouls."

To drown: for some reason Jane dreamed that night
that the poor trapped figure was Joanie's. Slowly, in the
dream, the face, hair flowing, turned malevolent, with a
smile that seemed to wait there below the water. Always
her old sin following. . . .

Nick, two weeks later, came for a visit, sailed with
Tommy (it annoyed Jane that Tommy never wore a life
vest anymore; Nick, of course, never had), returned to

tell Jane that this was where he should remain, here he could pull himself together. Then, borrowing the new Porsche, he drove it into a ditch. He'd had another blackout, he explained while Ted, in reproving silence, went off to rescue the car.

Men were walking on the moon, Jane pointed out, and Nick couldn't even manage the sun porch. Nick opened one of the windows, perched on the sill, spread his arms and dropped from sight. When she searched down the ten feet into the beach grass, he was on all fours and laughing.

"' The Eagle has landed,' " he told her.

Jane banished him to Greenwich. Meanwhile, *Legend of Their Youth* was opening simultaneously around the country and Dando had been correct. Day and night the lines snaked around the block where it played. People brought food, blankets, pillows, to lie on the sidewalk before the box office opened. Theaters around the country were held open continuously to accommodate the crowds. *Cinéaste* called it a landmark in film history. Everyone received kudos, with special mention for Joe Conti's astonishing performance.

But it was Nick they singled out as having fulfilled all his early promise. It would be difficult, the critics said, for him to top himself. A long article in *Film Comment* dealt with the influence Nicholas Spenser had already had, with only five films, on other actors. To comprehend this, one had to get past the remarkable looks. The writer mentioned the paradox that he'd been honored at Cannes and in England, but not in Hollywood. Was it, he wondered, something to do with Spenser's personal life?

Congratulations poured in. While Tommy visited a school friend in Maine for a week, Jane went down to Greenwich. The critical acclaim had brought a hush to Nick's frenzy as he wondered if his talent were irretrievably lost.

"I'm going to pull myself together," he vowed, spoke to Dr. Winkler on the phone, reported back that apparently it was she who had led him astray, trying to tie him to her by tearing him down. Jane threw a costly piece of bric-a-brac at his head. With the old agility, Nick caught it in midair, laughed, dropped to his hands and knees, began to bark and yap around her ankles. Jane's anger melted into laughter until he fell over in another blackout.

Gloria's announcement of the birth of her boy had, of course, depressed Nick. Joe Conti was singing again in Vegas, had been signed to a lucrative new recording contract, was considering several film offers, while Nick saw nothing worthwhile in the immediate future. Hollywood—and the country—were stunned by the Sharon Tate murders. Nobody seemed able to find out enough about the grisly details. Amid the body counts from Vietnam came those from Hollywood.

Also, from Tommy in Maine, a phone call, his voice strangely flat. He was asking if it were true, what his friend, some of the other guys were saying. That she'd killed her husband, his father. She'd stood trial for murder, had been acquitted only by some fluke. In fact, that —not motherhood—had ended her career.

"Is it all true, Mom?" He sounded young, defenseless. "Somebody said if I didn't believe it, I could look up old newspapers. They're kidding, aren't they? It's just the Sharon Tate business. And that you're in Hollywood so much."

At Christmas, she'd intended to tell Tommy, had hung back. Jane cursed the cowardice she'd let pass as inertia. "Tommy, meet me back at Wellfleet. All I can say now is—some of the details are right. Only the facts are wrong." She wondered, as she passed the familiar scrub pines of Route 6, if she should tell Tommy everything—even about Danny. Danny had said she'd always misplaced her debts to the living and the dead. Perhaps she owed her child all the truth.

It was amazing how he took it. The tide was low as they walked the wide ocean beach in early evening, the last sun glittering in pools the sandbars formed. It lit the fair down along Tommy's tan skin, the long, curly sun-bleached hair that blew around his neck. There was a strange lowering beyond the sun as though the sky held a distant storm. Half a dozen surfers in wetsuits balanced on their boards. Jane and Tommy walked with their arms about each other, the wind whipping strands of their hair together. Their feet left glistening prints in the wet sand that the foam erased.

She told him everything. Scott Williams. Sal Celucci. (Shock: "You were friends with the guy that killed Scott —the one that called you Amazing Grace?" As an afterthought: "Remember: that's the song at my funeral.") Clyde Simpson. How she'd come to marry Bill. The doomed evening of the party to celebrate their anniversary, Tommy's birth.

Of course, Tommy was horrified at Bill's murder, incredulous of the dangerous edge on which she'd teetered throughout her trial. It pleased him to know how much Bill had loved him. He liked hearing—as he had before—of Bill climbing the rigging of the yawl, Tommy in his arms, vowing to make a sailor of him. The part that moved him most, not unexpectedly, was Danny.

"He's my father!" he marveled. "And he knew me! Just from my pictures, he knew me!" Also, not unexpectedly, he wanted to see Danny again, and soon. Jane was silent. She didn't think, finally, that—despite Rachel— Danny could deny his son.

They climbed a dune to rest, slipped on the sweaters they'd brought along, leaned against one another to stare out at the dark hissing water under the risen moon. Gradually, Jane spoke again, about Nick, the hold he had on her life. She sensed a resistance in Tommy to this, then a giving way. He held her hand in his, startling her again with how large it had grown.

"I understand." He nodded wisely. "You can't desert him. Not now." Like an adult—like Danny—he pressed her hand.

Again, they were silent. A dog ran at the water's edge and barked. Jane watched Tommy. The wide-set golden eyes, so direct, so void of guile, always looked as though they'd captured the sun. Like Danny's. And still, that lift of the brows, the set of the lips, that was Peter. "What are you thinking?" she asked.

"You should go back on the stage. It's time. . . . Did you know I've decided to become a director? I'll probably go to Yale Drama School. On the other hand," he grinned, "I may join the Coast Guard."

They walked back at last, stopped in at the Bookstore

Restaurant for chowder, steamers, an enormous platter of fried onion rings for Tommy, agreed to go clamming next day at low tide. Faith and Ted were in Provincetown when they returned to the cove. Laughing, Tommy permitted Jane to sit on his bed, sing again his favorite lullaby from infancy.

> "Hushabye, don't you cry,
> Go to sleep, my little baby;
> When you wake, you shall have
> All the pretty little horsies,
> Blacks and bays, dapples and greys,
> All the pretty little horsies. . . ."

By the time she'd finished singing he was already asleep, his lips slightly parted. Jane remembered, as she bent to kiss the warm cheek, his plump bare feet in the wet morning grass of Greenwich, when they'd gathered raspberries.

For the first time in many months Jane slept late next morning. It was, she supposed, some sort of cleansing process, a form of healing that allowed it. There was a note from Tommy.

"I wanted you to sail with me but you were so sound asleep. See you soon." In what must have been an afterthought: "I love you."

There were whitecaps on the bay when she came out on the sun porch to drink coffee, read the papers. This meant Tommy would turn back soon. The foam at the water's edge rippled sideways as though a white serpent hurtled purposefully toward its destination. A long interesting article told about the new "auteur" type of director in Hollywood. When Jane glanced up, it was because she'd become peripherally aware of the sky darkening, as though a squall were mounting. The bay appeared fuller, swollen. Across the harbor, the red alert flag had been posted when she hadn't noticed.

Jane picked up the binoculars always kept there, saw only two sails riding far out on the horizon, one of them Tommy's Lightning scudding between Buoys Ten and Eleven. Tommy was hiking far out, his long curls skim-

340

ming the water, his feet in the hiking straps. He should reef the mainsail, she thought.

A sudden gust came from the opposite direction. Tommy raised himself quickly—did he notice the red flag?—and the mainsail came around with a speed almost impossible to conceive (yet, to her mind, also as slowly as the pendulum of eternity) so that the boom, in a sudden jibe, struck violently against his head.

For one moment, it was as though Tommy were dazed, suspended in some inviolate immobility, before he dropped slowly backward over the side and disappeared into the slapping waves. The boat came around, settled into irons.

Beside it, just below the surface, shimmered that face from her dream, the hair streaming, the malevolent smile that had to wait no longer.

Chapter XI

1

In the long living room of the East Hampton house—
Hugh Kirkland's wedding gift to Sybil Fox—mirrors alternated with oak panels. In each mirror, an extrava-
gantly dressed woman floated into view as she passed
among the party guests, a woman in wide silk culottes,
hip-length gypsy blouse tightly sashed at the waist, hair
done up in the latest fashion, chignon and loose tendrils
curling at each side of her face, à la Ingres. The woman
brayed raucously at whatever was said to her—though
much of what was said concerned a massacre, a carnival
of death in some hamlet in Vietnam, My Lai, the place
was called. It had occurred some time ago but only recently had it been discovered by the press. Jane wondered why, under her vivid makeup, the woman's face
revealed so green a tint, why—when she didn't laugh—
she went on visibly swallowing, as though something in
her throat one more effort might push down.

Oh dear, she recognized that woman. Mainly because of the man pressed suddenly at her side, whose
arms went around her hard, held her, his cheek against
her hair. He was always holding her these days, she
thought: this man whose youthful beauty she dimly recalled, whose almost ethereal comeliness ("Behold,
thou art fair, my love; there is no spot in thee") was
somehow faded, replaced by a more rugged handsome-
ness, a look more seemly to his age. But when he held
her like this, as he was always holding her these days,
he made the laughter stop—ah, so *she* was that woman!
—and when the laughter stopped, there was only that
splinter in her heart that hurt very badly.

Somebody nearby murmured: "I think she's dis-
graceful. Why do they invite her?"

Close to her own ear came *his* voice, in its slowest cadence: "How do I mourn thee? I will count the ways. . . ."

Another evening—she didn't remember the occasion —a woman, not knowing her, had sat quietly by her side, begun to speak very simply of her son. The family had been so relieved, this stranger had said, when their son had received his college deferment. No Vietnam for him. Then, driving home for the holidays, he'd been killed in his car.

"Eventually," the woman had said, "you begin to live again. You're just never ever completely happy again."

Later, when Nick had held her, Jane had beat against his chest with her fists. "I won't accept it!" she'd cried. "I won't."

Funny how the world out there had still time and passion to devote to her. Several had written to comfort. "Be glad your son has become a jewel of Jesus. He'll never have to grow up and know what real suffering is." But one had said: "You sure didn't care much about your kid. You were seen coming out of Bergdorf's the morning of the funeral." (Ah, yes: the black veil she'd needed.) Others had been patient enough to dig up that old headline: WAS JUSTICE DONE? They'd sent it along with their letters. "At last the Lord has seen to it that a murderess gets some of her own back," one had written. Another: "Did you think God would keep looking the other way forever and let you get away with it? Too bad your son had to pay and not you."

The publicity about the accident had brought another Joanie to the door, a blonde lush who insisted it was she who'd disappeared that day from the swing, been kidnapped, sold to white slavers. . . . The story kept changing.

As did her own control.

With the hate mail, with the woman impostor, she was oddly calm. When Nick took her to the Open Theatre, to Italie's *The Serpent*, when the young blond actor, as Kennedy in the dread moment of the Dallas motorcade, raised his hand to his neck, Jane rose from her seat with a confused tangled scream in her own throat, struggled past the people beside her, stood—Nick's arms around her—retching on the sidewalk.

Where was it, she wondered now, that he'd embraced her into silence like this only recently? Oh—some afternoon affair at a Central Park South penthouse. The young son of a well-known academic couple had talked to her of his college entrance exams. For some reason, she'd launched rather tipsily into a story of a famous actress who'd shouted denunciations at a guest for breaking an heirloom dinner plate. The poor man, Jane said—feeling her eyes bright with pain—had taken up the two halves to piece them together, found stamped on the back, "NRA."

"The NRA," Jane began, her smile fixed, meaningless, "that was . . ."

"Oh," the boy interrupted, eyes round behind thick spectacles. "I know. National Recovery Act. Under FDR."

This dear sweet boy, Jane had thought, through the haze pervading her. He'd learned everything the child of high-placed academics should. Also, he skied, he played Ping-Pong and tennis, he'd go to Amherst, Harvard or Haverford. . . . His face was young, tough, arrogant, scared. Let me love you, she'd told him silently, what's all of that compared to just being alive? She'd thought it had been silently till Nick had reached her, pulled her away from the boy who recoiled, transfixed, before her cries.

Oh, yes, she'd take such care of him! As she had of her own! "That's what you're thinking, aren't you!" she'd challenged Nick as they'd wobbled along the sidewalks toward Sixty-first Street. "Aren't you! Aren't you!"

He'd begun to speak about Tommy. Something about when Tommy had first been learning guitar, and later: the way he'd stood with his ass slightly out when he sang, like the Beatles. Only Nick spoke about him, ever, of his own accord. She'd learned quickly that look of unease that came across people's faces if she mentioned, ever so casually, even Tommy's name. Nick could talk about him and she'd listen. He knew, too, when she couldn't bear to.

Then, it was dimly consoling—ah, no! don't feel!

warned a voice: feel nothing!—to know his bereavement, too. All that time they'd put off the funeral, had waited for the body to be found—strange, she'd thought then, the days dropping so slowly into one another, like the taut drops of water that hang trembling from a tap—Nick's grief had been almost as palpable as her own. When the tides had finally washed the body in, it was Nick who'd gone to identify it. The fishermen who'd grappled in vain from their boats had warned him: it wouldn't be a pretty sight.

"Can the sight of someone you love, dead, ever be pretty?" The question rasped from her strangled throat. Which was better, she'd wondered? No corpse, as in Peter's case, or a mutilated one, in this? Nick hadn't permitted her to come along, had made certain the casket was closed, when the funeral took place at last. You see, I remembered, a tight little voice in her head repeated as the organ sounded out "Amazing Grace." . . . If it were only playing for me, my darling, the voice said. . . . I now *am* lost. . . . Across the room, behind Tommy's friends and as though across the world, stood Danny. He didn't look at her.

She hadn't gone on to the cemetery, had let Nick—and Danny—do that. That night, when it rained, she'd decided. It *was* better, she'd wept against Nick's shoulder, to go as Peter had. It was too pitiful to think of the rain falling on that newly dug grave. Nick had rocked her back and forth, held her close to him through the night. In the morning, the sunlight Tommy would never see again had hurt even more.

And, she thought now, here Nick was holding her again, her only support in the world, the only one against whom she could rage and tremble, her hair soaked with sweat, her mind dazed by Dalmane, Valium, drink. This pillar of her strength, whose strained pretensions of enthusiasm, of gaiety, by which he imagined he could cajole her, often simply gave way before his own constant anxieties. Poor Nick, she sometimes murmured aloud to him or silently to herself. He hadn't bargained for this.

Then, in a flare of anguished rebellion, the term "bargain" exploded in her mind. What bargain did life ever make? One had a child and signed away forever one's immunity against whatever the cold, implacable universe stored up. There was no escape anywhere—flailing against the coming awake from drugged sleep, against the hours that stood locked immovable each day ahead of her, or else that rushed by as though with the audible noise of a terrible storm. Her blood, she felt, had turned to water, her very bones to ash.

Now, as so many times before, Nick was taking her away with him. She was, as so often before, making a scene. How awful that those mirrors must reflect it all, the physical struggle, the woman no longer laughing but railing, that awful greenish face with the stylish tendrils at either side. . . . Well, for the sake of their host and hostess, the woman was haughtily asserting, a great show of false dignity, she'd not argue, she'd go quietly. She was passed from embrace to embrace, the pity so tactful as they kissed her. She was bundled into the Jaguar Nick had recently bought, they were off again into the glare of headlights, he was driving with one hand on the wheel, the other on her knee as though still to steady her, he said nothing as she pushed another capsule between her lips. But there was no way to get that down when she could barely swallow at all, and Jane rolled the window open to the bitter cold, spit the pill out. Resentment, the other pills she'd taken, drink slurred her speech.

"Fuck Danny," she intoned. "I'll take a night plane to Israel, shove his wooden leg up his ass."

"Right. You do that." Over the rushing wind that poured into the car, Nick's voice was distant, reedy and hollow.

"Who the hell does he think he is? Am I Medea? Did I kill my child myself? And who taught me to sail in the first place? I was never even *in* a goddam sailboat till he took me to Wellfleet."

That last word was a mistake. The splinter in her heart widened, pushed deeper and more piercing, so that she gasped, choked. Like the actor doing Kennedy, her hand went to her throat as the scene returned: the long sun-bleached curls hitting the spray of water as he hiked out on the edge of the boat, the swollen sea, that other face, hair streaming, waiting below, as the boom came around, the unheard smack of it against his head, the slow, dazed falling away, the boat settling around into irons. . . .

Why, she wondered, eyes stinging from the cold as it poured into the car, hurting her cheeks, helping with its hurt, had she no image of Peter reaching out, catching Tommy to him? Why was there always, instead, that image of a burial in space she'd seen on film, Tommy's body hurtling with incredible velocity far out and away, a speck forever lost? . . .

That image had ricocheted across her vision the day she'd snapped at Faith, Ted, Laura: "I'll fire the three of you. Today. Unless you stop the crying."

"But he was a golden child, a golden one," Faith had mourned. And added, for the first time: "Mr. Danny's boy. . . ."

Jane had stared, newly stricken. Then: "Put away all his pictures. Put them all away." As though, with that, his face would no longer look down on her to mourn his lost life.

She knew it was disloyal to remain alive herself. She must, she told herself over and over, hurry to join him before he was totally lost forever. Who would care for him in that cold space where his spirit floated? "I want my child!" she screamed out, at times, to Nick, as he held her. Then, very quietly: "It's not that I'm mourning all the years he didn't live. It's not that." Lips quivering: "I just want, once more, to see his cheeks. The way the hair of his eyebrows grew. Nick, you never noticed, did you?—his left eyebrow: it had a completely different arch to it, Nick, from the right eyebrow; I used to examine it while he talked to me, he . . . Nick! Nick! Do something! Help me!" Again, she was crushed, helpless, against his chest, screaming out, moaning, shuddering, the tears flooding forth.

Nick had selected one method to assuage her pain that was especially distressing. He asked her to be in a play with him. The two of them together, at last, on Broadway. "On, Off. I don't care. We have to do it. Now or never, Janie. Come on. Be a sport."

This pressure—she was an animal caught in a trap,

chewing at her own limb to free herself—was difficult to resist because it *had* appeal. The only moments Jane wasn't aware of that splinter that festered in her heart were when Nick reviewed the plays they might tackle.

"Are you afraid of trying?" he challenged. "Or afraid of feeling better?" He spoke of *The Seagull, Miss Julie.* Her scornful laugh brayed. Why such youthful roles for her? She was, after all, by now ancient as death itself. He was particularly keen on *Mourning Becomes Electra.* Ralph Gurney—surely in another lifetime?—had agreed to direct her in that someday.

But it was Lavinia, the daughter, she'd have done, Jane argued, not really caring, as the winter wore on. Lavinia she should do, Nick said—to his Orin.

"I'm much too old for anything but Christine, the mother." That word—it tasted of ashes. The theme of the play—guilt—would be appropriate. Guilt was the theme of life. That was what the dead hold of the past was all about.

Only dimly was Jane aware of the scripts Nick had turned down from MCA. January's anniversary issue of *Variety* listed, as usual, the top moneymaking films of the year, and *Legend* led them all. Among the top moneymakers of all time, *A Rose at Christmas* continued in the first ten. Nick reacted with his usual complaint of feeling used, of being wanted by Hollywood not for his talent but for his star quality. He was ready, he told Jane, to return to the stage, if she'd come along. It was as though, each day, he coaxed her reluctant feet along the path of the living.

It was only after the 1970 Academy Award nominations were announced, Nick not even named, that Jane gave in about the play. What did it matter, after all, what she did? Others shared her consternation: *Legend* nominated all the way down the list: Best Film, Best Direction, Best Editing, Best Sound, Best Cinematography, Best Supporting Actor (Joe Conti)—and Nick not even named. Crowds still waited to see *Legend* all across the country. It was Nick's performance, surely, that had drawn it all together. To console Nick, Jane—recognizing the mistake as she did so, but not caring—agreed to play Lavinia.

2

From the moment she stepped onto the stage of the Phoenix Theatre, the script trembling in her hands, Jane knew they were courting disaster. They'd cut the drama drastically, to compress performance to one evening: each of the three plays now one act, each act a scene. Learning lines temporarily eased Jane's mind of its pervasive grief although always, even without thought, there was that sense of a massive slab of concrete weighing on her chest. Steve Hearn, who'd brought with him to Tommy's funeral reconciliation with Nick, would do Captain Brant, and Nick would direct.

Yet, as the days progressed, Nick turned increasingly to her, and Jane was finding it difficult enough.... "A woman on the verge of forty-five," she imagined the comments of cast, critics, audience, "playing a girl of twenty-three." Not that it mattered, that inner voice repeated. Nothing, anymore, mattered.

Nick preserved a grim frenzy of organization, the only presentiment of trouble his harried, unkempt appearance, his impatience with the crowds that stood on lines several blocks long on Second Avenue as soon as tickets became available. "They're not here for O'Neill," he grumbled. "They're salivating to see a fucking Hollywood star."

Rehearsals had fallen into chaos when James Hooper came in, brought some order to them. Still, Jane read in his anxious face the preview of what lay ahead. The woman playing her mother was younger than she, the roles should be reversed, her old confidence, the will, were gone. "I can't *hear* you!" Hooper repeatedly called from the rear of the theater as she ran her lines.

"Leave her alone!" Nick flashed. "She's perfect!"

Jane rather began to think she might pull it off, after all, by the first week of May when they were to open. Hadn't Bernhardt, in old age, played young women? There came news of shootings at Kent State, pictures of young bodies on the TV screen and the papers. The searing rush of her own agony, only damped down, returned, the waves of grief and loss. The night of the preview, Jane sensed a wall of hostility in the audience each time she appeared onstage.

"Those aren't Hollywood fans out there," she stormed at Nick during the first intermission. "Those are the best of the theater world. And they're watching me betray everything I ever stood for." (Still that voice persisted: What does anything matter?)

"Fuck 'em," Nick mumbled. "You're doing great."

The reviews were worse than she'd feared. "One hundred thousand marchers protested United States involvement in Cambodia this week," said one. "A few should protest the fiasco at the Phoenix Theatre which may, after this, never rise again."

More painful were those who forebore, perhaps for old times' sake, to tear her apart, confined their remarks to the complaint that she was simply miscast, couldn't be heard. Many praised Nick but one pointed out: "An actor cannot return to the stage for a one-month run after more than ten years and hope to be instantly great again, let alone adequate."

For her, it had been more than fifteen years.

Because so many fans did wish to see Nick, the run was extended through July and slowly, almost against her will, Jane saw her own performance rally. Old admirers even returned, they told her, several times. Nick was now impatient to have it over with, to be freed from humiliation, get back to serious drinking. But it was, Jane perceived, much like what had happened to her onstage in *Zeal for Thy House*. The reality that had always existed behind the curtain, that had always summoned her, had that time long ago delivered her from the cold armor in which she'd encased herself against feeling for Peter's death. Now, the act of confronting so much death and talk of death, the act, too, of playing sister to Nick—who had so replaced Peter—the binding him to her as the drama unfolded, then fighting to be free of him, began to appear to Jane like an allegory of her life, working through to another epiphany.

Those were, many of them, Nick's weaknesses that flowed across stage to her as he spoke Orin's lines and, each evening, Jane discovered a stronger identity with Lavinia who stood, in some ways, like herself, so alone.

There were certain words that flashed from her that caused a new flicker in Nick's eyes, as though they were not onstage speaking written dialogue, but reworking their own relationship. At Nick's incestuously jealous questions, she flared: " 'I'm not your property! I have a right to love!' " Her sobs at his threat to tie her to him came to seem as though she were, indeed, weeping for the bonds that held her to him in life. Nick, with new feeling born of her own, admonished: " 'Don't cry. The damned don't cry.' "

One critic who returned wrote glowingly of her performance, cited the moment when she stood, eyes closed, and spoke as though to herself: " 'The dead! Why can't the dead die!' " Another remarked she'd created the exact blend of pity and terror with: " 'I've got to punish myself! Living alone here with the dead is a worse act of justice than death or prison!' "

This was largely what she'd done, Jane knew, much of her life. Pulling over herself the robe of guilt, she'd ignored, in some important sense, the many-colored cloak that Tommy's presence had spread over her. She understood that now she'd finally, perhaps, grown up, had at last given over that yearning need of the spirit for her lost childhood, for Peter, for all that Nick had come to symbolize. Without Tommy, she faced, at last, the fact that, at its core, each existence was essentially solitary, and that what she had always asked was some form of magic it could not give.

This did not signify that Nick's role in her life was diminished. Need and obligation were complementary. But though, offstage, she was still the sufferer, the bereaved, onstage she was groping toward that release for which she'd waited in vain the day her trial had ended. And she could act again: that was the light shed around her as she bowed before the acclaim that gathered increasingly each evening. They were coming to see her now, not the film star. It was possible to think that perhaps, someday, in the future, when she had Nick back on his feet . . .

There wasn't, of course, enough of this new audience to keep the play going and Jane sensed only Nick's relief when it finally closed. She saw how deeply the mortification of his own failure had dug. Nick called now for reservations at restaurants with the terse announcement: "This is Nicholas Spenser. I want a table for two in a few minutes," hung up with a curse when they didn't tumble, didn't fawn. Their car halted on upper Broadway beside that of a young actor he knew, someone who'd made it big that spring in a comedy, was contentedly on his way to the theater. Behind the shouts of greeting, the quips, as the stop-and-go traffic kept bringing them together, Jane recognized the pain and envy in Nick's eyes.

She was, herself, weary, she sensed in the restaurant, when a sound man from Universal leaned from the next table to flatter Nick—weary of the way the man's eyes were apparently unable to penetrate beyond the barrier that stood between herself and film stardom, even simple recognition of her presence. It annoyed her to see Nick respond so eagerly to the attentions of the owner, the waiters, the free liqueurs brought after dinner. What a fall was this. . . . Beneath the weariness, the annoyance lay always the hope of renewal she'd found onstage, like a gift only waiting to be unwrapped, its tentative pleasure put off to another day.

Meanwhile, it was too easy, here in New York, Jane reflected, for Nick to yield to whatever he wished, with little concern about the gossip columnists of Tinsel Town. He'd taken in a new lover and, lying alone at night, Jane gave herself up to fantasies about Tommy.

Tommy was still alive, had taken up skiing, was trying to teach her. He laughed—curls escaping his woolen cap—as she flopped on her rear, the skis pointing toward a cloudless sky. He'd entered Yale, she was seated in the third row—first row or third row?—for this first attempt of his at directing. Awfully pompous, she recognized her own reaction to his fantastically intuitive touch, just as she'd bristled with pride over his early swimming at Wellfleet.

No. . . . He wasn't at Yale, he *had* joined the Coast Guard, was trying very hard to hide amusement at her inability to comprehend his explanations as they trod the deck of a Coast Guard cutter. There was a girl there, too—Jane struggled to see her: dark hair? blonde?—the girl was obviously all but incoherent with her passion for Tommy, just a bit leary of the mother-in-law role Jane appeared to represent. Jane tried to reassure her by her own manner, her easy smile: really, I'm only too happy. . . . I don't want to interfere, but you do realize that Tommy's favorite jelly is blackberry, he absolutely loathes cherry. . . . No, that *was* too mother-in-law-ish, she scrubbed all that, began over as the nighttime hours ticked by and she turned and turned in bed.

Surely, it was too soon to regard her throbbing grief for Tommy as pathological? Not quite two years yet, she told herself, and wondered if there were only bones now in that grave she still couldn't bring herself to visit. . . .

When Nick's new lover left—"I don't have to put up with this shit, even if he *is* a superstar!"—Nick complained to Jane that he'd now become an old man, in a few months would turn thirty-four, was finished.

"Balls." Jane was busy picking up the scripts that littered his house. Helen Eustace had quit during the last lover's sojourn, telling Jane:

"I don't know how you take it. I can't, anymore."

Whether Helen had meant jealousy or outrage wasn't clear. After all, both before and after this last affair, Nick had gone to bed with whomever he chose, male or female. Often he didn't choose: whoever happened to undress him when he passed out usually ended the night with him. Daisy still flickered in his life, coming to see him past the groups of fans that beseiged the house. She maintained that air of dignified tenderness, complained behind Nick's back to Jane about him, to Nick about Jane. It was Jane, she insisted, who's got him hooked on cocaine.

"Listen," he told Daisy. "Jane's my best girl, see? Aside from the White Lady. You get a real speedy high from snow, Ma. No aftereffects like from speed, Ma. When I'm on the stuff, I get this radiant glow of self-confidence back, what you gave me as a kid, Ma. You were the original White Lady. It almost kills the pain of being me. Get it?"

"You'll damage your nasal membranes," Daisy said.

Gloria arrived to make a film on location in New York. Jane strolled down with Nick to Fifty-second and Eighth Avenue one morning to watch. Gloria had to start a small car along Eighth, turn left from the right lane into the path of an oncoming van, with a screech of brakes narrowly miss collision, bounce to a halt on the sidewalk diagonally across, emerge from the car, start running, return to collapse in tears over the hood of the car.

Despite the crowds gathered to watch behind crewmen's ropes, Nick went unrecognized as he slouched, unshaven, a worn cap on his long dark hair. In the muggy heat of early morning, the crew worked with their usual air of calm bustle. They lugged heavy cameras back and forth across the avenue, the soundman wheeling his equipment in a makeshift combination of wheelchair and shopping cart, studio rental trucks moving back and forth, while the police casually warned spectators back from the action. Gloria, red hair cut short and curled, was professionally patient as she redid the scene, each time deftly missing the van, arriving up on the sidewalk. The scene had to be shot many times before they got a take in which the cameraman beside her wasn't visible. An old lady with a thin dark mustache pushed up against Jane, tapped her on the shoulder.

"All these police around and they don't arrest someone driving like that? I don't know. . . ."

Jane turned to smile toward Nick and recognized the pained envy with which he watched Gloria's involvement. Chewing gum, Gloria grinned over at them and winked. That evening, she joined them at Nick's house.

"So, sweetie-pie. Ready to go back on the work force in something big?" Gloria asked.

Nick grinned. He was always happy, Jane reflected somewhat sourly, with Gloria. "You find me the right part."

"You'd make anything right, luv." Gloria leaned over to smoothe the dark hair from his forehead. Her heavy breasts brushed against his arm.

"Hollywood has my number. They'd tear me to bits out there. You know Dirk Bogarde was a matinee idol one time? Till he *played* a faggot onscreen? That finished him. . . ."

"So he had to stop being a matinee idol and become a great actor," Gloria argued in her little-girl voice.

"I thought *I* was one. What's the percentage—if you never feel rewarded?"

"Anyone who's one fuck serious about movies has *always* said you're the tops. Besides, you need the money, chum." Gloria placed her rather short but shapely legs on the coffee table.

"And I hate living out there. I like New York."

"Mother of God! It's like playing tennis. I rush to one side of the court to hit back a ball and you come back with a slam way over on the other court. Stop being such a prick, will you?" Gloria gazed at him fondly. Nick slid a hand up her leg under her skirt, fondled her thigh. Jane crushed out her cigarette, lit another.

"Am I a prick, Glory darling?" Nick asked, tenderly.

Gloria laughed, arched her lovely white neck, raised her ringed fingers to her hair. Then she was pulling it about her face, without warning sobbing: "Oh, shit! Don't mind me, please! It's just that it's so great to be here with you and I'm so goddam frigging unhappy with Ken! He goes on treating me like a fucking child and goddam it, I don't need a father-figure anymore. . . . His career's going down the fucking drain over here, too, and I feel so guilty, and I don't know what in hell I'm supposed to fucking *dooo!*" She leaned over, collapsed across Nick's lap.

Nick stroked the luxuriant red hair, murmured soothing words, made her lie full-length while he massaged her back, later fed her hot milk. Gloria sat up suddenly.

"Shit. My eyes better not be red tomorrow," she announced matter-of-factly.

"There's my little trooper." Nick smiled. "Aren't you staying over, Glory? Everything's ready for you here."

The green eyes slid a glance toward Jane. "I'm working class, buster. When you're in a movie with me again. . . . Not till then."

3

It was August when Nick prevailed on Jane to sail for Europe. The two years are up now, Jane thought as she paced the deck in the morning, watched the shining swells rise toward the horizon. Mourning beyond two years was regarded as abnormal. Nick joined her, placed his hand on the back of her neck.

"Two years," he said, with his startling intuition. "The pain's there. But is it different?"

Jane shielded her eyes from the wind and sun. Nick looked nervous, unkempt, older than thirty-three. Almost for the first time, she saw that his hair was thinning, thought—not for the first time—how many hours she'd spent with him when she might have been with Tommy. Guilt, clenched in the dead fist of the past. Guilt and regret. Real life had no plot, yet Fate appeared to fling it into orbit, only to snap it inexorably back by some hidden thread. The hidden thread, perhaps, was always guilt—and regret.

"The pain's there," she conceded. "But it's different."

Europe, she saw as soon as they arrived, was a mistake. Tommy hovered everywhere, the trip they'd taken together when she'd thought she might break with Nick. In the middle of the Place Vendôme, Jane suddenly broke down, Nick had to maneuver her to safety. They flew back, went off to Mexico City. Nick mounted the Pyramid of the Sun, recited Shakespeare, soon disappeared from the Zona Rosa, ended up in a Mexican jail from which Jane had some difficulty rescuing him. Instead of Acapulco, they returned to New York.

Jane was preparing for another winter of discontent —new rumblings of trouble in the Middle East, India at war with Pakistan, all charges against the National Guard at Kent State dropped, intensive United States bombings of North Vietnam, here in their two houses disarray—when Gloria suddenly came through.

"It's just a stinking soap opera," she told Nick on the phone, Jane on an extension. "But you'll get your million again. And we'll be together again. You do it for me, chum, or all bets are off."

"Um, um," Nick began.

"Um, um," Gloria broke in. "Up yours! I've already rented a house for you and Jane on Dawn Ridge Road. The studio's sinking the national debt into this one, on the strength of us both being in it. Your little fat-ass agent'll probably contact you any minute. I just wanted to lay it on the line to you now. Yes? Or yes?"

"Christ, I look like hell," Nick mumbled to Jane after he'd agreed. "I look like Father Time. How can I show myself on film?"

"We'll get you in shape," Jane promised. To him, and to herself. She had him sign up again at a gym, watched his liquor intake, went over the script with him line by line when it arrived. Yes, she agreed with Gloria on the phone: it was a shame preparation for *Long Division* took so long. Nick was growing increasingly nervous. Despite his new disciplined regime, he'd wrapped his new car around a tree on Fifth Avenue.

"At least," Jane said, "he's sworn not to drive anymore himself. He says he's hiring a chauffeur when we get to the Coast."

They reached there in late spring in the midst of a heat wave. The settling smog made Nick's sensitive eyes water while he went off in the chauffeured car for costume fittings, publicity stills. All news continued ominous. Wallace, stumping for the Democratic nomination, was gunned down at a Maryland shopping center. In Rome, someone crying out, "I am Jesus Christ!," smashed the face of the Pietà with a hammer. In Washington, five men were caught installing eavesdropping equipment at Democratic National Committee headquarters, in a building called the Watergate. Endless small problems continued to delay *Long Division*, a story of the Reconstruction era in the South, of families pitted against one another to stay on and rebuild, or to move west with the frontier. Nick, with Jane's help, went on making script changes to be relayed to Rasmussen—a choice for director that rendered Jane uneasy. Of course, she pointed out to Nick, Rasmussen *was* good.

"Yeah. And hates our guts."

The delays became a signal for Nick to resume his drinking. The producer called one day with a warning. Nick, who promised to behave, was affronted to discover the producer had taken out an unusual one-million-dollar insurance policy against production breakdown.

It was better once shooting began. Then they rose each morning before six, rode in the chauffeured car to Culver City. Each day, Nick complained about the smog, the lights on the sound stage—how bloodshot these made his eyes.

"Not drinking?" Jane responded. "And the pills?"

Gloria, she knew, considered Nick's behavior at her house—his rudeness to her guests, his eating from their plates, his incoherence—due "only to the sauce," as she called it. She remained somehow unaware of the trunkful of pills in the house on Dawn Ridge Road, the capsules Nick secreted on the set.

Still, Nick was happy, no doubt of that, to be with Gloria. On the set he laughed continually at her casual jokes, went over almost every day—Jane often stayed away—to her house. The Hearns were in Hollywood for a picture Steve was doing, and often joined them now. Nick enjoyed Gloria's boy—almost the same age Tommy had been when Nick had come into the nursery that first day, had ridden Tommy on his back, imitated the gaping mouths of the goldfish, walked across the room on his hands, done a somersault, Tommy had tried to imitate him. . . . It was awful to find herself fleeing that family scene. Jane wished no harm to Gloria's child. It was simply too hard, at times, to take. . . .

What Nick found difficult in the house on Benedict Canyon was the way Gloria and Ken took turns keeping him up half the night to discuss their marital problems. Despite the good times, a price was exacted from Nick, and Jane sensed in him a fundamental depression. Above all, he needed more sleep.

"You know you're always burning yourself with your damned cigarettes?" Jane warned one day on the set.

Nick glanced at his blistered fingers. "I don't feel them. Honest. I keep forgetting I'm holding them." He appeared shamed, wandered the set with his wide staring gaze. When Jane found him back in his dressing room, he'd taken something again that turned his gaze blank. At least the shooting for the day was over.

A different element troubled Jane, a paradox they'd never discussed all these years. So far as she knew, Nick —despite his wide and varied experience with others— had never taken Gloria to bed. As Gloria's marriage deteriorated, Jane brooded. She didn't doubt Gloria still loved Nick, would leave Ken in a moment if Nick would promise, at last, to marry her. Jane was growing weary, herself, not only of playing watchdog on the set, but of listening through her own hours to Ken's complaints while Nick was off with Gloria. Ken put it to her one Saturday evening.

"You know I'm most awfully fond of Nick. But—I have to ask. Is he having it on with my wife?"

Jane had known jealousy before. The searing wave that swept her now was shaking. She feared, Jane realized, no one so much as Gloria, no one existed so fundamentally threatening to her own hold over Nick. (Which, she sometimes wondered, was binding the other?) It surprised her she'd never framed it herself so clearly before. There'd always been, from the first, that spontaneous affection Gloria elicited from almost everyone. But what was that, compared to this rush of fear, suspicion, envy? The freedom she'd thought she wanted, the freedom to open that waiting gift appeared suddenly worthless. She had an image of herself, teeth bared like a dog, then self-pity: I'm almost forty-seven. I have nothing else. She can't have him. . . .

Jane smiled. "You want me to spy?"

Ken winced. He was stretched on the couch to relieve back pains. "I really couldn't bear to think of them together in bed." He sent her a sharp glance. "Could you?"

The drive down from Benedict Canyon was replete with twisting winding roads, over which a strong wind blew at night. Jane, angry at the tears that blinded her, maneuvered her own car—Nick was out in Gloria's, hadn't driven himself for months—carefully down. Poor little rich girl, mocked a voice in her head. When Nick returned to Dawn Ridge Road in the early morning, she was waiting, raring for a fight.

"Shit, we were with the Hearns the whole damn time!" Nick's tone was injured, plaintive. "You want to call up and check?"

"Of course, I'll do just that!" Queasy from cigarettes, Scotch, Jane paced the floor. "Shit, shit, shit. . . . You're beginning to sound just like Gloria."

The gray eyes stared, bloodshot. "Anything wrong with that? I thought you liked Glory."

"Liked, liked! Of course! I *love* Glory. Who could help loving *Glory*? Glory, Glory Hallelujah!" A despicable woman was reflected in the long windows bared to the dazzling view of lights below. Probably she *was* menopausal, as Dr. Winkler had suggested years ago.

"You're jealous." Nick's wondering tone only incensed her further.

"Jealous!" Jane laughed mockingly. She stopped, looked at him. It was as though sparks flew from her. "Shouldn't I be? You don't think I should be? What am I supposed to do here? I mean, after I spend the evening propping up *Glory's* husband, so *he* can take more shit from her. . . . *He* hasn't any more balls to lose."

"Some guys beg to get their balls busted." Nick's eyes had turned bright, wary.

"Oh, brilliant! And what do *I* do? Just wait around for you to haul my ashes when you're good and ready? Or do I get on line behind the young boys in the crew? Is that what I should do?"

She was shaking. She'd never spoken to him quite this way before. Nick continued to stare up at her from the chair in which he sprawled. She sensed the conflict in him of fury and pity, fury and self-pity, too. It was curious, she found herself wondering coldly. Which would win out? She rather opted for the fury.

Instead, Nick slipped to the floor. He came toward her, a shamed grin on his face, on all fours. In a moment, he'd be yapping at her heels like a dog, expecting her to capitulate, to take him up, laugh, fondle him. He moved close, his face damp, the eyes glittering—But I love him! a voice mourned somewhere, this was the face, above all, that she still loved—and Jane put out her foot, kicked him sharply in the chin. It wasn't the force that made him fall over. He lay, watching her quietly, as she strode across the room toward the stairs.

4

In New York, despite the heat wave of early September, her hands were continually cold. Terrorists forced their way into the Israeli dormitory at the Munich Olympic Village, eleven team members and hostages were killed in a shootout. The Democrats were seeking damages for that Watergate break-in and accusing the Republican finance chairman, others, of conspiracy to commit political espionage. McGovern's campaign against Nixon— "This is the most corrupt administration in history"— had been damaged at the outset by the Eagleton affair, didn't seem able to get off the ground. In *Variety,* Jane read that location shots for *Long Division* were delayed: Gloria had badly sprained her back.

Probably in bed with Nick, Jane decided. She imagined to what excesses such delay might lead Nick, reminded herself she didn't care. Rasmussen's bald dome must be glittering with frustration, she told herself with satisfaction. Steve Hearn called, said Nick was drinking, depressed about the film, about Hollywood, felt he had no control over anything, was depressed about *her.*

"Tough titty. What else is new?" Jane asked, hung up.

Walter Raney's doglike devotion, which she'd accepted with humorous skepticism all these years, brought with it now a dim security, a comfort she needed. He still halfheartedly pressed the case for marriage, more urgently her return to the stage.

"You've never been more beautiful," he insisted.

Indeed, mirrors reflected back to her a strangely youthful bloom—perhaps, she thought, her last. Hugh Kirkland heard she was back, wanted her to play the mother in a revival of *The Glass Menagerie.* After a meeting at his office, Walter walked beside her toward the Algonquin, suggested she sell the townhouse, with all its memories. Perhaps he sensed it, too: Tommy's spirit still brooded, as though mourning his lost life, floated above the stairs, was present in reproach everywhere. It was as though she knew she must make the step now, reemerge into her own life.

It was like the plot of some tightly constructed opera when, in December, a denouement she'd never expected arrived. (Nixon had won a sweeping victory, had now ordered the heaviest bombing raids so far in the war.) Walter brought it to her—the letter that had been sent to her at the castle. Postmarked New York. No return address.

"Jane Belmont." The letter was written in pale ink. "When you read this, it means I'm dead. I been wanting to let you know for years now about your sister but how could I take a chance about you coming after me with the law? I don't blame you if you hate me but try not to hate me too much. I was always seeing all of you in the park like that and having to take care of this little girl and I thought to myself she sure can't have any parents that care that much if her brother and sister always have to take care of her. But I didn't plan it ahead, though. That day when you were busy looking for a ball or something I just got up off the bench and took her off the swing and led her out of the playground. I said what came into my head about her mother was very sick and wanted her to come right home. I told her you two knew and you were coming right along. Maybe she believed me because I knew her name from hearing you two calling her other times. I had my car parked pretty near and in the car I told her really what her mother had was contagious and she was supposed to come with me not to catch anything and somebody else would bring you two along later. I had this old, rundown place in Pennsylvania my sister left me—I knew I better not bring her to my room over on Columbus Avenue—and that's where I took her. I never meant her any harm at all, I wasn't one of those perverts or anything.

"When we were there a day or two and she kept asking where you were and all I told her you had first gone home and everyone in the family got sick and you all died. I said I was supposed to take care of her from now on. I guess a five-year-old kid will believe anything. We went far out enough in the country nobody really noticed anything. I changed her name to Elsie, just in case. In case you're upset, nobody ever took better care of a kid than I did. The sun rose and set on that little girl. We never had too much because I only worked as a general handyman but I gave her everything I could. When I sent her to school I told her not to talk about anything about New York because people would think they'd catch something from her. Later I just told her

her family didn't want her anymore because they couldn't afford to take care of her. I don't know what she really believed. I think when she was twelve or so she tried to call you all but the call never went through. Then when she was fourteen the Lord really punished me. The school bus she was on in June '44, last week of school, too, there was an accident, lots of kids hurt and my Elsie one of them killed.

"I never got over it to this day. I know the Lord was punishing me but I don't see why He had to take it out on her. Anyway, I'm giving this to someone in town to mail it to you from New York once I'm dead, no questions asked. I always followed you in the news and I know you had plenty hard luck. I never thought you killed your husband and I sure was sorry about your boy. I just wanted to say I hope you don't hold all this too much against me."

There was no signature, obviously no way to trace the letter. Yet, intuitively, Jane knew it to be authentic. For some moments there was only silence as she held it in her hand. The thought arose: I must tell Tommy. Then she heard the squeal of the bus tires, the thundering impact that had crushed Joanie—the same month that Peter had died.

No, not the crash of a bus but another terrifying sound, a swishing across the room. It started at the far corner, coming through the air toward her, cutting it with a rushing boom, a gigantic wooden swing. Hot hands were on her forehead, pushing her down, the roar through her head was noiseless thunder, and she sank, sank for hours. . . .

Yes, she assured Walter later. She was lying on the couch, he holding her hand. It was better to know. Knowledge is Power: that was what the sign over the portico at Julia Richman High School had announced. For some moments it appeared to her she could feel Joanie's warm body on her lap, smell her babylike smell, as they sat at the small maple table in the bedroom on West End Avenue. That image drifted mistily into one of Tommy in her arms as an infant.

Then, both were gone. There was no village, no house, no place to make one last contact, no grave at which to mourn that lost child of her own early past. She had, Jane knew, mourned Joanie all her life. A different sort would be in order now. Also, in some sense, she was free. It occurred to her, when she woke in the early hours as usual, how much she would like Danny to know what had happened. Danny had been with her and Peter that day, with her through so much after.

But Danny hadn't forgiven her. Across that first loss of one childhood lay the long shadow. *Their* child, like their love, was vanished.

5

She was listening to the early news on TV while she dressed to go out with Walter. Tomorrow she would sign the contract for *The Glass Menagerie* and, in celebration, Jane was wearing a new dress, the low-waisted silhouette in fashion since the film of *The Great Gatsby*. She was pulling up the zipper in back when Nick called.

"Just wanted to say hello." He sounded distant, tired. "I guess I just wanted to hear *you* say it."

"How's everything out there?" Her hand was tight on the phone, her throat was tight. It angered her to feel that flow of tenderness well up in her belly at the sound of him.

"I'm drained. . . . We finally began shooting again. Leaving for location soon in West Virginia. The schedule's really intense, making up for lost time. And that damn Ken's over almost every night to carry on about him and Gloria. If he's not here, Gloria wants me there, so *she* can complain." (A mental note: he hadn't called her "Glory.") "I really feel as though I've had it. Just got off the phone a minute ago: first her, then him. That I have to come over for dinner tonight. I told them. Absolutely not. Tonight I'm going to bed early. Already gave the chauffeur the afternoon and night off. And *I'm* certainly not driving after all this time. I'm just going to

study my lines for tomorrow, and go to bed. . . ." Pause.
" 'And, Honey, I miss you. . . . And I'm being good. I'd
love to be with you. If only I could.' "

She was silent. He asked: "You still there?"

"Yes. I'm happy to hear you're being sensible." Stiff-
necked crone, she thought: that's what *she* was being.
"Why not have a nice warm meal—drink some milk—
watch a little TV, and go to bed?"

"Yes." Only Nick could stretch such a short word.
Then: "Janie. Please come back."

Something in her leaped upward. She pressed her
lips together, as much in denial of herself as of him. "I
don't think so, Nick."

"When am I going to see you again? I'm so lonely."

In general, or specifically for her? "Oh, when you get
to New York I'm sure we'll run into each other."

"Run into each other? Like two ships that pass in the
night?"

"Mm." She considered telling him about the part she
was going to do, about Joanie, sensed a holding away
from him. "I really don't have time to talk now, Nick.
I'm just dressing to go out."

It was his turn for a moment's silence. "Will you ever
have time again?"

"Please, Nick. I'm not in the mood for character analysis. It *is* good to hear from you. What time is it out
there? Just a little after three? Why don't you swim, do a
little exercise, then go on as you've planned, get to bed
early." She had no right, she knew, to patronize him so.
She imagined the frustrated consternation widening the
gray eyes, the full lips open near the mouthpiece. She
shouldn't, she told herself, imagine those lips, the lean
cheeks.

"Well, okay. I'll be seeing you, Jane." The connection went dead.

They were seeing *The Godfather* that evening, she
and Walter, going to late supper at Elaine's. The film
was so long, so full of violence that Jane pleaded a head-
ache, asked Walter if he'd mind awfully skipping the
restaurant, taking her home. He'd have liked to stay on,
but she sent him off after a sandwich and coffee. Auto-
matically, she clicked on the TV as she undressed, was

listening to an almost exact repeat of the earlier news, when the announcer broke into the sportscast.

"We interrupt this portion of the news with a special bulletin just received from our wire service. The movie actor, Nicholas Spenser, well known for his acting achievements and his unusual good looks, has been severely injured in a car accident. He was driving alone, leaving the home of his friend and co-star, Gloria Randolf. We understand, as of right now, that he's expected to live but that he received extensive injuries, especially to his face. . . . We now return you to our regular news."

There was a ringing in her head. No, the phone was ringing. Her arm seemed to travel ahead of her, detached of her own volition, but bringing her body with it, her stiff fingers reaching for the phone. Her voice was dry, like paper crackling, as she answered.

"Jane, this is Steve. Have you heard?"

"Just now, on TV. What happened?"

"Oh, Jesus!" A muffled sound, a sob. "Jane, you don't know. . . . Oh, Christ!"

"No. I don't know. Tell me. . . ." Rather, don't: turn back the clock to before whatever it was had happened.

"Nick wasn't going to come. Goddam it, he wasn't going to come to Gloria's. Gloria and Ken were after him all day. . . ."

"Yes." Lips dry, barely framing the word, wishing it back so Steve wouldn't guess her responsibility in this. He wasn't, of course, alert to her reply, went on in a high despairing voice.

"He even told them he'd sent away what's-his-name —the chauffeur—and no way he was driving the car himself, after all this time. I don't know *what* in hell made him change his mind, Goddam it." I do, a small voice inside her said. "But suddenly he shows up. It was only Ken and Gloria and me. Kathy was home with Nicole. So far as I know, Nick had one damn glass of wine, and he wouldn't even sit down. Just kept hanging out by the door. Hadn't shaved, looked like hell, just kept muttering and staring around. Suddenly, he says he's leaving, it's dark already, will I just guide him down that steep grade as far as Sunset Boulevard? Gloria was begging him to stay just a little longer, just to eat, but I could tell he really wanted out. So I said, sure." That muffled sound again. "I was going to take care of him!"

Jane floated on the moment's silence. She said: "It's a bad road there. In Benedict Canyon."

"And it was foggy. Fog had been coming in all day over the ocean at Malibu. Nick was obviously knocked out as hell. He talked to me outside a couple of minutes. How low he was feeling. The film. Everything." She wondered: had he mentioned her? his phone call? her rejection? "Anyway, then we got in and Nick was following me. I kept watching him in the rear-view mirror and thinking: now why the hell does he have to tailgate? On that twisting steep road, with the fog and all. Suddenly, his car gives mine a little push. I started going faster. For all I know, he was going into one of his blackouts. I remember making that first turn and then, right away, coming on that real treacherous next one. Nick's car was swerving from side to side, I could see his headlights. Then a terrific screeching sound, and the next thing I hear this awful crash. All I could see was this cloud of dust. I stopped and ran back. God! I'll never forget the sight of that as long as I live."

It wasn't patience that held her silent. Each moment of not knowing held at bay the image that would be planted soon in her own vision, never to be erased. Like that image of the boat, Tommy hiking out over its edge. . . .

"His car was crumpled around a telephone pole with the engine still going. I smelled gas so I turned it off. The car must've smashed first into the cliff and *then* around the pole. Glass everywhere, wherever I moved I was crunching on it. But the worst of all: when I leaned in to turn off the engine, I couldn't see *Nick!*"

"Oh, yes. He never wears a seat belt. Was he thrown clear? Was that it?" Stupid questions. Hadn't she already heard the newscast?

"I had to run back and turn my car around and drive back and shine my headlights on the wreck. That's how I found him. The dash was all crushed in, all the wires hanging down, and Nick scrunched up under it. Jane, I can't describe it. His face was stripped off. I mean, just a bloody pulp. There *was* no face. You know, I thought

he was dead. . . . I got back in my car and drove on up to
Gloria's. I was banging on the door and Gloria opened
it. I said—I don't know what I said. . . . 'A terrible accident. I think Nick's dead. Call an ambulance. . . .' Ken
and me tried to keep her from coming back down with
us but she began screaming and just raced down the hill
on foot. She couldn't open the driver's door but she got
in back and crawled over the seat. By the time we got
there she was crouched down on the floor with his head
in her lap and he was moaning. At least we knew he
was alive. He was starting to choke, he pointed to his
neck. . . ." (That image of the actor playing Kennedy,
clutching at his throat, she staggering from her seat, Nick
following, holding her . . .)

"Why was he choking? The blood?" It was Gloria's
fault he'd come out that night at all. No, it was her own
fault, Gloria who'd held that poor faceless head in her
lap.

"He'd got two bottom front teeth knocked down his
throat. Gloria actually reached in and pulled them out. I
never saw such courage as hers, such calm. Some doctor
showed up then. It took him and Ken and me half an
hour to get him loose and he was conscious all the time,
bleeding like the end of the world. Gloria rode with him
to the hospital. Cedars of Lebanon. He kept telling her
he had to get to the studio, he didn't want to make Rasmussen mad. And she kept that calm till he was in the
operating room. Then she got hysterical."

"The operating room. Is he out yet?"

"Just a while ago. By the time he got there, his head
was swollen about as wide as his shoulders. You couldn't
see his eyes. . . . The doctor just told us: his jaw was
broken in four places, his nose is broken completely in
half, one cheekbone was cracked. . . . And the amazing
thing: the rest of his body's pretty much okay. He hasn't
suffered any brain damage, the doctor's fairly sure. He's
completely sedated now, of course, and all visitors are
barred."

"All?" She remembered driving the Pacific Coast
Highway after *Legend*, how she'd feared the geologic
fault on which all this lay, had recognized even then the
displacement of that fear.

"As of right now. The reporters have set up a state of siege. You'll see. And I hear the studio—the publicity department—they've already notified AP he won't be scarred at all, he's only a little banged up, the film's just going to be delayed a few weeks!" Steve's laugh was short, bitter. "Jane. You'll come, of course?"

"I'll take the first plane. But Steve, what do *you* think?" Courageous people always wanted the truth. Jane recognized, with great clarity, that she wasn't courageous.

"What do I think?" For the first time, Steve's voice slowed. "I'll tell you what I think. God's gift to us is Nick's life. . . . God's gift to Nick might be his death."

Chapter XII

1

Nick would see no one. Rather: he didn't wish to be seen. Heavily sedated, he'd been restless, the doctor told Jane—walked, till they raised the bedgates, in his sleep. He was, by now, one day after the accident, in traction and his jaws wired shut.

"But as of now, the bones in his face are really just pasted together. He doesn't keep that neck of his stationary, they'll come apart. With luck and good behavior, he won't need plastic surgery. You the lady with influence over him?" Almost as an afterthought: "Just had to tell him this morning. Reason he's in such pain: the jaw wasn't set right. Looks like we'll have to break it and set it again."

Jane had flown out immediately. After the bitter cold of the east, the humid warmth here wove itself through the texture of unreality. Like ominous sentinels, the palm trees drooped sullen, dusty under morning smog. Thermos in her large canvas shoulder bag, pills in an envelope, Jane had pushed through the sweating mob of reporters, photographers, fans—many weeping—ordinary curiosity seekers that thronged the hospital lobby. Nick had sent her a message as soon as she'd arrived:

"I'm suffering. You smuggle me martinis and Demerol, you get to see the freak show."

Jane availed herself, before pushing open the swinging door of Nick's room, of several deep breaths. She was aware, leaning against the door frame, of all the flowers. This allowed her only gradually to concentrate on the figure in the bed, the swollen face infused like a balloon stretched to the breaking point. Through the poor, ruined lips, Nick drank some concoction from a straw. His eyes, staring wide and frightened toward her, remained the only familiar contact point. Those, and the bony fingers fumbling at the sheet.

She didn't, couldn't speak. Nick watched as she lifted the thermos out, emptied the styrofoam glass into the toilet, refilled it with martini. She shook a Demerol into his uplifted palm, waited as he slipped it between the wired jaws, helped him to insert the straw. It was just possible to glimpse where he'd lost the bottom four front teeth. While he sipped, slowly, she sat, glanced about at the flowers. A strangled sound indicated he was trying to speak, and she leaned close.

"Fucking funeral parlor," she made out.

"Mm. You don't have to worry about the film, you know." Polite conversation, to a stranger. "The studio spoke to the director. They're shutting down production. For at least six weeks."

Choking guttural sounds. Again she leaned close.

"What'll they shoot then? Back of my head?"

"Oh, by then you'll be much better." The pretense of a smile.

The gray eyes glittered. "Not. Never be okay again." Nick's gaze wandered toward the windows. In the air-conditioned breeze, the drapes rustled. He looked back at her. She couldn't make out the next words and his effort brought out a few drops of sweat on his forehead. Then she heard: "Always had it so easy. Took good looks for granted. . . . Now I'll find out, how it is. . . . Joining the people who walk in darkness. . . .

Back in the house on Dawn Ridge Road, as emissary from the east, from the possibility of the new life she'd contemplated, Walter Raney arrived. She'd never liked this house, Jane reflected as Walter leaned forward on the hassock before her. Hollywood *moderne*, Nick had dubbed it: the muted beiges, ivories, ochers. "It needs a streak of blood," he'd commented once. They had that now, she thought. A nerve in her left eyelid kept twitching.

"Jane, I beg of you. Don't get enmeshed again. It's not just me. Hugh Kirkland insists I not come back without you. He's counting on you for *The Glass Menagerie*. You'll never escape again. If you don't now. . ."

Jane smiled grimly. She was prepared, this time, to

pay her debts to the living. Tommy, too, had insisted she couldn't desert Nick. The nerve in her eyelid twitched. It was said that, between the galaxies, where space appeared black, light hidden to the human eye irradiated the darkness. She couldn't yet see that light. The press agent had jeered at her that night: "This it? This what you meant by epiphany?" Perhaps that didn't come ever, of itself, all in a moment. . . .

Defeated, Walter left. Two weeks after the second operation—a total of five in the hospital—Nick was moved back to the house on Dawn Ridge Road.

"I can't bear to look at him." Steve Hearn walked beside her to his car. They'd left Nick on a chaise by the pool. "I don't mean just his face. I mean what he's doing to himself. Can't you stop him?"

"You don't understand. There's still so much pain. The concussion. The splits in his skull. Not to mention the bones in his face. The skin doesn't show it—but they're still cracking back into place, underneath." This sounded feeble, perhaps, against what Steve had observed. The liquor, the pills, the stupor in which Nick lay back, staring at the cloudless sky. Nick dosed himself not only on what the doctor gave but also from his own store of medication. Sometimes, when he slept, Jane wondered if he'd ever wake. "You don't know," she flared at Steve. "Half the time he's shaking all over with pain. The agony's incredible."

"But doesn't the booze work against the healing?"

An ocean breeze swayed the eucalyptus trees that obscured Nick from their view. Jane slumped against the side of Steve's car. "Look. I've tried to convince him: forget the damned picture—it's just meaningless crap. Come back to New York. Get well. Let them collect on the insurance. . . . Do you know they come by every day to see if his face is 'ready' yet?"

They exchanged glances. She didn't add that she understood why Gloria and Ken—now in the process of divorce—stayed away. The twisted, misshapen mouth, the once-perfect slightly aquiline nose curved now and angular, the left side of the face immovable due to the severed nerve in the cheek, the swelling on the right side where a loose tooth had abscessed. . . . Aurelia had put it bluntly.

"It's as though all his features have somehow enlarged and coarsened. You can still see it's Nick. But he looks like some peasant cousin of the real Nick Spenser. Someone he might have been with generations of malnutrition and inbreeding. . . ."

Jane had hissed at her to get out, not to return. With unsteady fingers now, she lit a cigarette. "You said—that day—God's gift to him would be his death." She lowered her voice as though Nick might hear. "You think he's killing himself now. Well, if he doesn't finish that picture, I'm afraid he really will."

It was ten weeks, not six, before production resumed. Rasmussen arrived with the new schedule—his first visit—a day when Nick was still in great pain. His jaw remained wired, made snapping noises when he spoke. Rasmussen made no effort to hide his shock.

"I really don't look *too* different, do I?" Nick pleaded.

Rasmussen's gaze didn't shift from the ruined face. His voice was deliberate. "Oh, not too. . . . What we'll do: we'll use mainly shots of the right profile. I'll speak to the cinematographer. We can use the diffuser—that sort of gel. Plus a lot of soft focus. We'll concentrate more on the eyes." He saw: the eyes were the same, wide, gray, though shining with pain.

It was an added burden that the film, half shot, should have to move to location in Harper's Ferry, West Virginia. Between takes, Nick sat reading the script over and over, while perspiration soaked his body. He was relying on speed and Demerol to see him through. He'd begin the day with a false high, barely—by afternoon— win the struggle back to his dressing room. *Variety* came out with a headline Jane wasn't able to hide from him: BEAUCOUP NIX RE STAR'S SCARS.

The next morning she had to summon a doctor to bring him, lying stuporous, a cigarette between blistered fingers, out of whatever it was he'd taken. From his labored breathing, the paralyzed diaphragm, the doctor reasoned it was lack of sleep and depression, fed by Nembutals, that had brought on the coma. He ordered a resuscitation machine, vitamin shots, oxygen held ready on the set at all times and questioned Jane about the depression.

How could he ask? "It's the rushes. The director was counting, at least, on his eyes. But they film so differently now. A sort of dead, glassy quality."

"What do you expect? All the drugs he's on? They'll show up in the eyes, no matter what tricks the camera tries."

That was the day she heard the rumors circulated by the tabloids. Someone else had taken Nick's part in the film while he lived, hidden but severely maimed, in the same nursing home that held James Dean. A cult in Northern California preached that the devil had twisted the wheel from his grasp, the night of the accident. Photographers and reporters besieged the set.

Yet, when Nick grew a beard for the last scenes, lay asleep on the grass between takes, someone took a snapshot of him that made Jane privately weep. He looked in it almost the same as before, peaceful in oblivion, the twisted mouth, the scars hidden. He found her, hastily wiping her eyes, gave her his old slow smile.

" 'Don't cry,' " he said. " 'The damned don't cry.' "

Shooting ended at last, they returned—at Rasmussen's request—to spend some time in Beverly Hills. Nick rested in his darkened bedroom—it smelled like a hospital—or by the pool, where he lay staring, unseeing. His face was still healing but at least the jaw no longer snapped, the swelling in his cheeks had subsided. When Dando dropped by with scripts, he sat removed, listened almost fearfully, once simply covered his face with his hands. Later, he said to Jane:

"Tell me the truth how I look, damn it. Don't I look like I was born with a harelip and had a lousy repair job?"

Jane murmured evasive denials. The upper lip *was* the worst, along with the deep facial scars, the general appearance of thickened, coarsened features—Aurelia had been right—in the once-elegant face. Rasmussen called. He needed Nick and Gloria back for some low camera angles, to replace a few earlier high ones, taken before the accident. Jane prepared for an especially bad evening.

Nick, strangely somber, returned, went to his room. After a time she followed, found him kneeling by the bed, and tears running down the thin cheeks.

"Darling, what is it?" Jane stood by the door.

Nick looked up at her, the immobile side of his face so at odds with the twisted pain of the other. Strangely, he smiled. "I went for some pills. All of a sudden I really examined myself in the mirror. . . . You know, I wasn't sure before. I thought I'd finish this lousy picture and then, that would be it. . . . But I know now. It won't ever be like it was before. But my career doesn't have to be over, Jane. I'm an actor. I can still act."

That light, irradiating the darkness. . . . She went to him, took him in her arms.

2

Back at the house in Greenwich, Jane saw to it that Nick swam, took walks. In return for such behavior, she shared his reading of possible scripts. In July, quite suddenly, a former presidential aide revealed that all conversations and calls in the White House and Executive Office Building had been taped. On the same day, the Defense Department admitted that the United States had carried out thousands of bombing raids on Cambodia before the so-called incursion of that country in 1970, that records—at Nixon's and Kissinger's request —had been falsified.

"This fucker's going to get himself impeached," Nick crowed in disbelief as Nixon defied the subpoenas issued by Cox, the special Watergate prosecutor. "I'm not the only one bent on self-destruction."

"At least you don't hurt other people. Only yourself."

"You know," he said slowly, "I never told you this before. But that day—after I called you in New York and you rejected me? The day of the accident: I'd taken some pills to sleep before I called you. Before I decided to go over to Gloria's, after all. . . ."

In the dim light of early evening on the terrace, they stared at one another. Fireflies flickered and a low throb of crickets floated from the flowerbeds. Beyond, wind swayed and bent the trees with a soft sighing sound. A terrible sadness such as she thought she'd never known pervaded Jane, seemed to flow out to meet his.

It was as though the full impact of what had happened awaited them in New York. On the street, the recognition, the furor that had always amazed, even terrified Nick at times, now changed to inattention, puzzled glances at best, shock at worst. There were startled cries from passersby: "My God, that was Nicholas Spenser!" "You're crazy!" "No, I swear." One screen magazine announced: "Nick Spenser looks—let's face it—very different."

Nick took down the mirrors in his house, made a point of avoiding Jane's. He spent hours—when not visiting a physical therapist, an orthodontist—simply playing records, staring at the floor. He held off Daisy, her assaults of flowers, fresh fruit, advice. As though to wound him further, Daisy liked to point out news of Gloria's new lover.

In October, Israel was attacked in what came to be known as the Yom Kippur War. Kissinger was awarded the Nobel Peace Prize—shades of 1984 and Newspeak, Jane thought—and Washington was newly stirred by what they termed the Saturday Night Massacre. By December, amid jokes about the eighteen-minute erasure on the Nixon tapes, Ford had been appointed vice-president. The first snows were falling when word of the sneak preview in San Diego of Long Division filtered east.

Audience reaction cards indicated that the film was, indeed, a three-hour "turkey." Still, it would make money, because everyone wanted to see it. The game was to pick out before-and-after shots. Rasmussen had instructed his film editor to splice together as many of those frames as possible. But it was said that every close-up of Nick indicated which was which: that intensity, that sense of looking past the camera into the spectator's soul was evident in the early scenes. Wearing the identical costume, assuming the identical pose, the "after" shots revealed a face immobile with illness, shock, defeat. "Is that him? That can't be him!" people murmured. At the first glimpse of the "after" face, it was said, many in the audience had gasped.

Newsmen requested interviews. What, they wanted to know, had Nick had to do to cope with what had happened? Mentally and spiritually, that is. Was he seeking help?

Oh, yes, Jane reflected, he was seeking it. Dr. Winkler, she'd recently discovered, permitted Nick to bring his thermos of vodka, crushed Demerol, and fruit juice to the office, where he polished it off during the session. That, Nick explained impatiently, wasn't what was important. What was was that Dr. Winkler was prodding him to accept his homosexuality openly, and he couldn't. He was impotent, anyway. And who'd want to lay him now, he asked: such a goddam ugly queer, who couldn't move his upper lip, or the whole left side of his face. . . .

His regular doctor warned Jane: amoebic dysentery and colitis had almost finished off Nick's intestines, liquor was giving the final touches. In the morning Nick often threw up from excessive drinking and smoking, swallowed Miltown, Valium, whatever was nearest to hand. Twice they'd had to leave the theater early—*A Chorus Line, Equus*—because of his chills and nausea. Despite Nick's remonstrance, Jane called Dando, in Hollywood.

"Look, bubba," Dando laid it on the line. Jane imagined his face that had always looked as though it were pulled on too tightly, like a mask, over his tiny buds of ears. "He's a known quantity by now. A pillhead, an acid freak, a boozer, a queer, he picks fights, people say he's turned spastic. He's more of a risk than any heavy breather"—the industry term for a ham actor—"and, in fact, he scares people. Need I say more?"

By the end of a disastrous summer, when Nick had had himself beaten up on Fire Island, Jane hired a tall, muscular relative of Ted's to look after Nick. Before Christmas, it was again Gloria who came through. She'd taken up now with Billy West, the diminutive but flamboyant director, and he'd written a screenplay for her. In Nick's living room she was radiant, more made up than ever, the green eyes flashing bold inquiries toward a youth from Fire Island who hovered, apprehensive, by the bar. At least, Jane consoled herself, Nick was no longer impotent.

"I told Billy no way I'd roll—in either sense of the word—without you," Gloria announced to Nick. "Are you up to it, lover? You sure look like hell."

"Nobody wants to see me in a film anymore." Nick was having a hard time controlling his spasms.

"Nobody wants to see me in a film anymore," Gloria mimicked. She slung one leg up on the coffee table. A new ankle bracelet glittered as she shook loose the heavy red hair over her shoulders. "Billy West wants me, he knows he has to take you."

Nick shook his head. Still, the gray eyes bulging in the pale face lit up with hope.

"Now, look, chum. No insurance company's going to pass you. We both know that. But you—uh—come on along to Shepperton Studios alone"—a glare at the blond youth—"with Jane, of course"—a smile for her—"and show 'em you're a big boy again. They'll have to deal with me if there's any shit. Gotcha?"

A whimper floated from the blond boy. Floyd Jackson, the black retainer, appeared with a tray of canapes and Gloria scanned him. Dignified, Floyd returned the scrutiny. Gloria grinned.

"And bring the Emperor Jones. . . . Anyone ever tell you you're the spittin' image of Paul Robeson?" she asked of Floyd.

"I've heard that." Floyd passed the tray to each of them except the blond youth who burst into tears, left the room.

Nick's salary for *After the Fact* was half what he'd earned on *Long Division*. On the flight over, it was Floyd who saw to it that he didn't drink. Still, when they alighted at Heathrow, Nick staggered so visibly that the morning papers reported him incoherent, completely soused. Nick didn't like Billy West—"He looks like he wouldn't know at which end of Gloria to start"—and, on the set, chaos quickly took over. Nick, who'd always prided himself on his quick memory, now had trouble with the long scenes his role demanded, would get through perhaps one line of the half page West wanted to shoot in a single take, blow the next. As West's anger mounted, so did Nick's agitation, his sweating and tremors.

"Jeez, Billy, have a heart." The second cameraman had just taken the flashbulb from his mouth after peering into a faulty camera, while West bawled out over and over the latest line Nick had blown. Nick sat hunched over, dripping wet, while Elizabeth Burns, the highly respected older actress, massaged his shoulders, took out her own lacy handkerchief to dry his forehead. As usual, Nick brought out the mother in women.

"Have a heart!" West boomed. "That's the trouble. I have one and it's breaking! I want all the coffee in England over on this set to counteract whatever sauce this lush is on." He strode to Nick's side, picked up the thermos of "orange juice" on the table, hurled it to the floor.
. . . The producer arrived, saw the early rushes, announced Nick had to go.

"Up yours," Gloria retorted. She'd already won several shouting matches with West. They were watching Nick across the set. At moments he resembled a wound-up robot, at others a thin, hunted animal with sudden curled movements of the body, the premonition of mortality in its bright shining eyes. Visibly shivering, he took his place now for the master shot of the next scene, didn't remember where he was supposed to stand. The assistant director patiently moved him about like an inanimate object, while West literally tore at his own hair.

The scene began with a tracking shot—Nick, holding himself steady an obvious effort of will, delivering a long history to Elizabeth of his childhood relationship with Gloria. He kept stumbling over lines. West now sat hunched over in his director's chair, back to the set, ostentatiously worked on a complicated doodle. At only one point, he looked up.

"Hey, sweetheart! How about an I.V. of acid and martini? Maybe we could work it into the script."

Nick began to tremble again. Elizabeth smiled encouragement. He fixed his wide staring eyes on hers, managed to get through the scene. West stood, called, "Okay, we're rolling on this one!" Then: "Thank God for small favors. That's a take."

Gloria sailed up to him now, spit in his face.

Despite everything, by the time the film was wrapped, Jane felt that Nick had turned in a competent performance in a role different from any he'd played before. She arranged to meet him on New Bond Street in front of Elizabeth Arden's. ("Why are the muscles so tense?" the masseuse asked, working painfully at a knot below her neck; under the Scotch hose, Jane had barely felt able to cling to the steel bar for support.) They'd tentatively planned a trip to the Lake District to rest up, advice that was all Nick anticipated from the doctor he'd just visited. The doctor probably wouldn't be able to explain why his eyes gave him so much trouble, why— aside from the effect of all the pills—he fell down so often.

"Guess what." As they walked slowly in the spring sunshine, his shoulders twitched uncontrollably. "Now I got premature cataracts. The doctor *said*. He said he never came across cataracts in anyone thirty-eight. And there's something the matter with my *para*thyroids."

"What?" Jane halted. A red double-decker bus lumbered by. "What's the matter *now?*"

"Low calcium level. That's what causes the muscle spasms and cramps. *And* the lack of balance and coordination. I told him to send West a note. West was always so sure it was the booze. Man, oh man!" A false elation at this new discovery masked the manifest fear. "Nobody knows the *tsurris* I've seen. Even the trouble with my memory comes from that."

"Well? What can we do?" Handsome dignified men hurried past in bowler hats, lovely women with the pure English complexion swept by in trim tweed suits. An Arab in flowing robes, followed by a retinue of women, scowled toward the shop windows. Perhaps he was annoyed that he didn't yet own their contents.

"Vitamin D shots. Extra calcium. But he doesn't promise I'll ever be 'normal' again. The balance thing —and the memory trouble—he thinks they'll always be there. Maybe even get worse."

"And your eyes? What about your eyes?" Why did everyone else seem to be hurrying toward delight, only they always toward disaster? Jane recalled the time when her chin had lifted in involuntary pride to be seen beside Nick, his beauty shedding light around her.

"Well, I won't need a white cane and little tin cup.

Yet." He smiled, the lower lip twisted away from the immobile upper one. "There's nothing they can do about cataracts, you know. Not till the cornea's completely covered. . . ." At the terror in her face, he relented. "Don't worry. That won't be a while yet. Meanwhile, I just keep falling down and don't see right. . . . Hey, how about a drink?"

No, Jane murmured, she didn't want a drink—she, with her newly waxed legs and her pedicure, her flesh still tingling from the massage and Scotch hose, her hair and face newly done. What did her appearance matter anymore? A man who resembled Walter Raney passed, sent her an admiring glance. They were passing Harrod's already, mannequins attired in tennis clothes, and she had a sudden image of herself running off a court with Walter, laughing together, they'd just finished playing doubles with Hugh Kirkland and Sybil Fox, there were cold drinks and sandwiches waiting, newspapers to read, favorable reviews of the play in which she'd just opened. . . . Danny, she'd heard from Sybil, had sent a play to New York, one that had had a great success in Israel. He'd probably be coming to the city soon himself —with Rachel. . . .

Two tall young boys, probably down from Oxford or Cambridge, passed by, laughing. Nineteen? Twenty? If she'd allowed him to visit Danny in Israel that summer, Tommy would still be alive. Those boys were Tommy's age by now. Tommy had wanted to go to Yale. "Of course, I might join the Coast Guard," he'd teased. How many sentences from the last had that been that he'd ever spoken to her, to anyone? Bells chimed from a church nearby, they'd turned off, were headed toward Hyde Park. Jane stopped with a sudden stitch in her side.

"Where are we going?" she asked. Her voice, her eyes, held an air, she knew, of helplessness. Nick stood motionless, adrift in his own montage of pain and loss.

"You tell me." The high reedy voice was hesitant. The wide, staring eyes reminded her of the first night she'd ever seen him, when he'd rendered those words from *Ghosts* that expressed the end of hope: " 'Mother, give me the sun. . . .' " A critic had said of him in *Long*

Division that he'd resembled those staring, sightless statues in a museum. A creeping coldness settled inside, curled up in her belly. Jane took his arm.

"Come on. We'll pay for chairs by the Serpentine and bake in the sun. It's almost seventy degrees. Let's take advantage of the heat wave."

Nick smiled. The smile held in it an element of pity for her that surmounted his own fear. They walked in silence for a time, passed a pram pushed by an English nanny, two small boys in short pants and carrying bookbags, an elderly gentleman walking his dog.

"Why do you do it, Jane?" Nick asked. "Who assigned you to Calvary?"

3

Jane supposed it had had to come. When they returned to New York, it was she who unexpectedly collapsed. Mononucleosis, indicated by the swollen glands, low-grade fever, lethargy. In the *Times* entertainment section, she read about Danny, now consulting in New York with producers about his play. Evidently he could write again, without her as inspiration. His wife was expected to join him soon.

While she was laid low, Nick spent some days at Mt. Sinai for what was diagnosed as alcoholic hepatitis. It was shortly after he was discharged, she herself still intermittently in bed, that the bloodiest terrorist incident in Israel's history took place: a blast in Jerusalem's Zion Square killed fourteen Israelis, wounded nearly eighty. Jane didn't imagine it possible that Danny's life could in any way be involved. It took several days to discover that his Rachel had been among those killed. *Zeal for Thy house has consumed me. . . .*

To her brief note about his new loss, Danny—as she'd almost foreseen—sent no reply, had left immediately for Israel. Jane and Nick went to the opening of his play, a drama about Americans settling in that narrow strip of the Mideast. In it, Jane heard the new authority, the voice of Danny's maturity, was not surprised at the strong critical acclaim accorded it.

All the winter of 1976—it reminded Jane of that time of recurring illness after Peter's death—she stumbled from one malaise to another. Ted left her off for a party at the Dakota and the large brown building floated with menace before her. In the elevator, she ran into Owen Durant.

"After all these years of our paths not crossing! What in God's name has he done to you—your Prince of Darkness?" Owen saw her lean against the wall, a film of sweat dampening her forehead. "I think I'd best get you home." Sweeping back his cape, he placed his arm around her, supported her to a cab, sat silent on one couch in her living room while she lay back on the other. It was as though they'd never been apart when she gazed apathetically across at him. The full pouting lips twisted in the old disdain, the hair swirled about his head as though to express the familiar indignation. He saw her watching him.

"This is the year, isn't it?" he commented. "You've attained to a full half century of folly?" Jane barely nodded. "I must say." The bright eyes that had often reminded her of black olives snapped. "I've never found anyone quite so much to my fancy—God knows why— as you. I don't suppose, after all this time of your personal firestorm, you'd let me take you away from all this?" He sighed. "Hidden behind the orphaned refugee camouflage, I detect the fine bones that first lured me on." His gaze slid along her body, inert on the cushions. "If I'm not mistaken, you're resting on that same fine round ass. How about deep-sixing your big enchilada? I may be ready to bite the bullet and make an honest woman of you."

Jane almost smiled.

Again, Owen sighed. "Stonewalling as usual, eh? Little did I know, that first night I found you dancing with your snotty little debutante, that the real smoking gun still lay in the future. . . . Guess you'll struggle on with that dingbat till he's permanently spaced out. Then what? You'll be left, you know. Twisting slowly, slowly in the wind. . . ."

In the spring, *After the Fact* opened to poor reviews. Box office was good only because people wished to see Gloria, who—embroiled with a married man, a leading actor of the Royal Shakespeare Company—had taken on the *persona* of dangerous lady. Interest still ran high in Nick's appearance. The kindest critics pointed out his unnatural stiffness, robotlike movements, exaggeratedly staring eyes. One complained that he was tiring of Spenser's perennial vulnerability.

From the theater where they'd sat together in silent embarrassment, Jane dragged herself with Nick to the newly opened Studio 54. Twelve landing lights from a Boeing 747 and colored strobes lit up the cheering gaudily dressed crowds, moving to the hustle. For a time, the beat of the music sent out by the deejay ignited her, too. Then Jane collapsed in exhaustion, lost sight of Nick as he moved off to dance first with a woman in a sateen jumpsuit, then with a man in cowboy boots, chamois pants, suede vest. Not unexpectedly, she found herself going home alone.

Nick called next day, asked how she'd like to come to the Coast with him, help him out in a minor role. There'd be many big stars—and himself.

No, Jane said, she didn't think she was up to it. This time out, he could play it on his own. With Floyd. It was rather like the first time, when she'd sent him to do *The High Mountains.* Even the location was similar—Nevada, now—and Nick would again play a cowboy. She knew the same guilty apprehension as he left her.

Jane watched the Fourth of July Tall Ships parade on the river, the fireworks for the Bicentennial with Hugh Kirkland and Sybil Fox, toasted the Israeli commandos who made the daring rescue of hostages at Entebbe. A peanut farmer from Georgia was chosen in New York to head the Democratic ticket for president. At Greenwich, she gave several quiet dinner parties, sensed her own slow physical recovery, punctuated by encouraging reports from Floyd. Compared to what John Gordon, the director, had to deal with with Hooper's wife, Floyd said, Nick was coming off as a boy scout.

Also, John Gordon wanted Nick to play the lead in the film whose script he'd been working on for years now—*Jude the Obscure.*

John Gordon, Jane warned when Nick returned—with great caution: she didn't wish to appear to dampen his hopes—might have lavished care and praise on him when Hooper's wife was the focus of difficulty. Nick did realize, didn't he, that Gordon had a reputation for picking, in every film he made, some one actor to abuse? Nick must be wary of attracting that lightning to himself.

It *was* a relief that Gordon had chosen to rely primarily on the Astoria Picture and Television Center in Queens. About two dozen films were being shot in New York this year and there were five sound stages out there, one more than two hundred by one hundred feet. For such a long, important venture, such a demanding role, it would be healthier for Nick not to be cooped up on location somewhere far from home with Gordon.

The first problem appeared with the script Gordon presented to Nick. "This stinks," Nick announced. "This isn't Hardy. It isn't life. It isn't art. It's nothing but unadulterated *merde.*"

Gordon—small, rotund, professorial, constantly sucking on a pipe—was enraged. He reminded Nick: he'd had his best writers working on this script for years.

"Yeah, well, find some of those honchos who answer the matchbook ads about learning how to write. You might do better with those."

Immensely keyed up to this role, Nick was eating less, drinking more, despite Floyd's efforts to hold him on course. Gordon, it turned out, had always heard rumors about Nick, had previously attributed them to malice. Now, with Nick's attacks on the script, he apparently decided to believe them.

Gordon, Floyd reported to Jane, had laid it on the line. During filming of his masterpiece, there'd be no homosexual shit, no older woman coaching Nick, no pills, no sauce. "Otherwise, we can cut right here," he'd stormed. "I don't need some brain-damaged alcoholic queen ruining what I've got."

Humiliated, Nick agreed.

In those first weeks, Nick worked well. But there

385

were constant script revisions—Gordon had seen what Nick meant—and Nick's memory was giving him trouble. He couldn't give Gordon the long uncut takes he wanted, Gordon—still smoldering at his discovery about Nick—alternated between frenzied impatience and cold scorn. Deirdre Blake, the tall, beautiful actress who played Jude's cousin, Sue, came by one evening to see Jane.

"John Gordon's going to kill Nick." Deirdre's large eyes were lustrous with tears. "There isn't a day he doesn't hand Nick a rewrite to learn just hours before shooting. And every single evening, there's a third or fourth revision we have to study till three and four in the morning. *I* can't take it. I don't see how Nick can. And he's such a darling person, he's so generous, so giving. You know, I just figured it out the other day," she added. "Why Nick hugs me—hugs everyone on the set all the time—so hard. It's partly to keep from falling down, isn't it?"

Surreptitiously, Jane visited next day, stood to the side where the continuity girl had smuggled her, watched as Gordon called, "We're rolling on this one!" fifty times before he was satisfied with one short scene between Nick and Deirdre. Nick, trying to placate him, was incoherent from fear, humiliation. Gordon suddenly spotted Jane. She hurried to Nick's dressing room with Nick, began to lay cold compresses on his forehead while he shivered. Without knocking, Gordon burst in.

"Listen, you little shit queen! You're going to remember your lines or I'll fracture any bone in your body that's still unbroken from that drunk accident. I'll ram your vodka bottle so far up that ass, no fag'll ever want to travel that way again."

Nick slumped in his chair, bloodshot bulging eyes upturned to Gordon. "Go ahead. Go on."

Gordon's face was wild. Jane tried to stare him down, felt herself pressed to the wall by the impact of his hate. As suddenly as he'd entered, he slammed out. She and Nick looked at one another in the mirror, then away.

Variety initiated weekly items on the lateness of the film, cost overruns. The set, it was reported, alternated between a maniacal deadly calm and complete chaos.

New dialogue was now written on the backs of doors and walls, on boards in front of the cameras. Nick, his eyes troubling him more as the stress mounted, couldn't see them. The studio, under pressure from Gordon, threatened a lawsuit. While Nick, unable to read the idiot cards, stumbled in humiliation off the set, Gordon calmly turned the page of the racing news.

"The point is, I have to be allowed to finish," Nick said to Jane. His forehead was damp with sweat, his limbs trembling. His jaw was again giving him tremendous pain. Nobody, Jane told herself, mentioned his courage.

By the time the film was finished and Jane had carried him off to Greenwich for a summer of rest, the studio had launched its suit against the insurance company. The movie had cost twice as much as had been budgeted, shooting had taken exactly twice as long as planned. The six months of litigation that followed divided the cinema world into warring factions. In the end, the studio lost. But the publicity and litigation had done it: Nick was now completely uninsurable.

Jane didn't mention it to Nick: that Hugh Kirkland now had in hand another play by Danny. He wanted her —unexpectedly with the playwright's approval—for the lead. When she turned it down, Hugh Kirkland stared.

"This," he said, "even after everything, I don't believe."

4

Jane read the newspapers to Nick as he lay in the hospital after a series of operations for the cataracts. He appeared to take a sour delight in the stories about Gloria and her English lover, Edgar Lathrop, with whom she was starring in a big historical romance in Italy. *Paparazzi* divided their time between following them around—"the most glamorous couple in moviedom"— and trying to discover what Lathrop's spouse felt about it all. Gloria was condemned, admired, envied. Only Jackie Onassis, perhaps Queen Elizabeth, came in for more publicity.

By the time Nick was released, he wore thick-lensed glasses, had lost all peripheral vision. These days his old movies were attended as cult films, he had an enormous underground following. But he was drinking heavily again, roaming the streets at night, picking up men, picking fights. . . . Danny's play, Jane heard, was held in abeyance.

Jane now allowed Owen to escort her here and there, to take her to bed. With him, she attended several parties at 30 Rock, passed up the grass and Quāāludes, the coke laid out in bowls with golden straws. Out of curiosity, they went to a punk concert, saw *Saturday Night Fever*, dropped in at Studio 54. Sometimes now, alone, Jane entered buildings under construction, asked to look at apartments as though she were really interested, wandered through the gerrymandered rooms and imagined, as she often had before, a new life. She was almost fifty-three.

This—a new life—was what Floyd, with heroic persistence, insisted he was going to give Nick, whether he liked it or not. He asked Jane if she'd come with him, confront Dr. Winkler.

"I want to see, once and for all, if this dude's going to let it all hang out."

At the office on Central Park West, Dr. Winkler rose from his desk, allowed Nick to grab him, hang on him as he often did to maintain his balance. While Jane and Floyd watched, Dr. Winkler embraced Nick, exchanged kisses, then turned his icy gaze on them. Nick, slumped in a chair, had had only one vodka, yet he was already drunk. That was all it now took.

"We're here," Jane said, "to have you tell us. Are you ever going to deal with Nick's drinking?" Nick watched slyly, a little smile on his twisted puffy lips. It occurred to her: from the first, he'd charmed even his therapist into complicity, acquiescence.

Dr. Winkler turned to Nick. "How many drinks have you had today, dear boy?"

"One," Nick whispered. "Only one."

Dr. Winkler turned back to Jane, his eyes narrowed. "I've heard all this from you for years. What drinking?"

Jude the Obscure was finally released. For the furor it had caused, critics wondered what it had all been about. Only a couple, the more serious reviews, speculated that Nick's performance would eventually, in the minds of film aficionados, join the array of his other great ones.

By summer, Floyd himself needed a period of recuperation. The last week Nick had been escaping him, going off Floyd said he didn't know where. She'd take Nick to Greenwich, Jane decided. Floyd could join them there after his holiday. Floyd packed Nick's bags, stowed them in the Porsche while Ted held the door open for Nick—neatly arrayed in a light gray suit—to step in beside Jane. A woman in a blouson dress, spiked heels, stared as though she recognized Nick. Two joggers went by. Nick leaned in toward Jane.

"Listen. I'll be right back. There's a guy always has coffee two blocks over this time of day. One of those new young directors from film school. You know?" At her hesitation: "Really. This fellow trained with Roger Cormin at A.I.F. It could mean a part. I was keeping it a secret to surprise you. These new kids—they're willing to take a chance. Even on a has-been like me."

It was difficult to refuse this sweating, trembling specter. Jane shrugged and nodded, met Ted's deprecatory gaze as he slid in behind the wheel. To avoid that glance, she lit a cigarette, watched two children across the street play hopscotch. Ted's voice startled her.

"See that?"

"See what?" Jane leaned forward as Ted swung the car from the curb.

"That checkered cab. Wouldn't you know? It made the light. . . . And your boy. He's inside it."

The anxious constriction in her belly denied Jane's initial disbelief. "Can you catch him? Where does he think he's going? What in the world is he up to now?"

Ted was silent as he tried unsuccessfully to pass an enormous truck. Its driver leaned out to shout cheerful imprecations. Horns blared as they sat out two red lights without moving. At last, Ted volunteered:

"Floyd's been telling me. Says Mr. Nick gets away from him, hustles himself over to these bars on Eleventh Avenue. Ones where they get the sailors and dockworkers. Jetsetters slumming. Pimps. Hookers. Damn!" The light had changed again and they passed the intersection but the cab had disappeared. "Now we just gotta travel and look. Hold tight and keep your eyes peeled, Miss Jane."

By the time they reached Eleventh Avenue, were cruising slowly southward, the errand appeared fruitless. There were too many sinister-looking bars, too many winos lolling on the corners. Jane, braced tensely forward, was about to suggest they simply turn back, wait for Nick to reappear on his own. But Ted's unspoken urgency underlined her own desperation, defused from it its essential sense of futility. In numb gratitude, she delivered herself to his persistence, stubbed out one cigarette after another as the car, pursued by impatient blasts of horns behind them, moved slowly on. As they reached Fifty-first Street, she heard Ted's quick sibilant intake of breath.

"That fast!" she heard him murmur as he pulled the car over, turned off the engine. Then Jane saw.

On the sidewalk, Nick lay curled in a fetal position, his neat clothes in disarray, his eyes shut in unconsciousness to the bums who hovered about him. Their hands picking at him reminded Jane of pigeons clustering excitedly over a sudden bounty of food. As Ted sprinted from the car, they fell back as swiftly as birds taking flight. Jane heard Ted's oath that scattered them to holding positions, heard another sound: a guttural noise as the vomit rose in her throat. Nick, naked on the tray at Bohdan's house. The beautiful swan . . . roasted black.

Then Ted had thrust his arms under the fragile body, had gathered Nick—he weighed only a hundred and thirty pounds now—to his chest. He swung the unconscious bundle into the backseat beside Jane, hurried in behind the wheel. Glancing back, as Ted swung the car down Fifty-first Street, Jane saw the disappointed predators regroup, shout obscenities after them. She held Nick's frail body close to her, wiped the sweat from his temples as the breath rasped uneasily from his trembling lips, glanced away—it was too painful to watch—from the pale stuporous face.

In the gutter, newspapers swirled past. A drunk lay asleep on the sidewalk near a church. Between Ninth and Tenth, an extremely goodlooking boy—perhaps twenty—cap on his light brown hair, dark blue eyes dreaming, an innocent smile on his lips, emerged from a tan brick building with fire escapes. Jane's blank mind followed him a moment as traffic stalled the car and the boy walked nearby on the sidewalk.

An aspiring actor, she thought: he probably worked as a waiter somewhere, took acting lessons, voice, dance. He lived a couple of blocks from the theater district, perhaps was on his way now to buy theatrical makeup at the place on Forty-ninth and Broadway, or on his way to a dance studio. . . . The boy glanced toward her, the smile of a child on his lips: he was lost, too, but in his own hopes, his hurtling future.

Nick woke in Greenwich, remembered nothing of the day before. Jane had slept poorly, dreamed of walking the corridors of those buildings she'd visited as though in search of an apartment, found herself treading halls with huge windows that gave a view into various rooms, all with their own clear high windows open to the sunlight that flooded in. In one, Nick rose from a couch, Nick radiant, smiling, clean, neat and shining as he'd been in his early twenties—like the boy on the street—he gathered up masses of *Playbills* that spilled from his arms, and she knew he'd been in all of them, all those plays, as he smiled toward her, a dreamy smile on his young lips, like the boy on the street.

She woke up, sobbing.

The house began to fill up with the syringes Nick left about. The doses of Demerol frightened Jane—addicting as it was—and the way he combined it with the liquor he always managed to smuggle in. It was a relief to have Floyd arrive, see the summer end, return to the city. To Nick, his surroundings didn't seem to matter.

"Once he was your demon lover," Owen commented. "Now what is he? Your child? What is he to you?"

"Everything," Jane said. That day they'd rehearsed together a recording for Caedmon Records. At the pain and hope in her face, Nick had lifted his thin hand to her cheek, his voice soft.

" 'She loved me for the dangers I had passed. And I loved her that she did pity them.' "

Again it was Gloria who came to the rescue. She descended like a comet, flashing diamonds from her ears, throat, wrists, fingers, laughed triumphantly at the fact that she was acknowledged the most important star in the industry, that—whether the world liked it or not— she was having her cake and eating it, too. For their own safety—people would kill, she giggled, just to glimpse them—she and Edgar Lathrop were being smuggled in and out the service entrance of the St. Regis. All this in Nick's living room, where Lathrop brooded beside her, his hand on her thigh, his good-looking Scottish face full of covert suspicion of Nick, of this wraith whose power over Gloria evidently troubled him.

Gloria could make Nick laugh again with her stories about how the press pursued them and condemned them, of the wedding ceremony on the *Queen Elizabeth II,* of the studio's fearful pleasure about all the gossip. She patted Lathrop's cheek. "Dig the animal magnetism, would you?" she observed, in her little-girl voice.

To Jane, in the pantry, Lathrop murmured: "I know. The lass *likes* me. But it's that one she *loves.* . . . He's supposed to be only forty?" Lathrop raised skeptical brows.

To Jane, Gloria wept. "He's dying! Nick's going to die if he doesn't work soon. Nothing else can save him."

Jane didn't like her own thoughts put so clearly. "You know no studio will have him."

"Balls!" The green crystal eyes were clouded, tears clung to the thick lashes. To Nick: "Listen, the bottom line is this: I can have anything I want. Can you learn a part? Can you go long enough not zonked out to learn a part?"

"I'm a has-been," Nick began. Still, the blank gaze underwent a change.

"Don't lay that trip on me, buster. You stay put. Edgar and me—we'll do the jawboning. . . ."

In the end, for the film Gloria selected for herself, Lathrop, and Nick, she had to put up, in lieu of insurance, her own fee—the largest of any star—as bond for Nick. Money, Jane reflected—not for the first time—was the one benefice he would not accept from herself. Nick, lying on the floor with the script, alternated between fears that he could never really act again, and outpourings of wonder that Gloria's affection could abide so steadfastly.

"She makes me feel loved again," he told Jane.

"Oh," Jane said. "You've been loved. That you've been."

There was the usual delay in production. Nick kept calling Gloria in Hollywood, kept badgering her either for reassurance or to express his gratitude. It was only when the shooting date was set for January that Nick seriously turned over what he termed "the last leaf in my book." They'd be leaving immediately after Christmas for location in England, went together one evening to an after-theater party upstairs at Sardi's. Unexpectedly—oh, yes, she'd read he was at Columbia for the year as Visiting Professor of Drama—Danny stood before Jane. His curly hair and beard, she noted quickly, were all gray, and there was a new wry twist to the lips.

"I was just looking at that drawing of you on the wall," Danny said.

Now Jane saw how, though his face was lined, the familiar intensity of those golden eyes—Tommy's eyes —warmed her like a benediction. Perhaps, she thought, her legs unsteady as the press of people pushed them close to one another, he'd finally forgiven her. It was as though, momentarily, Tommy breathed there between them, asking that they love one another. Then, a touch of vanity brought her hand to her hair. She wondered how she looked as she murmured, with something like shyness:

"That was so long ago. . . . How are you?"

Briefly, Danny smiled, took a sip from his drink. "Still the insulted and injured. You turned down my play."

"Oh." She was like a girl, trembling before him. "I

don't act anymore." Inanely: "I'll be leaving for England soon."

Danny's gaze wandered to where Nick stood alone, away from the bar, a glass of Fresca in his bony hand. "So I've heard. . . . You never even read it, did you? My play. Actually, I wrote it the way I wrote *Zeal*. For you. . . . I even pictured seeing it put on in the same theater. Where we did *Zeal*."

No recrimination revealed itself in his regard, only a profound understanding of her. This she needed almost as much as the old concern she thought she also saw manifest. Jane hesitated, her glance traveling back to where Nick slouched against the wall. A sudden release of emotion clarified his image from the obscuring detail of ruin. Actors, she thought: they lay themselves bare, greedy to express their talent, hungry for adulation, naked to the eye of the stranger. They could not be judged like others.

"You know," she explained to Danny, "he did it. At his greatest, he laid himself on the line. He went all the way. Do you see?"

Danny's hand was on her arm. "I know. I understand." With those words, with his eyes, his hands, it was as though Danny comprehended, embraced her entire life. Then, others intervened, they were separated. Jane saw that Nick searched her out. She took him home.

In November, by murder and suicide, almost a thousand cultists died in Guyana. Immediately after, a disgruntled city worker pumped bullets into the mayor of San Francisco and the leading political homosexual. Nick, working hard, pausing only long enough to buy expensive Christmas gifts for everyone he knew, had completely stopped drinking, was undergoing new agonies with the tremendous cutdown in pills. The sweep of deaths shook him, like a prophecy.

"Why does death take the young away?" he asked Jane. "And why do people throw life itself away?" He regarded her somberly. "Why did I? Why did I destroy myself?"

Jane studied the ruined face. She recalled the time in the days of the David-Jonathan play when she'd feared that his star would streak so far he'd be lost to her. He seemed now in 1978 more like a planet flickering feebly in outer space, its orbit traveling always further, soon to be lost. He sensed her sadness.

"Listen." His face brightened. "What was the greatest moment of your life? I mean, what moment, if you could, would you relive?"

They were in his bedroom, the black drapes drawn as always, the room dark except for one lamp. She sank back on the bed and thought. Moments with Peter rose up before her, passed. Danny, in that brief interlude before his marriage. The first time she'd held Tommy in her arms. Standing on the stage in *Antony and Cleopatra*.

"Give me my robe, put on my crown: I have
Immortal longings in me. . . ."

Nick was watching her. Suddenly she knew.

"It was a night in Greenwich Village. I was sitting at a table with Ralph Gurney and Mary Nodine. They'd asked me to come along, to watch a young actor they were considering for their new play." As though across those years, they smiled at one another. Her heart was very full, tenderness, pain, both, she wasn't certain.

"Jane!" The ashen face flushed in the lamplight. "Guess what I want to do!"

"Kinky sex?" she asked doubtfully.

The old bark of laughter. "I want to act it out. Let's make believe this is the place again. Sit up. You're at the table. With Ralph and Mary. Come on." Jane pushed herself up, dutifully crossed her legs, "You were drinking, weren't you? Sure, you must've been drinking." He peered toward the door, ran into the bathroom, brought out a bottle hidden in the toilet tank, together with his toothbrush glass. "Okay. You smoked then, didn't you? Got to get the smoke-filled room!"

Jane lit a cigarette. Nick was tremulous with fevered excitement. He laid aside the thick spectacles, disappeared behind the dark drapes, in exaggerated stentorian tones announced:

"Ladies and gentlemen, the featured attraction a lot

of you've been waiting for. A nice hand, please, for Nicholas Spenser."

Jane laid aside the cigarette, clapped, emitted a whistle, stamped her feet. The black drape was pushed aside. Nick stepped out, slouched toward the stool Floyd often sat on to massage him. He settled himself upon it, made as though he were adjusting a microphone, gazed around with the old large unblinking stare, as though he were memorizing the faces before him. He gave a shy somewhat awkward smile, that smile she'd guessed even that evening was the result of conscious practice.

"Folks." His voice was a little high, a little reedy. He gazed around with that wide stare. "I give you Jack Kerouac." The left hand he raised trembled slightly before he thrust it in his pocket. It flashed through her mind: Kerouac was dead now, a suicide.

Nick recited the old lines, just as he had before, the wide gray eyes searching her out, making certain she understood, inviting her. Then he paused. The lamplight illumined the gaunt, ruined face. Jane held very still, couldn't smile, couldn't applaud. He rose, made as though slightly to raise the mike, softly announced: "Poe speaks. *William Wilson*." She remembered that moment, the hush in the house had deepened as he'd raised his right hand, the beautiful lean young face had grown haggard, haunted, damned—the face before her now.

" 'Men,' " he informed her slowly, " 'usually grow base by degrees. From me, in an instant, all virtue dropped bodily as a mantle. . . .' " He hesitated, couldn't find the next lines. Then: " 'Death approaches; and the shadow which foreruns him has thrown a softening influence over my spirit.' " Again that pause, the search for words. A shake of the head as they didn't come. His gaze wandered, returned to her. " 'It was Wilson. . . . I could have fancied that I myself was speaking while he said: *You have conquered, and I yield. Yet, henceforward art thou also dead—dead to the World, to Heaven, and to Hope! In me didst thou exist—and, in my death, see by this image, which is thine own, how utterly thou hast murdered thyself. . . .' "*

She was tremendously moved. He saw, when he came to her arms, how her eyes were wet with tears, and

396

he kissed them from her cheeks. She thought, as he lay nestled close to her to sleep, how she'd always felt cheated of it: Amazing Grace. Perhaps she'd had it all along, had found it, when she'd found Nick. Was that why, she wondered, she'd chosen to relive that evening, above all others? She wished she could tell him that, but he was already asleep, like a frail child, in her embrace. She lay awake, holding him.

What was grace, after all, except continuing love?

5

In the morning Jane woke early. Nick gave her a quiet smile as he opened his eyes, turned over. She slipped noiselessly from the room, agreed with Floyd over coffee that it was a good sign Nick could sleep this long. The air was cold, crisp, the sky blue when she reemerged, showered and changed, from her own house. She walked up to Madison Avenue to Blanchard's to have her hair done, on from there to Henri Bendel's to finish her Christmas shopping.

It occurred to her that she and Nick should walk along Fifth Avenue before they left, look in at the holiday windows. About those, Nick had always been like a child. Tommy, she remembered, had often laughed at Nick, pushing his way—shoulders hunched in a short winter jacket—to a front position before those displays. She thought, too, she should invite Danny over before she left: show him all the pictures, all the artifacts of Tommy's life. . . .

A crowd had assembled before Nick's house when Jane turned down Sixty-first Street again. The crowd at first obscured the ambulance parked there. Her steps quickened, then slowed. She didn't want to know. Police cars, too, their beacons whirling. Jane sensed her feet dragging, as though she wore heavy iron shoes, impossible to lift. It must be the result of Nick cutting down on all the booze, she told herself, all the pills, so drastically. They'd probably have to delay their departure, Laura Crowell would have to see to the plane tickets. The studio would be in an uproar but Gloria would know how to placate them. She came close now to the crowd, read from the elation on their faces that, of course, the news was really worse than that. Somebody shoved her.

"Look out, lady! I was here first!"

No, nobody was here earlier than I was, came an unbidden voice. Jane looked up toward the draped windows as though Nick could lean out—as he'd leaned there the morning he'd first come there—could tell these obdurate people to let her through. Floyd stood in the doorway, suddenly noticed her, reached out his arms. She saw his face, the dark hooded eyes always so calm, now wild with a refusal to accept whatever it was that had happened. The crowd parted for her at last— the police helped, of course—and Floyd gathered her close. He'd always been so strong. Strange to feel those arms quiver as they went about her, to hear him sob.

She stood before him in Nick's living room. He repeated it over and over as though she'd tell him: No, what you're saying is a mistake, I'll go up there and you'll see, it hasn't happened. . . . He'd been worried by noontime, Floyd was saying, had gone upstairs with a breakfast tray. Nick had been lying there with his glasses on, the script for the film beside him, his right arm rigid to his chest, his fists clenched.

"I thought he was just passed out. The way he sometimes was. What he was going through these last days— cutting down on everything. No food for so many hours. I was going to carry him to the shower." Floyd wiped his eyes. "I started to lift him up, to carry him to the shower. Then I saw. I saw he was dead. . . ."

Nick's doctor came down the stairs, took her hands. "His heart. It was his heart. Just gave up the fight. . . ." His eyes were so full of pity—for her, for Nick—she didn't know. Jane nodded.

"I want to see him," she said.

The doctor hesitated. "Do you think you should?"

Sharply: "Of course." Floyd made as though to follow her. "Alone."

Someone—the doctor? Floyd?—had removed the spectacles. Nick had been wearing slacks, a shirt, while he slept in her arms. She didn't know if he'd undressed himself when he'd waked to study the script, or if the doctor had stripped him. He lay bare-chested, the sheet pulled up to his armpits, his face staring up blindly, as though listening.

Lathrop had been right, she thought dully, studying him. Nobody would think him just past his forty-first birthday—this gaunt, scarred face, the wizened body, the thin arms rigid upon the sheet. He looked, she thought, as though he'd been dead not hours, but years, had been mummified.

As she stared, dry-eyed, the body seemed to stir upon the bed. No, not this dead body, but another, a ghost that rose and gathered itself together from these bones, this tired flesh. The apparition clothed itself as Nick, the shining and beautiful one he'd been, came toward her, gathered her to him. He laid his forehead against hers, pulled her arms around his neck, began to move with her in a slow dance. He was singing and smiling, a sardonic smile for what he sang, but holding her close. *I'll remember this one day,* she'd thought at that time.

"I came home unexpectedly
And caught her crying needlessly
In the middle of the day,
And it was in the early spring,
When flowers bloom and robins sing,
She went away. . . .
And, Honey, I miss you,
And I'm being good,
And I'd love to be with you,
If only I could. . . ."

Everybody called. People from everywhere, New York, Hollywood, London, Rome. From Paris, Gloria sobbed: "He was my best friend in all the world, my brother, my soulmate." Somehow, the press got hold of that, played it up, as they did all news that concerned her.

Daisy was enraged that Nick's instructions left Jane in charge of the funeral, was barely placated by Walter

Raney's announcement that Nick had left his mother three-quarters of his estate—down to less than a quarter of a million dollars—the remainder to charity, with special large gifts to Floyd and to the godchild, Nicole. For Jane, there was what she valued most: his scrapbooks.

She decided to hold the funeral at St. Thomas's Church on Fifth Avenue and Fifty-third. That should accommodate those who'd come out of loyalty, out of love, those who'd come from curiosity, even revenge. The details she left to Walter—with the admonition that Nick had wanted "Amazing Grace" to be played.

"Like—like the other time?" Walter always had difficulty saying the name.

"Like Tommy," she said.

The morning was bright, clear and cold again. Snow still hadn't fallen, though it was almost officially winter. Yet all sounds seemed curiously muffled in the house, had seemed so since Nick's death, as though the world were buried in snow. Faith, Ted, and Laura had gone ahead to the church, with Floyd. She'd be traveling alone, with Walter.

Jane recognized, as she passed from one room to another, as though she were leaving the house forever, that she was simply putting it off—going. She didn't know why, really. The casket, by her order, was closed. She wouldn't glimpse Nick again, in death anymore than in life. She supposed she was looking to see if any part of him would be here for her when she returned. She wondered how she'd get through it again—those moments when the bagpiper she'd asked for, the organ, played the music of "Amazing Grace."

What she must cling to, when the time came, she supposed, was the memory of holding Nick in her arms that last night, what her thoughts had been. In that way she might convert those strains of mourning to a temporary truth. She had known that grace. . . .

Epilogue

No one, except perhaps Walter, had seen her leave Nick's house, the reception still in progress after the burial. Jane wasn't certain, as she walked in the wet snow, where she was headed. But she couldn't go home, not yet. The streets she crossed were all streets she'd walked, at some time, with Nick, and the tears that had not yet come clogged her throat, threatened to mingle with the snow on her lashes.

At Fifth Avenue she turned south, was soon passing the stores with their Christmas displays. She'd planned that Nick and she must look in those windows one more time before they left for England. Despite the thinly drifting snow, groups were still gathered to peer in at the scenes set up like small stage sets, excited children were held up to view the moving puppets. Jane was walking briskly now, to stay warm, to ward off the ghosts from the past.

Perhaps it was the image of those small stage sets that led her to turn west at Forty-fourth Street. She soon found herself mingling with the theater crowd and her steps slowed, a wanderer without purpose. It occurred to her she might drop into a bar. As she glanced inside at the press of people gathered before one, a man noticed her staring. He smiled and beckoned. Jane walked on.

Amid the impatient blare of horns, taxis discharged passengers under theater marquees, umbrellas were opened, snapped shut, friends met one another, huddled together before passing inside. Jane saw the billboard pictures, critics' reviews posted beside them, proclamations of how long this play and that had been running.

She understood that her wandering had not been

aimless after all, knew where her steps were taking her. Past the theaters of all Nick's triumphs—this was her best farewell. Here he'd stood onstage with the Gurneys in *A Dead Language*. Across the street and a few paces on, he'd played David in *The Sceptre and the Harp*. She walked on to stand before the theater of his final Broadway victory, *Romeo and Juliet*.

Then, she'd passed them all, was turning north on Eighth and headed for Forty-fifth Street. Across the avenue, the Martin Beck's last audience was just filtering inside. It was easy, for a moment, to imagine that marquee lit up, not with *Dracula* but with another title— *Zeal for Thy House*—easy to see herself not among those theatergoers pressing into the lobby but slipping in through the stage door, with her own life, her own career still before her.

Jane hesitated, before crossing the avenue, at this self-indulgence. Still, why not slip just for a moment into that past? When she'd acted in that play, the past had held her prisoner. Now that she had, as it were, grown up, she might release herself to traverse it again. The past must, after all, give birth to whatever her present might yet become.

But she hadn't expected this: not that, as in that past, Danny should detach himself from the thinning crowd. As though he'd known, before she had, that she must arrive at this place, at this moment. (In a park long ago, as she and Peter and Joanie had walked the windswept paths, a voice had shouted, "Hey! Peter!" There was Danny Edelman coming toward them and Peter gave a slow, casual wave down near his waist. Immediately, the ball came sailing to him and he leaped. To Jane's relief he caught it and she trailed Joanie toward the swings but walking backward to watch how Danny—a damned good-looking kid, she told herself—swung the bat.)

On the church steps today, he'd told her she was not alone. But Jane stood motionless as Danny slowly approached.

("Joanie's gone." Her voice trembled. So did her knees.

"What do you mean—gone?" But Peter glanced quickly about, the immediacy of his response at once soothing and frightening. He came toward her, trailed by Danny, whose interested glance at her loose knee socks and frayed coat made her blush. . . .)

Danny didn't touch her now, didn't take her arm as he had there on the church steps, only watched her in silence. Under that gaze, Jane bowed her head. Finally, she looked up at him.

"Was this where you were hoping it would open— your new play?"

"You know that," Danny said. "My play—and you in it."

Her voice caught a moment. "Do people deserve a second chance in life?"

"Everyone deserves a second chance—and more."

(Once, descending the hill to West End Avenue, she and Peter and Papa, all of them silent as always, they came abreast of Danny Edelman. He stopped, appeared to take in at a glance everything about their situation and, in solicitude, raised his light brown eyebrows. . . . Later, years later, he held her: "Why can't I stop loving you?")

Jane slightly shook her head. She saw how the snow touched his curly gray beard, as it set ablaze diamonds in the lights above them. The black veil slipped from her hair and Danny lifted his hand to it, then held that hand to her cheek.

"Don't you know that work is everything?" How long ago he'd told her that! Now, he added the rest of it: ". . . but only together with love."

That past in which she'd wronged him, wronged her- self held Jane hesitant. From that past, which she'd known must give birth to her present, the ghosts of those she'd most loved appeared to gather. Tommy, Peter . . . and Nick.

She didn't know which of them now pressed closest. Perhaps it was in concert that they helped her over a moment's reluctance, a moment's false pride. Then she lifted her own hand to cover his against her cheek. She remembered Ralph Gurney's praise as he'd handed her the Tony for *Man and Superman* and how she'd stood onstage beside him, spoken in answer her last line from that play. She smiled at Danny and said it, now with no love withheld:

" 'Go on talking.' "